## BLUE RIBBON COMPETITION

**Jim,** the great rider who dazzled Diana with his skill, and finally trusted her with his shocking secret . . . **Hugh,** the handsome, womanizing tycoon who taught Diana the ecstasy and treachery of passion . . . **Philippe,** the irresistibly charming Frenchman who introduced Diana to his jet-set world of sleek yachts and sophisticated sin . . . **Steve,** who gave Diana more than she could repay, but less than she needed . . . **Bill,** the brilliant doctor and perfect lover who had everything— including a wife . . .

**Diana Winston was riding to fame and fortune on a trail of grit and glamour, hurdling over all obstacles and odds . . . but on the perilous path of love, she found how easy it was to ride to a fall. . . .**

# *TROPHIES*

# TROPHIES

## Ainslie Sheridan

A SIGNET BOOK

SIGNET
Published by the Penguin Group
Penguin Books USA Inc., 375 Hudson Street, New York,
New York 10014, U.S.A.
Penguin Books Ltd, 27 Wrights Lane, London W8 5TZ, England
Penguin Books Australia Ltd, Ringwood, Victoria, Australia
Penguin Books Canada Ltd, 2801 John Street, Markham,
Ontario, Canada L3R 1B4
Penguin Books (N.Z.) Ltd, 182-190 Wairau Road,
Auckland 10, New Zealand

Penguin Books Ltd, Registered Offices:
Harmondsworth, Middlesex, England

First published by Signet, an imprint of New American Library,
a division of Penguin Books USA Inc.

First Printing, August, 1990
10  9  8  7  6  5  4  3  2  1

 REGISTERED TRADEMARK—MARCA REGISTRADA

PRINTED IN THE UNITED STATES OF AMERICA

PUBLISHER'S NOTE
This is a work of fiction. Names, characters, places, and incidents
either are the product of the author's imagination or are used
fictitiously, and any resemblance to actual persons, living or dead,
events, or locales is entirely coincidental.

BOOKS ARE AVAILABLE AT QUANTITY DISCOUNTS WHEN USED TO PROMOTE
PRODUCTS OR SERVICES. FOR INFORMATION PLEASE WRITE TO PREMIUM
MARKETING DIVISION, PENGUIN BOOKS USA INC., 375 HUDSON STREET,
NEW YORK, NEW YORK 10014.

To Jim

# Acknowledgments

I would like to thank Henry W. Vaillant, M.D., president, Emerson Hospital medical staff and member of the faculties of Harvard and Tufts medical schools. Through his personal example he has shown me that no matter how marvelous the technology, the most beautiful elements of modern medicine continue to be care, respect, sympathy, and love for one's fellowman. This book could not have been written without him. William C. Steinkraus, individual gold medalist in Olympic show jumping and chairman of the board of the United States Equestrian Team, took time from his busy schedule to answer numerous questions about the puissance event. Alan S. Trueblood allowed me to quote from his translation *Antonio Machado: Selected Poems* (Cambridge, Mass.: Harvard University Press, 1982.) I would like to express my admiration for Grand Prix rider Michael Matz, whose rescue of two children from the crash of United Air Lines Flight 232 epitomizes the courage and heroism I hope the reader finds in several of the characters in this story. Anna Lenos, Stephanie Millham, Sandra MacKay, Holly Van Borst—thank you for being there when I needed you. And, finally, to my childhood friend Daisy, who was destroyed but never lost—we made it over that wall at last.

# Contents

# Hampstead

It was an expensive New England horse farm, which meant it didn't generate wealth, but the reverse—wealth generated it. Complete with acres of four-board enclosed pasture, mirrored indoor riding arena, and custom-made jumping course, Hampstead Farm had been given by Robert Snyder, president and CEO of Premium Computers, to his wife, Barbara, as a birthday present and, rumor had it, a salve to his conscience. The only sign of Mr. Snyder's presence was an early-morning and late-evening helicopter that appeared on the lawn of their Greek Revival manor house to ferry him over the crush of lesser commuters.

By the mid-eighties, Hampstead Farm had developed into a top East Coast training facility. Stabling more than eighty horses—show jumpers, working and conformation hunters, children's ponies, and broodmares—the big H logo became as familiar as the name Hermès. Hampstead's clients won at shows, won because they bought quality horses and quality training—in short, because they had time and money.

The inside of the main stable looked as immaculate as its shining white exterior. A cathedral ceiling gave the aura of an entire underground village. Solid oak stalls, perfect reproductions of eighteenth-century English ones, resplendent with metal grillwork and burnished brass balls on their corner posts, presented a large, roomy appearance. In the aisles, red terrazzo laid in herringbone pattern caused the grooms who swept them to curse. But the tiles seemed aesthetically pleasing to everyone else. And swept clean they were, not a wisp of hay evident, everything in its appointed—and understated—place.

Down a side aisle, a red wheelbarrow stood at one stall entrance. Every few seconds a forkful of manure would travel several feet in the air and plump into it. Wielding the pitchfork was nineteen-year-old Diana Winston, lowest rung on the ladder of Hampstead's hierarchy. Just two weeks before, she'd left her job as groom and sometime instructor at a local riding academy, hoping that by hard work at the top facility—making herself invaluable—she'd get a chance to demonstrate her talent and an opportunity to ride and learn from the best. Beautiful and tall, she had an erect bearing and confident manner that conveyed a sophisticated, mature presence. Intense dark eyes suggested a woman who would get what she wanted by sheer force of will. And her goal—determined at the age of twelve—was to become the best show jumper in North America.

Closing the stall door, she patted the black gelding on his neck. "Rocco, did you know I didn't even make my bed this morning so I could get here in time to make yours? And yes, you don't even care, do you?" Diana pushed the wheelbarrow down the aisle. But just as she turned the corner, she had to swerve sharply to avoid hitting Courtney Snyder, daughter of the stable owners, leading her massive Hanoverian, Grunewald, a gelding imported from the best stud farm in West Germany. The heavy barrow overturned, spilling its contents over the floor.

"Why don't you look where you're going?" said Courtney haughtily as she stroked the startled horse. "Well, you'll just have to clean it up," she commanded, "and here, Grun needs to be cooled out too. Mother's taking me into Boston for a fitting and I'm late already." She stuffed the reins into Diana's hands and stalked away. Without turning, she added, "Do a good job of cooling him or I'll know who to blame if he colics."

"Spoiled brat," Diana hissed under her breath. Holding the reins, she attempted to right the wheelbarrow. But the big gray gelding startled and rushed backward, taking her with him. "Easy, boy. See the mess I've got to clean up?" As she spoke, she saw the horse was still hot and soaked. "You've got to be walked." At the same time Diana knew she couldn't.

"Can I help?"

She turned to see one of Hampstead's many grooms. Steve was Mexican (he had adopted the English form of his "Esteban") and had been at Hampstead six months. Polite but reserved, he spoke only when his work compelled it. Seeing his dark and kind face, Diana instinctively felt attracted to his manner as well as his powerful body, tanned from hours of summer work. She failed to note a cast of perpetual sadness in his eyes.

"My problem's pretty obvious," she said with a self-conscious laugh, relieved that somebody cared.

"Here, I'll see to the horse. You do what you can about that." He nodded toward the overturned mess. Then he took Grunewald's reins from her hands and began to walk down the aisle.

"Thanks," said Diana. She stared at the manure-covered red tiles, then picked up her pitchfork. "I hate this terrazzo."

After mucking nine more stalls, she decided she'd had enough. She had come here to ride. In exchange for mucking, she'd been promised lessons from Herr Gunther von Engerson, three-time winner at Aachen, six-time European champion, and former member of the West German Olympic Equestrian Team. Into the office of the stable manager she marched.

The red-haired, round-shouldered man hunched over his desk, then looked up. He was updating each horse's medical chart—who needed worming, or the farrier, or who needed teeth floated or special dental work. He didn't like interruptions. "What is it?"

"May I have five minutes of your time?" asked Diana.

Bob Sloan glanced at his watch, set his beefy pale arms on the desk, and said, "You got it: no more, no less."

"Mr. Sloan, if you remember, you hired me as a working student. I work in exchange for instruction, and you let me know when my lessons are."

"Yeah, that's right."

"Well, Mr. Sloan, could you tell me, please, when the first one is?"

"Susan . . ." began Sloan patiently.

"Diana."

"Well, Diana, then. How long have you worked here?"

"Three days."

"And how much does one hour of your work count toward a lesson?"

"Four dollars and twenty-five cents."

"That's right." His bug eyes conveyed that she had the answer as to why she hadn't yet ridden.

"But when will I have a lesson with Mr. von Engerson?"

Sloan's face now flushed with anger "Su . . . er, Diana, do you know how much our clients pay for one session?" She stammered something vaguely negative. "I didn't think so. Eighty bucks."

"Eighty?" Diana asked with amazement.

"Eight, zero: *eight*-ty. I got your name right. Now get the numbers right."

"Just for one riding lesson?"

"One riding lesson, but not just. Von Engerson's the top. To train with him is an honor, see? Training with him is learning the best. That means—"

"Mucking out one hundred stalls," said Diana softly, shaking her head.

"What'd you say?"

"For one hour with Herr von Engerson, I muck out approximately a hundred stalls."

"Diane . . ."

"Diana." Her voice now became edged with impatience, though the coarse-fibered man barely caught it.

"Diana, minimum wage for minimum labor. We need to keep costs down. Running this establishment is expen-

sive, and Mrs. Snyder isn't even trying to turn a profit."
(Bob Sloan declined to go into the tax advantages on that
score.)

"How about a scholarship?" she asked timidly.

"Scholarship?" he retorted, sarcasm rising in his throat.

"Yes, I have riding ability but not the money to develop it. Perhaps you could explain this to Herr von
Engerson? He's a teacher, he might understand. I could
ride for him—show what I already know."

Sloan stood up, impatience giving way to exasperation.
"Diana, von Engerson's here one year. He trains our
clients on their horses. We make money from this, but
that's not the half of it. Our clients take what they learn
into the show ring and they—and Hampstead—win. For
every thirty hours of yours—we need to deduct taxes and
medical coverage—we're allowing you one hour of Herr
von Engerson's time. And for what? You won't likely do
us any good. We even supply your horse, which you
might injure. And you can afford only one lesson a week.
Any advancement will be slow. So be grateful this farm is
willing to sacrifice an hour of its famous instructor's time
for an aspiring rider who'll remain exactly that—an aspiring rider." He sat down and looked intently at a positive
Coggins test that had sent shivers up his spine before *she*
came in. "Five minutes, Punto."

Diana stood shaking and hoped her voice wouldn't
crack as she spoke. "Mr. Sloan?"

The man looked up, surprised and irritated she hadn't
understood the dismissal. "That's all I have to say."

"Mr. Sloan, when is my first lesson with Herr von
Engerson?"

Near exploding, he concluded the best way to get back
to work was to answer her question. He got up and paced
over to a training schedule posted on the wall.

"Next Monday. You'll have twenty-nine hours by then.
Three o'clock. Ride Exeter."

"Thank you," replied Diana, turning to go.

"Oh, and, Diana? Either plan on getting here an hour
early or skip lunch. Your lesson bites an hour out of the
workday."

Diana nodded and walked away. But as soon as she turned the corner, she kicked at the hay bales stacked for evening feed. "Damn this place!"

A gentle nicker greeted the swearing. She peered into a dark corner stall. Every show horse's mane is trimmed to four inches, the tail crisply banged at the hocks. But this mane and tail had grown to natural length and fullness.

"He's an Andalusian—their manes and tails don't get pulled." Diana turned to the voice and saw Steve. "Aren't many in this country," he went on, stroking the silky white mane. "I'm sure you've seen them in the bull ring."

"Andalusian?"

"Brave and agile. Soldiers and knights rode them because they can turn so quickly. You've seen in a picture that Napoleon favored one?"

"The one in brandy ads, that portrait by—"

"David," finished Steve.

"You know!" said Diana incredulously.

His blush and glance down conveyed that she shouldn't pursue how an underpaid wetback groom could be acquainted with French art circa 1800. She turned back to the stallion. "And who's he?"

"This gentleman, Navarro, he belongs to the Spanish ambassador. As you see, he is very beautiful."

"Shouldn't he be in Washington?"

"His wife and Mrs. Snyder went to the same school."

"In Spain?"

"No, some school near Washington, D.C.—Foxcraft? Yes, I think Foxcraft," replied Steve, obviously pleased at calling up the name.

"You mean Foxcroft?" asked Diana, smiling at the suggestive mistake and feeling increasingly drawn to this sweet man.

"Yes, Foxcraft, you know it?" Now it was his turn to be surprised.

"It's the top rich-bitch prep school in the East—of course I know it. Each girl has her own horse, but do they get them ready to ride? Good heavens, no! Why get a dirt line under your manicure when our counterparts down in D.C. can?" she asked sarcastically.

"My little friend, you make me feel sorry when you speak like that." He put his hand on her shoulder.

"Sorry?" asked Diana, shrugging off his gentle touch. She didn't want his pity.

"Yes, you're so pretty and—"

"Are Andalusians used for anything other that bull-fights?" Diana cut in, not caring to hear any more. Anger at Courtney and Sloan had spilled over into her conversation with Steve, and she was mortified that this gentle Mexican saw through her toughness to the hurt beneath.

Steve went on to describe the great Spanish riding school in Jerez where Andalusians train in dressage, its *haute école*, and perform airs above the ground—the famous levade, capriole, and courbette.

"Can they jump?" asked Diana, her thoughts turning to the competition that obsessed her.

"You ask if ballerinas can jump? And Nureyev or Baryshnikov, can they jump? It's the same. I must go back to work now." Abruptly ending the conversation, he turned and walked down the aisle.

"He's a different sort of groom, isn't he, Navarro?" Diana stroked the white neck, but the horse stared down the aisle in Steve's direction and didn't heed her admiring touch.

That evening Diana opened the back door of her house and greeted her mother in the kitchen. "Hello, darling, how did the lesson go?" replied Mrs. Winston. A pleasant woman, slightly overweight, her hair and eyes a faded color of her daughter's dark brown, she carried her body and spoke in a manner that suggested half-contented resignation with life.

"Fine, Mother."

"What did you learn?"

"Oh, I'm working on flying changes of lead at the canter," Diana lied. She knew her mother would be shocked to find out that her daughter hadn't yet received a single lesson. So angry, in fact, she'd try to get her to quit.

"That's nice. Of course, you know I'm not a horse person. I'm sure your father would have known what flying changes are. How about fixing the green beans for me?"

Diana took the colander and plastic bag of vegetables to the table, pulled out a chair, and sat down. She thought of Courtney, spoiled and rich, with everything at her fingertips. "Mother, when did we lose our money?" The sudden question filled the whole room.

"What did you say?" Mrs. Winston's body froze, indicating she'd heard the words perfectly but needed a few seconds to answer.

"When exactly did we—I mean, did Dad—lose our money?"

Diana's mother squared her rounded shoulders, and drew measured breath. It was time for the inevitable conversation.

"A few years after you were born, your father put most of his savings into venture capital and stock options. He did it against everyone's advice, but, well, you know, he was such an optimist."

"But he had a family. He risked us all. He was irresponsible, wasn't he? And now we have virtually nothing."

"Diana, your father was imprudent. He made a mistake. But he wanted some things so badly that he couldn't bear to hear he was going about getting them in the wrong way. He wanted a lot for us and worked very hard. As for having nothing, that's preposterous."

"But, Mother, we did have *a lot*, didn't we? I remember Dad going off to ride dressed in his pinks. He kept a string of terrific horses. You used to serve hunt breakfasts. I even had lessons on Tally from the master of the hunt, went to Nashoba Brooks—lots better than Southfield. And I remember the ferry to Nantucket and staying at the inn—the Jaffrey, the Jeffery . . ."

"The Jared Coffin House. Yes, I remember all that—

and more." Mrs. Winston looked out the window wistfully. "But we lived on borrowed time. When one venture failed, he'd attempt to bail it out by investing in another. It was just more credit to gamble. But your father loved us more than anything else."

"So, where do we go from here? I've got nothing. I need something so I can make it more." Diana wadded up the plastic bag and spiked it into the trash, annoyed that the violent force resulted in such a light descent.

"Diana Winston, I don't want to hear, ever again, that you have nothing. Your father and I saw to it that you're getting a fine education. You went to Boston for plays and concerts. You've been well-fed, well-clothed, and I think, all in all, your life has been pretty pleasant."

"I want more than a pleasant life. I want . . ." Diana's voice trailed off.

"What *do* you want?"

"I want to succeed," said Diana emphatically. "I want success."

"Then you'd better get off to college."

"Some second-rate place? Not me."

"Diana, just because you couldn't get a full scholarship to Radcliffe or Bryn Mawr doesn't mean there aren't other places just as good."

"I don't want to spend four years sitting in classes debating whether or not the Old Man and the sea was Jesus Christ. I want to learn to ride and I want . . ."

"What *do* you want?"

"I want success," Diana repeated emphatically, "in what I want to do—no delays, no deviations."

"Then you should get a job. You have remarkable abilities. I don't want to see them wasted. You should at least get involved so you might meet some nice—"

"Future husband? No, Mother. I'm where I want to be and learning what I need to learn. I love my sport and refuse to see it as a habit to be supported by a regular job. It *is* my job and it's my life. The husband will have to come later."

"But riding takes money and you don't have any."

In the wake of learning that she'd have to muck a hundred stalls for one lesson, the truth hit hard, but Diana felt herself gather strength in the face of it. "I can't—I won't—let myself get cut out of what I love because I don't have any money."

"Well, money isn't everything, of course. I just want you to be happy."

Diana knew that when her mother resorted to clichés the conversation was winding down. Moreover, she had to thwart her desire to shock her mother by telling her that she knew her father really didn't love his family and that he'd been no paragon of virtue. He selfishly squandered his money—their money—money that could have kept up the place, paid for lessons at Hampstead, and money that could have made lots more money instead of dropping into some unscrupulous broker's pocket.

The evening he drove his Trans Am into the turbid Nashua River, John Winston hadn't been alone. When she was thirteen, Diana looked up the accident in the newspaper files at Southfield library. The lurid news story described his secretary, Meredith Parsons, as the sole passenger. There it was in the *Patriot Ledger*, nauseatingly clear. After autopsies revealed high levels of blood alcohol in both, the Parsons family sued, and a discreet out-of-court settlement meant more money gone, more shame. This side of her father had been completely hidden from Diana until then. Perhaps her mother knew all along. Diana didn't dare ask. She did know her mother desperately wanted her to cherish her father's memory. If Mrs. Winston believed that her daughter knew nothing of the illicit activities, then the older woman could more easily forget the truth that had caused so much grief.

"Excuse me, Mother, I forgot. I've got to feed Tally!" Diana stood up from the table and ran out the door toward the red barn before her mother could protest. It was a large, well-constructed building in need of paint and repair. Of twelve stalls, only one was occupied. The liver chestnut Tally had been John Winston's favorite horse, and once the top conformation hunter in the North-east. Diana had learned to ride on him. Now she occasionally got on his back, but at twenty-four and arthritic in both hocks, the veteran couldn't take rigorous exercise.

"Tally, things will change because I'm going to—I've got to—change them back to what the Winstons were before joint ventures and young secretaries. Mother's right: money isn't everything, and I don't need everything. I just want back what was ours. I've seen what money can do—it pays for all the shoveling in the world, and right now I'm the one doing it, but not for long."

Next Monday Diana had her lesson with Herr von Engerson. She shined her boots to a rich, flawless black and carefully ironed her riding shirt. As she tacked up the thoroughbred, she felt an enormous sense of power mixed with anxiety. She was going to ride in the arena where Olympic greats rode—and on Exeter, a retired Olympic champion. She would listen to everything von Engerson said and she would perform spectacularly. As she walked Exeter down the aisle to the indoor arena, she saw Courtney Snyder with two male friends. One, a tall blond, looked like he'd just flown in from the islands—sunburned, white chinos, Top-Siders, and aviator sunglasses. The other, dark and tanned, had dressed for the occasion—Guess-jeans-and-jacket outfit.

"I don't know a horse's front from his rear," kidded the blond. The other chimed in that he knew a horse's ass when he saw one. "Do you really ride this thing?" the first asked Courtney. He jabbed a finger at Grunewald, who was absentmindedly chewing hay.

"Yes, of course, Paul. What do you think I do with him?" She fingered his polo collar, more to flirt than to adjust.

As Diana passed, Paul took Courtney's riding crop and rapped the unsuspecting Exeter on the hindquarters. "Is this a jumper, too?" The startled horse lunged and his foreleg caught Diana behind the knee, making her fall hard on the ground.

"Gosh, let me help." Designer Outfit offered his hand.

Shaken, Diana stood up and dusted off her riding shirt, but a streak of dirt wouldn't respond. "Look what you've done!" she said angrily. She struggled to suppress her tears.

"I said sorry." He made it sound like a command.

Diana glared at the trio. "Looks like this stable is now boarding jackasses."

"How dare you speak to my friends that way," huffed Courtney. "This is your last day of work at Hampstead Farm, whoever you are."

Conceited laughter followed Diana as she ran down the aisle, tears streaming down her face.

She had barely time to compose herself before she stood before the great man.

Herr von Engerson, a gentleman of the old school, disproved the common theory that there are none left. Originally of the Junker class, his family had for generations been among the elite of Germany's equestrian world. His brother conspired in the army plot to assassinate Hitler and was subsequently tortured and shot. Immaculately dressed in tweed jacket, boots, and cap, von Engerson spoke fluent but heavily accented English. He walked over to Diana and offered his hand. "Good afternoon, miss. I am Gunther von Engerson, and you are . . . ?"

"Diana Winston." His Old World courtesy and seeming interest in her eased her anxiety.

"I am very pleased to meet you. Well, let us see what we can do today." Her lesson started well. Herr von Engerson, a master of detail and finesse, showed Diana how, by a subtle shift of weight, the slight turn of a shoulder, and a soft but closed hand, she could get Exeter to trot, canter, and do flying changes with the least effort. "Fine, very fine! You have a good seat, wonderful hands, and superb instincts. Let us try a few jumps. First this crossrail, please, just to see. Head up! Good, good, *schön*! Now, Diana, a small course: begin with the oxer, then the in-and-out, followed by the coop, and last the gate."

Diana circled the energetic Exeter to organize both of them before she started. The proud former Olympian felt ready.

"Eyes up, Diana, up. More inside leg. Slow him down. He is now very excited to be doing this. You must control more. You be in charge, not the horse. Excellent approach. Head up on landing. Slow him before you ask. There!" After repeating the course a half-dozen times more, Diana trotted the big thoroughbred over to where von Engerson stood smiling. "Good, good. *Ausgezeichnet.* Timing is excellent, but there remain points of refinement that I perhaps could help you with. It is important—I cannot emphasize this too much—that when you do a course, it is like living your life. True. Jumps are goals, not obstacles. They are what you want, and you must look to the one ahead. Early in going over a fence, you put your eye on the next one. Ping! Immediately. If it is, for the moment, out of sight, look in the direction you believe it to be. That is how you get to it most quickly. In the ring it is not only getting over jumps without knocking them down, but how fast. *Die Zeit ist kurz, die Kunst ist lang.*" She hadn't the slightest notion what *that* meant. "Another thing I cannot tell you too much: how style counts in riding, just as in life too. Many people think style is something extra, the . . . what you call 'frosting on the cake.' But, Diana, style *is* the cake. It is from beauty of one's style that performance and then ultimate greatness come. Now, you ride a little like a cowboy, so determined to get where you want to go that you abandon your body to the four winds. Refine yourself. Horse and rider are not a well-matched pair—they are *one*. Exeter has excellent training, so he therefore has style. You understand, young lady?"

Diana nodded unsmilingly. She had tried her best, and wondered how she could acquire this style. "Thank you very much, Herr von Engerson." He then ungloved his hand, offered it, and after they had shaken, began to walk away.

"Diana." The aging instructor paused. He had stopped

and now turned around. "You are . . . very good—you could perhaps be one of the best," he added with quiet authority. "I think, yes, perhaps. We shall see." All business. His face had lost its smile. Diana's entire body welled up with happiness and excitement. The feeling didn't last long. Waiting just outside the Fibar arena by the benches stood Mrs. Snyder, dressed in an emerald suit, sunglasses, and pearls.

"Diana Winston?"

"Yes, ma'am?"

When the woman took off her sunglasses, her hazel eyes were beautiful and direct. Diana glanced at the mirrors and flags, thinking to herself that this would be the last time she'd see them. "I understand my daughter and you had a little incident." Diana nodded. "Well, you know I take Hampstead very seriously and cannot tolerate behavior that results in a horse running loose, reins hanging. If Exeter had caught a leg, he might have had a serious accident. Do you understand?"

"Yes, but—" Diana started to reply, overpowered by mortification.

"So I should like very much to apologize for the behavior of my daughter and her friends. They jeopardized a horse for which you had responsibility. Courtney assures me it will never happen again. And I assured her the same." The hazel eyes flashed angrily. "Now I'm afraid I must go. Nice to have met you."

Diana smiled, stroked Exeter's neck, and reflected that even though the daughter was a brat, her mother was quite nice. As she led the horse into his stall, though, she suddenly wondered: how had Mrs. Snyder known the real story?

"Excuse me, miss," said the person responsible. Diana closed Exeter's stall and faced the handsome red-haired Jim Williams. Unknown to her, he had witnessed the entire incident.

What she knew very well, of course, was that Williams was the gold medalist in Los Angeles, winner of two World Cups, and member of the United States Equestrian Team. She also knew his black mare Calliope was in training with von Engerson. Jim worked out of the USET headquarters in Gladstone, New Jersey, but periodically drove or flew to Hampstead and checked on Calliope's progress by taking a lesson or two with older pros.

"Well, hello, Mr. Williams," Diana said in mock formality, trying not to show how dazzled she was by her girlhood hero.

"How do you know who I am?" Her frank manner charmed him as his modesty did her.

"Awfully hard not to know who you are, Mr. Williams."

"And who are you?" asked Jim, playing his Cheshire-cat self, with the smile remaining.

"A person of little consequence in the horse world—at least at the moment." Diana's tone grew serious. Who was she kidding? she thought to herself. I'm just a horse-mad girl with unrealistic hopes.

"No doubt the moment will be short," he said, lightly touching her arm with his hand. She felt excitement, then shyness. "You know, you still haven't told me who you are."

Now annoyed at her own timidity, Diana further froze and stared at the ground. Before she could get out the first syllable of her name, he went on. "Look, since this obviously will take some time, why don't we find a more conducive atmosphere?" Jim glanced at her dirty breeches. "Do you have something else to wear?"

"Not anything much better. I've got jeans in my bike basket, but they're filthy from this morning's work." She self-consciously rubbed the smudges on her arm. Bike basket, she thought. I must sound like I'm ten years old. "My mother has the car today." She immediately regretted that admission even more.

"That's okay, we can take my car. I know a place where the dress code's not draconian. Why don't you pop into the shower while I get my things, then meet me in fifteen minutes?" He turned to leave.

"I can't use the shower—only clients and trainers, not muckers." She paused. "My name is Diana Winston."

His face reddened with irritation, but not at her. "Use the shower. Someone asks, you're my guest."

"Are you sure it'll be okay?" She hesitated.

"Absolutely." His firm dismissal signaled Diana that she didn't dare tell him why she really didn't want to use the Trophy Room—it made her feel awkward and out of place.

Making as little sound as she could, she opened the door just to the right of the main aisle. So this was the Trophy Room. Before or after riding, owners and trainers could relax, take a hot shower, watch a video (Joe Fargis winning the gold or *Beverly Hills Cop*—there was variety), or mix drinks at the spacious wet bar. The Early American decor in green and red, Hampstead's colors, had been featured in an *Architectural Digest* article on "working" show barns. Walls and shelves were lined and laden with ribbons and trophies from big competitive shows in the East. In the center, amidst primarily blue and red ribbons, hung a picture of eighteen-year-old Courtney Snyder on her mount Bonnie Princess. She had just captured second place in the Medal Class at Madison Square Garden. Her smile revealed a girl accustomed to winning, as if it were expected, if not her outright due.

Once in the dressing area, Diana did what she could, washing her face and combing back her dark hair. Just as she opened the door, Courtney herself stood there about to enter. "Just what the hell do you think you're doing?" she demanded.

"I'm getting ready to go out for the evening," said Diana coolly, gliding past her nemesis.

"The help aren't allowed to use clients' facilities," said Courtney, with her attempt at British grammar. "I'm sure Mr. Sloan briefed you when you were hired."

"A client gave permission," said Diana, "as *his* guest."

"Who'd be that nearsighted?"

"I guess I would."

Courtney turned to see Jim Williams staring at her, his impassive face barely concealing his pleasure as he watched Courtney squirm inside. "Oh, Jim, you're kidding—I was only teasing." Years of training in social ruses and mis-cues allowed her to control the damage.

"You two obviously haven't met. Courtney Snyder, I'd like to introduce you to Diana Winston." Both young women hastily exchanged glances. "Courtney, if you'll excuse us, Diana and I are going out to dinner." Jim, fully aware Courtney would give her eyeteeth to be in Diana's shoes, waited for a reaction.

But Courtney merely nodded as the two walked out of the stable. Embarrassment and anger gnawed at her, but mostly jealousy. She'd been after Jim since assuming junior female command at Hampstead. He'd always been polite to her and assisted her in riding, but acted uninterested—despite several overt invitations. Courtney decided that like a fair number of other men in show jumping, Jim Williams was most likely gay. Or was he? He seemed awfully interested in this little groom who'd caused trouble with Mother. It was too much. She threw her whip viciously at the stall across the aisle, causing the horse to shy. "Asshole!" she snapped at the startled animal, and left.

"I can't go in there!" Diana stopped in the parking lot outside the River Mill restaurant, among the finest in southern New Hampshire.

"Why on earth not?" asked Jim, looking serious but nonetheless amused at Diana's predicament.

"Look how I'm dressed!" She held her arms outstretched and gazed down at her riding clothes.

"You look fine. Believe me, fine—beautiful, in fact."

"Then why did you change out of *your* riding gear? You too could be beautiful." Her exasperation gave way to humor. He wore a blazer and slightly flared gray flannels, European cut—picked up during competition abroad. To Diana he seemed the height of casual ele-gance with power resting at the core.

Jim gently squeezed her arm with his hand. "Diana, a lot of horse farms and shows are in the area. I'm sure this restaurant has seen more stable clothes than a tack store."

"All right, I give up." She yielded more to the pressure and warmth of his hand on her arm than to his explanation. During dinner they talked with unceasing animation about their past, present, and future. Once they looked into each other's eyes, they could soon stand neither to look nor to look away. They discovered they shared many interests and opinions. Jim was happily surprised that Diana had a passion for Renaissance music, while she liked it that if he ever had children he would introduce them to painting by hanging prints of Raoul Dufy on the nursery walls.

Of course, the conversation included horses. He mapped out a program for her success. "You want to gain the trust of some owners at Hampstead who hire riders to show their horses."

"How do I do that?" asked Diana.

"You have to get Mrs. Snyder to ask you to exercise some of the horses." At her look of doubt, he smiled. "Don't worry, you're good. I watched you. It'll happen soon enough. And if you pay attention and give those animals your best, some owners will pay you to train them regularly with von Engerson. Then the sky's the limit."

"That 'if' is a big one."

"You're not giving me any credit. If you're going to lack confidence, please allow me to have some. I've been around, you know." She smiled at the Olympian's understatement. "I've seen you ride. Von Engerson told me he hasn't seen anyone with your natural ability in years, Europe or the United States. But unless you believe that you can be the best, you'll turn out to be your own worst enemy. You'll fail not because you don't own Grunewald or Exeter, but because something inside you spreads that rumor you don't deserve a great horse. You do—just wait a little and make more effort to get one." Diana looked at her lap and then out the window. "Am I right?" he asked, his green eyes warm and intent.

"I suppose so, it's just that . . ." Diana glanced at him, then down at the little wicker basket of rolls.

"It's just that . . . ?" he urged.

"Well, you say I need confidence, von Engerson says I need style, and I don't know how to go about getting either. The place is so intimidating—the flags, the names, the horses, and the money. See? Lack of confidence." Diana smiled nervously and fingered a sugar packet in the glass server.

"Do you want to know how?" He took the packet away from her and gently placed her hand on the table. "Ride your ass off. Ride any and every horse offered you, and keep mucking those stalls out until the owners kick in free lessons because they believe you're good enough to make their horses win. Clear? Stop biting your lip and tell me that's clear."

"Perfectly clear, Mr. Williams. I'll ride my ass off till there's nothing left." She smiled pertly.

"Please, don't go that far!" They both laughed.

The dinner slid leisurely by. She told him she'd never had filet mignon done so well, and the St. Emilion—well, she simply hadn't had good wine in a long while. Relaxed and happy for the first time in months, she felt her face flush as the alcohol warmed her body and gave every sense a dizzy new connection. And she liked the rush of physical desire, set off simply by watching Jim order Benedictines to complete dinner. A moist sensation between her legs and longing deep in her pelvis seemed delightfully out of control.

Jim opened the door of his Porsche and she got in, exhilarated by the shock of evening air. "Are you all right?" he asked as he put the key into the ignition.

"Absolutely fine," she answered, afraid he knew how intoxicated she was, how much she wanted him.

"Good, it just seems you're a little quiet." He revved the engine and turned into the night, evergreens marking the dark horizon.

"Comfortable," sighed Diana.

As they drove up Hampstead's long driveway, Diana groaned, "I don't want to come back here—really, can't we turn around, it's too . . ."

"But you love it, don't you?" he gently teased. "Being where the best are."

"I do, but not at ten o'clock tonight." Jim drove the red Porsche around to the barn where Diana kept her bicycle. "Don't you think it looks like a pumpkin?" Glancing at her rusty bike, Diana suddenly felt twelve years old. "You know, Cinderella." She glanced at her watch. "I hope midnight never comes."

Jim stiffened as the significance of her fairy-tale image cut through the haze produced by the evening's wine and liqueur. He'd gone too far. She had misunderstood the evening and wanted romance. She expected a kiss, at the very least, to close out the night. "I know what you mean. But I'm taking Calliope down to Gladstone tomorrow and have to be up at five to get her ready for the trailer ride." Without another word or glance in her direction, he hopped out of the car, opened the trunk, and fitted her bicycle in.

"Now, I know where Southfield is, but not your house. Should I take Merrick Road or One-nineteen?"

"Merrick," she answered softly. What had happened? Had she said something that made him change his mind about her? She'd half-hoped he'd invite her in for a drink in the USET rec vehicle that served as his home while he was at Hampstead. She'd been too forward. But could that alone have caused him to back off? Maybe in the end he simply didn't like her enough.

They didn't pass a single car as they drove the three miles from Hampstead to Southfield. "Tired?" Jim asked.

"Worried and lonely." She turned and looked out the window. Acres of newly tilled fields, dark trees, and black sky formed the dark night canvas.

"Why?" he asked, sympathetically touching her forearm. " 'Lonely'? I'm here."

"Oh, Jim, I've admired you for so long and . . ."

"And now we're friends. And we'll become good friends. I feel it."

"Do you mean that?" Diana felt a surge of hope.

"Yes, good *friends*. Given the crazy life I lead, we shouldn't expect more."

Though she sensed the qualification, Diana took his hand and held it in hers, but Jim almost immediately withdrew it. "I've got to shift," he laughed.

A few minutes later they drove up the lane to Diana's house. Yellow lights glowed inside the old white colonial. "Uh-oh, I've had it. Let me off here. I don't want Mother to see you or this car." Jim pulled over to the side of the road, jumped out, and deftly lifted Diana's bike from the trunk.

When she took the handlebars, she looked into his face, expecting a kiss. But there was none—just a brotherly pat on the arm. "Don't forget, ride anything short of a mule that comes your way," he said lightheartedly.

But as Jim returned to Hampstead, he felt anything but lighthearted. The thrill and delight of Diana's company—worse, the naive way she had showed her hopes about the two of them—gave way to confusion and remorse. How could he tell her the truth?

It had begun in seventh grade at St. Benedict's, a monastery and prep school north of New York City. One evening in the library, Doug Ryan, a junior, sat reading at the same table, but got up and called Jim outside. Doug was vice-president of the student body, almost certain to be valedictorian and, more important from the school's standpoint, would no doubt receive the Christian Leadership award. Jim felt flattered. Suddenly Doug was telling Jim how he had become interested in a girl at St. Philomena's. They would meet again at a dance that weekend. But he had a problem—he'd never been with a girl and she'd expect him to kiss her when they went back to her dorm. Maybe Jim could help him practice how to kiss so she'd like it. It was like girls practicing dancing together. At first Jim said no, and continued to refuse despite the boy's entreaties. But when Doug said that he'd tell Father Ambrose, their dorm head, that Jim, in fact, had tried to stroke his "private parts" under the library table, Jim got frightened. Doug Ryan, the school's most Christian student—so all the monks said. If Doug told on the younger boy, he'd almost certainly be believed. Jim reluctantly agreed, and they stepped out to the dark lawn and into privacy behind the hedgerow.

When the blackmail continued, it became clear to Jim that Doug Ryan had used the dance at Philomena's as an excuse. And though Jim objected to the coercion, he no longer objected to what followed. The encounters went on for several weeks, until Father Ambrose called him in, put a gentle hand on his shoulder, and said that he had noticed Jim hadn't received Holy Communion recently, and was there anything he wanted to talk about? Shortly thereafter, Jim admitted the truth. He felt better, but not completely free of guilt. He'd been unable to confess what had troubled him most about his encounters with Doug Ryan—he enjoyed them.

During the remaining years at St. Benedict's, Jim Williams convinced himself that Doug Ryan had been an aberration. He immersed himself in schoolwork and athletics. Primarily interested in history, he became fascinated by men of action and courage. His first hero was Winston Churchill. He identified with the traumatic childhood, the boarding-school life, and the unrequited love of a lonely boy for his mother. And like Churchill, he regarded the horse as the final and endangered symbol of heroism. In this connection, Jim started to ride.

Throughout school and most of college, he repressed his homosexuality, but the masquerade began to take its toll. He couldn't bear hearing himself make locker-room talk with college friends, or having himself set up with dates because those who cared about him thought he was too shy with girls. The one time he had sex with a girl at Princeton, it was terribly awkward and quick. Quietly and discreetly he entered the gay world.

Now, back in his rec vehicle, he poured himself a beer, flicked on a radio, and sat on one of the bunks. As he cradled his drink, he stared at the photos of the Olympic greats—Hugh Wiley, George Morris, Frank Chapot, Bill Steinkraus, Joe Fargis, and himself. He'd done well—he should be proud. But why such emptiness? He recalled Diana—bright, beautiful, energetic, kind, and inexperienced. What an enthralling combination. And yet he was gay. Could he be getting "better"? He'd lived gay for some years now. Still, he'd heard of occasional swings back and forth among bisexuals. Perhaps he was bi, not homosexual. He shook his head, driving the speculation from his mind. No, he preferred men—too many encounters had proved that. Yet, something about this girl made him urgently desire her friendship. It was too much to think about, so he quickly drained his glass, got back in his car, and drove up to Harpo's, a small gay bar in Nashua, just over the New Hampshire line.

"Diana, where on earth have you been? It's almost midnight!" Mrs. Winston stood in the doorway. "I was about to call the police."

"Mother, you're up," said Diana.

"I've been pacing for hours. Where have you been? I demand to know."

"I fell asleep, Mother. I had a difficult and tiring lesson, so I went to lie down in the hayloft and didn't wake up till just twenty minutes ago. I got one of the grooms to drive me home."

"Is that right?" Mrs. Winston intoned sarcastically.

"Yes," Diana replied weakly. It was the only unused story on open file.

"Are the salaries at Hampstead so lavish that grooms can afford Porsches? When are you getting yours?"

Diana gave up. "I'm so very sorry."

"Not as sorry as you're going to be if this happens again. I don't mind your going out, but at least have the courtesy to let me know your plans so I won't fret."

"I *am* sorry."

"The nights I waited for your father, and that one night he didn't come home." Mrs. Winston's voice cracked into sobs. Instinctively Diana hugged her.

"I didn't mean to make you worry. I promise it won't happen again. I was inconsiderate for not calling."

Mrs. Winston nodded her acceptance. "Well, let's get to bed." As Diana climbed the stairs, her mother called out, "Diana, you're all I have left. My hopes and dreams *are* you. You must know that."

"I know that, Mother, and I love you."

When Diana put on her flannel nightgown and looked around her room—the stuffed animals, horse statues, and Olympic posters—she felt out of place for the first time. She picked up the bear that had been hers since infancy, and sat on the end of her bed. His missing eye seemed to stare, and she remembered the ear that Bob—their old Lab, now dead—had chewed off.

"Reggie, today things started to change for me. I know what I want and I'm going to get there—I feel it. I'm too old for you, old friend—for all this. I don't want to hurt your feelings, so come to bed with me this one last night." As she held the bear, Diana recalled Jim Williams —his gentle face and soft touch and how he had spoken to her. This was the man her dreams told her she'd been waiting for. She imagined them both riding, training, giving lessons out of their own show barn. At least that's what she hoped for. But then she remembered what Jim had said on the ride home. Friends. He just wanted to be friends because of his packed show schedule. Of course, it would be better if he were at Hampstead permanently, but did he actually think love was based on logistic considerations? Or did he indirectly mean to convey that he did not love her and could not—ever? As she stroked the brown plush of her bear, her eyes filled with tears and she thought how Reggie must have looked the day he'd been placed in her crib, and how worn, outworn, he'd become.

# Grand Prix

After that first night, Diana didn't see Jim Williams as much as she had hoped. What she had thought might be the beginning of an affair now seemed the beginning of its end. Jim spent most of the fall at USET headquarters in New Jersey, driving up to Hampstead only three weekends. During winter months he competed on the Florida Grand Prix circuit.

For the next half-year Diana mucked out stalls and rode hard. The cold mornings fueled by coffee began to pay off. Under von Engerson's tutelage she ceased being a mere passenger on the horse's back and took charge, shortening and lengthening stride when required, signaling time to clear a five-foot spread, and calling for flying changes in midair over jumps so the horse landed on the correct lead. Barbara Snyder asked her to assist in schooling younger sale horses over low rails. Diana felt elated: she had gained the trust of Hampstead's powerful doyenne.

The proper training of a green horse over first jumps is essential. Small mistakes in a careless practice session will shatter confidence and ruin the prospect's career. The rider must expect the unexpected. Diana had to support, not interfere, urge but not excite, reward rather than punish. She did—and her charges responded wonderfully. Customers who came to Hampstead horse-hunting openly remarked how impressed they were with the confident manner of the four- and five-year-olds Diana guided over a two-foot-nine course. Sales shot up and Bob Sloan grudgingly recommended that Barbara Snyder import more animals from Europe, the big, bold movers that commanded high sales figures.

That summer Diana's talent and work propelled her into competing at A-rated shows for owners at Hampstead. Her first triumphs came in hunter classes, where the horse's style and form are judged, not speed or the height of obstacles. Her mounts never under- or over-jumped. She placed them to take off in a relaxed, fluid manner. At shows she would invariably run into Jim Williams and express her eagerness to move from hunters to jumpers. And at Lake Placid the "I Love New York Grand Prix" brought them close again.

"I don't care if you think hunters are not, as you put it, 'where it's at,'" scolded Jim. "They give you polish and style to gauge Grand Prix jumps when your turn comes—and it will. American riders excel in jumping because they're stylists. Take the English: with them you think of horses as much as tea. But their riding stems from field hunters who get over fences any way they can. Here we believe that if you proceed in the most elegant and efficient manner, jumps take care of themselves. Look." He pointed to a man in a red coat mounted on a gold chestnut just entering the Grand Prix course. "See how he hauls that horse up with his arms before each effort? Then he throws them away. Not aesthetically pleasing, is it? More than that, it's not going to help him get around. Watch when he enters the triple."

Diana saw the horse take two strides after the first fence, but when his rider tried to pick him up, he turned a shoulder and skidded a yard and a half, smashing straight into four rails. The sound of thick wood splintering filled the stands. "English?"

"English," confirmed Jim. He put his arm around her shoulders. "Keep riding hunters. They'll put the finishing touch on that fine von Engerson base you've got. Then those Grand Prix jumps will just happen."

"Just like you'll happen for me?"

"I don't understand."

"That first night at the River Mill I thought . . . I hoped . . ."

"That we would be more than friends?" he asked gently. The kindness in his eyes increased the pain. She nodded, afraid her voice would crack. "Diana, you know I feel strongly about you, but we can't get involved in anything long-term—it wouldn't work out."

"Why not?" she asked directly.

"I travel all over the place. Soon you will too. Remember what my schedule's been the last six months? I've seen lots of marriages break up under the stress of all the traveling."

"What makes you think I'm talking about marriage?" she asked, though she had to admit to herself she'd fantasized about it that night in her bed after the River Mill.

"Well, in the end, aren't you?"—sure she was.

"The problem with you, Jim, is that you impute your conservative beliefs and prejudices to others. I haven't given marriage a thought."

"I'm glad, Diana. My life is complicated enough." He looked away from her and focused on the jump crew repairing the rails demolished by the English rider.

Angry tears welled up in her eyes. "I didn't know you could be so arrogant and patronizing."

"Diana . . ." Jim entreated, trying to pull her close.

"No, really, I'm so sorry to have been an additional complication, however brief." She pulled away and strode toward the grandstand, hurt and confused. She didn't need anyone like Jim giving free—sometimes unwanted—advice. She succeeded at Hampstead because of her riding, not because she saw the world champion Jim Williams.

"Hello, lovebird!" The familiar voice caused Diana to shift her attention away from a junior jumper class. At the foot of the bleachers Courtney Snyder appeared with Grunewald and, farther behind in tow, a preppie wearing his Cornell letter sweater. Her greeting reeked of phony delight. She still hated Diana intensely, but also studied balance-of-power relationships. Any tilt away from Diana at the moment would fail—her stocks had soared way too high with Mommy. But they'd come crashing down eventually, and Courtney planned to catch the black day. She might even create it.

"Hello." Diana concealed her grief by responding with an icy minimum.

"Was that Jim Williams I saw with you a moment ago?" Courtney was certain of the answer.

"Yes." The monosyllable conveyed Diana's desire for Courtney to get on with her business, if there was any.

Courtney either failed to notice or ignored it. She turned to her young man. "You know, Phil, at Hampstead people thought that Jim Williams—he won the silver in L.A.—that he and Diana were quite the item. I guess one can't count on anything in the horse world. It moves so fast, and in such mysterious ways."

Courtney's friend of the day seemed confused and too dimly informed to catch up. "I'm sorry," he said in obligatory fashion.

Diana shook her head incredulously, thinking that Courtney's arrival came like jackals and vultures at the side of an injured animal. However derivative and predatory, it required skill—but then, it was her nature. God, how I dislike that voice, she thought, managing a smile at Courtney's awkward escort. She gets that southern-sugarpie banter from her mother, but with no accent to soften it up and make it slide down. Raising a bored eyebrow at Courtney, she asked once again for Courtney to come to the point. This time Courtney complied.

"Mother's waiting for you at Hampstead's wing of the stalls. The Canadian let her down and can't ride Aden in the Grand Prix. Some nonsense about his father having a heart attack. Anyway, he's gone, and Mother has this crazy notion she wants you on Aden."

Catch riding, like pinch-hitting in baseball, falls within the rules of jumping, and riders without horses often arrive at an event secretly hoping one of their colleagues will suddenly get the flu. But Diana had never considered that anyone would turn to her.

Courtney smirked. "You better get over there. She's frantic." As soon as Diana left, Courtney said, more to herself than to her friend, "I hope she breaks her neck. In this sport it's easy."

From the air a Grand Prix course looks as if a child has carefully laid out painted matchsticks, thread spools, and plastic blocks in a vague, asymmetrical pattern, all hemmed in by a neat rectangular border. Even on TV it gives the impression of a series of upscale playground sets in primary colors, the telephoto lens crunches distances so much. But walking it level the first time takes one's breath away. Here poles weighing close to eighty pounds wallop the average person right in the eye. A short woman can step under the high ones without ducking. The spread of oxers—two vertical fences set together—seems able to accommodate a half-court basketball scrimmage. The water hazard, which must be jumped clear, is longer than many living rooms. Very quickly the idea's communicated that this sport isn't on a human scale. Any freshman in physics might remark that the involved forces, speed, and momentum far surpass anything except motor sports. But here the vehicle has a mind of its own; if it breaks, you can't fix it, and nothing but air separates the competitor from heavy wood and hard earth. Some horses weigh as much as compact cars. Most try not to fall on their riders but don't always succeed. Jumping claims more serious injuries for each participant than any other sport in the world—skiing, technical climbing, boxing. It supports a lot of orthopedic surgeons as well as veterinarians. Outside of target shooting, equestrian events are the only Olympic ones in which men and women compete equally. In jumping, the field's perfectly level—it's just that it's above everyone's head.

"Diana, you're here," Barbara Snyder said with consternation and relief. "Michele Devereux had to leave because his father's seriously ill. I found out when he didn't turn up to walk the course. We've been looking all over for you." Diana waited for the key line. "Can you manage Aden?" Her face conveyed that she assumed an affirmative reply.

"He's only been at Hampstead two weeks. Mr. Adams' horse, isn't he?" Ben Adams, an independently wealthy New York film critic, had for years competed some of the nation's top jumpers on the eastern circuit.

"Yes," Barbara responded, her puzzled tone indicating that she didn't know what effect ownership had on the crisis at hand, or why Diana was telling her what she already knew.

"I've seen him at shows." She intended her tone to convey how dangerous she thought he was. Split personality, both bad, she thought to herself.

"Diana, you're so steady. How about giving him a try? I think you can do it."

"So do I." Diana turned to see Jim leading the huge black horse. "What did I tell you: wait and you'll receive," he said, smiling.

From six feet away she could feel the stallion's hot breath, and her hesitation evaporated. "Yes. I've got to get my coat."

"There it is," said Jim, pointing to the green wool lying on a hay bale. He'd obviously run back to retrieve it.

"You think of everything."

"Everything?"

"Yes," said Diana, pointing to Aden. Mrs. Snyder would never have chosen Diana for a Grand Prix ride and put a hundred-thousand-dollar horse at risk without a top professional recommendation.

"Let me help you on with your coat, and listen up. You know this guy's a steamhead—gives new meaning to the concept of jock. You've got to get him in place three strides before each fence. For the triple combination it's critical he jump precisely. Six inches off means more than six feet down." Diana didn't like the double meaning.

"When he tries to have it his way, hold him with your legs and seat. You don't want him so excited he puts in extra strides. Keep him going forward so his antics won't throw you. Force him to move on or he won't concentrate. The reason he's a thriller to watch is he's hell to ride."

When Jim boosted Diana onto the huge Westphalian, her legs came barely halfway down his barrel. As she adjusted the stirrup leathers, she noticed flecks of lather on his muscular neck. He knew exactly where he should be pointed and was already counting down. She could hear the T-minus clicks in his head and sensed how it felt astride a thirty-mile-per-hour acetylene torch.

"Am I forgiven?" Jim asked.

"If I break my back, I'll need the absolution." She noticed the concerned expression on his face. "What you need and have is my unending gratitude. Thank you, Jim."

As Diana and her seventeen-hand partner walked to the ring, Jim called after her, "Ride your ass off!"

"Till there's nothing left," she yelled back, trying to ignore the nausea rising in the pit of her stomach.

When she entered the ring, Diana felt Aden's body hesitate like a clutch mushy between gears. His walk stalled to an animated, collected trot, more energy revved up but less ground covered. She heard the announcer's far-off voice. "Ladies and gentlemen, a new face on the circuit, number thirty-six, riding Aden, Miss Diana Winston. She's nineteen years old and competing in her first Grand Prix."

Maybe my last, she thought, working her seat and legs in a vain attempt to get Aden to walk. They approached the judge, she saluted, and the bell rang. The allowed minute before jumping she used to scope out the course and figure what she had underneath her. The most difficult fence would be a narrow vertical following the water. To negotiate the long pool, Aden would need to extend his frame flat-out. Then in four strides he must round his back and go for height: a psychological and physical trick often played on open jumpers. Diana picked up the right canter lead and settled Aden into a quiet rhythm. He was obedient, at the moment.

At the first fence, an oxer of rustic poles, Aden crowded in close and caught one hind leg, rocking the pole in its shallow metal cups. Spectators took a collective breath. Next the pair fired over a deceptively simple gate that many horses had taken down, misjudging the height. The spread of rails seemed straightforward, but coming off a curve it required the rider to regulate stride skillfully. Then Aden picked up speed, tossed his head, and instantly exploded out of control. He wasn't looking at the next jump and would career through it unless he concentrated. Diana sat back and half-halted severely. With other horses her sensors always caught a split-second warning before the panic phase, but this one had flipped a superfast cut-in switch. She leaned back with all her weight to counterbalance his schizoid drive. Just in time Aden came on his haunches, eyed what lay ahead, surged forward, and put four and a half strides where the sane plan demanded three. Few horses could've taken any jump so close, but he vaulted up and barely cleared.

Diana had him back in her hands cantering down the long side toward an in-and-out—two fences, with room for only one stride in between. He made an enormous effort over the upright pole and brush combination, but landed too near the second element—parallel poles over barrels. He dropped his hind leg, giving the top pole a rap hard enough to bounce it in the cup. As it jolted up and down, the only thing heard in the expectant hush was an incessant clicking of camera shutters deep behind their huge lenses. Then, seeing the pole somehow stray back in its cup, the audience roared.

Next loomed the wall—hollow wooden blocks painted to look like bricks. But they'd tumble off at the slightest scrape. Diana approached perfectly and Aden cleared with room to spare. At the water, von Engerson's first speech to her registered and she looked beyond it. A hoof

in the pool meant four faults, so Diana let the horse
open up. They managed, and the difficult vertical rushed
toward them. She tried to pull Aden in, but the reins,
wet with both their sweat, slipped. Gloves . . . she hadn't
worn gloves! Again Diana grabbed and pulled. Again her
hands slipped hopelessly. Aden was approaching the five-
foot-three vertical wild and off-stride. Suddenly, with
unpredictable power, the Westphalian gathered himself
and flew almost straight up. As Diana slowed the excited
and soaking horse, she heard a familiar, urgent voice
calling inside her, but couldn't make it out.

Then the announcer's: "Ladies and gentlemen, a clean
round in thrilling style by Aden and Diana Winston. She
joins four others—Anthony D'Ambrosio, Leslie Burr
Lenehan, Tim Craig, and Jim Williams—in the jump-off.
Don't roam far from your seats. The new course will be
ready in ten minutes."

"Terrific!" Jim gave Diana's thigh a congratulatory
slap.

"I thought I was going to get burned into the rails,"
she puffed. "What a powerhouse." She glanced at Aden's
withers, all lathered up.

"You're in the jump-off." Jim smiled. "And you're
going to have to keep control of this guy while you pour
on more speed." Diana closed her eyes at the thought of
another round, faster, sharper turns, higher fences. "While
you were riding, they posted the course. The big decision
is whether to take a tight turn after the wall before the
triple. Saves a couple seconds, but I don't recommend it.
Aden's tough to place correctly and you're almost certain
to have a rail down. Take the safe route, you're in the
ribbons anyway."

She nodded seriously. Her first Grand Prix frightened
her so much that when she tried to take a deep breath,
her chest muscles froze and she realized that "choke"
wasn't a figure of speech. Never before had a horse or
jumping course made her feel, every moment, physically
at risk. Her helmet seemed to have the heft of papier-
mâché or eggshell. She'd take Jim's advice and after the

wall swing left of the oxer, allow more time, and hope for a clean round. A groom walked up with Schenectady.

"Learn from my mistakes." Jim smiled as he swung into the saddle. He gave her a thumbs-up and headed for the ring. A deep hush covered the crowd. Jim saluted the judge, the bell rang, and the horse started at full tilt to clear the first jump over water. Clean, Jim headed for the vertical with the correct departure, but at the last second Schenectady dropped a hind leg and rocked a rail, sending it down at an oblique angle. Diana groaned with disappointment. They cleared the wall with daylight and went clean over the first and second elements of the triple, but at the third, brushed down another rail. Diana buried her head in her arms. How could she expect to do better than or even as well as one of the world's greats, who'd ridden scores of Grand Prix and dozens of jump-offs?

"That's what I get for stomping on the throttle," Jim said when he returned and slid off the tall bay. Handing him to the groom, he immediately started a no-nonsense conversation: "Look, go for the shortcut too. The footing's started to give way just where you'd take the longer route. So don't. You might slip. Head to the right of the oxer."

"Are you sure? I'll have less than half a stride to set him up, or try to."

"You can do it. I rode Aden last year. Forget about von Engerson on that turn. There's style beyond the style book. You'll even have to set him off-balance first. Pivot him around your inside leg and keep the outside one strong so he doesn't shift his shoulder away. When he comes out of the pivot, half-halt with your seat and legs. Not before, or he'll miss the aid and run berserk. Got it?"

Diana nodded. "I'm afraid, Jim."

He put a reassuring hand on the calf of her riding boot. "That's normal. Just try to leave it behind when you head for the first fence. You can do it. I wouldn't be wasting my time if you couldn't. Just commit yourself to each jump and you'll get over. Don't lose concentration, and knock 'em dead!"

Knock 'em down is more likely, she thought to herself. She turned in her saddle to look at Jim, smiling and mouthing an unmistakable word with his lips: *win*. Aden considered all this old-hat, the signal to blitz through and book for home. The inside of his nostrils shone bright red from extreme dilation of arteries. He wasn't pumped up—critical mass for a fission reaction was more like it. He liked jumping even with no one on his back, preferred it actually, and several times had succeeded in making his preference known in the ring.

Leslie Burr Lenehan's horse stumbled and had a rail down at precisely the place Jim had warned Diana about. But Tim Craig took the quick route and secured a clean round in 35.32 seconds. Diana must not only jump clean but also beat the time.

"Diana Winston on Aden." By coincidence, at that moment she saw an ESPN commentator give the French shrug to his cameraman and point to a program in confusion. What was she doing here, anyway? No note card on her. Still nothing punched up in the computer. Even the technical adviser whispered that he'd never heard of her. The video crew might catch a spectacular spill.

Diana saluted the judge and headed straight for the water jump, no problem, then immediately gathered up the horse. Collecting his stride, she placed Aden perfectly and they sailed over the five-foot-six-inch vertical with lots to spare. At the wall Diana bit her lip as she heard a foreleg strike it. One block shifted, dislodged, but didn't fall. She pressed her right leg hard against Aden's wet flank. He turned and pulled up in the air in front of her, totally at a standstill. She clamped both legs and screamed "Yaaah!" As Aden extended his body, she sat back, pulled on the reins, and collected him again. His ears pricked forward and he visually locked onto the next jump. Diana partially released the reins and Aden seized the opportunity to pull hard through her hands. She grabbed back and asked him to put in a short stride.

But this horse you couldn't ask. He responded by exploding upward, clearing with two feet under him. The crowd's stunned gasp never found its way into a cheer. Diana approached the triple trying to calm the wild man down. They cleared the first element like a textbook photo, but Aden stumbled at the second, picked himself up, made the jump, then arrived far too early for the third. He put in a full stride and leapt. A hind leg struck the top rail—so hard its thickness flexed visibly—but it remained, and Diana raced to penetrate the clock's invisible finish beam. With the rail holding, the Seiko readout flashed 34.50. The early-summer throng leapt to its feet.

She believed it only when she heard the loudspeaker's authoritative statement. "Ladies and gentlemen, winner of the Mercedes Grand Prix, Miss Diana Winston on Aden. An unknown face has beaten the country's finest riders with a rare combination of guts and style. Congratulations, Miss Winston. Will all prize recipients please enter the ring." After the appropriate riders gathered on their mounts, the announcer continued. "We are honored to have with us today, presenting the first-place trophy, New York City's Mayor Ed Koch."

The controversial bald man walked over to Diana. "Good riding, young lady. If you didn't before, I guess you love New York now." He reached up to clip the ribbon on Aden's bridle, but the horse reared at its flapping streamers. Koch leapt back too. "Let's use him for crowd control." He tried again, but Aden wheeled to the right.

"Sir, I can do it," offered Diana.

The mayor good-naturedly handed the ribbon to her. She wrapped the dangling colors around the rosette, then quietly slipped it on the brow band. He laughed. "I could use your tact in my administration. You do the work, I get the credit."

They both laughed. When the other ribbons had been handed out, Diana and Aden led some of the world's best riders in her victory lap. As she galloped past the stands, she felt a rush of power and elation she'd never experienced. At nineteen—young, but not unprecedented—she'd won the first Grand Prix she'd entered.

"No more mucking out." She congratulated herself on that possibility as much as on the victory itself, and almost said it out loud. When she left the ring she jumped off into Jim's open arms.

"You did it, and on a tough horse—congratulations!" He hugged Diana and helped her off with her coat.

Barbara Snyder ran up, put an arm around her shoulders, and nodded in the direction of Ben Adams and a friend of his. "Here's one happy owner anxious to meet you."

"How do you do?" The distinguished silver-haired man offered his hand. "Absolutely magnificent ride, young lady. Where have you been keeping yourself?"

"She's Hampstead's secret weapon," Barbara said proudly.

"Not anymore." The other man stepped forward enthusiastically, his hand outstretched. His direct gaze and the lingering clasp caused her to flush.

"Ah, Diana, I'd like you to meet a friend of mine, Hugh Simpson." Ben Adams smiled. "Hugh already knows who you are." As Diana received the handclasp of this handsome man in his mid-thirties, she knew he was appraising her, but not as a rider. His fingers kept hers a few seconds too long and his eyes rested on her breasts, distinct against the soaked shirt. "Hugh's a Wall Street financier with a reputation as a cowboy among colleagues and clients, so you've got something in common." Ben Adams stroked Aden's streamlined neck.

Hugh seized the opportunity his friend created. "I'm sure we do, and I'd like to invite you, Diana, to join Ben and me for a drink to celebrate."

"A drink is exactly what I could use," said Diana, pointing to her parched throat. At this Jim Williams suddenly but quietly walked away with Diana's coat on his arm.

"You go on with Hugh, Diana. My wife's instructed me to walk Barbara to our car for a visit. We'll try to catch up with you at the bar."

"How's Pat been?" asked Mrs. Snyder.

"I'll let you see for yourself," he said, taking her by the arm in gentlemanly fashion and steering her toward the polo field—parking lot for the weekend.

Hugh, smiling inwardly, concluded that he might have maneuvered a better situation for himself, but for starters this would do. "Come on, we've got a lot to discuss." He took Diana gingerly around the waist and walked her through the crowd toward the big yellow-and-white-striped tent that served as the bar. They passed the mobile Miller's tack shop, a semi-trailer with awning windows on the side, but Diana didn't notice Jim at the entrance, bleakly eyeing Hugh Simpson's proprietary manner with his friend. Tim Craig joined Jim on the ramp, a broken bridle in hand.

"Jim, you were on the money about your new star. I thought you two would be celebrating. Where is she?" queried Jim's longtime friend and competitor. "I'd like to meet her."

"Over there." Jim pointed glumly to Diana and her escort.

"Doesn't take Simpson long, does it?" Tim shook his head in amazement. "Who was it last year—yeah, that little French rider. My brother's a tennis buff and told me Simpson followed Tanya Minova from continent to continent like a dog. Likes the little girl athletes, doesn't he?"

"He's repugnant—devours people. Once he's made his hit, he's on his way, next victim please. If they graded shit, he'd be government prime. 'Would you like a drink?' 'We have a lot in common, I think.' 'You've *never* been in a private jet?' Same crap."

"I agree the guy's got a problem, but it's one I wish I had. You said Diana was cute, but Jesus God, look at her, she's gorgeous—what an act!"

"Just shut up, okay!" snapped Jim.

Tim stared openmouthed at his already apologetic-looking friend. "You're in love with her," he exclaimed. "Well."

"I am not—you know I'm not." Tim was one of the

few straights Jim had confided in about his gay life. "And neither's Hugh Simpson." Jim seemed unaware of the irony.

"Stranger things have happened. From what you've told me, she's more than capable of handling that rich steamroller. She's over the age of consent." Tim shot his distressed friend a side glance. "Maybe your feelings go beyond the category of older brother."

"Please, let's not talk about it. I'm just a little worried. The first Grand Prix's a success for her, but that doesn't seal the lid on any other. You know, just more pressure. Some kids win one at eighteen and it's downhill from there."

Tim led Jim by the arm into the tack shop. "Come on, Papa Bear. She's got to learn to deal with it in the business. What's that?" asked Tim pointing to the green riding coat Jim was carrying.

"Oh, Diana's. I need to know her size." My God, thought Tim to himself: he's not in love, he's decapitated.

Hugh Simpson pulled out the white wrought-iron chair for her. "Now, Diana, what's your usual?"

Gin and tonic flashed through her mind, but she reconsidered. "I'll have a martini." That was a sophisticated drink.

"Sounds good—straight up or on the rocks?" Hugh scooped a handful of peanuts from the glass bowl.

"Uh, straight, I guess."

He beckoned the waiter. "Two martinis, straight up. And *very* cold, please. Gin. Twists."

"And could I have a couple glasses of water?"

Hugh smiled. "And a pitcher of ice water for this thirsty lady." Without another word he reached over and took Diana's hands in his. "So, young lady, that was a super ride on Ben's horse." He emphasized the first syllable and said it again, looking her right in the eyes. "Super."

"Aden's a great horse. He saved me out there a couple times."

"Looked like you saved him a couple more," Hugh said, letting go Diana's hands to take more peanuts. All his appetites were pumping full-tilt in the usual well-oiled fashion. And beneath it, he hadn't forgotten some special news out on the Street Friday—well, in on the Street, actually, and privy to few—news that invited action at tomorrow's opening bell.

"Oh," demurred Diana, "I'm just glad it's over."

"The lady's modest."

"I'm not modest, Mr. Simpson, just relieved."

"Hugh."

"Hugh, then." As his gaze settled on her, she felt uneasy, unaware that this was because he enjoyed her discomfort.

Hugh Simpson exercised great care in his appearance, but it didn't show as such. Twice a year he visited Anthony J. Hewitt & Co. on Savile Row (he disliked the larger, well-known establishments like Huntsman's or Gieves and Hawkes), and flew back on the Concorde for four or five fittings, even if no other London business demanded his presence, though usually it did. International money speculation had made Hugh a hundred thousand a day more than once. He had his ties done from exclusive hand-blocked silk prints out of northern Italy near Lake Como, his shoes on a Bari last; a haberdasher in D.C. that he kept secret made his shirts, Swiss cotton or Sea Island, depending on the weave and pattern he wanted. The result was that when men and women saw him, they didn't remark what beautiful clothes he wore or ask where he shopped, but simply came away with the conviction that he was a handsome powerful man, something magnetic about him. And any anxiety seemed a million miles off.

Right now Diana came within that aura. When their waiter arrived with the water and drinks, Hugh took his and smiled. "My I propose a toast?" Without waiting for a response from his red-faced partner, he went on, "To Diana Winston, next Olympic gold medalist. May she—"

"Mr. Simpson, I mean, Hugh, the Olympics aren't for

two years." Equestrian Team selections represented serious business. She was a relative unknown and hadn't a prayer. But he wasn't fazed a bit.

"Well, to Diana Winston and the 1988 Olympics!" responded Hugh good-naturedly. He raised his glass and took a large swallow. Diana still didn't like the toast. After all, she lacked the most important element for selection—a great horse. But it was well-intentioned and she said nothing. "So, Diana, other than a superb equestrienne, who are you?" he asked, his unblinking eyes driving into hers.

"That's all I am, I guess—a girl who rides."

"No, you're much more: you're a beautiful woman who rides, and who wins Grand Prix—against men."

"I've only entered and won a single Grand Prix, Hugh. And, as you saw, a number of women rode as well. Actually, I think it's the course one really competes against."

"How old are you, Diana?" His tone indicated an evaluation was at hand.

"Nineteen."

"A mere baby," he observed.

The patronizing tone annoyed her. "Does that frighten you?"

"Frighten—no. It excites me." He chuckled in a way somehow hard to condemn.

"Good."

"Good?" Hugh was amused by all this.

"Yes. I'd rather my age work to advantage." She felt a flicker of sadness as she wondered if Jim's being seven years older had been a negative factor in their relationship.

"I'm flattered you consider me an advantage."

"Ah." Diana looked down, drawing a finger along the rim of her glass, looking into it and waiting. Things moved along pretty fast with Hugh. She felt her face redden and grow warm.

He found himself taken by this plucky little rider who attempted to flirt hardball with one of the big boys. When the pace got too fast, she retreated into embar-

rassed silence. Or was it? She was a challenge. He signaled for another round, annoyed he'd let her glass go
empty without the next on hand.

"What do the cards hold for you, Diana?" he queried
as he took out a pack of Dunhills.

"I don't know what they hold, but I think I know what
I'd like," she replied, pushing the hair off her high tanned
forehead.

"And what's that?"

"I'd like to be a top rider."

"Already are. The top." Hugh took two glasses from
the waiter's tray and waved him off.

"No, I'm not. And nobody who knows anything about
riding would say I am, except to be polite or, perhaps, to
make a pass," she said, trying to regain control of the
situation.

"Are you accusing me?" remonstrated Hugh.

"I should think you'd like to be accused of being
polite," she countered.

As if reading her, he smiled in a boyish way and
added, "Today, at least, you're the top. Can't deny that."
She didn't mind hearing him put it in those words, and who
could dispute it? God, this kid's good, he thought. I can't
wait to slide my hand into those breeches. He felt himself
begin to thicken against his pants, and now paid more
attention to imagining her than talking across the table.

"Well, you're right there—it doesn't happen very often, I guess."

"But you're the top rider as far as I'm concerned," he
said, taking her hands again.

"Hugh, remember when Bjorn Borg first won Wim-
bledon?" She withdrew her fingers on the pretext of
taking another sip—vaguely aware the sips were mount-
ing up.

"Guess I do. I was there."

She didn't let it slip she was impressed. "Then you
remember a lot of people thought he was just a flash in
the pan."

"I know what you're saying, Diana, and you're abso-

lutely right. He had to go to beat the best consistently—
Connors, McEnroe, Vilas. And not just once, but in lots
of tournaments."

"That's what I've got to do to be confirmed a great, or
even competitive. There's an awful lot of work ahead.
And I don't even have my own horse." But with the
breezy coolness of martinis and the rising relaxation in
her body, work seemed farther off than when Aden
jolted the arena ground.

The drinks had no effect on him, and in a few minutes
he called for another round. "I've no doubt you'll succeed, Diana, but why concentrate your energy on horses?"

She was floored by the question's inanity. "Because it's
what I like to do." She hesitated to use "love" in any
context around this striking man. "Do you disapprove of
the sport?"

"Not at all. But I can see you're a person of enormous
intelligence, power, drive. You could do a lot better than
a high-class jockey. You'd be a super businesswoman
. . . or lawyer—from the way you've been handling me,
at least." Hugh laughed easily, his manner still in
control.

Diana winced inwardly; the racetrack couldn't com-
pare with the art of showing. "I certainly prefer my work
to an office routine, nine to five, watching my body turn
to flab all day." She couldn't help glancing at his midline,
punctuated by a belt of exotic leather, which she guessed
might be elephant, and recoiled at the thought. She half-
expected his stomach to bulge, but there wasn't any at
all. The shirt looked trim and hard, as if stretched on an
ironing board.

Her controlled, strong voice served as further erotica
to him. Most women he knew found him attractive—his
body, his personality, the power and money. And most
wouldn't dream of endangering their chances by contradicting
him.

"I work in an office, Diana. Is this flab?" He sat up
straight, allowing her an unobstructed view of the torso.

Embarrassed at being called on to assess his physique,

at the same time she couldn't help admiring the thickly ridged middle. "And what sort of office activity produces that?"

"New York Athletic Club three times a week, jogging in Central Park, squash—regular regime. Skip desserts, and I do some other exercises, too," he added, repressing a sly wink.

"In my work fitness comes with the territory," she commented, pretending to ignore the innuendo.

"Well, some of us have to pay to keep in shape." Hugh had just dropped ten thousand to be a life member at his club. He'd memorized the squash ladder, and his aggressive spirit had devised a plan for steady advancement.

"Are you wealthy?" Diana asked ingenuously.

He'd heard the question perfectly but was taken off-guard by its directness. Most women he dated, and both women he'd married, thought it more tactful to infer the quality of his life rather than inquire point-blank. They judged by the interior-decorating job in his Sutton Place apartment, his Bang & Olufsen stereo, custom Rolls and Lamborghini (more expensive of the two models), and how many decades back he would thumb the lists when ordering wine at Trump Tower restaurants. Diana cared either very much or not at all, and he was going to enjoy finding out which.

"Well, I suppose I'm rich in the sense that I can do what gives me pleasure and makes life comfortable, and gives others pleasure and comfort too." He paused a few seconds and waited for his thoughts to come together. "I guess I'm rich and not rich, since rich is letting your money work for you, and not being rich is working hard for your money. I do both." He smiled, pleased, for this was a rare occasion when he reflected and produced a pithy, accurate reply. "Really, let me tell you a little bit about myself." Hugh's hushed voice and sincere gaze conveyed he was about to hand over the keys to his psyche. "Ten years ago I was a Blue Angel."

"In the Navy?" asked Diana, profoundly impressed.

"One of those crazy jet jockeys," he replied with false modesty.

"How exciting! When we had our house on the Cape we went to see them at Otis Air Base."

"Impressive?"

"I practically held my breath the whole time."

"Well, I loved it. I worked hard to be a Blue. I made it my goal when I entered Annapolis. A lot of middies thought I was arrogant, but I never lost sight of it, not through flight school, not when I was ops officer on *Kittyhawk* during Nam. And it was great for a while—all the women."

"The women?"

"Of course, women loved us," Hugh stated unabashedly. "They threw themselves at our feet wherever we went."

"What a dull and put-upon life. Were you married?" Though her voice was light and teasing, Diana felt somehow threatened by Hugh's previous Navy fan club.

"Blues can't be married. Navy forbids it. The official line's that all the travel puts too much strain on family life. The reason is that they don't want Navy married screwing others, lots of others, when they're in the public eye."

"Sounds like it means the same thing."

"It was tough, Diana, accidents always riding on your shoulder. We had a PR officer traveling with us, and guess what he kept in his attaché with all the FLY NAVY bumper stickers?"

"Press releases?"

"Obits, our obits. Alphabetical order, whole thing. Neatly typed, updated periodically. Xerox copies ready to hand out. Lists and phone numbers of next of kin too."

"Incredible!" Diana was shocked by military efficiency.

"But true. So you see, the strain was great. We risked our lives daily to advertise the Navy."

"But you wanted it."

"Sure I did—don't get me wrong. I loved it. All those

gals coming onto you, and you let them because they were the release you thought you deserved for putting your life on the line. But you were attractive because of what you were, not who you were."

"Attractions of power," commented Diana, half-seriously.

"Guess so. Celebrities, fame. Screwing somebody who is something the whole free world knows about." Hugh looked at the little hands that had just guided a fourteen-hundred-pound stallion to victory around two difficult courses.

"Are you married now?" she asked, eyes cast down, watching her forefinger trace the top of her glass, getting empty once more.

"Present tense?"

"Present."

"Yes and no, again. I'm separated. Legally."

"I'm sorry."

"Don't be, I'm not. And you?"

"Me?" Diana laughed at the absurdity. "Don't see a ring, do you?"

"Thought you might take it off when you ride." He didn't miss a stitch. "Well, you're not too young. They say Juliet was twelve."

"Thirteen." She immediately regretted the correction.

"At any rate, you seem to do everything else early." The waiter brought a fourth set of drinks. As Diana lifted the glass and felt the soothing wet cold on her palm, a blissful sense of freedom coming from the heady combination of winning, exhaustion, and the company of a man powerful in every respect, rushed over her. It was time to relax and let go. She'd worked hard and deserved it. Desire began to override her apprehension.

"Look, I'm staying at the Placid Inn with Ben's other guests," said Hugh. "It has an excellent restaurant. Won't you please join me for dinner—let's continue the celebration."

"I'm sorry, but I've got to return with Hampstead. They'll be leaving about six. I didn't drive."

"I'll get you back."

"Back where?"

"Massachusetts."

"When?"

"Whenever you want. My plane's at the airport. Besides, it's quality time if you join me for dinner. You'll be home before the stable gang. From here to Hanscom Field is less than an hour, then I'll phone a limo."

The thought of returning in a private plane appealed enormously to Diana. And unlike the River Mill with Jim, this time she was prepared—she'd packed a dress. "I'd love it, Hugh, if you're the pilot."

"Well, it's no F-14, but I'll condescend as long as you're there to upgrade it," he said gallantly. "Ben can drive my car back to New York." He made a mental check to cut the drinking right then, and poured himself a large glass of water. He'd leave his fourth martini for her.

"I'd be honored."

"Tell you what. I'll get you a room at the hotel—that'd make dressing more comfortable."

"No, thanks, Hugh, I'll just shower in the rec vehicle. I'm used to it." She felt uncomfortable about a hotel room paid for by a man, particularly one she barely knew.

"It's *already* paid for. One of Ben's guests cancelled late. Don't make the inn collect double. They don't deserve it."

"No, Hugh, I'd rather stay here. I've got a lot to organize." Hugh's manipulative attempt to lay a financial guilt trip on her failed.

"You'd save me the trouble of coming all the way back from town to pick you up." He clasped Diana's forearm and looked at her with unblinking eyes, almost a command.

"Yes," she yielded, feeling uncomfortable, but unable to put off the man who offered to fly her home, then arrange a private car. An unnecessary trip for appearance sake was silly. All right, she thought.

"Wonderful, I'll meet you in Hampstead's wing in thirty minutes. Will that give you time to pack?"

"Pack everything?"

"Well, we may as well take it all in the plane."

"Sure," she replied, slightly dazed.

"Don't forget your trophy!" he called.

"I'm afraid that belongs to Ben Adams."

"Unfair. Absolutely criminal."

"I don't think so. Aden acted the better half. Besides, Mr. Adams put up the money."

"Well, he's got plenty. See you in thirty minutes." Hugh walked in the direction of the bar to have a ginger ale, his steps, however, still perfectly straight.

Diana returned to the rec vehicle, delighted with herself. All was right with the world. She'd won her first Grand Prix and was about to dine at the Placid Inn, costing the equivalent of mucking out four hundred stalls. On the way to the camper van, she stopped at a pay phone to call home. There was no answer. She checked the time. Her mother never missed the late-Sunday-afternoon cable movies. Loneliness had addicted her. Maybe she'd unplugged the phone in order not to be disturbed. Well, there'd be a chance to try again at the inn. When Diana stepped out of the rec vehicle, she saw Jim reading the message board set up to keep participants advised of schedule changes, social events, calls, and support—hay, farrier, vets. He was carrying a large rectangular package.

"Diana, where've you been?" He hoped she hadn't stayed with Hugh two hours. That guy, he thought, a solid gold snake in the grass.

"One of Ben Adams' friends was kind enough to help me celebrate—Hugh Simpson, know him?"

"I know of him. Look, why don't we go out this evening? I found a charming little Italian place, hand-cut pasta, best Chianti." Diana suddenly felt torn. She'd love a fun evening out with her friend and mentor. Perhaps proving herself on Aden had made her more attractive to him. Yet the idea of first-class treatment by an impressively rich and powerful man lured her too. Besides, she'd made that commitment already.

"I'm sorry, Jim. Hugh invited me to dinner. I—"

"Have a good time, but watch out for yourself." Jim's face grew serious and his tone kind, trying not to reveal the hurt.

"Why?"

"You've been on the circuit some. Have you seen the women he's been with? He's got a reputation."

"I've never seen him before. Are you implying I'm out of his league?"

He put his arm around her. "On the contrary, I'm implying Hugh's out of yours." He placed the box in her hands. "For you."

"May I open it?"

"That's why it's in a box—so you can." She took off the lid and folded back the tissue to reveal a Grand Prix jacket, striking red. Only riders who'd competed at that level or were USET members wore one.

"A real coat!" Diana hugged him. "What a wonderful and all-too-expensive present."

"You deserve it." He smiled, his face beaming.

"Diana." Now the cheeriest voice was Hugh's.

"Oh, Hugh, my bags are still in the RV."

"Don't move, I'll get them."

"Bags?" asked Jim automatically, unable to conceal his chagrin.

"It's not what you think. Hugh's offered to take me home after dinner." An awkward pause filled the air as Hugh went to fetch the luggage.

"He must be pretty devoted to drive ten hours for a dinner date," said Jim, instantly regretting it.

"It's not like that at all—he has a plane."

"I see," said Jim in a tone indicating he didn't.

"Ready?" asked Hugh, walking out with Diana's suitcase and gear bag.

"All set." She kissed Jim on the cheek. "Thanks ever so much for this." She gestured to the box.

"Sure," he said flatly, thinking Hugh Simpson had ruined the unique first time to share her red jacket.

As Diana and Hugh walked to the parking lot, Jim's feelings ambushed him—anger, jealousy, envy, and concern. Diana had allowed herself to be picked up—no other word for it—by the horse world's most notorious little girl chaser. And she was going back to his hotel. Jim felt positive she'd be used and would regret it. "My, your little Diana seems to be getting around." He turned to see Courtney gloating, the word "your" resonating in her throat.

"She's more successful at it than you are right now," replied Jim caustically, and walked away without waiting for a return comment. Courtney's face fell. She'd hoped Diana's demonstration had convinced Jim that Miss Winston was nothing but a low-class cunt. It obviously hadn't worked—yet.

"Nice car," Diana said as she slipped into the black Lamborghini.

"I brought it across on the *QE II*." Hugh hit several dash buttons and music filled the perfectly engineered space.

"Bolling's *Suite for Jazz Flute and Piano*." She identified the lively first bars. "So lively and happy."

"Great, isn't it?" He was pleased that things seemed to be going ahead and mused at the innuendo, Rolling with Bolling. Throwing back his head, he laughed. "Diana, you're a kick." When they reached the Placid Inn, Hugh moved her to the quaint cage elevator that took them to the fourth floor. "Here we are." He turned the key and pushed open the door. "After you." He'd tipped the bellhop not to come.

"What a beautiful room." Diana strolled about, admiring the decor and space. She'd never seen such a large hotel room.

"Take a look," said Hugh as he pulled the curtains back to reveal an incredible view of the Adirondacks. Whiteface Mountain caught the slanting sun. "Or, if you're thirsty . . ." He opened the unobtrusive refrigerator stocked with everything from Evian water to champagne and Petrussian beluga caviar.

"Pretty extravagant for this neck of the woods, isn't it?" asked Diana.

"Well, Ben flew in a few improvements for his guests." Hugh smiled. "Say, bet you don't have a bathrobe."

"It's in my bag."

"Oh, no." Hugh motioned dismissively. "Use Ben's supply. The terry cloth's so deep you'll need a passport. I'll have them send one up."

Diana walked into the huge white bathroom decorated with red trim and towels, the walls and ceiling completely mirrored. "Do they hold Valentine's Day parties in here?" she joked. The slightly vulgar decor made her uneasy.

"Something like that, I guess. How about a drink to relax before your shower?" Before Diana could say no, Hugh walked to the refrigerator and removed four miniature bottles of Scotch.

"Just one, please. If I drink more, you won't be hearing from me till morning."

"Can't let that happen, can we?" Hugh clinked his glass against hers. "Cheers." Now he felt secure he wouldn't be flying that night. As far as he could see, visibility on the ground was unlimited.

"Oh, no!" She put her glass down. "I forgot a boot-jack. I'll never pull these things off. New and tight."

"I'll get 'em off," offered Hugh, who couldn't resist taking Diana's innocent remark as a *double entendre*.

"I don't know. They're custom-made and awfully snug."

"Well, let's have a go. Sit down over here." He pointed to a straight-backed chair. "Take hold of the arms and hang on." Hugh took one heel in his hands and pulled hard. The boot didn't budge. "Diana, are you bracing your foot against me?"

"I stopped doing that when I was three. Glued on, isn't it?" She enjoyed the frustration in his voice. "I went through two pine bootjacks, so I use an oak one now." Hugh pulled again, clenching his teeth and tightening every stomach muscle. The boot slid off with a satisfying, barely audible swoosh.

"Very good," applauded Diana.

"One down, one to go. I have a better idea. Go and hold that bedpost. Now give me your other leg." Hugh smiled. He pulled and grunted, tensed and strained, but the boot didn't slide a millimeter. He stood up to catch his breath. "I feel like I'm in some weird Grimm's fairy tale. You know, those impossible love tests—guessing a name, fitting a slipper, unfitting a stubborn boot."

Diana laughed hard. "Try again."

"Another idea. Why don't you slide down and hold on to one of the bed boards? I'll brace against the mattress. That ought to work. I'll get more leverage."

Diana went along and pulled herself under the bed.

"Anything to grab?"

"Yup, holding now."

"Okay, give me the boot and stay fast."

"Roger, out." Diana held up her leg and giggled.

"Quiet, down there, don't make me laugh," commanded Hugh. "Serious business." He braced his buttocks against the mattress and pulled with his might. The boot glided off. They burst out laughing as he took hold of her ankles and pulled her out from the bed. But as she started to get up, Hugh pressed her back to the floor. "No, I want my fairy-tale reward."

"What's that?" she asked, feeling her blood quicken at his closeness.

"To wake Sleeping Beauty with a kiss."

"I'm not asleep," Diana weakly protested.

"This story has been a fairy tale carefully adapted for twentieth-century readers by . . ." Hugh pinned her shoulders to the rug and closed his mouth over hers with a delicious warmth.

"Ummm," Diana felt her whole self ache with longing.

"Thank you, Princess," said Hugh, getting up. She took the outstretched hand. He glanced at his gold-piece Corum. "I've got to make some calls. What if I return in a couple hours? Is that time enough?"

"Plenty," replied Diana, wondering how she'd amuse herself.

Hugh gave her a quick kiss on the cheek. "Enjoy your shower." As soon as he turned away, a broad grin broke over his face.

Diana looked around the room, then jumped onto the bed, landing flat on her back. "Ah, this is it—service. I love it!" She rested a minute, then bounded into the bathroom, glancing in the mirror. Dried sweat plastered down her hair, and wisps had fallen out of her braided bun. Time for that shower, she said to herself, and walked back through the bedroom, leaving ascot, shirt, breeches, and underwear where they fell. In the bath, she undid her hair and stepped into a pulsating jet of hot water. Her neck and back muscles began to loosen. She opened the little vial of shampoo and worked up a rich white lather, then sneaked a look at her body again in the mirror—strong and feminine. Legs skinny a year ago had become lissome, her buttocks firm and round, breasts full.

"Does riding do that, or do you come that way?" She stopped soaping and looked up. Hugh stood in the doorway. "I brought your bathrobe myself. Room service with a personal touch." She grabbed a towel and held it across her body. "I didn't think you'd want some strange bellboy bringing this."

"I could have used my robe, you know," said Diana, blushing. Her attraction to this man overrode any sense that her privacy had been invaded.

"That towel's hiding only your better half." He nodded to the mirror behind her, a perfect rear view. She gave up and threw the towel at him. "That's better. How long has it been since someone gave you a bath? When you were three?" Not waiting for a response, Hugh slipped his shirt and pants off, aware of her gaze. "I must admit to Nautilus machines in my office." He tossed his shoes in a corner. "I mean my office gym."

Diana looked at him, stiff and standing out from the strong body. He stepped into the stall and took the soap from her hand. As he lathered her neck and shoulders, she felt his cock brushing her rear. He laid the facecloth over his hand and worked it between her legs. As he pulled it back and forth, he slipped a finger deftly in and out. Diana moaned when he kissed her neck and pulled her body up against his. "Around," he said, and put his hands on her shoulders and turned her to face him, beginning to massage her breasts.

"Glad I forgot to lock the door," she said softly.

"Didn't. You forgot I had a key." He moved her legs apart, pulling the facecloth across her. He drew her up against him again and rhythmically stroked her. Diana felt his cock grow harder, teasing her hips and thighs. He cupped her ear in his mouth and whispered, "Like this, like this?"

He turned her around. "Hold on to this bar," he instructed. She took the chrome towel rack in both hands and looked in the mirror to see him bring his cock to her from behind. He positioned it at the base of her cunt and put his hands on her waist. "Let go now," he said. As she did, his arms pulled her upward, then down hard onto him. She screamed and clenched her teeth as she felt the tearing pain.

Hugh turned her around and looked into her eyes with a combination of concern and disbelief. "Are you . . . ?"

"I was," she replied, wiping the tears from her eyes.

"I'm sorry. I didn't know. You should have told me. I would have been different."

"That's okay." Diana felt embarrassed but glad of his concern. "I want you to come back in."

Without a word Hugh stepped out of the shower and held open a huge white towel. "Dry off first." As he rubbed her down, he felt his cock larger than ever. This girl still a virgin—who would have guessed? He dropped the towel and pressed Diana's body against the mirrored wall with his own, then fitted his penis between her legs. "Do you want me?"

"Yes," Diana panted, putting her hands round his firm hard buttocks. She gasped with excitement and pain as she felt his cock move unrelentingly up her vagina. Hugh withdrew, then slapped his pelvis against hers, shoving himself up inside. Pleasure now overrode pain as Diana groaned with each delicious thrust. Hugh covered her neck with kisses as he continued to move inside her, unceasingly. He took a hand off her breast and took her clitoris in his fingers. He then shifted the forefinger of his hand into her. Diana could barely stand. He shifted the forefinger of his other hand into her. She screamed for another release. He bit her shoulder as he felt himself start to come. He took his hands away from her and pressed her with more force until he felt her body shudder, and again. He couldn't stop as he slapped his pelvis hard against her. When he came, he bit her neck, leaving teeth marks that would last well into the night.

Diana stood with Hugh in her while they caught their breath. Finally, as he reached for another towel, she felt the limp, sticky thing slide down between her legs. He began to wipe off both bodies. "How did you like that?"

Diana hesitated because she felt somehow upset by the way Hugh had made love to her. She wasn't even sure you could call it being made love to. Certainly it was not how she'd envisioned losing her virginity. She had to admit she enjoyed the roughness, but not the underlying hostility. And she wondered about the pain she'd experienced, concluding that being aroused did increase one's pain threshold. She certainly felt pain now—her vagina, her nipples, her neck.

"Did you like it, Diana?" Hugh waited for his evaluation like a student expecting confirmation that he had, indeed, made the honor roll.

"Well, it certainly relaxed me. I'm exhausted," she said, nodding below his waist. "You're quite the lover."

He smiled—the reply was appropriate. Helping her with the floor-length white robe, he pulled the hood around her face and gently kissed her lips. There was a knock at the door. Hugh threw on his robe and left the bathroom. "Room service again," he called.

Diana ran a comb through her hair and walked out,

her moist toes enjoying the thick carpet. "Dinner's served," Hugh announced, pulling out a chair at a completely set table, obviously brought in during their shower.

"I thought we were going to the restaurant."

"Why, when the restaurant can come to us? I hope you don't mind—I ordered for you. Is lobster Newburg all right?" He nodded to a large covered silver tray and chafing dish warmed by a white candle. "And Taittinger champagne to celebrate," he announced, holding up a bottle just uncorked. Vapor wafted out of the green neck like a smoking gun.

"Everything was exquisite," said Diana finishing the last bit of amaretto mousse. She felt full and content.

"I tell you what, why don't we go downstairs to the bar for an after-dinner drink?"

"That sounds nice, but let me straighten myself out a bit." Diana tried to run her fingers through her hopelessly mussed hair.

"I need a fresh change of clothes from my room. How 'bout we meet in the bar—fifteen minutes?"

As Diana nodded, he picked up his things, put on his bathrobe, and headed to the door. "Hugh!" she exclaimed. "You can't go out like that."

"Watch me." He smiled and left. The heavy oak door clicked shut but Diana could hear Hugh talking with someone down the hall and moved near the door.

"What've you been up to, Simpson?" asked a male voice. "The inn pool's closed."

"Remember that little piece on Ben's horse?"

"The kid from Hampstead?" asked another man.

"I just got a little riding done myself, and I didn't even need a whip." Raucous male laughter followed.

"And this you're not going to believe. That gorgeous girl's a maiden mare." Hugh glanced at his watch. "At least she was until approximately ninety minutes ago." More laughter.

"So it worked out that Susan couldn't come?"

"Fuck that bitch."

"What happened to Susan?" asked the first man.

"She called after I got here, whining how she couldn't come because the Ford Agency sent her to Paris on some short-fuse booking. Tough."

Diana walked away from the door physically sick, too stunned for tears. More than used, she'd been violated—and as a substitute for some high-tone New York model who would have been used too. She'd enjoyed herself, but that obviously didn't count with the cadre of bastards she heard. And if they knew now, who'd know tomorrow morning? What mattered to Simpson wasn't just that he had scored with a virgin, but the advertising that followed. How could she have swallowed the bathos about being a Blue Angel? Now he was crowing about fucking the day's Grand Prix champion. Maiden mare—how sick. She recalled Jim's concerned face. He'd known, or at least suspected. Why hadn't she listened to him?

Diana slowly but deliberately moved to the bureau, picked up her watch, and began packing. She'd thought she might have sex with Hugh when they first had their drinks, but she hadn't thought she'd be raped by his attitude. She imagined him in the bar bragging how he'd managed to find a second-string lay to replace his Ford model. Men could be such shits! She flipped the lid of her suitcase and zipped it with fury, then picked up the phone. "Front desk? This is Diana Winston, I'm with Ben Adams' party. I'd like a taxi, please . . . . To the Olympic fairgrounds . . . . Ten minutes? Fine." She took out her wallet: thirty dollars. She wondered if after her victory she'd qualify above the poverty line. Immediately after dressing, she went into the hall, took the elevator to the lobby, and walked out the door. The cab hadn't arrived.

In the bar, the tall thin man in glasses asked, "So where's this horsewoman of yours?"

"She'll be here. She's crazy about me. I taught her an awful lot. Besides, she's smart, a scorcher. Where's Ben anyway?"

"Don't know. I expect he's still with that Snyder woman. They had a thing once."

"They did?" Hugh asked. He was delighted to hear such news about his sedate friend.

"A few years back, but it's over now."

"So why's he seeing her?" Hugh was puzzled by this waste of time.

"She's getting a divorce, didn't you hear? Not every man follows your credo of hump and dump."

"Is that a criticism or a compliment?" asked Hugh, tickled his seductions had been elevated to a credo. Next came a legend.

"A bit of both, I guess," responded the man with a touch of envy.

"Aw, Harry, lighten up. Have some fun. Take advantage of women's lib. It's an incredible opening, no pun." Hugh's eyes darted to his watch. "Wonder what's taking my rider so long? She doesn't strike me as the type to spend hours in the mirror. With that face she doesn't need to." He stood up. "I'll look in the lobby in case she misunderstood."

Diana was nowhere in the lobby, but as Hugh walked to the house phone to ring her room, he spotted her and went outside. "Where are you going?" He glanced at her bags nervously.

"Where I should have remained—Hampstead's van," she stated with as much aloofness as she could muster. It was either that or tears, and she wasn't going to give him those.

"What on earth's wrong with you?" As soon as he put his arm around her, she shook it off.

"I'll tell you what's wrong, but it's nothing to do with me. It's that men like you exist." A yellow cab drove up.

"Diana, have I done something?" asked the uncertain Hugh.

"Done something?" Diana repeated with baffled contempt. She opened the door and got in. "You know, Hugh, it's a pity you're not gay. Then at least you'd be inflicting yourself on your own sex."

She saw a flash of anger cross his face. "I hope you know by now that I'm certainly not gay."

She seized the opportunity with the reflexes of a bull terrier. "Oh, I don't know, Hugh. Haven't you heard what psychiatrists say about reaction formation?"

He hadn't the faintest idea of what she was talking about. All he knew was that he wanted to display Diana at the bar. "I've offended you. Over what, I don't know, but I apologize."

"You'd offend any decent man or woman. The next time you're in the market for a screw, chase down a thirteen-year-old Russian gymnast nymphet with an underdeveloped pituitary. Compete on an international scale and, as you say, go for it." Diana rolled up the window for a period, and the cab drove off, leaving the bewildered man in a cloud of blue exhaust. He walked back to the bar, where the two men in the hall had joined Harry.

"So where's Diana?" asked the suntanned one with curly hair.

"I'm afraid she's too exhausted to join us," responded Hugh with a "Hey, what can I say?" expression.

"You old son of a bitch!" Harry exclaimed.

"Now, don't call Hugh that. You know an old dog can't learn new tricks." Crude laughter filled their corner of the lounge.

The Hampstead van and rec vehicle had left just before Diana got to Olympic Park, so she had the cab drive to the spot where Pegasus Farm parked. She sighed with relief—they hadn't gone. Their destination would be Westborough, only ten miles from home—she'd catch another cab there. She asked the stable manager if she could bum a ride. But as the last of the crowd, Diana had to sit in the back with six horses, three on each side. The trip would be long, uncomfortable, and smelly.

As the van bumped and threw her about, and as the horses thrashed their hooves, she thought of her experience with Hugh. It had been humiliating and repulsive. But why? Before she'd heard about the model who can-

celed and her being a virgin, she'd considered it a lot of
fun. She'd enjoyed the rough sex—it was like rough play.
And wasn't that what counted, enjoyment? Why should
the attitude of Hugh and his cohorts make her feel cheap?
He had orgasms, she had orgasms—she'd been the pas-
sive one, willing to relax and let him do as he liked, so
long as he gave her pleasure. She hadn't even minded the
pain so long as pleasure subordinated it—like the salt
crust on a margarita rim.

It was still a double-standard world. Hugh would make
up some insipid excuse why she wouldn't have a drink,
and the boys would laugh and joke about women they'd
had. She wasn't anything to them. To Hugh she was
another statistic. It didn't count that she'd enjoyed it—
what counted for him was that he'd screwed her. It had
all been done to her.

A horse whinnied. Diana looked up at the animal
gazing curiously at his traveling partner. "I'd rather be
jolted around in this truck with you, fellow, than in some
Lear jet with a jackass." If only Jim had been more of a
friend, then Hugh Simpson would never have happened.
She could have lost her virginity in the arms of a man
who really cared. Then, the more tired she got, the softer
the shavings became.

After ten hours, tired and achy, Diana walked down
the van's ramp at Pegasus Farm and called a cab. Forty
minutes later, just past breakfast time, it scooted up her
driveway and dropped her at the back door. It was May,
still too early for flies and mosquitoes. The air blew
warm, not hot, and flowers opened everywhere. Diana
admired her mother's carefully planted tulip beds in full
bloom, white and red.

"Mom, I'm home," she called. The TV was on. Her
mother didn't usually watch anything until early afternoon. But there she was, sound asleep, back toward her.
Diana smiled as she approached softly.

"I won." She gently touched her mother's arm. Cold, it
fell stiffly to the lap, and Diana was filled with panic. She

shook the shoulders, but there was no response. She paused and listened. There was no breathing either. Diana screamed and shook her mother again. Tears running down her cheeks, she rushed to the phone.

When the dispatcher hung up, Diana sat on the side of the chair, put her arms around the body, and wept —for the pain her mother had just suffered, and for the pain she had endured so long. She hadn't lived a happy life, and she'd given up trying. Now she was gone, just when Diana felt her own career taking off and could share the success. And Diana wept for her own loss too. This was the woman who had stayed up all hours when she was ill, comforted her when her father died, and talked with her about what was right and wrong, and where life could take her. Now Diana was all alone—a virtual orphan at nineteen.

Next day the *Patriot Ledger* announced the sudden passing of Mrs. John Winston. It had been a heart attack. Only then did Diana remember that when she'd come home, the channel was tuned to the Sports Network that the day before had broadcast live coverage of the Lake Placid Grand Prix.

# Boston

Many Southfield residents came to the simple funeral. Though I-495 and beltway bandits like Digital were rapidly changing the town, it remained small, a farming community with old New England values. Reverend Martin, who had baptized Diana at six weeks, praised Mrs. Winston and how she'd discharged duties as wife and mother. He spoke of her commitment to the local hospital—Lancaster Community—where twice a week she read to children and the blind. He remarked on changing times and that society made many demands, all of which Mrs. Winston fulfilled admirably.

Diana felt comfortable in the little Congregational church among people she had lived with for nineteen years. Her mother's friends all came—Mary Blood, Sandra Wilke, Kitty Warden, and Maude Gunnerson. Some might have thought it odd that Diana sat with those friends rather than her only living relatives—Mr. and Mrs. Louis Winston (Diana's father's brother) of Beacon Hill. Incredibly, Diana had never met them. The one time she'd heard her father speak about his brother, he mocked the opium-trafficking origins of the China trade. Even in severe Boston finery, the Louis Winstons stood out like cardinals among a flock of starlings.

As Diana half-listened to the minister, she felt her insides torn apart. The body lay in a simple pine casket, now almost impossible to obtain, but the short will had specified it. Her kind mother bore the indifferent fingerprints of employees at the Carter Brothers Funeral Home (nondenominational). As the eulogy ended, the children's choir, dressed in red robes, stepped forward and sang "Hear Our Prayer." Diana, who had been a member herself, began to sob. Kitty Warden took a hankie from her purse and pressed it into her hand and cradled her head onto her own shoulder. "If the Lord didn't want her, dear, he wouldn't have called her away so soon." Had Diana's sorrow not been so penetrating, she would have been amused. That kind of fatalistic piety would never attract her.

The hilltop graveyard, typical for the area, offered a view halfway to the sea. Some stones dated back to the seventeenth century. It had always frightened Diana as a little girl—the carvings of winged angels and burial urns, ominous epitaphs which spoke of death's inevitability rather than of immortality. But on that day in late May it seemed different. The grass looked vibrantly green; the overhanging maple and oak branches sheltered the terse headstones. Her mother's would be located where she wished it—next to her husband's.

After the burial ceremony, everyone would walk over to Sandra Wilke's house for coffee and cake, but Diana lingered. She stood on the grass between her parents' graves and wondered: What was the point of their lives? Her mother's, it seemed, had been completely sacrificing, and her father's self-indulgent. Yet Diana's mother had forgiven him and she had been the grieving party. Suddenly anger flashed through her body. How could her mother have let herself be so downtrodden? There was a difference between devotion and subservience, but she hadn't seen the distinction. She, Diana, could never forgive her father: he had humiliated and dishonored her mother and their name.

She picked a daisy growing next to her father's stone. As she twirled the green stem between her palms, she recalled childhood memories—the time he hoisted her in front of him on Tally's saddle and drank sherry just before the call to hounds, the many times he fell asleep while reading her bedtime stories, and how he held her strong and sure, lifting her above the turbulent white rush of waves on Cape Cod. She remembered the afternoon she came home crying because a neighbor's sheep had butted her all across a field, and her mother holding her close, and then taking her downtown to Southfield Drug for a therapeutic ice-cream sundae, and how she acted so seriously when Diana announced the death of a mouse in the barn, and her willingness to provide a paper cream container to serve as the coffin. A good portion of their lives they had devoted to Diana, and now, suddenly, she felt unworthy and alone. Nothing for company but conflicting feelings of anger, guilt, loneliness, loss, and love. With her mother's death Diana had no one.

"Hello."

She shaded her eyes from the sun and looked up to see Jim Williams.

"How did you get here?" She dropped the daisy but remained standing still. She hadn't expected to see him.

"I drove over from Hampstead. Just arrived late this morning. It was there I heard. I'm sorry to have missed the service."

"It . . . well, it really was a nothing sort of thing," said Diana, looking down at the dirt piled nearby.

"Still, I would have liked to be with you." As Jim put his arms around her, tears started to fill her eyes again.

"Jim, I don't believe there's a heaven and hell, so where is my mother but down there!" She gestured toward the fresh cavity in the earth.

"Diana, it's all right. I don't believe things are that clear-cut either." He gently tilted her chin with his fingers. "But I do believe there's a spirit that connects us all, in a way we can never understand, and that no real boundary comes between life and death. We have no idea what time is. How can we guess at eternity?"

"I think you've been reading some of those out-of-body reincarnation books." A smile struggled past her tears.

"Diana, please . . ."

Now suddenly she was weeping. She'd heard his plea but it seemed far away. He felt helpless in the face of his friend's grief. "You know, with my mother gone, I've lost everything. I'm not going to be able to ride for three months. Everything's in a mess. She kept the family papers, insurance policies, mortgage, even the birth certificates, all tucked in photo albums around the house."

"What'll you do?" he asked.

"Mother named my uncle chief executor of her will. He suggested—and I guess it makes sense—that I stay with him and his wife in Boston while he sorts out the estate." Diana managed a half-smile. "They had nothing to do with any of us until today, and I'm not very happy about going, but I do feel at loose ends. I've got to do three months on Beacon Hill—Mount Vernon Street."

"Nice place to do time," he replied.

"Jim, don't joke. I'm so torn—I want to stay in my house, my parents' house, and continue working at Hampstead."

"Do you think your mother and father would want you to live alone?"

"I will anyway, three months from now. Wild horses couldn't keep me in the shadow of the State House."

"But it might be better for you to have a change." He felt relieved that she hadn't lost her humor.

"No, I need to be where my memories are. The idea of sponging off some relatives my parents didn't like and who probably won't like me is really hard for me. And they're so old—I'll probably wind up taking care of them."

"Diana, it's Boston you're going to, not Devil's Island. You're being very hard on these people. Maybe the story with your parents is more complicated than you know, and maybe they really do want the right thing for you. Besides, Boston's a wonderful city—make use of your time."

Diana stood up and brushed stray daisy petals from her skirt. Her eyes grew serious. "Jim, you are a dear friend. Thanks for coming by."

"I wanted to, and I also wanted to ease your pain somehow. Not very good at it, I'm afraid."

"Being here counts."

"I wish I could see you, but I'm obligated to conduct a series of clinics at Chesterland Farm in Virginia and I won't return till summer's over. But by then you should be on the back of a horse again, right?"

"Right," said Diana with conviction.

"So, good-bye for now." Jim drew her close and gave her a hug, holding her tightly.

As he walked down the hill and over to his red sports car, Diana said softly to herself, "How I love you, Jim." But then she looked at the daisy petals scattered on the grass, and the raw pain of her grief returned.

A chauffeur carried Diana's bags to the front door of the attractive eighteenth-century red brick town house. Before preceding him, she glanced down the narrow cobbled street. Similar houses lined the steep grade. Lampposts, later reproductions, were exact in every detail except for a natural-gas pipe coming up inside.

Her uncle met her at the door. "Diana, how lovely to see you. Welcome, and do come in." Louis Winston dutifully kissed her cheek and showed her into the small but beautifully appointed living room. Large windows with double white curtains let daylight fall on wood wainscoting, burnished with age and made lovely by its distinctive grain. Even with cars and trucks struggling up the hill a few yards away, no noise could be heard. She realized the walls must be a foot thick. On the ceiling a decorative plaster ingeniously gave the illusion of a larger room. Built-in bookcases with shelves spaced for folios indicated they were no recent addition.

A maid in black dress and white apron wheeled Mrs. Winston into the room. Diana's aunt wore a lavender silk dress with a heavy amethyst-and-pearl brooch. Her parchment skin was powdered pink, and the hair, such as it was, held in place by a gold clip over her left ear. That such a frail woman still made the daily effort to present herself in her own Brahmin fashion impressed Diana.

The red-cheeked Irish girl positioned the chair in the rays of incoming sun and left when Mrs. Winston waved her away. Diana felt a sting in the pit of her stomach. She was angered and embarrassed by her aunt's exercise of superiority.

"Hello, my dear," the old voice quavered, scratching like a record on a hand Victrola. "Come and tell me, how was your ride?"

"Very fine, Aunt Mildred," replied Diana politely and formally to conceal her shyness. "Your house is lovely."

"Thank you, dear. We couldn't live anyplace else. No, I'm afraid we really couldn't. You know, Henry James said . . ." Mrs. Winston interrupted herself: "You do know Henry James?"

"I haven't read any of his works," said Diana, recalling the exact location in her father's library of the two shelves holding the author's novels and critical essays.

"Well, I daresay you've got plenty of time for that. Begin with *Daisy Miller*. It concerns a beautiful and headstrong young woman. He, that is Mr. James, said that Mount Vernon Street is the most beautiful street in America."

"I'm sure he was right, Aunt."

"But how do you know, child? How many of America's streets could a mere slip of a girl like yourself have seen?"

Diana was taken aback by her aunt's assault. Hypocritical expressions of politeness didn't come easily to her. "You're right, Aunt Mildred. I haven't seen as many streets as you and Uncle Louis have, and on second thought I'm not sure it is in fact the prettiest of all the streets I've seen in my short little life." If she wants candor, I'll give her candor, Diana told herself.

"*Quite* right, then." Diana heard an amused chuckle rattle around and escape the blue-veined throat.

During the first few days, Diana walked all over Boston. She visited the historical sites—Old North Church, the USS *Constitution*, the Granary—but soon found herself more drawn to Back Bay. As she walked past the exquisite boutiques lining Newbury Street, she saw yuppies everywhere in L.L. Bean and Eddie Bauer gear driving their black Cherokees (for most of them their only extended contact with minorities). She started frequenting the Café Vendome on Dartmouth Street, watching the affluent outdoor crowd. She noted the captivating women and admired their way of dressing and carrying themselves. They didn't give up their sexuality in a quest to dress for success. Hats and gloves, high heels and accessories—Pucci scarves and simple but elegant jewelry from Shreve, Crump & Low. She had never been attracted to fashion because her job demanded she wear jeans and boots. Suddenly she found herself wishing she knew how to wear those clothes.

Diana recalled a Southfield High acquaintance who always dressed in outfit after outfit of Jordan Marsh mix-'n'-match. Her mother worked at Chestnut Hill Mall and got a discount. She was voted best-dressed in her class. At the time Diana had paid no attention, but now she vowed to do better. She'd get a job at an exclusive shop on Newbury Street.

The next morning she put on her black dress and entered Cipriani moments after it opened. The matronly woman in chignon and pearls smiled until she learned Diana wished to apply for a position rather than make a purchase. "I'm afraid we have no openings for college students. We're fully staffed." Her formal tone and French accent conveyed that she regarded this as an unpleasant task best dispatched brusquely.

"Well, then, we're both lucky I'm not a college student."

"That is different, then. You are so young-looking. Do you have a degree?"

"No."

"I am afraid we require a degree." Diana moved away from the door, about to be opened in order to hasten her departure.

"Ma'am, may I speak with you a moment, one woman to another woman?"

Madame Deladier could not repress her amusement at the mock-grown-up manner of this pretty girl. She nodded her assent.

"I'm not a college student, so I wouldn't quit and leave you high and dry without support this fall. But I am well-educated. I'm very reliable and have been inculcated by my parents, both of whom are now dead, with integrity and honesty. Additionally, and rather recently, I have trained myself to have excellent fashion sense."

Madame Deladier was disarmed by Diana's performance but managed to check her smile. "You have good fashion sense?" She looked at Diana's dress with a blank expression.

"I do, don't I?" asked Diana, nervously glancing down. She felt the disparity between what she wished she could wear and what she had on. If someone had asked her about the conformation of a certain horse, she wouldn't have blinked, but this was new territory.

"Well, not bad. Are you still in high school?"

"No, graduated, with honors. I can work all hours."

"I see. You are very young. It is important our saleswomen relate to the customers. We shall see. Please come tomorrow morning before ten so I can show you how to work the register. It will be quiet then. We shall see what we can do about working out some hours for you." Madame made a snap decision but felt confident she'd not regret it.

"Yes, thank you. What time, exactly?" asked the excited Diana.

"Nine-thirty."

"I can be here earlier," she offered.

"I can't," said Madame Deladier flatly. She held the door open.

"Oh, I was wondering . . ." But Diana waved her hand to cut short her own question. She'd ask about a clothing discount after the first day or two.

Madame Deladier misinterpreted the foray. "Your salary—your wage? Four dollars and fifty cents an hour. That is satisfactory?" Her face conveyed that Diana should find it more than enough and take her leave.

"Absolutely all right. Thank you very much. See you tomorrow." After Diana closed the door, a saleswoman with red hair walked over to Madame Deladier, who had begun pinning a Givenchy outfit on a wicker mannequin.

"Isabelle, did you hire that child?" she asked.

"Yes, I did." Her intonation was slightly defensive.

"But she is so young."

"Yes, you are right. Business sense may demand the opposite, but I like her. She was so . . . amusing. Such a performance. Here, help with this scarf. Jeanne, you've heard the term 'young man in a hurry'? I think we have a young lady in the same situation. And I think I'm going to enjoy helping her along."

The next day, after Diana had learned how to use the cash register and other menial tasks, Madame Deladier proceeded to the more important job of sales:

"Now, when a customer comes in, you must offer assistance. If you are busy with someone else, you must at least manage a pleasant greeting. You must never let a customer carry the clothes she is to try on into the dressing room—you must carry them for her. If she wishes to continue looking, take her things so she doesn't have to move them around. Also, don't miss an opportunity to suggest an accessory—a scarf, a belt, or jewelry.

"You are free to talk with any of the customers, but with someone in the store we do not chitchat between ourselves. It is bad form. There is plenty to do, color-coding and straightening dresses, folding sweaters, filling in scarves, and keeping the changing room neat and ready for the next customer. We do not lean on the glass counters—it looks sloppy." Madame Deladier gently touched Diana's elbow, which was resting squarely on one. "Do you have any questions?"

"What if a customer doesn't want help?" Diana recalled the uncomfortable moments she had been hounded by saleswomen.

"Then leave her alone. We want customers to feel like our guests. You're a clever girl—you'll get a feel for what each woman wants. Service is what makes us better than department stores. And that's why we must be more expensive. Also, service greatly deters shoplifting."

"Do you get a lot of shoplifting?"

"Our small size does not make us immune. The best time for a shoplifter is if salesgirls are chatting, or if they're busy with other customers. Soon you'll get a feel for what these petty thieves look like. They almost all wear full skirts so they can walk with a lot of clothing between their legs. They look like penguins when they waddle out."

Diana was stupefied. "Don't you stop them?"

"Such scenes discourage business."

"But you let them leave?"

"And why not? All they would get is thirty days, and then they're back on the streets, so to speak. Why try to save a thousand dollars' worth of goods if it results in the loss of five thousand worth of customer purchases? People don't like police and a lot of yelling. It is hard to be discreet with loud fools." Madame Deladier gave a shrug only a citizen of France could perfect. "Besides, some criminals turn out to be married to surprisingly important husbands."

"Between their legs!" That seemed the height of audacity to Diana.

Madame Deladier went on. "In fact, there is one woman—you will come to know her, she always wears a blue bandana around her head—who recently complained to Maria about the quality of this year's merchandise."

Diana looked at Maria, who smiled. "Pretty amazing, isn't it—the human race, I mean."

"Awful," commented Diana, appalled.

"Well, all this brings me back to my first point. Customer attentiveness strongly deters shoplifting. If there is anything a shoplifter hates, it's a solicitous salesgirl. So you understand, Diana, how a strategic advantage accompanies politeness?"

"A shopgirl!" crackled Mildred Winston, putting down her iced-tea spoon.

"Diana, if we need to give you more money . . ." offered her practical uncle.

"No, I don't need any more money. At least not from you. You've been more than generous. I'd just like to earn a little bit on my own."

"A shopgirl," repeated Mrs. Winston, convinced Diana's character had been fatally flawed by inferior maternal bloodlines.

"Yes, it's a good way to learn about fashion—I'm really excited by it," she said cheerfully, hoping to stave off what she knew was coming.

"But Boston," Louis Winston said proudly, "is not the city one comes to to learn about fashion."

"Oh, but you're wrong there, Uncle Louis. There are lovely stores. Mine carries Ungaro, Hanae Morie, St. Laurent, Diane Von Furstenberg." To him the names might have been randomly drawn from the western suburban phone book.

"And who is Von . . . What did you say?" asked her aunt.

"Von Furstenberg—New York designer. And I get a discount."

"A discount?" repeated her aunt with disdain.

"Forty percent," announced Diana proudly.

"Diana, your aunt and I are not going to prohibit you from working in this place, but don't you think you could put Boston to better use?"

"Uncle, I am putting it to good use. I'm learning to become a great lady like Aunt Mildred." Diana was a fledgling when it came to subtle flattery. Her aunt pounced.

"Grand ladies develop from within. If you become morally and aesthetically acute, the appropriate clothes will find their way onto your back."

"I . . . I uh . . ."

"Imagine, zipping up the backs of dresses on complete strangers! What do you think you are, an Irish chambermaid?" The old lady made an odd noise in her throat.

Diana could no longer control her irritation. "Aunt, I'm only going to use this job as a stepping-stone. You never cared about me before, so why the snobbish concern now? I thought there was no room for prejudice in this house. I wish you hadn't intervened in my life. You kept out of it for nineteen years. My mother dies and suddenly you cart me off here, which is exactly where I didn't want to go. You're hypocrites—I know about the opium and the Chinese. Don't talk to me about votes for women and nursery schools."

Diana turned and bounded up the stairs two at a time before her uncle could stop her.

"Millie, we must let the child do as she likes."

"A shopgirl," repeated Mrs. Winston, disbelieving.

"Perhaps we are a bit out of touch."

"Discount—can you imagine?"

"Now, it's not as if she's snorting cocaine and picking up boys on the Common."

"Louis, really!" exclaimed Mrs. Winston.

Shortly afterward Louis Winston knocked on Diana's door. "May I come in?" Diana put down *Daisy Miller*. "I must apologize for what your aunt said. I'm not proud of my comments either. We know this is just a temporary thing for you and that we really haven't at hand what it takes to keep an energetic girl occupied."

"Why is Aunt Mildred so dead set against it?"

"Never you mind your aunt. You take that job and buy as many pretty frocks as you can. I have a feeling that you'll be needing them sooner or later." He patted Diana on the head and headed out the door.

"Uncle Louis?"

"Yes?"

"Why did I never see either of you until the funeral?"

"Your father and I got into a fight over a woman."

"A woman?" Diana was shocked.

"Yes, a woman."

"What kind of woman?" Diana's mind raced up and down the potential inventory her father and uncle might have quarreled over.

"A marvelous woman."

"Uncle Louis." Diana's voice reproached him for teasing.

"We both very much loved Katharine Reilly."

"Mother." The word escaped Diana's lips involuntarily.

"The three of us met while your father and I were at Harvard. It was winter—a skating party on Walden Pond. In the end I lost, of course—and more than your mother, I'm afraid. There came to be bad blood between us. And then I disapproved of other things he did." Louis Winston didn't elaborate but turned and looked out the window. Southfield lay beyond the farthest ridge of hills, some forty miles distant. Memory still triggered the pain. "And that helps explain why your aunt is liable to criticism, Diana. She's always been jealous. It would have been quite another thing if I had rejected your mother." Louis Winston gently closed the door and went back downstairs.

Stunned at this new piece of information, Diana took a seat in a chair by the window. A large cabin cruiser headed up the Charles, and only a few sailboats remained on the water, which now reflected late-afternoon light. So her father's verbal assaults on his brother's immorality were merely a projection of his own. A wave of anger surged through her body. He'd betrayed her mother by the affair, and betrayed them both by squandering his money. Now, because he was dead, she could never tell him what a hypocrite she thought he was. And her mother—she must have known all along that the secretary he drove into the Nashua River hadn't been the first. How could she—how could any woman—put up with a man like that? A terrible feeling of loneliness and isolation set in as she confronted her past. She felt herself an orphan in desperate need of complete support, love, and understanding. But there was no one—just distasteful memories of her father and disappointment in her mother. As the twilight sun dipped below the river basin, letting the ocean shadows draw in from the east, Diana wept for the family she'd never had.

During the next several weeks Diana proved herself a tireless worker at Cipriani. Madame Deladier knew she could count on Diana if someone else became sick or if an imminent sale necessitated night work—taking inventory, noting markdowns, converting the office area into an extra dressing room. Her mature manner and ability to gauge immediately the sort of women she was dealing with made her very popular. For her part, Diana met some impressive women—individuals in federal and state government, private business, the arts, as well as entrepreneurs. And every paycheck she spent on clothing. With Madame Deladier's help she selected elegant items, but not trendy ones, that would serve her well for years. Her aunt did not mention Diana's work again, other than each evening to inquire blandly how her day had gone, thereby registering continued disapproval. But from her uncle she felt support, and on occasion showed him some of her purchases, which he invariably applauded.

One day, after working almost three months at Cipriani, Diana helped an energetic blond in a simple black suit to find a dress appropriate for a wedding on board a private yacht. After the woman expressed delight with the selections held out, her eyes hardened and seemed to evaluate Diana's features.

"Did I get something on my face?" she asked, peering into a mirror.

"Have you ever modeled?"

"No." Diana laughed at the absurdity.

"I think you should consider it." She circled Diana, continuing to take mental snapshots.

"Why?" While a number of Diana's friends dreamt of becoming models—devouring every book and magazine on the subject—it had never interested her.

"It's exciting work. Hard work, no doubt about that, and not as glamorous as most girls think. But someone like you could make quite a lot of money." Her eyes drilled through Diana's skirts in an effort to ascertain the exact outline of her body. "You'd have to lose seven or eight pounds, of course. How do you think your parents would feel about your living in New York?"

"I'm not sure how *I'd* feel about it."

For a fraction of a second the woman was taken aback. Then, with the shrug characteristic of someone who had only so much time, she took out a card, wrote an address on the back, and handed it to Diana. "Dear, you go and get yourself a portfolio at this studio. Just show them this card and they'll know what shots to take. And they'll charge it to my account." After she paid for her purchases and was on her way out the door, she turned to look back, as if Diana had become an afterthought. "You really should come to New York, dear."

"Who was that?" Maria put down the earrings she was attaching to the display case and walked over to Diana's side.

"Someone from the Eileen Ford Agency."

"Not just someone, Diana. That was Eileen Ford herself. You know her agency, of course." Madame Deladier began rehanging the outfit that Diana's blond customer did not take.

"No, not really."

"I thought girls your age knew all about people like her." Madame Deladier spoke in a friendly but chiding manner. "The Ford Agency books top models in the United States—many of international caliber. And the pay these mega-models get is phenomenal—Cheryl Tiegs, Christie Brinkley, Kim Alexis—all multimillionaires. If Eileen Ford suggested you get a portfolio, you must do it. You could be set up financially for life in one year."

"You think I should get a portfolio?" Diana asked excitedly.

"Of course. You're a beautiful girl—classic features.

And you eyes . . . well, they'd be hypnotic if they weren't so sharp and exciting."

"You've got nothing to lose," Maria added.

Two days later Diana walked up the steps of a dirty red brick building and followed the signs to Spectrum Modeling. The empty waiting room had no receptionist. She took a seat in a black chair with chrome legs. Framed in metal, black-and-white blowups of vaguely familiar models hung from the molding. In a matter of minutes a thin man in his forties wearing jeans and a T-shirt—Diana thought it was an undershirt—came out. He hadn't shaved and the side of one soiled sneaker flapped off the sole.

"Diana?"

She nodded and followed him into the white-walled, high-ceiling study. After an assistant brushed her hair and made minor adjustments in makeup, the photographer took control again.

"Sit down over there." He pointed to a black plastic stool, then began to look through his Nikon and adjust lenses. "Well, another Ford find. I'm sure you already know you'll have to drop some weight. Okay, we're all set. So, baby, just smile into the camera." Almost before she could move her facial muscles, he continued, "No, that smile belongs in a second-grade class photo. All right, your lover has just come in the room. Smile. He's over my shoulder now. Tilt your head right. Pretend you've just been paid the greatest compliment in the world—give me a one-hundred-watt grin. Now make like you're thinking about making love—serious, with just the trace of a smile, all thoughts inside your head."

Diana stood up and looked angrily at the puzzled man. "That's where most people's thoughts are, but let me tell you one of mine. I don't like the way you're talking to me. You're not coaching me—that I could use, I know—but you're trying to . . . to . . . seduce me onto film. It's demeaning—all of it—the words you choose, your familiar tone."

The photographer shrugged. He was used to tantrums, but not from novices. "Hey, you're the boss, babe, whatever works. Now, turn your head and pull your hair around the other side so Eileen gets a look at your profile. Terrific—the neck of a swan. Now the other side. That should do it. Okay, kid. We're in business. Now, I just need your name and address for Eileen and my files."

Two weeks later Diana received a letter from Eileen Ford inviting her to become a model in her agency. "I'm not going to do it."

"Why not?" Though Madame Deladier's tone conveyed surprise, there was an undercurrent of admiration. "You'd make a great deal of money and be the envy of women. Men would fall in love with you."

"I don't want to be envied and I don't care if men fall in love with my paper face. The thought of wearing pinned-up dresses and standing in front of photographers day after day leaves me cold. And who wants to live in Manhattan? It's getting to be like a third-world nation— only the rich and the poor."

"But you could have a wonderful apartment. And you'd travel."

"I'm going to have a nice apartment and I'm going to travel, but not this way. I want to get back to riding. I've been away too long as it is."

"Diana, you have all the time in the world ahead of you. A year or two in modeling could set you up for life. You said the Ford contract lasts only a year."

"Well, I'm not signing. But . . ." Diana paused, then smiled mischievously. "But I am going to model in Boston—runway work—for the Barbizon Agency. I went to see them yesterday. I go to a how-to class this afternoon, then I work a Laura Ashley fashion show at the Copley Plaza the day after tomorrow. I won't get paid as well, but I can still work here part-time for three more months. Then it's back to Southfield and riding."

"And you will use your modeling money to buy more

clothes here?" Madame Deladier asked, sympathetically and devoid of self-interest.

"Would that be unethical because of my employee discount?" she asked guiltily.

"Of course not." Madame Deladier waved her hand dismissively. "You have a bright future, Diana, and I am more than pleased to help you dress for it."

# In Training

The same afternoon Diana returned to Southfield, she drove to Hampstead. Bob Sloan sat at his desk entering bloodlines into the Decmate. "May I help you?" he asked glancing up.

"Yes, Mr. Sloan. Could you tell me what sort of training schedule I'm on now?" Her voice subdued, almost respectful, Diana was determined to start off on the right foot.

"Excuse me? Oh, it's you. You look different. Did you do something . . . uh . . . your clothes?"

"I cut my hair. I called Mrs. Snyder last month to let her know when I'd be back. Didn't she tell you?"

"No," said Sloan, still punching in the bloodlines of his latest Hanoverian Verband imports. He didn't look up and didn't continue speaking. It was a cheap exercise in power.

"I'll go find Mrs. Snyder. I'm sure she'll tell you what she told me." Diana was almost out the door when Sloan lifted his red, ball-shaped head.

"Mrs. Snyder's gone," Sloan said, then glanced down at the computer. "Goddammit, I thought that was the bold key." (Someone had just acquired a new grandsire.)

Diana felt a sinking sensation in the pit of her stomach. "How can I get in touch with her?"

"Who knows?" She turned in the direction of the familiar female voice. Courtney stood decked out in a black rhinestone-embellished Krizia jumpsuit. She walked a circle around Diana.

"Little Diana—how we've grown up. Did they have before-and-after sessions in Boston for *Seventeen* magazine?"

"I don't read it."

"Don't suppose you do. Well, it's nice somebody finally decided to give you an allowance."

"Where's your mother, Courtney?"

"Mother, you obviously haven't heard, is getting a divorce from Daddy. I should say she's divorcing Daddy. They're legally separated. Have been for two months. Mother needed to get away, so she's traveling. Some inn on Martinique. She's staying with an old Randolph Macon chum."

"So who's running Hampstead?" Diana asked as politely as she could, heartsick her chief ally was gone.

"I am, as always," said Sloan, looking at Diana's breasts. The kid's grown up, he noted to himself.

"I mean who's overseeing Hampstead?"

"I am," announced Courtney with overwhelming satisfaction, aware the impact her words had.

"Well," said Diana with an inadvertent touch of resignation, "whom should I ride?"

"No one," replied Courtney abruptly. "Go see Steve. I think he needs help mucking out."

Before Diana could open her mouth to protest, Bob Sloan intervened. "Courtney, Diana should start schooling the three geldings just in from Newburgh quarantine."

"Pam Warnke's assigned to them."

"Says who?" asked an irritated Sloan.

"Says me," countered Courtney tentatively.

"Okay, Diana, you go check in with Steve. I'll get back to you on your program. I'll never get these things entered." Sloan slapped his folder shut, and as Diana closed the door, she heard Courtney rant:

"You know I hate that little twit. I didn't think she'd be back. The only way I'm going to get rid of her is put her back in the manure pail."

"You're stepping into my job, and I won't have it. Remember what your mother said. Want me to cable her? She doesn't want your ax-grinding to hurt *her* farm. That kid, if you can still call her a kid, means big bucks to this place."

Courtney's face reddened and her voice jumped an octave. "You all think she's just so great because she won a Grand Prix once. Luck."

"With or without that, she's good around horses, especially the young ones. Between her salary and the prices these warmbloods command, we're making some real money here, just when your mother might need it. You find me someone else with her ability and then I'll sack her—not before."

"Thanks for your support, Bob," Courtney said caustically. "I'll be glad to help you sometime too." She slammed the door behind her. "I'll get that little bitch out of here."

Bob Sloan sat at his desk and flipped the Decmate switch. As he looked out the window, waiting for the machine to give him the cue with his disks, he saw Diana wheeling manure across the stableyard. Sack her is exactly what I intend to do, Courtney, but not the way you mean, he said to himself. He felt his freckled cock inflate like a bicycle tube as he mentally undressed Diana.

"Diana, my friend, how are you? Welcome back." Steve ran and took the wheelbarrow from her hands. "What a grand lady you've become. Your hair—and I see you are wearing makeup."

"Oh, Steve, stop." Diana blushed.

"You don't know how to take compliments. To be truly a grand lady, you must learn that."

"And how do I learn?" she asked good-humoredly.

"When I say you are a grand lady, perhaps nothing but a smile acknowledging what you already know to be true. Do you think if I paid the same compliment to Catherine Deneuve or Sophia Loren they would respond by saying, 'Oh, Steve, stop'?" Diana laughed. "No, they wouldn't. They would say, 'Get this man out of here' and I would be whisked away by their bodyguards."

"Steve, don't make me laugh so hard."

"It's so good to see you and to see your smile. I was sorry to hear about your mother."

Diana's smile faded. "Oh, well, we all lose our parents someday, I guess. Thank you for your card. It was very kind of you." Feeling a sudden jolt of pain, she hurriedly changed the subject. "How's Navarro?"

"Navarro is just fine. If he weren't a stallion, I'd say he was in foal. Too much grass, not enough work. The front field's his to graze, but he's due to leave next week."

"That's too bad. Where's he going?"

"Dressage barn outside Washington. Don't make such a face—your friend will be back in a month. You know Roger Merkin? Navarro will be schooled by him. They're going to try to take him into upper level."

"Will he succeed?"

"Oh, sure, if he's careful with his mouth. These Andalusians have difficulty with Germanic hands. But they are talented and forgiving of fools. Fortunately, Merkin's not one."

"Somehow I think nationalism's creeping into your opinion," teased Diana.

"No, no, I respect German riders very much. It's just that their horses are less sensitive than ours, and then the riders may become a little less sensitive too."

"Sounds credible. Anyway, I'll sure miss Navarro. Seems silly to say, but I've never known a horse with so much soul."

"Not silly to me. Breeders cherish character more than anything else." Steve would miss Navarro too, but didn't let on. From the day the horse had first stepped off the van, Steve thought he'd seen him before, but in the end dismissed it as similar breed traits. Yet the more Steve watched the white horse, especially the way he'd nuzzle his pockets for carrots and neigh when he saw him, the more Steve was troubled. When he stood and stroked the neck it was as if this almost mystical creature understood the man's past life—and was there to help.

Diana resumed an active training schedule, though now

and again Sloan asked her to help out mucking when a groom called in sick. He increased the number of imports, and though Diana knew how crucial establishing a foundation with a young horse was, she yearned to get back on the Grand Prix circuit. Training young horses was fine, but it didn't gain international acclaim. The most she could expect would be regional notice as someone to send your problems or promises to. And at that time there were no Grand Prix prospects available except Zanzibar and Flag, both already scheduled for the Lipari brothers. Diana decided she'd ask Sloan if he couldn't refer her to contacts at other barns.

"Come in."

It was the first time Diana had entered the office when Sloan wasn't at his desk. What a thick body he's got, Diana thought to herself. Apelike.

"Yeah, Diana, what is it?"

"Do you have time to talk about something?"

"Shoot."

"You know I did well on Aden. And since we don't have any Grand Prix horses competing from here at the moment, I wondered if you'd be willing to refer me to some people who might give me a chance on the circuit this year."

"I see." Sloan paused and looked out the window. Precisely what he didn't want Diana to do: if she were away, there went the underpinnings of his training and sales program. In fact, he had received two calls about Diana during her stay in Boston—one from Coker Farm, the other from Primrose. Both had new Grand Prix horses they wanted Diana to campaign. They'd be willing to send them to Hampstead and pay the board and training. However, that didn't quite equate to getting an import from Germany at twelve thousand dollars and reselling him in three months for twenty-two. Sloan knew exactly how to reach Diana, but told the farms she'd quit the business and gone to live with relatives in Boston. He wasn't about to lose her.

"Uh, sure, Diana. I can make a couple calls for you.

It's a little late in the season, so most horses probably have riders assigned. If only you'd come back sooner."

"I couldn't."

"I know that," Sloan said with a failed sympathetic smile.

"And, Mr. Sloan, we need to discuss my salary."

"Salary?" he repeated gruffly.

"Yes, I'm twenty and I've got some skills that deserve to be paid for."

"Okay, you're a big girl—time to start you off with a big-girl salary—twelve thousand. Congratulations."

"Landmark and some of the other big farms start their trainers at twenty."

"Why don't you go there, then?" Sloan immediately regretted his sarcastic recommendation. He had no desire to lose what von Engerson had told him would become one of the country's top riders.

"Right now, at least for a while, it'll have to be the minimum. Let's see how quickly we sell these three geldings you're working with." He moved closer to Diana, making her feel uneasy. He fingered her shoulder as he spoke. "You realize, Diana, ever since I've known you, you've had an attitude problem. Things would go a lot better for us if you could be more cooperative." With that Sloan forced her body against the wall with his and closed his mouth over hers.

Diana quickly shoved him back. Face flushed, she continued the conversation, though her voice failed to contain her anger and fear. "The ones I trained last year went for between twenty and twenty-five, and I know you got them from a breeding farm outside Munich for much less," she said evenly.

Sloan resumed his businesslike posture. "What we get them for is none of your business." He pulled out his chair and his body fell heavily into it. She saw the blue veins in the side of his neck stand out in agitation.

"Okay. Twelve thousand till the first group goes, but they'll go soon." As she walked across the courtyard, she saw Steve but looked away. She felt terrible that getting her salary settled involved a repugnant sexual advance, and was certain he would read the distress on her face.

During the next six months Diana occasionally went out with former high-school friends but didn't find the visits particularly stimulating. Sue was getting married and full of talk about invitations, in-law conflicts, and the best washer-dryers. Kathy and Gerry enrolled at Nashoba Valley Tech while Linda and Pam went off to college for the long haul. None seemed to have the aspirations, drive, and direction Diana possessed. They found her single-mindedness boring. They didn't understand the complexities of the show world and had no wish to. Where there'd once been gales of giggly girl laughter now existed either silence or awkward small talk. Most evenings Diana spent reading in the family library. She knew her mother would have been happy if she'd taken the thirty thousand dollars she'd left and gone to college, but she was going to be a top rider and would need that money and more. She'd educate herself at home and forget the idol of a degree. In less than two months she plowed through Ariel and Will Durant's *Story of Civilization*, bought herself a VHS system, improved her French, and began to learn Spanish. Once a week she went to the public library to read periodicals ranging from *Foreign Affairs* to *Town and Country*. She'd never allow herself to be found less than politically astute, or unaware of the comings and goings of would-be American aristocracy.

Jim Williams didn't come back as soon as he'd predicted. He extended the stay at Chesterland and from there went straight to Gladstone. Seven months passed before Diana saw him.

"Hello."

Diana put down the hoof she was cleaning.

"Jim!" They exchanged hugs. "I missed you. Where've you been?" How handsome he looked in his pale blue shirt and khaki slacks, she thought.

"Working. I've been engaged in the Puritan-approved pursuit of earning a decent wage."

Diana laughed. "I heard they gave you an offer that was too good to refuse."

"They did, in fact. My God, Diana, you've changed. Step back and let me have a look." Diana twirled a professional-model circle, flouncing her nonexistent skirt, then put her hands on her hips and strode down the barn aisle as if it were a runway.

"Tell you what—let's go celebrate your return to the horse world with a bottle of champagne this evening. How about the Harvest in Cambridge?"

"That'd be wonderful. What time can you come by?"

"I'll make the reservation for seven, since I still take it you're getting up early for these guys." Jim pointed to the black gelding.

At that moment one of the new grooms—a small Cuban-American—approached Diana. "Diana, I was sent to tell you that your ring time is in ten minutes. Mrs. Bunnell has the next hour and you know how she hates anyone in during hers."

"Thanks, Paul, I'll be right there. I just have to throw the tack on this guy." She turned to Jim. "I've got to go. But there's so much to tell you."

Jim put his arm around her shoulder. "Well, tell all tonight. Pick you up at six-fifteen." They exchanged hugs again.

Jim came promptly. "Diana, you are gorgeous. Where'd you get that dress?"

"It's a de la Renta—like it?"

"Like it? It's sensational. Made for you."

"Actually, I think it was originally made for a Rockefeller. Got it at a thrift shop for 'gently used' luxury wear. Anyway, you're the first to see me in it. I didn't exactly spend my time on the Beacon Hill upwardly mobile cocktail circuit while you were gone."

"And your hair's lovely. I'll never understand how women can get it to stick and roll over and do all those things."

"Styling mousse."

"Whatever it takes—looks great. You could be a model." She laughed and took him by the arm as they headed for his mud-spattered Porsche. "I'm sorry, I didn't have time to get a car wash."

"But the driver can't be improved on."

"Anyway, what was so funny? You do look like a model, you know."

During the fifty-minute drive into Cambridge, Diana told Jim about her retail-modeling ventures. "Why didn't you stay in it? The Ford Agency, my God, you could have made a bundle. It would have paid completely for this filthy habit you and I share."

"Didn't want to. You know Torrance Fleischmann Watkins?"

"Sure, we worked a little together on the Combined Training Team. Nice lady."

"She was a model."

"I know that too, believe it or not."

"Well, she modeled all day and then would take the train out of Manhattan to her Long Island home. Then she'd drive to the stable where she kept her horses and *then* trailer them all the way down to Hector Carmona's farm in New Jersey. She'd ride for two hours and then trailer them all the way back! Eight hours, not including the commute home on the train. And she only rode two horses a day. I ride six and I'm exhausted."

"No one's suggesting you follow that sort of gladiator program. But it seems to me if you took your riding easy for a year or two, you'd be in great financial shape."

"I'd lose two years—that's not what I call being in good shape."

"You act as if your world is perched on a house of cards. You've got to plan and invest you time, and even learn how to wait."

"No, Jim. I'm not going to spend one heartbeat doing something I don't want. Besides, I don't need the money. Mother left me with more than enough."

"You'll dribble that away if you don't get yourself a better position."

"You think I should get back on the Grand Prix circuit."

He kept his mind on the tricky intersection at Route Two, then continued, "Only if you can manage to keep your job at Hampstead at the same time."

"Why shouldn't I?"

"Chances are you'll be able to, and get a raise to boot. You're Sloan's bread basket. He's not going to make it easy for you to leave. But if someone calls you, he might feel compelled to give you a raise—I assure you it'd be 'minimal'—rather than lose you to another barn."

"God, did I just make a mistake?"

"How so?"

"A while back I asked Sloan to see if some of the other barns needed a Grand Prix rider."

"Well, that wasn't so much a mistake. No harm done, anyway. He just won't, that's all. You don't think if anyone called Hampstead directly asking for you he'd pass it on?"

"I guess not," Diana said glumly.

"You guess right." Jim patted her head. "Yuk, this mousse stuff's stiff."

"You're supposed to admire it from afar, dummy," said Diana in a friendly retort.

Over châteaubriand for two they caught up on eight months. And afterward they walked along the Charles River. The sun was just setting in a pink-and-blue sky, and the water reflected the evening light. A sailboat from the Cambridge Boat Club made its way up the river between the Eliot and Anderson bridges—its white canvas tinged pink in the twilight. "For not having a real campus, Harvard certainly is pretty. Look how lovely the Business School looks in this light."

"It does. Aren't you sorry you didn't go to college, Jim?"

"But I did."

"I had no idea." She was completely taken by surprise.

"No reason why you should. I went to Princeton, though I was accepted here and at Williams as well."

"Why Princeton?"

"Poor reason, I'm afraid. Close to Gladstone."

"Why did you bother with school at all?"

"I've got this anachronistic concept of the liberally educated man. I just didn't think I'd get as much out of life without an education. Fundamentally selfish, I suppose."

"No, I don't think so. I think you're broad-minded and your heart goes beyond your sport. That's probably why you're a better rider than most. Jim?"

"Yes?"

"Do you think I'm making a mistake, not going to college?"

"No, from what you told me about your recent monastic study habits, it doesn't sound like it. I'm basically lazy, and going to school was a way of getting my feet held to the fire."

"So you think I made the right choice?"

"I think, Diana, it's the right choice if the horse world is what you truly want. I believe it's what you want now. I just hope you don't change your mind. Anyway, there's time."

"I'm not going to change my mind," said Diana resolutely.

"Then you made the right choice. Many would envy your commitment and ability to set yourself goals and head straight for them."

They paused to watch a golden retriever swim out to fetch a stick his owner had thrown in the river. Jim put his arm around Diana's waist and drew her against him, closing his lips over hers and gently working his tongue inside her mouth. Afterward Jim held her close, his head against hers.

"I love you," she said quietly.

He looked into her eyes and smiled as he stroked her cheek. "And I love you in my way too, Diana."

She sensed the odd qualification but didn't want to spoil the moment by pursuit. "You know, there're so many women in the horse-show world, and it seems just about all the men are fags."

It was as if she had punched him in the stomach. "A lot of gays, that's for sure," he replied.

"Why do you think that is?"

"I don't really know. Perhaps it has something to do with riding being an art."

"And also, don't you think it might be because English riding is considered sissy in this country? God knows why, it's so dangerous. I'll bet it's our 'Marlboro Man' mentality."

"I really doubt its image has anything to do with that. I hang my hat on the art theory. Remember, I'm from that world in New York. Gays predominate."

"I guess so." Her tone was disinterested.

"Diana, I think we'd better head home. I've got a long day and I know you do too."

"Okay," she said, surprised. Things had been going so well. But then maybe, just maybe, he might be planning to ask if he could spend the night with her. "Jim?"

"Yes."

"I'm glad, with all the crazy people in the horse world, that I have you."

"I'm glad I have you as a friend too, Diana." He hoped his tone registered more conviction than he felt at that moment.

Jim did not ask to spend the night with Diana when he stopped the car in her driveway. He didn't even turn off the ignition. As he drove back to Hampstead, he felt about as alone as he'd ever felt. He had thought he might tell her soon—that night even—that he was gay, but that would never happen now. He'd thought she'd be sympathetic, but he'd been wrong. "Fag." How he hated the word.

It was four weeks before Diana would see Jim again. He decided to visit his mother in New York, then fly to Cancún with some friends. Diana, of course, didn't understand any of these comings or goings. If they were such good friends, if he loved her, wouldn't he linger at Hampstead with her, or even ask her to go with him?

And why didn't she meet his family? Or any of his friends? He never introduced them to her at shows, except for Tim Craig. He seemed to have compartmentalized her. They had a marvelous evening, but that next day he was off again. What did their kiss mean to him?

During this time Diana received her salary. She was paid twelve thousand a year for forty hours a week. She felt elated because it began to symbolize her worth, though far below it. Bob Sloan consulted her more on his imports: she would review videos of what the breeding farms in Germany had to offer. One glance at a horse's shoulders told her whether he had the extension necessary to get a first in the ring. One look at the back and she knew whether this was a horse that could clear five feet with a rider.

Slowly and surely Diana learned what it was to be professional. Cardinal rule number one was to be as candid as possible with clients about strengths and weaknesses of their horses. There was no sense in encouraging someone to pour thousands of dollars of training into an animal that lacked either the mental or the physical ability. Cardinal rule two was never to relay these weaknesses to anybody else—whether farrier, vet, another trainer, or particularly another client. People could be very emotional about their horses, and if after a frank discussion they still felt they had a Genuine Risk or Bally Cor, then they should be left to their dreams. One instructor at Hampstead continually bad-mouthed an Anglo-Arab in public for its lack of ability, hoping the owner would get the message. In fact, the owner good-naturedly took all these remarks, or so it seemed, until one Saturday a van arrived to pull away with the horse (and two others the owner boarded there). They went to another barn, where the trainers were just as candid with the owner but tight-lipped to others. And of course the bruised man bad-mouthed Hampstead every chance he got.

Diana did learn to hedge when discussing a horse with

prospective buyers. Not because she didn't want to be honest but because Sloan would have nailed her otherwise. So if a horse toed in with a particular hoof, she might put on bell boots during the demonstration ride. Or if he had a tendency to spook, she would ride him last thing the night before and plan to show him after he'd been turned out in his pasture a couple of hours and exercised at the end of a lunge line. If a horse had a serious problem—one crazy mare would rear over backward rather than halt squarely on all fours—she just wouldn't make herself available for conversation. She'd dismount, hand the horse to a groom, and let Sloan take it. She didn't want anything to do with life-threatening transactions. Even though she knew *caveat emptor* was the horse-seller's motto, she couldn't bring herself to become involved in gross deceit.

And like a house that sells better on the market if it's nicely furnished, Diana saw to it that each horse she presented was groomed to the hilt. Its coat would shine with Prosheen; its mane had been recently pulled, its whiskers, ears and fetlocks trimmed, and its hooves oiled and its tack immaculate. It would at least look like the winner she wanted the client to believe it could be. Diana also took care to dress herself. She'd bring a clean pair of breeches and change into them just before riding. Her shirt would be neatly ironed and her boots shining. She didn't have proof-positive that it helped sales, but didn't see how it couldn't. Diana also began to learn about the difficult world of employee relations. As she worked with grooms, telling them when the horses had to be ready and how the tack was to be cleaned, she began to realize how good she really was in her mucking days. It would never have occurred to Diana to call in sick when she wasn't. It wouldn't even have occurred to her to call in sick when she was. But now she had to deal with people who had no sense of commitment. Sometimes they didn't show up at all, and even Sloan would have to take a turn with the shovel. One girl called to say her ant farm (the vicious red African variety) had died and she needed the

day off to clean it out and bury them! Diana let Sloan
pick up on that call, and to her amazement, he didn't
bounce her. He shrugged and said that good help was
hard to find and harder to keep.

Late one morning, exhausted from a particularly difficult session with an eighteen-hand blood bay Oldenberger,
Diana decided to take a break. Rather than have her
lunch in the client lounge, where she was now permitted,
she climbed to the loft, where the solitude would help
her recharge. As she went up the ladder, she heard hay
rustle. Stepping forward, she worried that a boarder's
child had come up. But as she turned past a large stack
of bales, Diana to her horror saw Jim with Paul, the
Cuban groom, who now lay across several stacked bales
while his partner thrust his penis in and out of his buttocks. She gasped involuntarily and both men looked up.
    "Diana!" Jim called. But she'd left before her lunch hit
the floor. She ran into the first stall she came to, sick and
sobbing. "He's gay," she said to herself again and again,
trying to absorb the shock. "My God—he's been gay all
along."

For the next several weeks Diana tried to drive Jim
from her mind, but couldn't. After all, what did it say
about her? What was wrong with her that she'd been
attracted to him? Jim didn't even look or act gay—at
least, not until that scene in the hayloft. She'd been
tricked. She'd been attracted to the facade of masculinity
he'd established to allow himself to walk around mas-
querading as a real man. She'd been the temporary object of some fantasy. She understood it all now—why he
kept his life with her so compartmentalized and why he
never took her to social gatherings with friends. She'd
actually thought she was in love with him—what a miserable joke. She'd never feel that way about men again.
She'd had it—Hugh Simpson, Sloan, and now Jim Williams. All had used her.
    She kept an eye out on Jim's comings and goings and

took pains to stay out of his sight. In fact, Diana decided, Jim now avoided her too. Once she saw him crossing the stableyard out of the corner of her eye, but when he caught sight of her he changed direction. He didn't even have the courage to apologize for his self-centered charade. Diana felt nothing but contempt for the young man who had shown her so much kindness and love.

Others observed fragments of the drama from outside. Courtney's antennae picked up something amiss. She didn't know what—only she felt delighted, real *Schadenfreude*. Herr von Engerson simply made mental notes not to schedule their lessons together. But Steve noticed much more. He knew Jim was a homosexual, which in itself didn't revolt him. But the fact that he was sexually active with other men and, possibly, with Diana, did. It seemed such a violation of the natural order of things. And yet in a homophobic society, who would choose to be gay? Aside from sexual orientation, Jim's character was unassailable. Infinitely kind, Jim had always been generous to Steve, speaking as an equal and a knowledgeable friend. And he was like that with all stable employees. And even if it meant a lost ribbon, he would never push a horse if there was a hint of lameness or loss of confidence.

Late one afternoon Steve found Diana cleaning tack at a furious clip.

"You'll rub the leather away and pretty soon you'll have nothing but stuffing to sit on." Diana looked up, pleased to see her friend.

"How goes it?" Diana stood the saddle on the pommel to get at the gullet underneath.

"Okay. And with you?"

"Lot of horses to ride. Almost got bucked off by that new Oldenburger this morning."

"What's his problem?"

"He's three years old, going on two." Diana's smile made Steve think of a proud mother complaining—but really bragging—about the exploits of an ambitious toddler.

"Did you convince him to grow up?"

"I had to," said Diana half-sadly, recalling that she had had to resort to the whip, something she never did easily.

"I'm sure you know growing up is difficult for all young things—horses, dogs, people."

Diana stopped soaping and looked up at Steve. In all the time she'd known him, he'd never tried to open a conversation as obliquely as this. "Okay, Steve, what's going on? Did I forget to take somebody's halter off when I put him in his stall? Is Sloan after me for taking a personal check without getting the phone number?"

"No, it's just that I'm sorry you no longer seem to be friends with Mr. Williams."

"That." Diana resumed her saddle soaping. "What's that have to do with young horses and dogs, anyway?" Her curiosity had gotten the better of her. And though she couldn't admit it, she'd been alone with her pain too long.

"Nothing really." Steve decided she wouldn't react kindly to his analogy.

"No, tell me—please!" Diana insisted.

"I guess I know why you're so angry at Mr. Williams."

Diana felt horrified. Could her love life be an open book at Hampstead? Did Jim tell about her feelings for him? That would help underscore his "heterosexual" image. "And why's that?" she asked, applying soap to what they both knew was a totally clean saddle.

"I think he disappointed you."

"He did."

"You must try to be sympathetic."

Diana was outraged. "Me sympathetic, what for?"

"There are few in the world who would choose to have his conflicting feelings, and even those so misunderstood."

"You mean the feelings of a rich Park Avenue New Yorker who got to go to Princeton before going to the Olympics?"

"No, I don't mean that." Steve registered her depth of pain and involvement.

"You mean gay," said Diana, her tone indicating she'd known all along what agenda Steve had drawn up.

"Yes, and also very kind," Steve said softly.

"His conflicts didn't seem such a strain to him when I saw him in the loft with Paul. For a while it seems Mr. Williams enjoyed the best of both worlds. Well, the masked ball's over. I want nothing to do with him." She turned and addressed herself to some dirty bridles hanging on a hook. But Steve wouldn't let go. He thought too well of Diana to allow her not to examine this harder side of herself and scrape it off before it became a comfortable callus. At the same time, his words conflicted with his own feelings.

"Diana, you are a very strong person—at least, that's how you present yourself, but you're not. It isn't easy to say someone hurt you and made you angry—and this man did. Because I think so well of you, I feel angry at Jim for the pain he caused. But despite his amiability, he's a very isolated man. You have so much empathy—I see it when you train these young horses—but where is that feeling for the man who's done so much for you?"

"Where were his feelings for me?" Diana retorted, her voice cracking. "Didn't Jim have any idea how I'd react?"

"I'm sure he thought about it. Perhaps he was afraid he'd lose you if he told. I don't wish to intrude on your private life—it's at such a painful juncture now. I just want to tell you that life holds a lot for you—it will hold more if you are less sure of what motivates others."

"Steve, you can't begin to imagine how awful I feel. There's really no use talking about it."

"All right, then. Mr. Williams will need you someday, just as you've needed him. And he was there."

"I said enough!" Diana tossed her sponge in the bucket and ran into the aisle, tears streaming down her face.

Steve squeezed the sponge and laid it out to dry. He then closed the door of the tack room and walked down the aisle, upset at his own hypocrisy. Though he believed what he said about Jim, he couldn't help but feel rage at the man he was sure had taken Diana's virginity.

* * *

Diana threw herself into her work even more. When she wasn't riding, she groomed, cleaned tack, observed other lessons, and learned from the vet when he made weekly rounds. She could recognize the incipient stages of colic or give a shot of Banamine to alleviate the accompanying pain. Dr. Miller taught her to insert plastic tubing through a horse's nose, down past the esophagus, and into the stomach in order to worm him. It was a delicate procedure—the danger of inadvertently blocking the trachea clearly possible. She also assisted in foaling. She came to know when a mare was near term. When the mare's udder bagged up, foaling would be in a few days, but when a mare's teats started to drip, it would usually be a matter of hours. When a delivery became difficult, Diana learned to tie two ropes around the protruding hooves and pull whenever the mare strained. To tug without the accompanying contraction risked rupturing the uterus. She learned to break the bag—the tough membrane that serves to protect the foal in its dam, but suffocates it if it isn't torn open during delivery.

At home Diana made sure she scheduled every last moment. When she wasn't reading or studying, she was cleaning, cooking for the week ahead, ironing, and meticulously arranging personal items so the minimum time would be spent later during a rush. If she couldn't get to sleep, she'd read more. If she still couldn't sleep, she'd go for a run and then take a hot shower. She'd wasted a lot of time with people like Jim Williams and Hugh Simpson and was going to see that they didn't intrude on her life again. That was what she thought, anyway: she couldn't deal with the pain of being hurt by someone she loved, and loving him couldn't be admitted at this point. Such openness would concede she was frail and vulnerable —and that was too full of risks for her. Dreams about her mother continued.

# Sea Change

Diana never did ride Grand Prix that summer. Sloan's self-serving inaction was one reason, and it exacerbated the other: most people in the jumping community credited the veteran Aden for having won at Placid, despite the burden of a green rider who, after all, had the advantage of a coach—Jim Williams—to tip her off about the slick spot that fooled other competitors in the jump-off. She found herself back on the hunter circuit riding mostly Hampstead horses, not a bad place from an objective perspective. It enhanced her reputation as a stylist able to make the most unwilling mount look polished and a pleasure to handle. But she felt impatient and thought her career might already be heading downhill. Lots of athletes had seen the peak before they reached twenty. Riding hunters protracted everything. A series of Grand Prix victories seemed like a mirage when there wasn't even a second Grand Prix.

In July she won the Working Hunter Championship at the prestigious East Hampton Classic. Long Island provided a perfect backdrop—shimmering dark water, endless beaches, and flat green lawns with white picket fences and purple hydrangeas. Salt air and sea wind permeated the showgrounds with freshness and vitality. They acted as a cure with immediate results. Mrs. Ethel Sedgewick, president of Meadowbrook Hounds, offered her a job. She wanted Diana to show and manage a private barn of eight hunters, as well as her husband's string of polo ponies. It paid twelve thousand a year and rent-free use of an estate cottage house. Mrs. Sedgewick generously added that Diana could use the *out*door pool as long as it wasn't between eight and ten in the morning, when she and her husband did laps, or when they entertained—often enough, as Diana observed.

Perhaps she should have considered the proposition more seriously. It translated into an opportunity to appear consistently on some of the nation's top hunters. Yet somehow she felt she'd get pocketed away with small chance to get on the jumper circuit. And what really bothered Diana was Mrs. Sedgewick's purportedly generous pool offer. The attached conditions, repeated obsessively, underscored the servitude. She was not to be seen or to mix with the Sedgewick's guests, or to appear as if she were attempting to inject herself into their hermetically sealed social stratum.

"You turned down Mrs. Sedgewick?" asked Beebee Jones, stupefied, when she ran into Diana at the Hampton Classic's hot-dog stand.

"Yes," Diana said flatly. "Could you hand me the mustard, Beebee?" She'd closed the book on it already.

"Whatever for?" Beebee slid the glass container down the aluminum counter.

"I like mustard," she deadpanned.

"Cut it, Diana," shot back Beebee, used to schoolgirl repartee and dying to get the nitty-gritty.

"Oh, she's just an old fossil." Diana shrugged, taking a bite out of her hot dog.

"But an old fossil with clout. She's got terrific horses and a lot of political influence with the judges." Beebee's first bite sent mustard oozing down the leg of her white breeches. "Shit!" she exclaimed, furiously dunking her napkin in Coke and trying vainly to dilute the yellow into oblivion.

"I agree," said Diana, and handed her a baby-wipe. Now she knew she'd made the right decision. She didn't want to bias anyone about the quality of her riding by showing for someone with an alleged "in." Even if it weren't true, the rumor virtually made it so: no difference in the result. The show world drove a vicious gossip mill, and even if Diana consistently won on Mrs. Sedgewick's horses, in the end her success might well be written off to the old bat's political inroads.

"Hey, these baby-wipes work," exclaimed Beebee.

"I never go to a show without them," said Diana, pleased at having demonstrated one of her countless methods of staying clean at inevitably dirty competitions.

"Maiden hunter on the flat, please report to ring number three in fifteen minutes."

"Diana, I gotta go! Thanks for the wipe. Think you're making a big mistake turning down old lady Sedgewick. Good luck." She bestowed a social kiss. Before Diana could reply, Beebee jammed the hot-dog end in her mouth and ran off, leaving the concession owner to clean up the paper plate, discarded pre-lunch gum, and half-empty soda cup.

"Sometimes I wonder who you people think you are," he growled as he swiped at the mess with his worn cloth.

"Here, let me help," offered Diana, grabbing the cup. For some reason, she felt responsible for the negative image horse people like Beebee projected.

The Hampstead van left next day at noon after the Conformation classes, but they took the long way back in the slow-moving Mercedes truck. Ordinarily they'd hop the Orient Point ferry across to New London. But the Sound chop made it potentially stressful for horses. So they labored westbound on the Long Island Expressway, over Throgs Neck into Connecticut, then north to Massachusetts. They lumbered up the long drive and entered the stableyard after seven. Everyone noticed an unusual amount of activity for the hour. Horses still stood in pastures, the yard hadn't been swept, and Diana could glimpse lights shining in the main barn. As she walked Moonglow, the hunter she had ridden to the championship, toward his stall, she saw Courtney doling out evening feed.

"Diana, I'm so glad you're here," puffed Courtney as she pushed the cart carrying assorted oats, bran, corn pellets, and sweet feed. No hint of the usual sarcasm tinged her greeting.

"What's going on?" Diana inquired.

"Can you believe it, Donna, Paul, and Steve—that creep's *never* sick—all have the flu. The first two called in and Steve had to be sent home. He was almost puking in the water buckets and just got in the way."

"Your concern for employees is touching," commented Diana as she slipped the halter off Moonglow. "Well, what should I do to help?"

"You'd simply be my guardian angel if you put Navarro in his stall and finish feeding the aisle."

"Okay. Is he still on Selenex, or is Clovite enough?"

"I guess the Clovite. Shit, how am I supposed to know? Can't you check the chart?"

I'll have to, Diana thought to herself, knowing if she hadn't come along Navarro probably would have gotten neither. "Have the mares been fed?" she asked, thinking how easily Courtney could forget the brood mares that spent days and nights in the far pasture.

"Steve got them before he left. Thanks, Diana, I truly do appreciate this. I'll make it up to you. God, I hate stable work." Courtney slapped her hands together in an unsuccessful effort to clean them.

Diana watched as Courtney's attractive but aching body disappeared. Chinese dowager-in-training, she commented to herself, then grabbed a lead shank off the wall and headed to Navarro's field. The large white stallion galloped up to greet her, obviously concerned about dinner status. A groom usually led him in before five, and a horse's internal time clock ran better than any manmade movement Diana had owned. To stop the impatient fellow from stampeding past, she climbed the fence and clipped the shank to his halter.

"Hungry, boy?" As if to reply in the affirmative, Navarro bucked and pranced all the way back to his stall. As soon as she unhooked the lead shank, he moved toward his bucket. "No, you wait till I get this halter off. I wouldn't want you to hang yourself." She unfastened it as quickly as she could. Navarro thrust his head into the feed and spilled a portion on his bedding. Diana closed the top and bottom latches of the door, hung his halter on the adjacent wall, then returned to the cart, bringing another half-measure of pellets. "Here, you. Try not to be such a pig." She closed the door again and finished the rest of the aisle.

Perched on the higher diving board of the large pool, Courtney watched Diana drive down the long private approach to Hampstead. Just a few minutes before, an enthusiastic client had been singing Diana's praises to the sky—how she'd won at East Hampton, how she could ride a mule and make it look like poetry in motion—everything that galled Courtney, forced to stand and smile weakly. And the poor man thought the daughter of the farm owner would be pleased for the establishment. But Courtney's envy only recoiled at another goad. You'd think Diana would treat me with a little respect, she boiled inside. What's she got? It's what I've got that counts. Jim Williams hardly comes here now, and I'm sure it's because of her. Watch, missy. I'll fix your wagon so even Sloan'll believe this place better off without you. Courtney went through all the clichés of hate, then glanced at the beads of water on her tanned and oiled arms, stood up, and executed a flawless jackknife, slitting open the water with a well-formed body.

The next morning, when Diana got out of her car, an enraged Courtney confronted her. "You'd better get your butt over to Sloan's office right away." The order came in her most disagreeable and proprietary fashion.

"That's some thank-you for last evening." Despite the coolness of her reply, Diana felt uneasy.

"It's because of last night that you'd better get your ass in there."

"Says who?" Diana had become accustomed to Courtney's panics, most of them caused by spotty knowledge of stable management and ignorance of emergency procedures.

"Says Sloan, and says me, in fact."

Without another word, Diana walked to the office and worried that something must be going on. Courtney had outstripped herself in nastiness.

As soon as she walked in, Sloan stood up from his desk and shoved the chair against the wall. "You're fired!" he yelled loudly.

"What for?" asked Diana, astonished.

"That Andalusian got out of his stall last night because you failed to close it properly," thundered Sloan. His face flushed several shades redder than normal.

"I closed the latch—top and bottom. I always do," replied Diana firmly.

"You didn't this time. And you want to know something else—we've got a stallion who'll never do dressage again, or anything else for that matter. He ripped his suspensory jumping the fence to get in with the mares." Diana's face paled, not from guilt—she knew she'd locked the latch—but from what she'd just heard. The suspensory ligament never really heals, and if he got in with the brood mares . . .

"Three aborted this morning. I'll bet he raped every last fucking one. We stand to lose six more foals because of your negligence." Sloan kicked the file cabinet and the floor shook. He could imagine calling Barbara Snyder with the news. And by now the story ranked number one on the grapevine, so he'd need to call quickly.

"Mr. Sloan, I'm very sorry this happened, but I had nothing to do with it. I'm sure I closed both latches. I'm very careful about that sort of thing."

"Careful, huh? If you're so fucking careful, tell me why you left him in the stall with his halter on."

"I always take the halters off and I clearly remember taking off Navarro's," countered Diana. "He was making an enormous fuss about getting at his food." She didn't have a precise recollection of the latches because such measures were second nature. But she envisioned again removing the halter because of the way Navarro attacked his food. She looked at Courtney, who'd come in, fixing Diana with the superior look of a prosecutor.

"I took his halter off," she repeated, this time to Courtney, who responded with a Joan Collins shrug of disinterest.

"Get your things and get yourself out of here," stated Courtney, her cold voice for once conveying firm control over a crisis. "I want you off the premises in one hour. Make that half an hour. Now, out—you've cost us thousands." Diana started for the door.

"Naturally," added Sloan, "you can forget working anyplace else. By the time I'm done telling other farms who was responsible, you won't be able to set foot within a mile of any feed bucket on the East Coast." Diana silently closed the door behind her.

Sloan cleared his throat and turned to Courtney. "And you'd better be damned right about this. There wasn't anybody else around that late except Diana and you?"

"No, just one owner and the van driver. But he was practically in his car before he'd turned off the ignition in the truck. I went swimming."

Sloan glanced at his heavy steel watch. "Great, I've lost a stallion, God knows how many foals, and the trainer of our young horses—and it's only eight-thirty."

"You sound like you might regret firing Diana, Bob." Courtney tested his resolve.

"Glad to be rid of her—nothing but a prima donna. Just wish I had a replacement."

"How about me?" Courtney asked.

"You?" Sloan couldn't prevent a laugh escaping his beefy throat. "Your mother would kill me if I put you on anything less than perfectly schooled," he said, impressed with his diplomacy. Courtney had neither the talent nor the tact necessary to ride impressionable horses.

"Mother wouldn't care. Besides, she's not here, remember?"

"Sorry, Courtney. No young horses—that's firm."

"Bob, you're such a poop!" she exclaimed in the best pout she could muster, then went out the door, far happier than she'd felt in months.

*      *      *

Diana waited for the insolent click of Courtney's riding boots in the main aisle, then stepped in front of her. She spoke evenly, but her face grimaced with barely controlled rage. Courtney shuffled back and attempted to put on a calm veneer. "Why, Diana, I thought you'd be busy getting your things together," she said uneasily, noting the fury conveyed by the other's body.

"You sabatoged me!" Diana pressed her own arms tight against her sides to help keep her temper.

"You made a mistake. A bad one, that's all. Don't pass it off just because we don't get along."

"You deliberately destroyed that stallion to get at me. You get right back into Sloan's office and tell him you put the halter on Navarro and walked him to the broodmare field."

"I did no such thing. Who'd want to hurt an animal intentionally? If you'll excuse me . . ." She attempted to pass, but Diana blocked her path. With a furious shove Courtney pushed Diana awkwardly with such force that she stumbled and fell backward over a tack trunk. Before she could get up, Courtney grabbed a pitchfork off the wall and hurled it straight at her. Diana immediately ducked as the angry prongs struck a metal bucket, sending it noisily down the red terrazzo. Diana gasped at how close the tines came to ripping her side. An anger she'd never felt before now instantly seized her. She rushed Courtney and threw her to the ground. Courtney tried to clutch Diana's hair.

"You lied! Go tell Sloan you lied!"

"The hell I will!" Courtney tried to bite Diana's knee.

"You fight like a liar too. Go to Sloan!" Courtney slapped Diana's face with a hand she managed to free. But then, with adrenaline flowing, Diana swiftly yanked Courtney up. She twisted her arm behind her back and up. "Tell Sloan," commanded Diana. Courtney placed her leg behind Diana's knee in an attempt to trip her, but failed. Diana pulled up angrily on Courtney's arm. "Get up and get back to Sloan."

"No way!" cried Courtney, tears streaming down her face.

Diana spotted a half-filled plastic manure tub and dragged Courtney over it. "You know, Courtney, you're nothing more than a real shithead!" She took the arm up higher and pushed her face into the greenish-brown ooze. Courtney sputtered and coughed. Diana pulled her out. Somewhere underneath the shit were tears. "To Sloan!" As Courtney nodded, Diana let go and backed off. Courtney stood up, wiping her face. Diana tossed her a grooming towel. Slowly Courtney walked down the aisle toward the office, but then turned and faced Diana.

"I'll never tell Sloan. And believe me, I'm going to finish you. If you ever poke your low-class snout into this world, I'll ruin you every step. Navarro's just the beginning!" Courtney turned and ran, her frame simultaneously shuddering with rage and sobs.

Diana brushed the hair off her own face, walked to a faucet, and ran cold water over the bloody tracks that four manicured nails had gashed. She felt destroyed—she was: all the dreams evaporated because of one miserably jealous and spiteful girl. She surveyed the mess on the floor. "Someone else can clean it up for once!" she shouted out loud, running down the aisle in a futile attempt to escape her defeat. She turned into the last empty stall and burst into tears. "I've worked so hard so many years!"

After a quarter-hour she remained in the stall, staring blankly at the boards, without energy. "Are you in here?" Steve still looked terrible from his flu. Courtney had passed him on her way to the ladies' room, and he suspected something had happened, but couldn't find Diana.

"Yes," she responded weakly, not wanting to see anyone.

When he caught her face and disheveled appearance in the shadows, he inferred the rest. As usual, the first to arrive, even sick, he'd been the one to find Navarro limping in the brood-mare field. He walked over to Diana, took a bandana out of his pocket, and handed it to her.

She started to cry again. "Steve, I've been fired for something I didn't do."

He sat down and pulled Diana close, putting his arms around her. "I've heard only one story. Tell me what you think happened." She took a deep breath and told him exactly what she'd done after she got back from Long Island, and what Courtney must have done afterward. "I will go to Mr. Sloan," he offered. "I will tell him what you told me."

"I already did—he doesn't believe me. Besides . . ." Diana hesitated.

"Besides, what?"

"I have a feeling he's getting back at me." Diana made an effort to regain her composure.

"What for?"

"He made a pass at me a couple weeks ago."

"A pass?" Steve felt uncomfortable with the term.

"Actually he tried to blackmail me into bed with him," Diana said with shamed impatience. Steve, always leery of Sloan, now exploded in anger. "I see," he said flatly.

"So, you do see. There's no use." Once again tears streamed down Diana's cheeks. He took out a comb and began straightening her hair.

"That's better. Diana, why don't you just take the rest of the day off and leave things to me? Maybe I can do something for you."

She put her face against his chest. "I don't think there's much you can do, but I love you for trying."

"Don't give up." He tilted her chin with his fingers, afraid to tell her how important it was to him that she not cave in. He was afraid this setback might transmute her love for horses into bitter hate, then bitter self-hate.

"Steve?"

"Yes?"

"What's going to happen to Navarro?" Diana looked across the aisle at the stallion, gingerly testing his wrapped right foreleg on the shavings.

"That's up to his owner. He probably will be used for a breeding stallion. Now, please take my advice and go home." He stood behind her and held her shoulders, directing her out of the stall and into the bright morning air.

"Okay, I'll go home. This may be the last time I see you, Steve," she said formally.

"No dramatics. You won't get rid of me so easily. Go home—rest! Take a hot bath and a couple aspirin."

"Yes, sir, Señor Doctor," she replied, oblivious of the accuracy of her statement.

Steve stood impressively in the doorway of Bob Sloan's office, waiting for him to look up and notice. He didn't.

"Mr. Sloan?"

"Yeah, Steve. What is it? You better?" Sloan didn't bother to glance away from the bills he was sorting. Steve walked up to the desk.

"I think you should apologize to Diana," he said evenly. He struggled to cap his anger.

"Haven't you got it backwards—shouldn't she apologize to me?" Sloan now looked at Steve standing in front of him erect, and even menacing. No longer the self-effacing and withdrawn groom. He decided it might be best to temper things. "Okay, well, thanks for your input."

"You know Diana's work. She's not a careless person and she is not vindictive. Courtney is." He wouldn't be put off.

"You know what you're saying?" A threat hung implicitly in his question.

"I do."

"Why don't you get out of here, Steve? You and I have better things to do than waste time talking about the broads who are always screwing up this place."

"Diana rejected your advances and you're getting back at her."

As Sloan stood up from his desk, his face turned crimson, then beet. "Look, you goddamn wetback, you'd better get out of here before I call Boston. Sure, good grooms are hard to find, but you stick your chicken neck out again for that little cunt and it might just get lopped off. Your homeland's as close as the nearest phone. Some people say you get it on with her yourself, and she spreads real wide for you. Know what they call it? 'Spic 'n' Span.' "

Steve shook with pent-up rage and thought of hitting Sloan, but managed to keep himself in check. He didn't want to return to Mexico, but a call to Immigration from this crude man meant just that. He was an illegal alien. Then helping Diana would be impossible. "Mr. Sloan, you are a true gentleman."

Even Bob Sloan couldn't miss that kind of irony. "Shit, now, being a gentleman's something I've never thought about. You know why? It don't pay very well. Now, will you get outta here so I can get back to work?"

"What about Navarro?" asked Steve.

"The Andalusian—yeah, I meant to tell you. Charlie's going to take him to the rendering plant tomorrow afternoon. I made an appointment at three. You know how sentimental Mrs. Snyder is about the animals—not wanting them to stand in the corrals for hours without food or water before they get turned into dog food. The ambassador signed off on the horse."

"He's being put down?" Steve asked, unbelieving.

"Yeah, why?"

"He's valuable."

"Not him. Can't perform and his papers aren't worth shit."

"Why not?"

"The Spanish stud book's all fucked up. It's still run by Franco's military. Probably his papers are fine—the breeder the ambassador bought him from says they are, but the military says no. So he's useless. The ambassador just told me to get rid of him."

"But he couldn't mean that. You can't do it!"

"He speaks English. I don't need you to translate. Watch me—he's useless as a show horse and no Andalusian breeder in the U.S. would let him near any mares. Fine offspring, sure, but try to register them."

"He can heal." Steve didn't tell Sloan he was certain the registration problems could be ironed out. Navarro was full brother to his wife's horse, and *he* had papers approved by the military stud.

"Look, I'm a businessman. You know a suspensory is very iffy. Even if it heals, it's prone to reinjury."

"Give him to me," said Steve.

"What?"

"I said give him to me, then."

"You don't want him. Where're you going to keep him—your studio estate in Eastford? Landlady permit pets?"

"Mr. Sloan, I have a place to keep him."

"Okay, I think you're nuts, Rodríguez, but I'll sell him to you for what the killers get."

"How much?"

"Lucky for you the market's depressed right now. Horse meat's going for six cents a pound. How much would you say the guy weighs?"

"About six hundred kilos—thirteen hundred."

Sloan hit the calculator with his stubby red fingers. "Look, give me a hundred and I'll throw in the halter." Steve drew a wallet from his flannel shirt and handed Sloan five twenties. "Cash, great. I think you're a jerk, Steve, but he's yours." Sloan put the bills in the gray petty-cash box and felt pleased he'd made some money on the horse—even if just a little. A trip to the nearest slaughterhouse in Connecticut would have cost thirty dollars in gas.

"May I have his papers, please?" Steve asked.

"I told you, they're worthless."

"I know, and that is why I'm going to ask you for a receipt as well," Steve said firmly.

When Diana got home, she poured herself a glass of wine and sat in front of the noon news but didn't hear a word. She felt dead inside. She had no options. There wasn't a barn like Hampstead around for miles, and even if she tried to get a job elsewhere, they'd call and check on her and ask why she left. She had no horse and no job. Tally had died three months ago, plain old age. She'd almost broken out of the vicious rut of manure pickers, but in the end was thrown back into it by Courtney.

She pulled out her wallet and went through a stack of business cards until she found Mrs. Sedgwick's. The thought of exhibiting hunters now seemed far more attractive than it had the day before. She dialed.

"Hello, Mrs. Sedgwick, this is Diana Winston. You asked if I'd consider coming to your barn. Well, I've mulled it over and think I'd be willing to make the move." Diana heard the voice crackle and clear itself on the phone.

"Miss Winston, I'm very glad to hear from you after your mulling, but I must advise you that I've already taken on a new manager. Perhaps you know her—Beebee Jones? At any rate, I don't think you would have liked working for a—you put it so picturesquely—for an 'old fossil.' "

Diana didn't speak further, but softly hung up. *Dearest Beebee. I guess she knew what she wanted all along. Next time, she can go in the ring with mustard stain on her pants.* Diana sat on the living-room couch and put her feet on the coffee table. It seemed that aside from actually winning the horse show—what an irony—everything she'd done in the last forty-eight hours was a mistake, even if she hadn't actually done it. *From now on,* she decided, *I'll speak to no one about anything that matters.* Diana laughed self-deprecatingly. Not that any reforms mattered at this point. She had another glass of wine and slept badly in the middle of the afternoon.

Before going to bed that evening, Diana walked into her parents' room, where she'd cleaned out everything. The drawers were empty, the bedspread and sheets gone, and her mother's favorite painting off the wall. Diana thought she might run a B&B in an attempt to supplement her pay while at Hampstead, but now it would be her only income. Imagine, she thought, washing dishes, scrambling eggs, calling plumbers. She opened the walk-in closet and smiled wistfully as she remembered the hours spent playing in the "cave" behind her mother's evening dresses. There she had plotted her dreams and charted the course to realize them. In the corner of the closet Diana spotted a familiar bottle—Ma Griffe, her mother's favorite perfume. Her father had presented this specially to her on their twentieth wedding anniversary. He brought it back from Paris, the bottle of Baccarat crystal. Diana took it into her bed and loosened the stopper. The floral scent reminded her of her mother's physical closeness, but now only heightened her lonely isolation. She touched a drop to her forefinger and drew it along her throat, then left a trace directly beneath her nostrils. She pulled the sheet over her head and in the lost memory of warmth and security she cried until she fell asleep.

Several hours later, Diana jerked awake in the dark. She heard the roar of an engine in need of a muffler, then saw headlights flash on the bedroom wall. On her knees, she lifted the curtain and looked out. An old Ford pickup pulled a rusty horse trailer. Diana threw on her robe. Someone in trouble, she thought. They must have seen I had a barn. Vanning horses was always a delicate business, and if one had car problems, then one had horse problems of the worst logistic kind. Triple-A wouldn't provide a stall while the pickup was repaired.

Diana was surprised to see Steve's face in the kitchen window. She unlocked the door. "Steve, what is it? Are you okay?" Her face showed curiosity and fright.

"Get dressed and come out. I brought you a little present." He smiled.

"What's going on, Steve? It's one in the morning."

"Yes, and I'd like to get some sleep tonight, too, so hurry and get dressed. I'll wait here."

Diana flew upstairs. Steve had brought a horse. That was obvious, but what horse and why? Or was it just a used trailer? Or something else in it? She threw on her clothes and ran back downstairs. As she finished buttoning up her shirt in front of Steve, he glanced away in embarrassment. Diana blushed herself. "Excuse me, I forgot you're a man of the old school."

"I'm a man of no school, but I like to think I'm civilized." Steve smiled sheepishly.

"Steve, you can say what you want to other people, but you are a man of some school. I won't say any more, but I just want you to know that I'm not wholly unobservant."

He smiled and nodded. "Here, come outside and observe this." He took her by the arm and walked her out to the trailer. Together they unpinned the back ramp and placed it carefully on the gravel drive. Diana gasped when she saw the great white stallion.

"Navarro!"

Steve took a lead shank and unloaded him. He stood erect and noble as he surveyed the area. Then he neighed loudly, announcing to all potential stallion enemies that this was now his territory and they must stay away. Navarro would have lost, even if only an anemic stallion had been there to take up the challenge. He could barely stand on the foreleg. It seemed worse than before. Steve saw Diana's eye focus on the useless limb. "He stressed it more on the ride by trying to keep his balance."

"Poor thing, he's beautiful. But so lame," said Diana.

"Do you have a stall ready?"

"I just need to throw down some shavings and put in a bucket of water."

"Go do that while I show him his new home."

"New home?" asked Diana, open-mouthed.

"Yes, new home. Now, *please*. He's hurt and getting excited. He should rest."

Diana ran to the barn. One by one she emptied five bags of fresh cedar shavings into a stall. Then she filled a black rubber bucket from the hand pump and clipped it onto the eye hook. Navarro stretched his back and searched with his eyes as he walked into the barn. They watched as the stallion took a mouthful of hay. He stopped chewing just long enough to neigh another claim at the vacant landscape.

"Tough guy, isn't he?" said Diana, amused and inspired by his confident majesty.

"He thinks he is, and he will be again. He must stay in this stall three months."

"Three months!"

"At least, but that's only the beginning if he's to get well."

Diana took him by the arm. "Okay, Steve, what's this all about?"

Steve took an envelope out of his pocket and handed it to her. "Open it."

Diana took out a beige sheet. "His registration papers. And a receipt."

"But the papers supposedly aren't any good—at least not right now."

"Why not?"

"The military stud in Spain won't recognize them for some reason. I think the pedigree documentation on the back is fine, but that's of little importance right now. Here—sign." He handed her a pen.

Diana turned the papers to the owner-documentation side. "Steve, this says you own Navarro."

"I do, but only for a few more seconds. Sign and you'll have a first-class show horse, if you can learn patience."

"Wait, Steve. I could barely afford to keep Tally. Navarro tore his suspensory. That's permanent."

"Serious as the injury is, it can heal with the right care. But you'll have to take my advice—no one else's. Now, sign, my friend. You've been wishing for a jumper of your own to ride—and now you've got one."

Diana was caught for a moment between her own caution about taking a seriously injured animal and the high regard she had for Steve's instincts and knowledge.

"Steve, why are you doing this? I—"

"Believe me, I will help you. You must trust me, just

as Navarro will have to learn to trust you if we are all to succeed."

Diana shook her head, smiled, then kissed him on the cheek. She laid the worn beige paper across her leg and signed and dated the owner column. "I don't know quite what to say. I don't know quite what I've done." She shook her head in disbelief.

"About suspensories. You know it is a ligament and ligaments cannot regenerate." Diana nodded. "However, the body is an amazing thing, and to replace the ligament, connective tissue will grow and attach itself to the sesamoid bone. It will act in the same manner."

"How long does it take?" she asked.

"Three months for a solid base of recovery. Connective tissue will never be as strong as a ligament, so any trauma could set him back to the beginning, or worse. Also, if the tissue gets torn, it will regenerate again, but not as completely. That cannot happen—one more tear and this horse will never jump again. We must treat this injury with respect."

"I thought he did dressage," said Diana.

"Yes, but you're interested in jumping, so he'll learn that too. The dressage background can only help." Steve didn't have to explain. She knew that dressage taught a horse to respond accurately to the lightest aid—a shift of weight, the application of leg, a hair's flex of the rein. It also taught the horse to use his muscle, particularly the hindquarters, effectively. And it was the hindquarters that propelled him over obstacles. Beyond that, a rider with some dressage training could generally get more out of any jumper.

Diana glanced at the stallion, who was checking out the quality of water in his bucket. "Ninety days in there?" She shook her head.

"Yes, and we must hope that he has the patience of Job. He mustn't buck or rear. He must adapt himself to his . . ."

". . . cell," finished Diana.

"Well, you will be here to help him. You can give him

toys to keep him from getting fussy and bored. Toss in a football . . . I mean, soccer ball. He'll bat it around with his nose. Do you have an old Clorox bottle? Plastic? Put in a few pebbles and tie it to the ceiling so he has a punching bag. He'll be very grateful."

Toys for horses, Diana mused. "Twenty-four hours a day, seven days a week, for three months. That's tons of mucking, Steve." She thought how used to it she'd become.

"I think, I'm not one hundred percent sure, but I think you'll be pleased with this horse." Steve walked into the stall. Navarro thrust his head into his arms. As he cradled the massive white head, he scratched Navarro under his jaw. The horse half-closed his eyes in pleasure. "He'll be fine," said Steve as he came out and closed the door. "Lots of carrots and attention." As he walked down the aisle, Navarro neighed and began to circle in the stall.

"Steve, he doesn't want you to go. He's going to hurt himself," said Diana anxiously. Steve ran back and Navarro quieted down immediately. Diana stood by the door, trying to make out what Steve said to the horse. But he spoke too softly and in Spanish, then left again. This time the animal remained calm, his dark eyes following every move. "He seems to like you," said Diana, impressed with the bond.

"We're both just Hispanics—*compañeros*."

"Very unusual friendship, even for *compañeros*."

"No, you'll see," commented Steve. "This is not just a horse. He is a soul mate. But he will give himself to you only if you give yourself to him. Now I must go or I won't be able to pick up a rake tomorrow—or rather today, I should say." He opened the door to the pickup. "Oh, and I'm sorry to come by so late, but I needed to change the plugs and points before this thing would work. I borrowed it."

"Who'd you get it from?"

"It doesn't matter," Steve said, closing the door.

"What happens in three months?" Diana tried to make her voice heard over the engine's roar.

"We shall see."

"We shall see?" asked Diana. "Ninety days of muck-ing, and 'we shall see'?"

"Yes, and we shall also see that you acquire a little patience." Steve waved as he backed the rusty vehicle out the driveway. She shook her head in disbelief. That day, she had thought, was the worst in her life—no family, no job—just despair. But now, because of Steve—and only because of Steve—she felt hope. Running down the drive after him, she yelled a tentative thank-you above the racket that broke the farm's quiet.

In the next three months Navarro went through eight Clorox bottles, several soccer balls, and a number of planks in his stall that he chewed out of boredom. Diana felt compelled to muck out at least twice a day because the stall got so dirty. She'd bring him grass from the pasture whenever she saw him look longingly out the door into the inviting autumn light. He seemed to under-stand his confinement was temporary and had something to do with helping him. Though Diana gave him vitamin supplements and groomed him each day, taking care to rub out the manure stains, his coat lost sheen and his muscles atrophied. The normally straight back became slightly swayed and he developed a hay belly. Diana cut his grain to help keep him quiet, but then had to increase his hay ration. His leg seemed to improve slowly, and by the end of the second month he could put full weight on it.

Steve stopped by every other week to check his protégé. He felt around Navarro's injury, noting with relief that there was little calcification on the sesamoid. That sug-gested the connective tissue was attaching solidly. Though Diana would ask him to stay for a drink or dinner, he never would. At most he'd pause for a glass of lemonade, tell a few horse stories, then be on his way. Once Diana asked him why he had left Mexico. Steve obliquely said that like most immigrants, he'd been dissatisfied with his economic situation. Diana joked and said it must have been really bad indeed, if working at Hampstead meant an improvement. But Steve would go no further, and Diana, though curious, wouldn't pry. She knew there was more to his story. He was an educated man of refined sensibility. The average groom didn't know the portrait of Napoleon by David, nor as much about veterinary medicine, no matter how long he'd been around barns. Diana suspected some sort of trouble—unhappy marriage, drug dealing, brush with the law—something.

As each month went by, she grew more fearful about her situation. She wasn't earning money and her savings now went to feed herself and the horse. A bale of good hay, the first cutting of the season, cost four-fifty; grain ran about ten dollars per hundredweight. With minor barn repairs and electricity, she spent about one hundred and seventy-five a month to sustain the horse. And there were other expenses. She had to administer a paste wormer to kill a variety of intestinal parasites, then the farrier and vet expenses—spring shots for eastern and western encephalitis, tetanus, rhino, and rabies. Perhaps the whole thing was a farce. Maybe Steve was wrong. She never should have accepted Navarro, but gone back to modeling instead, made some quick money, and moved out of New England, perhaps to California, where she could get a job at a jumper barn that hadn't heard the dirt. She could sell the farm and realize a good bit of money— enough to buy a condo in Pasadena or San Luis Obispo. And yet there was something about the strangeness of Steve, an unknown quantity, this extraordinary Andalusian stallion, and her desire to push forward with her life. She hung in and took risks, despite what her bankbook and common sense urged.

One Saturday at the end of three months Steve appeared in the stable while Diana was rigging up the ninth Clorox bottle. "I think you can start hand-walking him today," he said after running his hand up and down the foreleg.

"Okay!" she said, pleased the poor horse would finally get out and feel sun on his back. "How much?"

"Today just ten minutes. Tomorrow the same. But

from then on add five minutes a day for the first two weeks, then keep that up." Steve stood and gave Navarro a pat of satisfaction.

"That's more than an hour of hand-walking a day!" exclaimed Diana, thinking ahead to the tedium of circling the pasture for over an hour a day every day for a month.

"You're a strong girl, good for both of you." He smiled as he said it.

"Oh, now I'm a big strong girl. Whatever happened to the grand lady?" Though she wouldn't admit it, Diana wanted Steve to say it again.

"She's there too. Somewhere inside—there." Steve laughed, pointing at Diana's heart.

"But right now what 'we' need is a big strong girl," quipped Diana. "Steve?" she asked softly. "Who'll help me train this horse, and who'll train me? I can't pay for lessons." Even top riders, like the best tennis pros, periodically took lessons and received coaching. They had the skill to know that no one is immune from bad habits.

"I will," Steve said, evenly looking at his hands that lay folded on the stall door.

"You ride?" asked Diana, knowing full well she was knocking at the gate of Steve's previous and private life.

"I did."

"And you rode well, didn't you?"

"I rode well. And I am familiar with this breed. My credentials were at one time quite good," he added, anticipating her thought. "But enough of that. Take the lead shank and let's see how he does his first ten minutes." As Diana moved the stallion into the sunshine, she felt his body come alive with power and energy. He started to trot in place.

"Diana, he must walk. He'll kill that leg if he doesn't."

"Easy, boy. Let's just take a quiet tour." Navarro walked a few steps but then trotted and threw a buck.

"Bring him in here—this isn't going to work." She led the stallion back into his stall, but he wouldn't settle. He'd had a taste of freedom and sky and wouldn't give it up. "Hang on," called Steve as he ran to his truck. He came back with a syringe.

"Are you going to tranquilize him?" Diana asked.

"Yes, and so will you for the first week. Otherwise he'll tear all that tissue and be worse off than he was three months ago. This is Rompun—it's effective almost immediately and wears off in an hour. No side effects except a little headache."

Diana watched as he detached the needle and placed it directly into Navarro's neck. "Make sure it goes into the muscle tissue and not a vein. If there's any bleeding, you'll have to reinsert." As he talked, Diana thought he must have given injections a thousand times it all went so smoothly. As if to cover his practiced technique, he said, "Anyone who cares can learn to do this well."

Diana watched as the fluid flowed out of the syringe and into Navarro's neck. Within five minutes his lids were half-closed and he shifted weight uneasily from left to right, fearful he was going to lose balance. "He's a very dizzy boy," Diana commented.

"Yes, but take him out," Steve said as he capped the syringe and tossed it in the trashcan.

"Like a baby." Diana smiled, relieved how easy her job had become.

"He doesn't look like much of a champion now, does he?" Steve asked, saddened by the sight of the docile, dizzy, and compliant horse. "If you're uneasy about giving him the shot tomorrow— "

"I am," Diana interrupted. Though she'd given shots many times before, she thought Navarro might unsettle or rear. He was too valuable to take chances. She had no money to call a vet. Besides, she wanted Steve to come back.

"I'll drop by and watch you give it. How will that be? Around five?"

"Fine."

"Then I shall see you tomorrow." Steve fished in his pockets for the keys. As she watched the blue-black exhaust from the pickup hang in the evening light, she said to herself: Thank you for all this. Then she shook her head quizzically. But I wonder what "all this" is, or will be.

Steve arrived promptly at five the next evening with a box of Rompun syringes. Diana looked with apprehension as Steve held them out and told her to take one. Her stomach was knotted and she felt her hands go cold.

"God, it's on awfully tight," Diana commented. For some reason, she had a case of nerves.

"Work it back and forth slowly," he advised.

But working things slowly was alien to Diana's nature, particularly when she wanted to get things over with. She pulled at the cap with as much force as she could muster. The cap came off, but she jerked her hand forward again, impaling her palm on the needle. She screamed as she saw the needle go in like one big iron stitch. Two thin lines of blood streamed out. Steve immediately put an arm around her shoulder and drew her close. "Hang on," he said as he took her hand and pulled the needle out. "Do you have some alcohol?"

"In the bathroom cabinet," Diana said, her eyes fixed on the streaming blood, which gave no sign of stopping. Once they were inside, she bit her lip to keep from crying out as he poured the alcohol over her hand.

"Gauze?" he asked.

"In there." Diana nodded toward a cupboard. He wrapped a line of gauze several times around her palm, then knotted it expertly.

"Here, let's sit in the kitchen until the bleeding stops."

"You mean *if* it stops," commented Diana darkly, simultaneously embarrassed and frightened by what had happened.

"Melodramas do not suit you." Steve smiled. "How about a cup of coffee?"

"I have only tea. In the cabinet."

But when Steve opened it, several cereal boxes and tins fell out. "Diana, you're not a very good housekeeper," he said as he watched a can roll across the floor. "You'll not make a man very happy if this is the way you run his home," he teased.

"One step at a time, Steve. I'm not going to be fit for any man unless I'm happy." Diana glanced at her hand. "And I'm not feeling very happy right now."

She reached for his hand and squeezed it affectionately, but Steve withdrew it almost immediately and looked at her directly. "Diana, our friendship will work only if you don't expect too much out of it."

She felt heartsick. Could Steve also be gay? Was that the reason he defended Jim? "You mean don't expect love?"

"I loved a great deal once and it cost me dearly. I don't want that to happen again."

Diana put her hand on Steve's shoulder. If he'd been hurt, she was certain he could love her. She would never do anything to harm this wonderful man.

"No, Diana, unless you understand that, I can't work with you and this horse," he said gently but firmly, and removed her hand. His family, María and Carmen—he'd done nothing to help them. He wouldn't let himself get that close again.

# Mexico City

Steve later ate alone—a quick supper at the local Papa Gino's—before returning to his one-room apartment in the small farm community of Eastford. He said good evening to Mrs. Morris, the elderly landlady, and headed up the stairs. It was more like a monk's cell—plain dresser, single bed, and a squat two-shelf bookcase, empty except for a Bible thoughtfully supplied by her. Nothing hung on the walls. He turned on the small black-and-white television he'd bought at a local flea market. The evening news was on and it was depressing. Over thirty dead in a Beirut car bombing, and the AIDS epidemic was invading inner cities. He sighed, flicked off the set, walked over to his bedside table, and took out a photograph from the drawer. As he lay back on the bed, he looked at a striking woman holding a delicate and pretty little girl of about four. He stared at the happy faces, then held the photo to his chest and spoke softly, *"Dios mío, mis recuerdos y pensamientos están todavía llenos de tristeza y dolor. Desde hace diez anos*. My heart can't forget. *Necesito ayuda, pero no puedo creer más. No puedo continuar viviendo así."* Steve closed his eyes. The tired body slept, but his tormented mind still active, his eyelids began to twitch as he dreamt.

*"Buenos días, Papi,"* called out the enchanting raven-haired girl as she ran across the patio of the stately hacienda-style house. She leapt into her father's outstretched arms.

137

*"Buenos días, mi ángel."* Steve laughed, hugging and swinging his daughter. "Now, what day is it today?"

"I am going to see a big hospital with Mama, and they are going to see me," answered the little girl, fingering the lapels of her father's cream-colored suit.

"Yes, darling María, they're going to see you and look at your pretty throat and take out that little ball making it so sore."

"And I'm going to get ice cream," exclaimed María, taking his face in her hands.

"Lots of ice cream. Just don't eat so much you explode, all right?"

"Oh, Papi." María's tone admonished her father's silliness.

"Esteban!" Carmen Rodríguez walked down the path, resplendent with pink camellias and yellow rhododendrons. She was about twenty-five; abundant black hair artfully framed her fine and carefully attended face. She was exquisitely dressed in a turquoise suit and pink silk blouse.

"Here you are, you two!" she said in feigned scolding tones.

"Yes, finally, now we all are here, family of Dr. Esteban Rodríguez, the best pediatrician and virologist in all of Mexico City," proclaimed Steve, keeping up the kind of mock ceremony only families who love each other very much can carry off.

"I am surprised you don't say in all Mexico."

"Perhaps early for that—tomorrow, maybe."

"Mami, Mami." María had grown impatient.

"Ah, here—with me, my dear." María let herself tumble into her mother's waiting arms.

"When will we go to the hospital?"

"Very soon. That's why we got you up so early. There will be many cars on the road and you must be there first thing. Carlos will take us because Papi must go to his laboratory before he goes to see you at the hospital. Come, there's Carlos and he's waiting." Carmen Rodríguez put the protesting María down and started to walk toward the house.

"No—I want Papi to go with me too!" María ran to her father and wrapped her arms around his leg.

"Darling, Papi will be at the hospital too, a little later. He must help other children who need to see him," placated Carmen.

"No!" María shook her bright curls stubbornly. "I want to be with Papi when he's at *his* hospital."

Steve picked up the little girl. "Darling, Papi will be there when you wake up from the dreams that the hospital sleep is going to give you. And you know what I will have with me, don't you?"

"Ice cream!" exclaimed María, clapping her hands in happy anticipation.

"Ice cream, of course, and perhaps a doll who would like to have a little girl for a mother."

"Oh, Papi, a dolly!"

"Now, go with your mother so I can find the dolly in time to give her to you when you wake up." Steve lifted his daughter into his wife's arms.

"No, no," the little girl repeated firmly. "I must say good-bye to Helénico or he will miss me." Steve looked at his wife with hopelessness.

"All right, you shall see Helénico, but only long enough to give him a lump of sugar. One. Promise?"

"Promise."

Steve took her again and walked with his wife down the tiled path leading behind the house. A beautiful white horse cantered to the fence when he saw them.

"Tico, Tico," the girl exclaimed. The stallion dipped his powerful head into the tiny arms. "Papi, the sugar." The girl beckoned with outstretched hand, not taking her eyes off the horse. Steve opened a British biscuit tin, now replenished with equine treats. He handed María a lump of sugar. The stallion lifted the morsel from the child's palm with his careful muzzle. After one satisfying crunch, he looked up.

"More, Papi," María clamored.

"No, dear, too much sugar is not good, and besides, it will teach him to nip. It's off on your big trip with Mama." The family walked around front. For the last time Steve placed María in the arms of his wife. "Carmencita, take care of this little miracle and I will see you at Juárez, about six." Steve kissed his wife and daughter and waved as their driver, Carlos, drove the black Ford Falcon, small but immaculately kept, out the wrought-iron gate. "I will be with you soon. Go with God." As Steve closed the gate and walked toward the house, he thought how lucky he was. He had obtained his medical degree at San Francisco in the United States, completing his residency at Stanford Medical Center. Though modesty compelled him to joke, he was, indeed, the best pediatrician in Mexico and one of the world's leading virologists. And what a lovely and loving family he had. Carmen was the perfect wife and mother. And how beautiful she was. He recalled the first time he saw her, a riding demonstration at the Army's equestrian center. She put a black stallion through upper-level dressage movements with ease and perfection. She was Carmen María Marcos de Vargas and now she was his. A fine rider himself, in the Army he'd worked with the military stud's string of accomplished dressage and jumping horses. In this connection he'd arranged a formal introduction.

He recalled the riding lesson Carmen had given María the day before. The girl practically disappeared on the great stallion's back. A bit nervous in the trot, María would glance at the ground, only to be reprimanded by her mother, who, from the ground, demonstrated correct posture—body erect but not stiff, eyes, chin, and jaw up. It was the look of a queen in training. He smiled as María held her body in a manner advanced for its years. The patient stallion trotted about the ring, aware how fragile his cargo was.

Thirty minutes later Steve was in his modest Fiat driving down the Avenida Juárez in front of the Presidential Palace in Mexico City's rush hour. Monday, so there was little of the brown industrial smog that enshrouds the city from later in the morning through Saturday. He could see the great snow-capped Sierra Madres outlined against the clean morning sky. He glanced at his watch—seven-fifteen. Good, he'd have time to get samples of his tissue cultures off to the virologists at the Institut Pasteur in Paris. This was an important juncture in his career. He was certain his technique on grouping viruses in tissue culture would receive international plaudits, perhaps even a Nobel Prize. To celebrate his mailing, he might even grab a cup of coffee and talk with old Velásquez about the Jacinto case before making rounds.

Suddenly he felt the steering wheel slide through his hands as if an invisible passenger had reached over and snatched it. His thoughts flashed: the car overdue for a tune-up; or a blowout. But simultaneously he saw a huge seam unzipping the black asphalt in front of the hood. It was an earthquake of horrific proportion. He slammed the brakes and leapt out, seeing the ground ripple like an underground ocean gone mad. Lampposts bent like molten toys on a train set. Lines were falling everywhere—snapping and popping with menacing sparks and flares. The sounds were awful—buildings moaning, glass shattering, metal splitting, and people screaming, suffocated by greater roarings. As a power line fell by his feet, Steve yelled to other drivers who could hear him, "Get back in your cars; the tires will insulate you or . . ." The sound of the Continental Hotel collapsing floor by floor drowned out his voice. Brown smoke filled the air. He could see nothing. Steve jumped into the car and planted his feet on the rubber floor mat. The car rolled like a carnival ride. He heard the searing of metal as his bumper hit the car in front. His head struck the windshield with a vicious jerk. Shards of glass tore into his scalp. He slumped backwards unconscious.

When he came to, thinning smoke revealed a terrible sight, an unreal city. Shattered glass, metal, and concrete strewn everywhere. Where buildings had been, collapsed accordionlike ruins tumbled into each other. People were

running around crying in pain or attempting to find loved
ones. "My María and Carmen! Where are you?" Later
Steve could never remember whether he muttered his
terrible question to himself or shouted it in agony. He
tried to open the car door, but it was wedged shut. A
chunk of concrete blocked the other door, so he slipped
out the window, its jagged shards tearing his suit and
slashing his abdomen. He ran the eight blocks to Juárez
Hospital, oblivious of blood streaming down his face and
onto his tattered jacket.

"Surely God lets a hospital stand," he told himself as he
stumbled over rubble in the middle of what he thought
was the street.

One block from the hospital, a motorcycle policeman
stopped him: "Señor, you must go to the Military Hospital if you need treatment."

"Why?" puffed Steve. "I work here."

"You are a doctor here, sir?"

"Pediatrician."

"Then, sir, I must instruct you to go to the Military
Hospital, where you will be assigned to the rescue."

"My wife and child are here. I must go in."

"I am afraid, Doctor, there is . . ."

Steve didn't wait, but pushed past and ran further
down the street.

". . . nothing left," finished the policeman, shaking his
head and gazing around.

Juárez was gone, all that remained of the twelve-story
hospital a fifty-foot-square tomb of debris. Stretchers had
been jettisoned out and lay awkwardly on the ground.
Blue-green surgical gowns hung on the jutting edges of
the collapsed frame in eerie suspension. Rescue workers
already hacked at the skewed beams and shattered walls.
Several bodies had been placed on slabs of surrounding
cement with "*Muerto*" chalked next to them so medical
teams wouldn't waste time. Steve ran over to the body of
a little girl, but stopped when he remembered María's
pinafore had been pink, not yellow.

"My God, my God—my family is in there!" Steve ran

to the outpatient pediatric wing of the hospital. A line of rescue workers moved sections of concrete and steel cable. Steve jostled to the head of the line.

"My daughter and wife are here. Have you found them?" he asked pleadingly.

"Señor, please, it's better if you go." As the rescue worker wiped sweat and grime from his face, he glanced at Steve's bloodstained face and matted scalp.

"You need attention." For the first time Steve became aware of the sticky warmth trickling down his face.

"I must find María and Carmen—I will help!" He bent over and tried to remove a piece of concrete weighing two hundred pounds. It tore his hands and fingers and didn't budge.

"Sir, you cannot help, you are preventing us now—please go. Survivors will be sent to the Military Hospital, or you can check at the stadium, where the dead are sent."

"No, they're here. I must dig." Steve pulled again at the unyielding rubble. "Listen!" Steve commanded, putting up his hand for silence. A terrible sound of muffled moans came from within, but the direction was hard to guess.

"We know. That's why we are here." The worker signaled a policeman. "This man has lost his wife and child here but he is now preventing us," whispered the man, turning away from Steve and then back to dig.

"Señor," said the policeman with his hand gently on Steve's shoulder, "you must come away."

"No!" cried Steve, yanking away from the grasp. He began to tug at a twisted metal coil, which sprang back and slashed his wrist.

The policeman motioned two other officers to assist him. "Wait, I know this man," called someone in a white lab coat. "He is a doctor here."

"A doctor where?" one of the rescue group asked ironically, surveying the rubble.

"Esteban, you must come with me. Many need your help."

"Pedro, my Carmen and María need me. They are in here," he said, pointing downward frantically, then pointing again as if his finger were a divining rod.

Pedro Saavedra remembered that today Esteban's daughter was scheduled to have her tonsils removed. He put his hands on Steve's shoulders and looked him square in the face. "If they're alive, they will be rescued. These people are professionals. There are ambulances and doctors. You must come with me to the Military Hospital. You're hurt yourself." Dr. Saavedra took him by the elbow, but again Steve pulled free.

"I am a doctor—with my family and patients here, I still cannot stay?" Steve looked at his friend with a pained, incredulous face. He started to dig again, but collapsed onto the unyielding dust and debris.

"He's lost blood. Send an ambulance and take him to the Military Hospital. Quickly. We don't want him in shock. Tell them he's Dr. Esteban Rodríguez. He must be attended immediately because he must help others." The policeman directed rescue workers to help carry Steve off the pile and back to the makeshift street.

"Doctor, we're ready," called up the nurse, her white uniform covered with blood and grime. Dr. Saavedra nodded and climbed the ruins to the section that was the maternity ward. A woman lay pinioned under a steel girder. He would amputate her legs in an effort to free her. They had just taken her newborn son from her arms, not letting her see he was dead.

"Be quick," he said, rolling up his sleeves and permitting the nurse to pour near-boiling water over his arms and hands. "The vessels must be ligated before excess toxins build up."

When Steve woke up, he found himself on Ward D of the Military Hospital. His friend and teacher Dr. Miguel Quintero sat at the end of the white wrought-iron bed. "Esteban, you gave us a scare with that back. Seventy stitches and four units of packed blood cells." The white-haired doctor moved to take Steve's hand.

"My family?" implored Steve, trying to prop himself up but failing in weakness.

"Esteban, we don't know yet." The old man took his hand gently and firmly. "It would have taken a special act of God. It's been twenty-eight hours since the quake. My heart is with you and it aches." The kind and exhausted doctor walked to the bedside table and handed Steve a glass of water.

"No!" Steve waved his hand at what the old doctor said, not the glass. "They're alive inside. They're strong and good and are spared. I must go to them." He managed to sit up and shift his legs over the side of the bed.

"No, my son. Go there again and you will surely be forced away or arrested. Believe me, everything possible is being done. But you must not insist. Juárez is a tomb. If by some chance God wills a miracle, let it surprise you. You must accept the worst has happened. Minister to yourself and these others—these children who lie around you and come hourly by the hundreds." Dr. Quintero gestured to four rows of beds. Only then did Steve hear the cries and labored breathing of the rescued. He glanced at the next bed. A young boy about eight slept fitfully, his head bandaged and both arms in casts. "His entire family was buried. He had run to the neighborhood store to get milk for his infant sister," said Dr. Quintero, hoping another's tragedy might bring Steve a little away from his own. It didn't work.

"I'm a father and a doctor. My first responsibility is to save my family," Steve cried out, looking on the floor for his shoes.

"You are a man and not God," Quintero said sharply, restraining Steve's search by taking his shoulders and steering him gently back in bed. "The work now belongs to jackhammers, winches, cranes. And prayers."

"Not doctors?"

"Doctors, too, and workers and nurses and search dogs, but not this doctor," said Quintero, putting his hand on Steve's forehead. "Rest one more day so that we may put you to work. Many children, many without parents, desperately need you."

"If you hear anything . . ."

"I will let you know," finished Quintero.

"Right away," demanded Steve.

"Instantly."

Dr. Quintero stopped at the nurses' station on his way out. "Señora Ortega," he said to the elderly nurse putting pills in little paper cups.

"Yes, Doctor," she said, holding a final count to herself to avoid losing track.

"Keep especially close watch on Dr. Rodríguez. He may take it into his head to get back to Juárez. Use this sedative if necessary." He handed her a slip with instructions.

"I know, Doctor. I've already taken his clothes and put them in the staff locker room."

"I see you understand. Thank you." Dr. Quintero opened the door that led down the hall to the cafeteria. He hadn't eaten a thing in thirty hours.

"Dr. Quintero," asked Nurse Ortega, "is there hope for his family?"

"I think not," said the old doctor sadly. "There have been no survivors in Juárez except in the first hours. It would take a miracle."

"There were seven floors on the maternity wing alone, each with forty cribs and forty beds!" Nurse Ortega's body shook with dry gasps locked in too long. She had seen everything in thirty-five years, but one day was worse than those twelve thousand together.

"We must be as strong as possible now. There are the living to think of." Dr. Quintero patted the nurse on the arm and went off the ward, deploring the inadequacy of his exhortation.

Steve passed another day in bed, trapped between a medicated body that needed rest and a mind that demanded he punch through the hazy block keeping pain at a tolerable distance. But those first few minutes of clarity brought no news, no word of his wife or daughter. With some hesitation a nurse granted his request and brought a radio to his bedside. The facts alone caused broadcasters to weep as they reported the destruction of the quake, 7.8 on the Richter scale, and cruelly selective: the largest public-housing project had been reduced to a "collective tomb." Ten government buildings, two hundred schools, and many hotels had been destroyed. Ironically, hospitals became the worst death traps with twelve hundred at the Centro Médico y Mexico General Hospital presumed dead (including those in its dormitory for medical residents), and nine hundred doctors, nurses, and patients at Juárez. Steve drew no comfort from learning that the National Palace, the National Cathedral, and the Templo Mayor Aztec relics remained intact.

The next morning, as he had said he would, Dr. Quintero put Steve to work. Starting at seven, he ministered to a never-ending line of the most innocent victims, children. With skill he treated burns, abrasions, lacerations, concussions, and infected wounds, seeing many into surgery for punctured lungs, ruptured spleens, and amputations for crush injuries. Always he would talk to them—and take the most time with those who would not talk themselves but looked at him with vacant, darkened eyes. These children had lost their mothers, fathers, and often their entire families. Steve could eventually ease the shock. They would tell him what had happened, how they felt, and he could get them to cry.

Dr. Quintero carefully watched Steve, trying to find a balance point between the acute emotional needs of his former student and the constant influx of emergency cases. At first the old physician thought that by treating the children's grief, Steve would confront his own—as he made the children talk and cry, so he would too. Instead, Steve protected his own pain from the subtle psychological scalpel he used to lance the emotional abscesses of the children.

He no longer spoke to the hospital staff about his family: they mistakenly believed Carmen and María had been lost. Their expressions and gestures gave them away.

Nurses responded a fraction too quickly to his questions about patients, medications, and operating-room schedules, afraid the conversation would take a personal and difficult turn. Colleagues invited him to their homes for dinner as if he were a widower, which he denied. Soon he stopped mentioning Carmen and María. He knew the truth if others didn't. After all, every day at noon he went to the Social Security ballpark, the city's impromptu morgue, and walked down the rows of bodies surrounded by blocks of melting ice. And since the authorities sent all the dead there, and he hadn't seen them, they were still alive.

After a week and a half, Dr. Quintero called Steve to his office. The elderly doctor sat for the first time in fourteen hours, his desk piled with administrative tasks. He yawned despite the unpleasant queasiness in his stomach caused by the job at hand, not an administrative one at all. When he heard the all-too-lively knock on the door, he drew a deep breath and waited. "Miguel, hello." Steve's energetic, cheerful manner conveyed that he was ill-prepared for anything but light conversation. Quintero motioned for him to sit.

"Esteban, in the short term it might be better for the hospital if I allowed you to continue this way."

"What way?" Steve asked, his tone offhand but his face conveying for an instant that some bad truth was at hand. "What way?" he asked again breezily, the emotional dike repaired and intact.

"Carmen and María are dead—you must know this." Dr. Quintero looked directly into Steve's eyes.

"What station have you been listening to, Dr. Quintero? I have a radio, they've been pulling people out of Juárez daily. All those 'miracle babies.' " Steve turned and looked out the window. Five floors below, a young couple was necking on the hospital's green lawn.

"Yes, Steve. But they were babies and they *are* miracles. Adults were saved only in the first hours. Then, by God's grace and the dissipating warmth of their dead or dying mothers, ten infants lived. But now no more. This morning Juárez . . ." Quintero paused, summoning the strength to tell the young doctor news that would shatter his delusion and open the floodgates of pain. "This morning Juárez was bulldozed."

"Bulldozed," Steve repeated softly.

"Yes."

"Why bulldozed?" Steve's voice rose with shock and anger.

"The government fears infection. They were going to do it three days ago, but waited. Thank God. They pulled out one last infant, though it's doubtful she'll make it."

"My God, bulldoze Juárez? My wife and child are in there!" Steve's face turned red as he gasped to recover his breath.

Quintero walked over and embraced him. "They are dead. Those to be rescued have been rescued."

"No!" Steve shook off the man's thin arms and the unacceptable truth they conveyed. "Bulldoze a hospital? Are we still in the Dark Ages? Do people believe that decomposing bodies cause epidemics? No, my wife and child have been murdered because certain smells offend Mexico's officials. It's too ludicrous." But then Steve leaned back against the wall and sank to the floor.

Quintero sat next to him and took his hand. "As doctors and scientists, we know there would be no plague. Yet, you said it yourself—the smell. Listen to what you said. You, too, know it's over. No one lives in there now."

Steve gasped as the truth finally confronted him. Of course they were dead—all dead—the patients and staff of Juárez. The dead in the ballpark weren't *all* the dead, just those bodies pulled from the rubble. There was no hope; hope had become a delusion. He tried to catch his quickening breath but couldn't. Overcome by dizziness, he tried to stand but failed. Dr. Quintero brought a basin, and, after the vomiting was over, gently wiped the perspiration from Steve's face and held him while he cried.

* * *

Together with his relatives, Steve attended the mass burial of an undetermined number of corpses from Juárez at San Lorenzo cemetery. There was no funeral for his family. Even his lab had been completely destroyed—culture strains, research files, correspondence. Years of work gone. Finally, rather than continue to sleep in the on-call rooms used by residents, he went home, and with Carmen's brother and sister began packing clothes and toys to donate to relief agencies. He asked his wife's best friend to take the stallion Helénico. Laura de Bonilla had lost her entire family in the quake—a husband, two sons, and an infant daughter—and Steve hoped that riding would help her through her pain. Laura, an accomplished equestrienne, accepted the talented Andalusian, making it clear that Steve could reclaim him anytime. But he signed over the registration papers, imploring Laura to sign as well. She then realized Steve had to remove the stallion from his own life permanently. When she and her groom came to pick up the horse, Steve didn't come out to help (as he always had when the two women went to dressage exhibitions). Rather, Laura noted, he remained behind the curtain, his bent silhouette outlined by lamplight.

On his daily commute Steve noticed that most of the buildings razed or damaged were less than fifty years old. Yet architects had supposedly incorporated a "sway factor" designed to withstand strong tremors. And Mexico had one of the toughest building codes in the world. *Mordito*, bribery, that silent and accepted institution employed in everyday business, had killed and maimed. Steve's anger over the failure to save his wife and child fused with anger at this government and country. He saw himself as a conspirator with Mexico—partners in murder. Over the next few months his anger turned to depression, and as he conducted office hours and made hospital rounds, he grew more isolated. His memory slipped—he missed meetings, couldn't remember what he'd written on patients' charts—and he began to misdiagnose. Quintero was not surprised when the reluctant vice-president of nursing finally complained. He'd already observed his friend's weight loss and abstracted manner. Again he summoned Steve to his office.

"Esteban, I want you to take a vacation." He motioned toward a chair.

"Vacation? You can't be serious. The wards are packed, and for each child discharged, we admit five more. I start rounds at six in the morning and finish after ten at night. A vacation?" Steve shook his head in disbelief.

"When was the last time you took one?"

"A while," he replied defensively.

"A long while, not since your wedding trip to Florida. Years. Conferences in Cancún or New York may count as vacations for most doctors, but not for you. I want you to take one now—four weeks, no less. Get out of the miserable tomb that envelops us. Go to the U.S. I know you like it there. Let the naive materialism distract you for a while. Or go see your friends at Stanford." Quintero lit a cigarette and drew on it, glad for a few seconds of relief.

Steve now understood. Doctors didn't take vacations when wards were double maximum capacity. And administrators didn't send any doctors away unless they were in trouble. He felt even more guilty now, more defensive. He shot back:

"The quake was here, not San Francisco. I've been working sixteen hours a day. But you don't need me? I'll help out in the emergency room if you like. I've gotten by on four hours' sleep before. The other doctors are exhausted. You need me!" He stopped. "Miguel, what have I done?"

"Indicated that you need a rest. This earthquake has ripped your heart just as it did buildings, and your heart needs time to heal. If you're uncomfortable with the term 'vacation,' we'll call it a leave of absence." Quintero's face looked sympathetic but implacable.

"Leave of absence? You want to get rid of me any way you can. It's you who'd rather call it a vacation. Easier for the administrator." Steve's voice cracked. "What the hell is wrong?" Quintero crushed out his cigarette and took a deep breath. He hated to tell a friend he was failing at the one time he desperately needed to succeed, for himself and for everyone else.

"Your suffering shows—memory loss, missed meetings— and you know it. You write Ritalin prescriptions for yourself. And now I learn you're prescribing medicines for children you haven't even examined."

"Who told you that? What child—when?" To give himself strength, Steve mortared his broken pain with anger. "God in heaven, what's happening? I'm killing myself with work!"

"So I'm sending you away before you kill others, and to help yourself in the bargain. Just for a while, until you come to terms with your grief."

"Look, Miguel. My family is buried. My lab—the culture strains, hope for any recognition—is buried too. All I have left is saving others."

" 'Saving others'? You prescribed a lethal dose of morphine for the Romero boy. His nurse reported it to her supervisor, and thank God she did. People lose confidence, the halls fill with whispers." Steve recalled the little boy's spinal-cord injury but had trouble remembering details. All his cases ran together in a haze. Quintero touched his shoulder. "You must get help. Let me call Fuentes—he studied post traumatic stress disorder."

"You're confused, Miguel. I don't get help, I give it. Either let me do my job or take the job away from me."

"Take a thirty-day leave of absence and get help."

"No vacation, no leave of absence, no euphemisms," Steve threatened. "If you want me out, say so—in writing."

"All right. Thirty-day suspension of privileges," Quintero replied quietly but abruptly. "You're dangerous to patients and yourself. If I looked the other way, I wouldn't be doing *my* job. I shall inform the other hospitals about my decision. You'll get official notification tomorrow. Meanwhile, I beg you, change your mind."

As Steve closed the door, he hurled a parting shot.

"You know, Miguel, an optimist would be grateful. Now I have the proverbial clean slate: nowhere to go, but up, right? Too bad Mexicans are seldom optimists. You've taken the last shred of life away from me."

Dr. Quintero sat at his desk and buried his head in his hands. He considered Steve the best pediatrician he'd ever known—intelligent, meticulous, unflagging, compassionate. He could treat a child's fear and pain better than anyone else he'd seen in over forty years of medicine. And this was because Steve knew—no, he felt to his very core—what the child went through. This identification meant that any improvement or cure became a time of unbridled exultation. But the impact of failure—or death—resulted in immobilizing depression.

When Steve had taken the position at Juárez after completing his residency at Stanford, he confided in Quintero and told him how difficult he found the work with children. He thought pediatrics in the United States would be easier—new facilities, higher standard of living, more money. But this triumph of affluence meant that the majority of children on the wards were less susceptible to cure—immune deficiencies, muscular dystrophy, malformations of the heart, terminal cancer. Some needed treatment for social or maternal neglect. In Mexico the hopelessness was ironically mitigated by hope. So much could be done—immunization programs, postnatal care, supplementary milk-powder programs. A doctor could see tangible results in days.

The pain of making rounds at San Francisco caused Steve to retreat into the world of virology. Stanford awarded him a two-year research fellowship, during which his work culturing unusual viral strains became well-known. For his third and final year the school tapped him to be chief resident of pediatrics. Of course the rounds could still be heartrending, but at least the attending physician acted as an emotional shield.

And now Quintero had to deal with the defect of Steve's virtue, in which acute powers of empathy drew on acute emotional vulnerability. The loss of his family had opened a wound that continued to fester. Switching on the Dictaphone, Dr. Quintero gave the date, subject ("suspension of privileges"), and Steve's name. The bureaucratic juxtaposition of that subject with his friend's name pierced his heart. Immediately he clicked off the machine and, filling his briefcase with less painful tasks, walked out the door. Tomorrow, he thought to himself, tomorrow would be soon enough to fire a doctor who had turned bad simply because he was so good.

The arrival of Quintero's letter spelled out an even bleaker situation for Steve. His feelings of self-worth had derived from family and work, and now both had vanished. He took it with seeming fatalistic acceptance, yet his severe depression prevented it from truly registering. To fill the now empty hours, he found himself at Rubén López's stable. He and Rubén had served together in the Army and successfully competed in show jumping and exhibition dressage. Rubén invited him to work with some young horses bound for export to the States. With Mexico City shut out by the twelve-foot white-washed stucco walls of an arena, Steve began to ride again. Just to place his feet in the stirrups, he had to force himself through depression-induced fatigue. But when the horse strode forward, his heart beat faster, his face flushed, and he came alive. The task of the moment—leg yield, half-pass, pirouette—demanded total concentration. For several weeks he schooled horses, each evening driving home, sleeping fitfully, waking to depression, then riding again.

One night Steve's tired body failed to put his mind to sleep. For the first time since the earthquake, he felt excited, but couldn't put his finger on the source. He pulled back the covers and walked quickly to his study. The shelves held scores of books and periodicals—Nelson's *Pediatrics*, Cecil's *Medicine*, and Beaumont's *Studies on Alexis St. Martin*. How nervous he'd been in those days—studying medicine in another language at top institutions. Slowly, as he assimilated thousands of pages and listened to thousands of hearts, his insecurity diminished and he knew the profound satisfaction of diagnosing and treating patients. And now Quintero had taken it away from him.

A small, muffled bang followed by the vibrating flutter of wings startled him. A monarch butterfly had caught itself behind a metal window grille. "You've come the wrong way. You should be heading north." Steve took the butterfly in his gently cupped hands. As he walked to the front door, he felt the light creature's frantic struggle. On the patio it remained on his now open palm, its fragile wings expanding and closing like the abdomen of a child in deep sleep. Steve took them between his forefingers and gently tossed the insect into the night air. Orange and black fluttered in the window's shaft of light, then disappeared.

Back in bed, he wondered why the monarch had gone off-course. This time of year they migrated north by the hundreds of thousands from Tamazunchale to the American Southwest. The horses sold would travel through Tamazunchale and, in the company of waves of monarchs, head north too. In an attempt to sleep, he next turned his mind to his routine—the horses he'd ride, their abilities and stage of training. But only after he heard the birds at dawn did sleep come. And by then he knew that he too must return to the United States.

The next day he drafted a request to Marshall Simpkins, chairman of pediatrics at Stanford. Steve had kept his California license and could set up practice there, but in order to pursue his specialty he needed to complete his exams and apply to the American Board of Pediatrics. Simpkins would write him a glowing recommendation. As Steve licked shut his letter, he noticed a streak of bright color across the address. He looked at his hands, the forefingers brushed with orange powder. Automatically, turning to get a new envelope, he stopped, then changed his mind. Perhaps the butterfly dust was a good omen.

Steve felt sure he'd passed his boards—written and oral—with distinction, and waited for his application to be accepted. Dr. Quintero called and wrote inquiring

after his health and imploring him to take steps necessary
to return to the hospital. But Steve had no desire to
revisit the site of his humiliation, so he cut the conversations short or did not reply. He rode at Rubén's, even
taking one horse to a Grand Prix, where the young
gelding made a favorable debut. When Steve got home
that evening, there—after two months of waiting—he
found a letter from the American Board of Pediatrics.
But the opening words "We are pleased" failed to appear. His heart plunged when he read on through the
stark black lines.

Dear Candidate,
    After reviewing your application for the American
Board of Pediatrics, we regret to inform you that we
are unable to recommend your certification.
    This decision was not made as a result of your
performance on the written examinations, but rather
on the basis of materials submitted by your preceptors and peers. We regret that these documents are
confidential and cannot be released to the candidate.
                              Yours very truly,
                              Grant Fisher
                              Chairman, American Board
                              of Pediatrics

That night Steve jerked awake many times, his subconscious unable to resolve the conflicts, losses, and injuries.
A couple of Percodan slid him into bad sleep. In the
morning he awoke too exhausted for despair. An hour
later at Rubén's he was forcing a filly to execute dressage
movements her adolescent physique couldn't sustain.

"Steve, what's gotten into you?" shouted Rubén, running to the middle of the arena, shocked and angered by
his friend's behavior and the irreparable damage he was
inflicting.

"She'll do it—she learns quickly," Steve countered,
forcing her into a half-pass.

"Get off—now," ordered Rubén. His sharp tone surprised Steve, who dismounted and handed the reins to the groom. The slender chestnut left the ring, her head hung in exhaustion and her body soaked with sweat. "I did that?" Steve asked himself after a few minutes, disbelief and realization dawning in his face. "Rubén, I don't know what got into me."

"You need a change. The gelding you rode at the show leaves for Texas tomorrow morning. Why don't you go along for the ride? Help me out—it would make a good impression on the buyer."

Texas. That suited him. California was out anyway. Back at home, a sudden wave of fury shook his frame. He raced to his study, pulled diplomas off the wall, and heaved them into a trashcan. The sound of shattering glass gave him perverse pleasure. He'd guessed why Simpkins couldn't be bothered to write back. Simpkins had done him in—professional jealousy. No one could duplicate his culture media and painstaking techniques, so the next-best thing for an envious colleague would be to bash him privately. Steve shook his head with disbelief. The man who'd tapped him to be chief resident had finished him off. And they say gringos are honest. Who could have known?

That evening Steve dined at a neighborhood restaurant. He finished by picking the sugar skull off his flan and disdainfully tossing it into an ashtray. All Souls' Day, the second-saddest day on the liturgical calendar—he'd forgotten one of Mexico's favorite holidays. He hated its fascination with death—bread shaped into bones, skulls of tissue paper, and skeletons rigged with fireworks: offerings to placate God. It all conveyed an acquiescence, an acceptance of powerlessness. He heard a distant explosion and out the window saw faint tracers rise—red, green, silver, and gold—rise, then fall into black nothingness.

In the predawn light he drove to Rubén's. The van would leave at five. Arriving early, he helped get the horse ready—leg bandages, head bumper, and a sheet to keep him warm in the cool morning air. Later, lulled by the rocking motion of the pneumatic ride, Steve fell asleep, his head against the cold window, unaware of the familiar landmarks and receding images of Mexico. Unlike the monarch butterflies, he'd resolved not to return.

That same night Dr. Quintero went to the hospital chapel. Working late to prepare for an accreditation visit, he'd neglected his prayers. The demands of the living with their loud cries had claimed priority. November 2—the Day of the Dead—had passed. Still, he offered one prayer for the souls in purgatory, hoping his earnest words might ease their condition. The sound of a child's scream broke the silence. Soothing adult voices followed, then receded into the distance. His thoughts turned to Steve—tomorrow he'd call him again—no, go to his house. The old doctor offered a second prayer, this time for his friend. Then he left the dark stained-glass room and walked out into a whitewashed fluorescent corridor, unaware that he'd prayed for Steve twice.

# Navarro

Every evening for the next five days Steve came and watched Diana inject Navarro with tranquilizer. On the sixth he phoned her to find out how the horse was. By then Navarro's walk lasted thirty minutes, with previous walks under sedation having taken the edge off his spirits. He enjoyed these hacks and the five-minute intervals in which Diana allowed him to graze. As days went by and the walks increased in length, Navarro regained his muscle tone and the eyes grew sharp with life. His leg seemed to cause no further distress, and Diana prayed the new tissue would be dense and strong. One evening, five more weeks into the convalescence, Steve stopped by again.

"What do you think?" Diana asked hopefully, walking up with Navarro, his muzzle green with foam from the early-spring grass he'd eaten.

"I would say, do this two more weeks and we'll see if you can start riding."

"Two more weeks!" Diana exclaimed. "I know we need to be careful, Steve, but when will I get to ride?"

"Two more weeks, *maybe*," Steve said firmly.

Exactly fourteen days later Steve stopped by again. "Well, can I ride?" were the first words out of Diana's mouth.

"Yes, in two weeks more." Steve didn't bother to look at her. In fact, he avoided eye contact, stroking Navarro's neck and waiting for her reaction.

159

"Two *more* weeks? Why don't I feel surprised?" Her eyes filled with tears of reaction.

"No, I want this horse to last for you," he said. "Two more weeks, Diana. He's almost there, but not yet."

"If I didn't know better, I'd say you planned from the start for me to walk this guy for a month but were afraid to tell me," Diana commented, wiping her face with her fingers. As Steve drove off, she led Navarro back to his stall. He knew I was going to have to walk you this long. I'm sure he did. He just was afraid I wouldn't go through with it. She suddenly realized she'd been outsmarted for her own good—and possibly for her career's.

At the end of two weeks Steve told Diana to get on Navarro's back, from where she could walk him yet another two weeks. He wanted Navarro's muscles to develop as slowly and correctly as possible, so they'd be able to alleviate stress, not only from the injured foreleg but also from any part of the body that could incur trauma from exercise. Steve had seen many young horses pushed early to make a quick sale, particularly true in the racing industry. Before their bones fused, many two-year-olds carried riders in tough workouts, even races, and developed the muscle to see them through. But in a few years their genes and training betrayed them and many were ruined by navicular, bowed tendons, arthritic joints, or stress fractures. The number and kinds of injuries were endless. Some track rejects at one time found homes in the hunter-jumper world, but that was now rare. Veterinary medicine had "progressed" to the degree that injured horses could be forced to run several years longer, rendering them useless for anything else but the dog-food industry. In dressage and jumping this helped to account for the boom of imported warmbloods from Germany, the Netherlands, Denmark, and Sweden. Steve and Diana discussed the necessity of taking time with Navarro. Psychologically it wasn't easy at first on the energetic, hard-driving twenty-year-old, but in the end—because of her sensitivity and need for quiet—Diana looked forward to these walks. They brought back memories of childhood rides with her father and reminded her how beautiful New England could be.

One of her favorite rides took her along the Nashua River, where she saw the great blue herons that returned season after season. Beavers and raccoons went about their separate lives. Further upstream she'd come to Groton School boathouse, and if she rode in the afternoon she'd trot along the bank, keeping company with the elite prep-school shells. On her way home she passed a small graveyard where several horses from the Southfield Hunt were buried in the early 1900's. Near the individual headstones a large tablet read, "To the horses, hounds, and foxes of Southfield Hunt." Diana sometime stopped for a rest at a gigantic granite picnic table. It was peaceful—the slow winding river, the rhododendrons mixed with pines, maples, and oaks. Grand Prix was on another planet. And this horse, light and airy, was like no other she'd encountered.

"It's the breed," commented Steve on one of his evening visits. "They're very responsive."

"Incredible. There's something antigravitational about him," exclaimed Diana.

"Wait until you jump." He smiled. "Then you'll see how 'antigravitational' he is. Do an easy canter along the fence line, half-seat, so you won't pinch his back."

Diana leaned forward, but just before she applied her leg behind Navarro's girth, he began to canter. "I didn't even ask yet!" she laughed.

"Yes you did. You moved your body in some way that told him he was going to be asked."

"It's a wonderful feeling," Diana called out as she came up to him.

"Yes, but presents its own problems," he cautioned. "Andalusians, particularly this one, respond so quickly to the slightest aid that even the competent rider must know exactly what he's asking of the horse. You mix signals with this gentleman and you're apt to wind up on the ground. Canter him no more than five minutes in each direction, but do it each day for the next two weeks.

Continue the trails, but only at walk and trot. We'll hope this prevents him from being too excited when he starts to jump. But all in good time. I must go now."

"Steve." She felt yet another sudden urge to get closer to this man, and asked abruptly, "Won't you stay for dinner? I'm not a good cook. But I can make some chili."

Steve looked at her with amusement and a sly reproach. "Yes, you know we Mexicans *love* chili. It seems whenever I'm invited out, people give me chili or tacos. Hmm umm!"

"I'm sorry, I didn't mean to stereotype. Chicken, a steak, macaroni—there's something in the freezer. I have a microwave."

"No, thank you, Diana. I really must leave. I shouldn't even have stopped tonight. I'm late."

"Then why did you stop?" she asked gravely.

"To make sure you two don't mess each other up," he said with a smile.

"But, Steve . . ." She paused. "Why're you doing all this?" Her tone conveyed frustration and genuine puzzlement.

"All what?" Steve asked innocently.

"Helping me, vanning Navarro here, checking on us."

"Diana, a friendship needn't have an ulterior motive. I want you both to do well. I'm attracted to underdogs."

"Thanks," Diana replied with good-natured sarcasm.

"I want the best for you. You're a pretty couple."

"And . . . ?"

"And I want you to win," he finished. "To succeed. I know what it's like to lose." He turned and walked to his truck, leaving Diana to feel badly for having touched his unknown pain.

He won't let anyone near, she thought. You approach, and down comes the iron gate with a clang. Navarro, oblivious of Diana's presence, continued to gaze out the door in the direction of the setting sun.

All those evenings, Steve truly did have things to do. He worked hard to ensure he wouldn't sit in his studio surrounded by the sterile walls which compelled him to turn his thoughts inward—thoughts inevitably going back to Mexico City or his situation at Hampstead. He wasn't safe there. Sloan's unveiled threats convinced him of that. But where else could he go? Even the shadiest employers were increasingly reluctant to hire illegals. Immigration had begun cracking down. Besides, another job might pay less, and he'd be forced on the street, unable to qualify for anything, not only because he lacked a green card but simply because he lacked a home address. Yet he didn't want to remain at Hampstead, vulnerable. Besides, why stay around horses anyway— especially Navarro? A masochistic impulse? He hadn't known the full brother to Carmen's horse would show up at the one barn he worked in. He hadn't even known that a full brother existed until one night after Sloan had left he sat behind the computer and called up Navarro's file. He'd been right all along about Navarro—there was something familiar about him and it wasn't simply breed similarities. Were he still a believer, he'd have thought God was intervening, that a purpose lurked in all this. But he no longer had faith. He drew no comfort from coincidences, but saw them as a mockery of existence. And were he a believer, he would have considered it God's irony.

For months nothing but sorrow had deadened his heart. But Diana startled him, like a brave young lioness who leapt from boulder to brush, claiming and protecting what was hers despite the cost. He'd seen her knocked down, but she always stood up with newfound resilience. Steve envied her self-reliance. He'd never known a woman like that; in fact, he'd known few such men. He had needed his family so very much, and embraced them with generous and spontaneous love. But they were gone. So he remained busy from his early-morning work at Hampstead to his late-night movies, or bowling, local plays, music festivals, and lectures. Once or twice—on a weekday—he stopped in at the local Catholic parish, but felt conspicuously alone and uncomfortably close to the

God in whom he no longer believed. How he envied Diana, with her future entirely ahead of her. Time was on her side. He wished he could have a future too, but it seemed impossible. He considered himself one of the living dead, without profession, friends, or joy—without anything but this girl and the white horse he'd found for her.

After four more weeks of gentle trots, canters, and long hacks, Steve started Diana and Navarro on "gymnastics"—simple jumping exercises devised to give horse and rider confidence and help develop the skills to jump a demanding course. For the first exercise Steve set up an easy in-and-out, a pair of low fences about two feet in height and eighteen feet apart. The second obstacle he placed thirty feet from the pasture-fence line. After the second jump Diana was to canter and halt at the fence, rather than let Navarro fire up with the excitement of jumping. "Let's trot him over this," he said, placing a rail on the grass immediately in front of the jump. It made a ground line so Navarro could gauge the depth of the fence. He slowed, looked, trotted over it, then cantered to the next one, leaving the ground at exactly the right spot. "Very good. Make a big fuss over him. That's the sort of attitude we want."

Diana patted Navarro's shoulder. "Fine fellow, what a good jumper." Maybe he was more than good. She felt herself well up with hope and excitement.

Steve made Diana repeat the exercise three more times, and each time Navarro strode perfectly. He didn't break from his trot until he landed after the first fence. Then he cantered on, nicely taking the second and responding quickly to Diana's request for the halt. "Diana, no more than ten minutes each day for the remainder of the week. I can be here next Tuesday, and then we'll start on exercises that help you at the same time we're building him up."

"Help me?" Diana couldn't suppress the question. She'd been training hunters and jumpers for more than a year and felt she didn't need elementary improvements. She'd learned from the best. She didn't mind Steve's advice on this injured Andalusian—he seemed to know a lot about medicine and the breed—but the idea that he'd teach her something about jumping when she'd never even seen him ride . . .

"Yes, I can help you become better," he offered, aware he was on tender ground. Years of experience with riders had taught him to beware of large, fragile egos. "You ride very, very well, of course, but you could perhaps get more out of your horse if you'd keep your seat back in the saddle an inch or two and free up his shoulders. They must be as loose as the air to lift off."

"I know different trainers have different things to teach." Diana tried to sound positive, but Steve didn't miss the note of skepticism. He'd hit her pride.

"Diana, you're a failure at pretending. It's one of your best and worst qualities. And one of many reasons I like you so much. You judge for yourself. I know you will. But if you ride as I advise, you'll get at least a foot more from this big fellow."

"That sounds good. Tell you what—I'll take your advice, no questions asked, no skepticism, if next time you promise to stay for supper. I'll put steaks on the grill and make a fresh salad. No chili." Diana felt her heart pounding as she waited for him to respond.

"I can't. Thank you again for the invitation, Diana, but I've got things I must attend to."

"Isn't there one night you're not busy?" She shook her head with disappointment and a sense of hopelessness.

"I don't think so," he said vaguely, aware how weak his objection sounded.

"Steve, I know you don't have a lover and I know you go out all the time by yourself. I see your car parked—at the movies, at Pheasant Lane Mall, and outside Kelly's—so don't, by the way, tell me you don't drink." All this was an educated guess. She'd seen Steve's car outside the bar only once. "I saw you get out of your car at Kelly's. Alone."

"Perhaps I didn't leave alone."

"Perhaps," she said, suddenly nauseated at the thought of Steve going out with another woman.

"Well, I did leave alone. And yes, I accept with pleasure your kind invitation to dine." He gave in to the pain on Diana's face. "When is good for you?"

"Anytime." Her face was bright and smiling. "Anytime the past two months has been good for me. How's next Tuesday, after these gymnastics you're putting me through?"

"Yes, a promise."

Tuesday afternoon Steve arrived carrying a bottle of Jerez sherry and wearing a starched white shirt under his khaki windbreaker. Diana thanked him and took the bottle. "I'll be right with you. Navarro's ready. I've just got to throw the saddle and bridle on."

Steve walked to the barn, nervously rubbing his hands together. He knew Diana had feelings for him, but he didn't want any more complications in his life. A relationship with her would certainly mean that. Besides, he had nothing to offer her. He laughed to himself: an illegal alien and a groom. *That* kind of groom. No woman who might interest him would take notice of a man like that. But her frank attention made him nervous because she was perceptive and knew a sharp disparity existed between what he was—what he had been—and what he did now. He felt at once exposed and attracted, and he needed someone to hold, and to hold him.

"We've been practicing those little jumps, and this fellow hasn't taken a false step all week," Diana said joining him in the barn.

"Terrific. I can see he's muscling up. Let's make things a little more complicated today." Steve adjusted Navarro's nose band.

"Isn't that a bit loose?" she asked. "You'll spoil him."

"I do not spoil this horse, I indulge him. There's a difference, you know. That is something you learn only after having been around these creatures for years. You will learn it yourself when you become a mother. Just believe me—it is far better to ask rather than demand a horse to do something. You may have some training days when you feel like you've accomplished nothing, but in the end you'll accomplish far more."

Diana took the reins from Steve and led Navarro out. She thought Steve's theories differed radically from those of the Germans, who were not unkind but certainly firm, if not downright severe. Which was better? she wondered. Maybe it depended on the horse.

"All right," said Diana, confident Navarro was ready. She circled and led him to the first jump at a trot. The long line of eight fences excited him and he jumped large, arriving too close to the second and forcing him to pop up. But after that he was fine.

"Don't worry about that first jump. He hasn't seen these things before. But you can help him shorten strides by sitting into him more. Try again."

Diana placed Navarro perfectly at each fence this time, but Steve wasn't happy. "No, no! You shortened his stride with your hands. Don't hang on his mouth like that. You'll deaden it and you'll both be in trouble when you need good hands for Grand Prix. You'll inhibit him from stretching his neck over the fence, and he won't be able to jump high and wide. Use the dressage training and don't spare your legs and seat. What we're trying to do here is to get him to propel himself forward and up. Please, try not to bother his mouth."

The next time, Diana sat back from the center of gravity and almost behind Navarro's motion. Von Engerson would kill me for this, she thought as she approached. As Navarro took off at the first fence, she sat back, shooting her arms forward to allow Navarro's neck to stretch. Her shoulders rounded—a serious equitation fault. But Navarro completed the series perfectly in balanced frame and rhythmic stride.

"Perfecto!" called Steve as he walked toward her.

"Perfect for Navarro, but I felt—and must have looked—like shit."

Steve visibly winced at her language. "Look, I know

you feel uncomfortable about riding this way, but you guide too much with your hands, some with your legs, and not enough with your seat. There is an exercise you can do to help. Jump without any hands."

"Steve, I jumped with no hands when I was a Pony Clubber."

"With arms outstretched?" he asked.

"Yes, with arms outstretched," Diana replied. Hurt and annoyed, she felt Steve had underestimated her ability. After all, she'd won the first Grand Prix she'd entered.

"Well, I'd like you to go over with your arms locked behind your back."

Diana fell silent. She thought about it for a minute. Going over jumps with hands behind one's back was a different matter. Balance would be far more difficult. And yet, as she thought about it, she could see the logic in developing the proper hip angle, not just during take-off but particularly on landing. Hands behind the back, Diana repeated to herself. Again she felt her admiration—and affection—for this man increase.

"Think it's a good idea?" Steve asked.

"If I don't fall off." As she approached at trot, she put her hands behind her. Feeling Navarro waver, she instantly applied leg pressure. He thought it a cue to jump and took off early. She tried to recover, but without her hands or outstretched arms to balance, she suddenly felt the thud of pasture on her back and shoulder. The blue sky looked big, strange, and close.

"Are you all right?" Steve yelled, coming toward her with Navarro in hand.

"Absolutely fine." She remounted and with increased determination rode Navarro through the first two jumps perfectly, but at the third he chipped in too close and popped straight up, propelling Diana over his right shoulder. Diana's head knocked the standard with a resounding crack. Steve ran up and unfastened her helmet. He looked critically at her eyes.

"I'm not hurt. These helmets are padded," Diana said. She touched her Saratoga—the same headgear jockeys use. But as she stood up, she had to catch Steve's arm to prevent herself from falling.

"Here, stand still a moment. Let me hold you." As Diana put her slender arm about his waist, he felt a surge of desire. It had been two years since his wife held him. And now, what was this? A twenty-year-old girl with a possible concussion that he'd caused.

"I'm okay. I'll go get Navarro and try again." Diana walked in the direction of Navarro, who was grazing placidly.

"No, you hit your head. Let's let it go for today."

"Absolutely not, Steve. You know I've got to go again," she responded in a surprised tone. It was against the rules to quit riding after a fall. The horse had to be left with a successful schooling or he could lose confidence. The rider needed it even more, for the same reason.

"Are you sure?" He'd done it again: a person had suffered because of him.

"Are you afraid, Steve?" He didn't respond. "For me or for you?" she pursued. As she refitted her helmet and swung up in the saddle, she didn't wait for an answer, but trotted for the fences. She jumped them with Navarro's strides perfectly cadenced and her own position flawless, hands locked behind her back.

"Terrific!" Steve exclaimed more from relief than from excitement. "I could see your torso adjust itself all the way through. A few of those each time you ride for a couple of months and you'll be able to place a horse perfectly."

After Diana started the grill, she took steaks from the refrigerator, then got two sherry glasses. "Dusty," she said distastefully as she evaluated the Waterford, unused since her father died. She ran them under the tap, then wiped them with a paper towel. "Fuzzies," she said, shaking her head at the transparent sides with little fibers on them.

"Need some help?" Steve leaned against the doorjamb.

"Please, come in. Already I'm not being a very good

hostess." Diana held the glasses toward him, showing Steve the problem.

"You have a dinner napkin?" He took the glasses from her hand. She walked to the dining room buffet and took out two Irish linen napkins. "Very pretty!" he commented, and began cleaning the glass.

As Diana admired Steve's deftness, she suddenly felt a rush of dizziness. She backed up to lean against the counter. It didn't help. Steve put the glass down and shored up her disoriented body. "You feeling okay?" he asked with concern.

"I'm fine. I just got dizzy."

"Here, let me help you." He scooped her up and placed her on the living-room sofa.

"Steve, I can walk," she protested weakly.

"Now I must attend to the grill, so if you'll excuse me . . . I insist," Steve ordered in mock firmness.

"Lovely dinner," Diana said as they finished the bottle of Médoc. She'd been touched by the way Steve had taken charge of the evening in order to take care of her. She'd never been treated that way by a man before, and she liked it.

"Now I'll do the dishes. Just tell me where the soap is."

"You will not! The least I can do is our dishes." But as Diana started to get up, she felt more dizziness accompanied by nausea. Her knees buckled. "Steve . . ."

"Sit back," he ordered. He placed her shoulders against the sofa back and took one of her hands, pressing the palm gently with his thumb.

"Do you feel that?" he asked. Diana replied that she did. "How about this?" He did the same with her other hand.

"Fine. Steve, what are you doing?"

He ignored her. "Now, I want you to follow my forefinger with your eyes. If you can't see it, tell me." Her eyes followed the slow-moving finger to left, then right, up and down, stop and start, and then return. Suddenly her eyes stopped and she looked him dead in the face. "Did it disappear?" he asked worriedly.

Diana covered his finger with her hand. "You're a doctor!" she said in a hushed but excited tone.

"One doesn't have to be a doctor to know medical tricks," he replied, evading her gaze. "Now, follow my finger: I think you've got a concussion."

"You're a doctor," Diana repeated, her voice softer still. "And all the while I thought that medical knowledge you showed around horses was secondhand from vets."

"It is. Follow my finger, please," he urged, suppressing a desire to tell her everything.

"Is that what vets tell horses—'follow my finger'? You've been around some pretty smart horses." Then she laughed as she envisioned the absurdity.

"Diana, I'm no doctor. Doctors save lives. I don't," Steve replied emphatically.

"Where did you learn this?" she asked with gentle insistence.

"As I said, one doesn't have to be a doctor to know something about medicine. I think you ought to rest a few days. No horses, no stable work. Let it go. You probably have a concussion. Bed rest. Watch some of those videos you've got stacked by your VCR. I'll drop by to feed and turn out Navarro."

Diana enjoyed surrendering to the care of her concerned friend. Medical tricks? she thought to herself. I don't think so. Maybe a malpractice suit ruined him. At the same moment she felt: if that were true, then it wasn't his fault. He's too responsible. She looked out to the kitchen and watched him wipe the counter, a white dish towel wrapped around his waist. And besides, she concluded, he's too nice ever to have done anything wrong.

"Now, listen to me, Diana." He sat down next to her. She was lying lengthwise on the couch. "What you have isn't a serious injury—at least, I don't think it's serious. But it could have been. You know that Massachusetts requires certification to instruct in riding. I don't have it."

"Steve, we know about that certification process. All you have to do is have a warm body and they pass you.

"I could get in trouble," he said, genuinely worried.

"How?"

"If you got injured."

"What's this all about, Steve? I don't pay you. I wouldn't repeat anything. I'm your friend. You just give me advice. You— "

"If you got hurt—"

"If I get hurt, I get hurt. I'm the rider. I put my feet in the stirrups. It's because I don't ride really well that I got the concussion. It was an accident and your teaching will help me avoid others. Really, Steve, it's not as if you're God. Allow me *some* responsibility, please."

You are a man, not God! Steve recalled Dr. Quintero's admonition. He turned to Diana and smiled. "You're right, of course." She took his hands in hers and he felt himself warm with desire.

"Steve, I owe you a lot. You've brought me a wonderful horse and given me some extraordinary teaching. For a while I had no hope. I felt such despair."

"Despair is a horrible thing," echoed Steve as he rubbed Diana's hands. She looked inquiringly, but he changed the subject.

"I'm glad to have you as a friend."

"Steve, I've done nothing for you. You've been so good to me I . . ."

"You exist—that's enough."

There was an uncomfortable silence. It was the moment, they both felt, to kiss. But Steve stood up. "I've got to go."

"Can't you stay a little longer?" she pleaded.

"No, I'm afraid not. You know I start work at seven. It's already eleven." She felt a surge of loneliness. She wanted to hold him, but he was leaving—again.

"Diana, what is it? Is it your head?" he asked, quickly sitting down next to her.

"Nothing. I just feel disappointed, that's all."

He wiped her tears with the tips of his fingers. "You had a good ride today. You shouldn't be disappointed."

"Riding isn't everything. In fact, sometimes, these days, I think it's nothing." She stopped crying but her lower lip trembled. Her dark eyes looked into his for a half-second. He lowered his head and stilled her lip with a kiss. His lips traveled across her cheeks, kissing away the remaining tears. He stroked her face with his fingers. "I must go." He smiled sadly.

"Stay with me—please."

"I can't. You should rest." Steve pulled on his windbreaker. "I'll drop by tomorrow to take care of the horse."

"Why are you so nice to me?" Diana asked softly. He didn't answer, but kissed the tip of his forefinger, pressed it to the tip of Diana's nose, then walked out the back door.

She watched the old truck drive away. He'd finally kissed her, but why? It seemed almost an apology. Or perhaps pity. But she wished it had been love. She sat back down on the sofa and cried softly.

Steve walked into his room, turned on the light, and sat down on the bed. Driving home, he felt alive for the first time in months, not an empty shell going through the motions of life. Diana was beautiful and she'd wanted him to make love to her. As he kissed her lips and felt her fresh skin, his whole body had shivered. But he couldn't stay, despite his heart urging him that he belonged there.

He washed and took off his clothes, turned out the light, and lay facedown on the bed. He recalled his kiss with Diana and he moved slowly up and down with love and imagined closeness. It had been such a long time. Not since the night before he sent Carmen and María to the hospital. Then Steve lay still, his penis now soft between his legs. As he closed his eyes, tears ran down his cheeks and onto the cold sheets. But there was no one to kiss them away.

# Newport

For the remaining spring months Steve reestablished a friendly but businesslike attitude toward Diana. He showed her how to locate any potential spasms on the horse by pressing her fingers along Navarro's vertebrae. He taught her to massage tightened spots by taking the skin between her forefinger and thumb and working it through. He insisted that she put a quarter blanket under the saddle and over the stallion's loins so his muscles wouldn't contract during exercise in the crisp New England air.

But all the body work and attention went to the horse. There were no more kisses; Steve saw to that. Even were Diana's lovely lower lip to tremble and tears fall, he wouldn't be caught again. It had been a harsh winter: December snow not melting until mid-March. The barn pump cracked, compelling Diana several times a day to carry heavy buckets from her house that inevitably sloshed on her pants. But then spring arrived from the south all at once. Dying arms of snow uncovered bright grass, daffodils and tulips quickly succeeded purple and yellow crocuses. Diana had worked hard but still harbored serious doubts about Navarro's career as a jumper. After all, he hadn't cleared anything of particular height. Between the frozen ground and the horse's injury, Steve wouldn't have it. But after the earth softened under the longer-lingering sun, he put Diana and Navarro over some sizable fences—not huge, about three-six. The horse jumped efficiently and with confidence. The jumps were combined with long hacks and occasional hops over fallen logs, and thus the white stallion progressed to a "serious" level.

The first week in May, a truckload of brand-new, expertly crafted show-quality jumps rumbled up Diana's driveway. She ran up to the sunburned teenager who'd begun unloading. "I think you've got the wrong place," she said, her hand over her eyes as a visor in the strong light.

The young man consulted a clipboard. "This isn't the Winston place?"

"Yes, it is," she replied in a surprised tone.

"Well, I've got the right place, then. Unless there are two Winstons." Without waiting for a response, the boy continued to take down exquisite jumps: coops, rolltops, targets, gates, and wing standards, all painted blue and white—the Winston farm colors.

"Who ordered these?" A quick survey of what already stood on the ground and the remainder in the truck told Diana that at least three thousand dollars' worth scattered itself in front of her.

"Ma'am, I just deliver—and they don't get delivered until they're paid for. So they've been ordered *and* paid for."

"Can you tell me who paid for them?"

"Don't know. Say, d'you suppose you'd have a glass of water or a garden hose?"

As she walked from the kitchen with water, Steve's pickup rolled in. She handed the glass to the young man and took another look at the beautiful assortment of jumps, then walked over before Steve had cut his engine.

"Do you know something about this?" she asked with an exasperated smile.

"I see you've got new jumps. Nice selection." He got out and began examining the striped poles. "May I see the invoice?" he asked the boy.

"Sure." He took a crumpled yellow paper from his dirty denims and handed it to Steve.

"Where's the wishing well?"

"I'm gonna drop that off next week. Sam got a little bogged down. No delivery charge, of course."

"Okay," replied Steve. He turned to Diana. "You like them?"

"Steve, you did this. Why? There's a few thousand dollars here. I can't pay for this."

"Already paid for." The boy looked up, as if to underscore that he'd reported that before, and couldn't she get the point?

"I can't pay you back," replied Diana, the pain of debt apparent in her tone. "You know I can't."

"I don't expect to be paid. In fact, I expect not to be."

"Steve, I can't accept this. They've got to go back."

"Impossible—no return on custom-painted jumps. See, blue and white. Pretty, don't you think?"

"I'll have to pay you."

"Absolutely not. These are a gift."

"I'll consider it a loan. Give me that invoice, please." But as Diana reached for the paper, Steve stuffed it in his pocket.

"Friends should never be bankers." He smiled. "Come on, help me set up the jumps in your field."

"I don't know, Steve." Her voice was hesitant and her uncomprehending hurt look made him regret the comment.

"All right, this is the only deal I'll make. When you win the Newport Jumping Derby, you pay me back. Total prize money this year is sixty-five thousand."

"That's a long way off," she protested.

"August 25."

"This August? Do you think in four months that Navarro, much less I, could possibly enter that obstacle course with any hope of placing, much less winning?" Diana's voice carried disbelief shot through with hope and excitement. The Newport International Jumping Derby, modeled on European derbies, presented America's fine version of such famous ones as Great Britain's

Hickstead. The course ran a mile-plus, with twenty-eight obstacles, a number of them "fixed"—meaning if a horse struck one, chances were good that horse and rider would strike the ground, while the obstacle remained firmly rooted and unmoved. In ten years of Newport Jumping Derby history, only twenty-six horses had managed to jump the course clean. The name of one jump, Pulverman's Grob, advertised the dubious distinction of being so difficult that it had killed its inventor. But the year before, Steve had been there and observed how large-lunged thoroughbreds had an easier time completing the course. Their warmblood counterparts huffed and puffed, frequently incurring time penalties. Navarro had an enormous chest and barrel, indicating great air capacity. With a winter of long hacking behind him, he had aerobic ability to finish under the clock.

"I don't think you can do it," replied Steve. "I know you can."

Diana placed a hand on Steve's arm. "But Newport, Steve. That's a Grand Prix and about the most difficult. The course is the longest in the country, and the jumps— Vichy Double Banks, double ditches, and the Grob! I know there's a thrill in facing death, but why rush to the front door when it knocks?" She felt herself breathless at the prospect. Diana's fearful words gave him pause. She hadn't jumped anything challenging since the East Hampton Classic, so now any proposed scheme might loom especially big. She could do it, he knew that—but she had to know it. And that explained why he had paid thirty-five hundred dollars for the jumps. Talent, even great ability, without confidence meant trouble. He spoke softly but convincingly. "Didn't you spend all that time hacking and repeating jumping grids for a reason?"

"But, Steve, those were *low* jumps."

"So? Navarro has a rear on him like a set of rocket boosters, and a pair of bellows for lungs. He'll make the Derby look like a Sunday-afternoon frolic. What we needed to do we've done. You've done. His leg, all his legs, are strong. All that's left is to school a bit over these—not much." He nodded toward the jumps.

"Ma'am, if you could sign here," interrupted the boy. Diana shook her head with disbelief as she scribbled her name on the receipt. "Thank you." He left without her noticing.

As the empty truck drove to the main road, Diana looked at Steve, regarding the rolltop with an amused, self-satisfied smile. She walked up and kissed him on the cheek. Startled, he blushed. "And thank you, Steve. You're the most wonderful friend I think I've ever known, but I can't help wondering—and worrying—where our friendship's going to take me." She looked at him intently.

"Funny, I feel the same way about you," he said lightly.

"Well, why don't we have a beer together after we get all these jumps into the field."

Steve stayed for a beer—just one—and then his vehicle made its way into the flow of late-afternoon traffic.

On Friday, August 23, Steve and Diana drove Navarro in a rusty, beat-up borrowed trailer down Glen Road and onto Glen Farm, grounds for the Newport Jumping Derby. Diana gazed at what appeared to be an open-air village, activity everywhere—red-coated riders on long-limbed jumpers, spectators walking with animated excitement and craning their necks to glimpse an Olympic rider or horse. The Newport flag—a pineapple, symbol of a sailor's return and hospitable welcome—fluttered atop a huge green-and-white striped tent. Though not visible, the sea's unmistakable harbingers—flat, sandy fields, pines, and salt air—signaled its proximity. The Mercedes International, the one Derby event in which they entered Navarro, took place Sunday, but the horse needed to adapt himself to his new environment before competing. A stallion, he was entitled to a permanent box stall in the main barn. Geldings and mares would find themselves in temporary quarters—wooden slat stabling erected on the polo field and roofed by a large green-and-white tent.

Stallions might reduce that arrangement to kindling if given half a chance.

Anyone who was anybody in the horse world came: Katie Prudent, Michael Matz, Joe Fargis, Conrad Homfeld, Jack O'Dell, Hiro Tomizawa, Bill Steinkraus. Diana never had seen so many heavy hitters at the same event. She and Steve bought sodas and sat down at a table next to Paul Newman and Joanne Woodward. Diana quickly consulted her program. The Newman's daughter Clea would ride in the Pin Oak Farm Junior Jumpers. Diana had seen her in the Garden two years before. What pleased her most about this excellent rider was that Clea always patted her horse after a round.

Diana soon found out that the Newport Derby included more than other large horse shows—it meant a major social event, which, given the people competing and viewing, expanded into a sort of week-long controlled free-for-all. Impromptu seductions could be fun. "The Avenue Crowd"—those inhabitants of Bellevue Avenue—made it such. They passed the summer in architectural monstrosities called "cottages" ("mansions" by plebeian definition), the remnants of Newport's golden era—before the airplane came to whisk the rich and the not-so-rich through time zones to their newest watering holes. And if the respected denizens, ranging from Auchincloss to Pell, turned out, everyone else turned out too—from yuppies inhabiting harbor condos to millionaires stepping off launches lowered from their private yachts.

Horse shows draw heavy concession business, but in addition to the usual Miller's and Dover Saddlery vans, Packard trailers, equine portrait painters, private jewelers, and custom photographers, Mercedes displayed its newest S type with a low-key representative standing by in gold-buttoned blazer and gray slacks. Corporate entertaining at sports events, whether Cadillac, Michelob, Insilco, Volvo, or Paine Webber, meant conversations with important clients, a little vacation, and contact with new prospects in a relaxed atmosphere. All those empty seats at sold-out tournaments? Companies simply purchased whole blocks or series of rows for their people. If not everyone showed up, it might not look the best on TV, but the tournament directors got their money and everyone felt well-served—plenty in the coffers for invitations and prize money to multiply and flow next year. Here at Newport, Piaget and Rolex trucked in their respective booths. Horse shows, notorious for dried hamburgers and burnt hot dogs, now turned to clam chowder, quahogs, lobster salad, and fruit cups in clear tumblers.

Jim Williams ran into Diana moments after he arrived. She stood out in crowds. "Hello, Jim. How are you?" She responded flatly to his appearance and hid her shock in the bare salutation, struggling to organize her emotions. So single-minded had her training with Navarro become that somehow the thought that she'd likely run into Jim at Newport had escaped her. But old feelings—complicated feelings—quickly resurfaced.

"Hello, Diana, Steve. Still keeper of the keys at Hampstead?" Steve stood up and clapped Jim on the back.

"Oh, they don't have any keys to entrust to anyone," Steve replied in a self-deprecating but critical tone. "How are you? You've lost a little weight—haven't you been well? Come, sit down." Jim glanced at Diana for advance approval. She nodded. But Steve was right. Though deeply tanned, Jim looked painfully thin and his eyes sunken.

"I'm just fine, Steve—at least now. I'm just getting over . . . well, a bout of pneumonia. Took a lot out of me. That accounts for the weight loss, I guess." Though Steve wore sunglasses, Diana sensed the intensity with which he was looking at Jim.

"What brings you both down here?" Jim asked. Neither Diana nor Steve responded. "What's going on? Steve, I know you've never been talkative, but—"

"I'm showing a horse in the Derby on Sunday," Diana cut in hastily.

"Why, Diana, that's wonderful. Whose horse?" he asked excitedly. He doubted she would be able to ride for anyone again—at least not on the East Coast. Once more, Diana and Steve didn't reply right away.

"Diana's horse," Steve said matter-of-factly. The studied, reticent tone conveyed anything but a cut-and-dried situation.

"You've got a horse, Diana? Who is he?"

"Navarro." She watched his drawn face closely for the first sign of disapproval.

"Navarro?" Jim asked, obviously scrolling through all the Grand Prix jumpers he had filed in his head. "Sounds familiar, but I don't think I've seen him compete."

"You haven't. He did dressage. He was at Hampstead— last stall on the main aisle—remember?" Diana asked, beginning to think the idea of her going into the ring with Olympic horses and riders totally mad. If it weren't suicidal to her reputation, it was just suicidal.

"I remember him now. That big Andalusian. He's a jumper?" he inquired gingerly.

"He is now," Steve said, his lips half-smiling at Jim's amazement.

"You're kidding. He can jump?"

"Like a gazelle," Steve said proudly.

"I've definitely been off the circuit too long. What have you competed him in?"

"This is his first Grand Prix."

This is his first Grand Prix, repeated Jim to himself. He took as deep a breath as he could manage. "Well, Diana, you sure picked a hell of way to kick off his career. I hope he doesn't get shell shock when he eyeballs the course."

"Who are you riding?" Diana asked, eager to get off the subject of Navarro. Clearly Jim thought that she and Steve were off their rockers. Anyone with knowledge about this game would. Who in their right mind would subject a basically green jumper to a mile-long course of twenty-eight efforts as his first competitive experience?

"Me? Nobody. I'm still recovering. I'd hoped to ride Rio, but I wasn't well enough, so Jack O'Dell got Katie Prudent to take him." Jim coughed into his fist.

"Excuse me," Steve said, getting up. "I must make a call. I'll be right back."

"A call? Steve!" exclaimed Diana. She didn't want to be left alone with Jim. Things were awkward enough.

Steve nodded. "Jim, would you stay with Diana until I return?" Then he ran off before she could protest again.

"Always the gentleman," Jim apologized.

"It's true. Steve can be quaint at times."

"Diana, how *are* you?" Jim asked intently.

"I'm fine, Jim. Really. I suppose you heard I got sacked at Hampstead. The why, the wherefore, all the gory details." She suddenly felt a need to talk about that terrible day. At least he would believe her.

"I did, but I don't believe any of it."

"Why not? Everyone else does. Even the honest ones." Diana's soda can buckled beneath the pressure of her tense fingers.

"Because I know you," he said softly.

"Yes," she commented, nodding her head with bitter-sweet sarcasm. "We've known each other."

"Diana, I do know you. I didn't apologize, but let me do it now. I should've told you I'm gay. It was unfair. And the way you found out—I felt so ashamed." Jim bit his lower lip. "Not ashamed I'm gay—but that I wasn't honest. I'm so sorry I hurt your feelings."

"Why didn't you?" Diana asked, peering at him. "Why didn't you tell me?"

"I was afraid you wouldn't let me get close to you," he admitted softly.

"You confused me so much. I felt so rejected." Tears from the old hurt brimmed up in her eyes. Her sunglasses hid them behind their large aviator lenses. Somehow she hadn't taken them off.

"You were confusing for me too."

"Jim, I'd never been close to anyone who was gay. I didn't know I could fall in love with someone who was."

"And I didn't know I could fall in love with someone who wasn't." They laughed gently over their mutual discovery. "Anyway, do you accept my apology?" He took Diana's hand in his.

"Yes, if you accept mine."

"Deal." He looked out across the waves of people sitting at tables, laughing and scanning about with their bright eyes. He summoned the courage to reestablish his friendship. "Are you going to the ball at Beechwood? I hear . . . well, I hear anything goes there."

"The competitors' thing in the old Astor mansion?" Diana recalled having read something about a social event.

"Yes, it's tonight. Come with me. We could go to dinner first on Bannister's Wharf—the Black Pearl. You'd love it, and so would I. I haven't seen you in such a long time."

"I can't afford that party," protested Diana. Tickets cost fifty dollars each.

"I have an extra. And the Black Pearl's my treat. Newport's too good to waste on the rich."

"I don't have a dress."

"Buy one this afternoon," Jim countered.

The idea of going to a ball in one of the mansions excited her now that it seemed possible. Mrs. Astor had been dominant lioness of nineteenth-century Newport. And Diana would love to dress up for a change. Didn't she deserve it after all that farmwork and mucking? She and Steve had been frugal—staying at the local Neptune Motel amid a spate of Dunkin' Donuts, Burger Kings, and McDonald's on the strip of East Main Road near Four Corners. An evening of fun and extravagance might be the only reward for the months of trial, so why not?

"Jim, I'd love to. What's the best women's clothing store around?" she asked, eager at the prospect of putting her hair up and wearing shadow and blush again.

"I'm not really sure about the best, but why don't you try Talbot's or the Narragansett? There're also some local and lovely older places near them."

"Thanks, I will." She looked up to see Steve walking across the grass, his hands pocketed in a windbreaker.

"A strangely wonderful kind of guy," Jim commented as Steve caught sight of them and smiled.

"You noticed too?" Then Diana reflected that Jim, of all people, wouldn't miss the enigma that was Steve.

"I also noticed he's in love with you." But before Diana could react, Steve reached the table. "Make your call?" Jim asked. He looked over at Diana, relishing her mute frustration.

"Yes, I did."

"Steve, Jim has asked me to go with him to the party at the mansion. Is that all right with you?" Diana felt awkward and annoyed. Awkward if Steve was indeed in love with her, and annoyed that she somehow felt she must clear her comings and goings with him.

Jim interjected, "I have transportation. I'll bring Diana back to the motel you're staying at unless . . ." Now he felt awkward as well. He wasn't sure what Steve's relationship with Diana was, exactly, but he'd heard rumors.

"No, no. I think that would work out fine. I really don't care for that sort of scene. What I'd like best to do is drive up to Fall River and get some flannel shirts at one of the mill outlets. Diana, would you mind?" Steve asked.

"Not if that's what you really want to do." Fall River, indeed. Steve had politely let her off the hook.

"I do. I'm in desperate need of shirts. Look!" He slid off his jacket and held up a dilapidated sleeve, split down the elbow. The collar flapped mercilessly in the breeze, little threads unraveling.

"Goodness, Steve, it's a wonder it stays on your back. Why wear it at all?"

"Penance, I guess." Diana and Jim laughed artificially. They both felt some distant truth in the reason he gave.

After a sandwich and Coke at Yesterday's, Jim returned to his room at the Sheraton Islander. He undressed and glanced at his Rolex: four o'clock—enough time for a shower and nap. Excited at the prospect of a

Newport evening with Diana (it would remind him of better days), he needed to rest first. As he walked toward the bathroom, his own image, caught in the large hotel mirror, arrested him. At home he knew where the mirrors hung and how to avoid them. Now the unanticipated glass confronted him with a full-length truth he couldn't bear. Every rib in his body showed, his collarbone clearly protruding from the transparent flesh. No muscle. He'd tried so hard to put on weight, but despite a calorie-packed diet, the scale dipped lower. Petty ailments plagued him—sore throats, flu, and a low-grade fever that hung around for weeks. Even in that condition he rode, rationalizing the weight loss as lack of exercise—his muscles had atrophied, and muscles weighed more than fat. That's what he told the doctor at Briggs and DePrete the rainy night he couldn't breathe. A lab technician scurried in. Blood drawn by latex-covered hands revealed a cell ratio totally out of whack. An infectious-disease specialist was summoned. More tests—Elisa, then Western Blot. Jim's immune system was collapsing.

Jim met Diana outside the motel office. Though he was only ten minutes late, and that due to bad traffic, she'd become the object of unending impolite stares from men checking in or going to conference rooms, and by now felt very uncomfortable.

"Sorry I'm late, Diana. Something going on at the Naval Base—a class graduating from Officer Candidate School or something. I got caught in a terrible snarl."

"You're just lucky I didn't get whisked off by a sales-man. Or someone bankrolling an America's Cup bid."

Jim laughed. This was his old friend Diana back—and in fine critical form. His eyes traveled up and down her floor-length black silk dress. Elegant and classic, it showed off her tanned slender arms, shoulders, and cleavage to full advantage, while emphasizing her slimness. "How could one blame anyone for whisking you off? You're beautiful."

He escorted her out to the familiar red Porsche.

As she slipped into the soft leather seat, she felt safe, secure, and happy. "I've missed this car."

"It's missed you." Jim gently patted her arm. "Look, we've plenty of time. Have you ever been along Ten Mile Drive?"

"No, I've never been to Newport."

"How about it, then? For a tourist it's *de rigueur*."

"I'd love to." Diana arranged the folds of her dress to ensure it would remain as crease-free as possible in the cockpit of the car. Music started.

"*Concierto de Aranjuez*," she commented. "I love it—so melancholy, but in the end, so . . . life-affirming."

"Anyway, this is in honor of you and your Andalusian—" Jim fussed with the fan adjustment—"Navarro."

Diana looked at the estates as they drove down Bellevue. The mansions, or what she could glimpse of them, loomed like great mortuarial slabs.

"This is a graveyard of grand monstrosities," commented Jim. The elms parted and he turned onto Beach Road and past Hammersmith Farm, now sold to an organization and unfortunately renamed Camelot as a reminder of halcyon politics in the early sixties.

"The Kennedy wedding reception was held there, and the ceremony at St. Mary's, just down the hill from the Tennis Hall of Fame." Diana turned her neck to get a better glimpse.

"Jacqueline Kennedy spent summers growing up there, too. She still keeps a small string of fine hunters at her place in Peapack, New Jersey. In the winter she ships them to the Mellon estate in Virginia. The Mellons won't let any horses but hers come on the property. So when she contracts a van, it must make a special delivery and Jackie pays for all the extra van stalls. Lucky horses."

"How do you know all this—you have a paparazzo for a friend?" Diana was surprised at Jim's celebrity info.

"Horse world's a small world."

Diana's tone conveyed resignation but also simmering anger. "Like some of the people in it."

"So small, in fact, everyone's wondering about this horse you've got. I'm wondering a bit too."

She thought then she shouldn't be going to this thing at Beechwood. She just wanted to relax and not think about the Derby, and didn't want to talk to anybody about Navarro. He's a long shot—why do people even bother, why do they care? She looked out the window at the spectacular, unending panorama of ocean and sky. Sunset colors muted themselves on the shimmering Atlantic palette. She rolled down the window, put her head out, and inhaled the clean salty air, watching as wave after wave rolled in and sprayed over black rocks. She felt a hand on her arm and so pulled her head in.

"Diana, I don't want you to catch cold. It's brisk this evening."

"I never get sick."

"You're very lucky," he said softly, more to himself than her.

"What's that island off in the distance—there, to the right?"

Jim took his eyes off the road for a moment, but failed to see anything in the blue haze. "I can't look now. Probably Block Island. You know, a few years ago the residents wanted to secede from Rhode Island because the state intended to permit mopeds on the ferry."

"Long live those islanders. And what happened?" Diana disliked the cheap, noisy commercialization of New England.

"They won," Jim said happily.

"Good for them. Living on an island might be nice: I prefer the ocean to the mountains. My family used to summer at Eastham on the Cape. But so much is built up now."

"Too bad. Think how relaxing and conducive to thought waves rolling in on the sand are, especially if you're alone."

" 'Out of the cradle endlessly rocking,' " Diana recited.

"Walt Whitman—exactly." But he grew suddenly silent and turned off Ocean Drive, heading back into town and toward the bustling and touristed wharf area, his face grim. He knew the poem all too well.

"This is Bannister's Wharf," Jim said, and took Diana gently by the arm, directing her across the courtyard toward an undistinguished building. It struck her as no more than an elongated shack. This area, one of the most congested in Newport during the summer months, attracted sailboats as well as cars and pedestrians. Many craft moored right there. Dress at the individual cocktail parties corresponded roughly to the different decks. Dinner dress on the new Sabre 34, Top-Siders and T-shirts (Ralph Lauren, of course) on the J-9s. The wharf offered places to dine, shop, see, and be seen. Fashion varied— from Swedish sailing gear to Paris originals—the only common denominator being expense. The atmosphere warmed with festivity, tanned faces with a final thin layer of sunburn, the real summer solstice, when pleasure was in full swing. Marine businesses mixed happily with import shops and restaurants. Cinzano umbrellas dotted the gravel patio of tables at the edge of the wharf. Salt air combined with rich cooking smells and the muted clink of glasses and ice at an outside bar. "Welcome to sailing center USA," Jim said.

She allowed his arm to guide her through the throngs and toward the undistinguished black building that housed the famous restaurant.

"So, how do you like downtown?" he asked, holding open the big wooden black door for Diana.

"I love it." Seeing all this happy activity, Diana realized for the first time that for most of her life fun had eluded her. It would be some time before she understood that people with her drive and ambition had to arrange to have fun.

"This way, please." The hostess motioned for them to follow her down a narrow hall to the right.

"I thought we were going to eat in that nice tavern area," said Diana. The bar and black-walled soup-and-sandwich area at first appeared to be the only room, but past the very visible kitchen an elegant room overlooked the harbor, its black and green interior reminiscent of an English men's club, crystal and white on starched tablecloths, and waiters attired in modified tuxedos.

"In there." Jim nodded ahead as they went past restrooms with "Buoys" and "Gulls" painted under miniature nautical representations. "Dressed like that, you deserve more than a burger on Syrian bread."

"This is lovely," commented Diana as the waiter held out her chair.

"I always make a point of coming here when I'm in town."

"May I get you a drink?" offered the waiter, one of the inexhaustible supply of college students who permitted themselves to be trained in the continental manner of service—for comparatively high pay. But the best fringe benefit of the package included mornings and early afternoons at Easton's Beach.

"Gin and tonic, please," Diana ordered with a sigh of relaxation.

"Perrier and cranberry juice." Jim smiled, hoping he wouldn't be asked about his abstinence.

Over pompano and salads, they caught up with the past year. Based in Manhattan, Jim traveled to farms in Westchester County, giving clinics as well as judging various A-rated shows. His black mare Calliope developed arthritic spurs in her hocks, so he retired her. Jim felt quite excited, however, because he'd just gotten her in foal to Abdullah, the gray Trakehner stallion Conrad Homfeld rode with marked success.

Lighthearted conversation had all been spent over the entrée. By dessert their talk halted in a series of awkward stops and starts. Diana put a fork of Sacher torte to her mouth, then took it away. "I suppose you're wondering about Steve?" Her low voice contained an element of embarrassment.

"Oh, I'm always wondering about Steve. He's interesting to wonder about, isn't he?" Jim dodged the question and bought more time by putting a sliver of cheesecake in his mouth.

"You know what I mean."

Seeing no escape, he swallowed and wiped the crumbs from his lips. "You mean about Steve and you?"

"Yes, well, what have you heard?" Diana put her fork down next to her coffee cup.

"The kind of thing you'd expect to hear in the horse world." Jim halfheartedly tried to avoid getting any deeper in the discussion, but knew she would persist.

"And what would that be?" Diana asked.

"They say you and Steve are having an affair." Jim hoped he'd be able to get away with just that, or less. He was wrong.

"What else?" Diana asked, not letting go.

"Why do you care? It's not worth paying attention to any of this, for God's sake." Jim became exasperated.

"What else?" Diana repeated firmly. "Jim, tell me, please." She felt a wave of dread.

"That he wormed his way into your affections by giving you some worthless stallion."

"I see," Diana replied. "I suppose in my naiveté I was tricked by this Mexican lothario into believing the horse had possibilities."

Jim nodded. "There never are any secrets in this business. Peripatetic vets and farriers see to that. And others, lots of others."

"For practically a whole year Steve's the only person in the horse world I've had anything to do with. I didn't even tell the farrier or vet that Navarro belongs to me." Diana split her dark rich cake in half with a fork.

"Well, Hampstead people knew Steve bought the horse from Sloan, and I'm sure word traveled back that the animal boarded with you. You supplied the blanks they filled in—as always, in the most malicious manner possible. What I heard was from George Reynolds—know him?" Diana shook her head. Another unknown name— talking about *her*. "See? And he's based in Virginia. God knows where he heard it from. Mayve Europe, or Arizona."

"These people simply don't have enough to do. I'm going to find out who's—"

"Diana, forget it. Don't waste your time and energy on them. Just tell yourself you're nobody if there *aren't* any false rumors about yourself. Your job is to prepare yourself mentally for Sunday." The waiter poured more coffee from a silver pot.

"But I'm so angry I—"

"Don't be. Life's too short. Leave it alone and let the trivial ones fall by the wayside as you gallop through. People who sling mud end up living in it."

"I know you're right, but it's so hard," she protested, shaking her head as she measured out cream. "Jim, I'm not having an affair with Steve." She wondered briefly what had motivated her blunt denial. Anger at the false accusations, old feelings for Jim, unrequited feelings for Steve—maybe all three.

He nodded, but wouldn't have been surprised if she had told him the reverse. Yet, at the same time, he felt relieved. He'd sensed a complexity about Steve, and right now Diana needed simplicity.

"So tell me about this Navarro and what the two of you, or rather, the three of you, have been up to. We can arrive at Beechwood fashionably late, or later." Over more coffee and a little Dewar's on the rocks, which Jim skipped, Diana told him about her winter of discontent, the hacking, the grid work, and the uncertainty. She went into detail about the training, and sounded out Jim's opinion on every aspect, including jumping with hands behind. "Sounds like he's got an incredible background in classic dressage and jumping." Her report at once impressed and puzzled Jim. A stablehand with such sophisticated equestrian education didn't just pick it up. He'd done it himself.

"Classic?" queried Diana.

"Classical riding emphasizes lightness and advances an ideal that the horse alone should be seen by the spectator. That is, the rider appears as if he has little to do with what the horse does. The aids should be virtually invisible, or completely."

"Navarro does listen—too well, sometimes." Diana smiled as she recalled how the horse surged forward at the touch of her leg.

Diana and Jim entered the Beechwood mansion and walked into warm light, music, and an animated sea of people. Everywhere hung a feeling of abandon, where five minutes might bring interest, fifteen an excited stirring, and two hours an affair. "All these horse people in tuxes and gowns," commented Jim. "They look like they've never touched a currycomb in their lives."

"Some haven't," Diana quipped. He turned at that moment to see her gazing at Courtney Snyder, dressed in a full-length chintz gown. Cut low, it revealed the fullness of her breasts and then nipped in severely at the waist. But rather than emphasize her narrow middle, which appeared cinched in the expanse of material that flared about her hips, it all made her rear seem on the large side.

"She doesn't have a wasp waist," Diana stated, her nose wrinkling in distaste. "But she's got a tail like one."

"Well, she *is* a Wasp," joked Jim. "And she's spotted us and is flying over."

Courtney swept in front of Diana without a word, grabbed Jim's arm, and kissed his cheek. "Jim Williams, it's been just too long. Where've you been keeping yourself? You didn't *have* to lose weight, you know," Courtney cooed, her voice pitched more for Diana's ear than his.

"New York." His tone, though courteous, conveyed disinterest. He might have been giving an address to United Parcel.

"New York, that's right. I'd heard you'd been ill. Nothing serious, I hope." She shot a heavy-lidded glance at Diana, designed to evaluate the reaction there.

"Just a cold."

"You must stay away from those naughty night spots

of yours." Diana looked hard at Courtney, trying to determine whether there was a homosexual reference there. "And then you've got those awful blowy Hudson and East rivers." Courtney nattered on in her artificial-sugar tones. No, Diana thought to herself, she doesn't know.

"And who's this girl—why, Diana? Is this Diana Winston? The absent presence finally presents itself."

Diana said nothing, letting her direct gaze convey that she considered this all so much crap. "Diana, you look surprisingly well. I'm sorry about the misunderstanding at Hampstead. But I hear you're starting your own *little* riding establishment. Do you rent out by the hour? I mean horses. And are there hayrides?"

"That's not true, Courtney. I'm not starting a stable," corrected Diana, looking over at Jim.

"I heard that Andalusian Steve gave you was intended as a foundation horse for your new enterprise."

So that's what this was all about, Diana thought to herself. She's prodding me. She felt Jim's hand press her fingers. "Jim, let's go check out the hors d'oeuvres." Eyeing Courtney's rear end, she couldn't resist a parting shot. "The spread looks better on the table than it does on some of the guests." Her voice matched her steady and collected demeanor. She took Jim by the arm and led him away.

"Three cheers for you, Diana!" Jim was pleased with her mature restraint.

"I wanted to knock her flat."

"But you didn't. And you didn't look like you did, so that's your victory. I'm sure all she wanted was a rise from you. Time's too valuable to oblige that sort." His voice, again suddenly soft, troubled Diana, but someone preempted her before she could ask if anything was wrong.

"Hey, Diana, tell us about the mystery horse you're riding." Diana and Jim turned to see Billy Jones approaching with a dark-complexioned young man she didn't recognize. Billy rode for Sand Dollar Farm in Tampa and, at the moment, was quite drunk. With his blond good looks and self-assured manner, Billy never lacked female companions. But the tension of competition had driven him to take hold of a bottle instead. He reeled forward and clasped Jim's hand.

"Diana, how are you doing? I'd like you to meet a friend of mine—Anthony Russo. He has seen the light and has left the West Coast to join us at Sand Dollar, where dollars are as common as sand."

"Hello, Diana. You're a new face on the circuit, aren't you?" He addressed Diana's perfect breasts after a brief glance at her face.

"You don't seem very interested in new faces, Mr. Russo," Diana countered, bringing him up short.

Billy, vaguely sensing delightful trouble, cut in. "I heard about your mount, Diana—very romantic, a *mystery* horse. I thought the Black Stallion was the last of those. Where'd you come up with him?" He lurched forward, cupping his ear with his hand, and waited for Diana's reply.

"You really don't need to know, Billy," Jim rescued her. "Besides, you wouldn't remember tomorrow if we told you," he said, shoring up the tipsy young man with his arm.

"Aw, none of that now, *Mister* Williams. I could tell lots of people about it tonight before I forgot." Billy slipped away from Jim's arm. "You may play for both teams, but I don't." Tony snorted and looked at Diana as if he'd discovered she was, in fact, unescorted that evening.

"Have you visited any of the mansions since you've been down?" Tony asked. He'd been on a bus tour that morning but wouldn't mind going again, even with the blue-haired "Golden Agers," if he could get Diana in the next seat.

"No, only got in this afternoon."

"You really should, y'know. I went to Belcourt, a place owned by one of those Perrys."

"Oh, that's right. Oliver Hazard Perry, direct descendant of Commodore Perry, who opened Japan in the nineteenth century." In her reading, Diana had found the history of the U.S.-Asian relations fascinating.

"Jeeesus." The man seemed stunned, then recovered a bit. "I didn't know you'd been to college, Diana."

Billy put an unsteady arm around Diana's waist. "Diana and I haven't been to college, but that doesn't mean we don't know the world. We do know the world, don't we, Diana?" He pulled her close and she felt amused at Mr. Russo's defeat.

"Diana," Jim said, playfully intervening, "I think you should mind your I's and Q's with Tony. Be considerate of your colleague's ability."

"Yeah, Diana, watch your I's and Q's." Billy wagged a disapproving and shaky finger in Diana's face. Suddenly he turned to Jim. "Hey, don't you mean P's and Q's? You meant P's and Q's."

"Right, Billy. Exactly what I meant," replied Jim. Billy was in no shape for anything the least taxing, even in his dry hours.

"Well, anyway, before we got onto this historical stuff, I was going to tell you about this Chinese . . . I mean Japanese guy's barn." Tony Russo tried to regroup. "It's the ground floor of his mansion, in fact. The stalls are humongous, gold nameplates on each one. And as you enter, two of the owner's favorite horses have the distinction of immortality by being stuffed, tacked in medieval armor, and stationed at the door. The guide told us they weren't bedded in straw or shavings—God, no, but pure linen sheets with the fucking family crest embroidered in gold thread on each one." Tony sounded impressed.

"I'd like to stuff the horse I'm riding tomorrow," commented Billy. "Shit, how do you muck out linen?"

Jim saw an opening to break away. "Here comes Jack O'Dell, Diana. You must meet him." He put his hand gently on the point of Diana's elbow.

"Jesus, Billy!" Tony said anxiously, "it *is* Jack." All eyes turned to the top hunter-jumper trainer in America, and clearly one of the world's best. Dark-haired and handsome, as a young man he had been a successful pianist for a while, but in the end returned to the equestrian scene. At the moment he held the position of consulting director at Sand Dollar. O'Dell practiced enormous dedication and self-discipline. He required nothing less in others. The horse he had scheduled Billy to ride came to O'Dell on consignment to sell, and he'd deal harshly with the young man if he saw him in a condition that would jeopardize the horse's performance and subsequent value.

"Let's hit it," Billy said, his voice panicky. "Emergency evacuation." He and Tony slipped out of the room.

"Jim, so nice to see you!" O'Dell stretched his hand to shake. He was accompanied by a striking man, tall, dark brown hair, a ruggedly handsome face softened by deep blue eyes, and immaculately dressed in a stunning raw-silk dinner jacket. Diana noted O'Dell wore a crimson silk bow tie. He was known for careful dress, and friends teased him unmercifully for the one time he'd been caught chewing gum by an ABC camera filming the 1984 Olympics. A stickler for appearance, he wanted his students to shape up.

"Jack!" Jim clapped O'Dell on the back of his shoulder. "Let me introduce you to a good friend, Diana Winston. Diana, Jack."

"Mr. O'Dell, yes, how well I know," replied Diana, thrilled to meet the man who'd prepared so many horses and riders for national and international victories.

"I know this young lady. I saw you win the hunter championship on Long Island a year ago." He shook Diana's hand firmly. "Stylish ride. Wish I had a video to show some of my cowboys."

"Thank you," Diana beamed. Her evening was made. It never occurred to her how much the top jumper people concerned themselves with hunters.

O'Dell turned to his friend. "Sorry, I've been rude. I'd like you both to meet my friend Dr. Bill Stanford. He's up in Newport on an extended respite from Manhattan hospital work. Bill, this is Jim Williams and, I'm sorry, is it Miss Winston?"

"Diana, Diana Winston. Yes."

Dr. Bill Stanford, chief neurosurgeon at the prestigious Briggs and DePrete Institute, averted his steady gaze and let go his warm, dry handclasp before his attraction to this woman—hardly more than a girl—could be detected. Though he was well-practiced at that maneuver, this striking, magnetic beauty caused him suddenly to feel self-conscious. But for an occasional horse show—his wife hated horses—he hadn't been anywhere socially without her at his side for fifteen years.

"Say, Jim, I do need to talk to you for a moment." Jack O'Dell's voice struck a businesslike tone. "Bill, could you keep Diana company for a minute while I go over Jim's Florida schedule?" Turning Jim away from his friend, Jack didn't wait for a reply.

Bill Stanford laughed. "You people are just as bad as, maybe worse than, doctors."

"You must mean how the professional intrudes on the social?" Diana smiled.

"That's exactly it. All shop talk." This lady's got a mind, he concluded. He noticed her empty glass. "May I get you another?"

"Yes, please. Gin and tonic." As Bill Stanford walked to the bar, Diana's critical eye followed. What a wonderful-looking man—handsome, marvelous dresser, sophisticated rather than pretentious.

The party moved into full swing. Conversation and music vied for dominance, and both rose to brush the Veronese imitations on the ceiling. People felt happy, and some were getting silly. That day's light and the next morning seemed equally far away. Diana leaned against the closed grand piano—a nineteenth-century Steinway—and idly wondered whether it stood there for its exterior or if the insides could still perform.

"So, tell me about this—are you a participant or just a lowly spectator like me?" Dr. Stanford offered her a cocktail napkin from its temporary perch in his top pocket. Diana found his thoughtfulness endearing.

"Spectator, I'm afraid," replied Diana.

"Oh, no," he corrected. "I mean at the Derby."

"The Derby? Yes, I'm a participant." Her voice became quiet.

"You seem almost embarrassed about it."

"Well, I suppose I am, a bit. Are you familiar with show jumping, Dr. Stanford?"

"Bill, please, and I don't know much. I try to get to two or three shows a year."

Diana recalled with a pang how Hugh Simpson had insisted on first names. "Well, I really haven't paid my dues. I should win a few Grand Prix and some European competitions before I dare set my toe here." She addressed this more to herself than to the doctor, who took a thoughtful sip of his brandy. He'd felt somewhat the same when he was tapped chief neurosurgeon at the "young" age of thirty-nine.

"If the equestrian world is anything like the medical, dues need be paid only by the mediocre. Most of the club never accept the excellent. Paying dues becomes a form of apology." Dr. Stanford remembered feeling almost guilty about being first in his class at Harvard Medical School.

"Success is what I want. It's all I want," she stated.

"I'd bet on you if you were a jockey," he said with encouragement.

Diane glanced at his left hand—a wedding band. "Does your wife like horse shows too?" She failed utterly at trying to sound casual.

Dr. Stanford's smile suddenly faded. "My wife? No, sport—of any kind—isn't her thing." He hoped his irony had escaped Diana. "Flowers, she likes arranging flowers," he added hastily.

Diana couldn't tell if Bill's darkened expression resulted from his thinking she'd mentioned his wife as a moral rebuke or if there were problems in their marriage. All she knew was she felt attracted to this man. "I like flowers. My mother had a beautiful garden." Diana immediately thought she sounded juvenile.

"Did she give it up? Gardens are a lot of work." An

outdoor garden—someday, that's what I'll have, Bill thought to himself.

"No, she died last year."

"I'm very sorry."

Diana looked at her glass and nodded in acknowledgment.

"Bill." It was Jack O'Dell. Jim was no longer with him. "Sorry to have been so long, but I'm sure you haven't suffered in Diana's company."

"No, not at all. I've got a vested interest in this Derby now that I've actually met one of the riders."

"Diana, I didn't even know you were entered. Who are you on?" asked O'Dell, his tone a combination of curiosity and politeness.

"A horse called Navarro," she replied. Hell, she thought to herself. Here we go again.

"American-bred?" asked O'Dell, certain it wasn't. He hadn't heard of him on any circuit.

"Spanish. He's an Andalusian. You've never heard of him, believe me. He did dressage."

"And now you've trained him up to be a jumper. Great. There's an Andalusian jumping really well in England. I wish you luck, and I hope you come in second to Comrade." Jack gave Diana a coachlike pat on the shoulder.

"Thank you—very much, Mr. O'Dell." She assumed Jack O'Dell was just being courteous in wishing her luck, but he spoke sincerely.

Jim came suddenly walking up. "Jack, I think you'd better come out back. Your Sunday jockey's just joined Cupid for a pee in Mrs. Astor's marble fountain. Security is trying to get him out, but he's being a little aggressive. Dropped a few of his duds, too."

"Shit. That moron." O'Dell's angry but unsurprised response conveyed that this fitted in perfectly with Billy Jones's track record. Diana and Jim followed him out back. Miffed at himself, Bill Stanford elected to stay behind. How he wished the conversation with Diana hadn't ended on her mother's death and that Jack had stayed away just a little longer. As Bill placed Diana's empty glass on a table, he caught the scent of her perfume—light, flowery, and fresh—and suddenly felt enthralled and heady that his uncomplicated, honest desire was to go to bed with her that instant.

It was quite a sight: Billy Jones standing next to Cupid, neither with a speck of clothing on. Oblivious to the entreaties of Tony Russo and the sterner command of a Pinkerton guard, Billy was awash in his cups. "Cupid's going to help me out this evening," he announced to the ever-increasing number of spectators. "I've just got to get him down from his pedestal." Billy gave the immovable object a tug. "C'mon, you ol' pisser, you." Diana couldn't resist a look at his penis, which swung loosely in front, while the statue's sent a constant clear stream into the pool.

"Billy!" Jack O'Dell's voice thundered across open air like the Old Testament God's. Billy ducked, then looked up for the source. O'Dell turned to Jim. "How are you feeling these days, friend?"

"Good, Jack. Better each day."

"You've got a ride Sunday if you want it."

"Thanks. I'll take it." Diana and Jim left Jack O'Dell to assist Mr. Jones with his soaked wardrobe.

"Are you well enough to ride?" Diana asked Jim as he pulled to the front of the motel.

"Absolutely. Nothing but a few lingering coughs. I'll be fine."

"You sure?" Diana still felt worried. She recalled how she'd continued on a hunt after a fall, unaware of a fractured vertebra.

"Worried about the competition?" he teased.

"Of course not," she replied with a smile. "But I am worried about the competitor."

Jim got out to open the other door. "Please don't. I want to think . . . I *need* to think you're with me because"—he paused and drew a deep breath—"because of our friendship from before. Tonight meant a great deal to me."

"To me too. And our friendship is why we're together now—not because a few pounds have slid off your frame." She touched his shoulder.

Jim tenderly kissed Diana on the cheek. "Thanks. I'm glad I still have you."

"We have each other."

Steve looked at the clock when he heard the door of Diana's room close. Three-thirty. He'd been afraid she'd spend the night with Jim. Of course, she had a perfect right to do as she pleased, but he wasn't worried about her rights or even about his own feelings. He worried about something else.

# The Enchanted Ship

Diana didn't sleep well those last few hours before sunrise. The Beechwood entertainment, coupled with the excitement, not to mention the anxiety of Sunday's Derby, prevented her from slipping back into sleep after the first rays of yellow sun crossed her face. That afternoon she'd walk Navarro around Glen Farm to get him used to his surroundings, then perhaps school him lightly over fences. And if time permitted, she'd like to look at the speed class. The horses would jump some of the obstacles used in Sunday's main event.

She wondered what sort of night Steve had spent and felt guilty about the evening without him. Mill outlet, she thought to herself. Poor Steve. He never had any fun. Well, she'd try to make up for his night alone by getting him a gift—some small measure of appreciation for all he'd done. Perhaps, if he couldn't accept her love directly, he could accept a manifestation of it. The luminous green numerals on the clock radio read 8:28. She groaned in anticipation of afternoon fatigue—a delayed reproach for having less than five hours' sleep.

After a quick cup of coffee at the Howard Johnson's counter, she stepped into the morning air, still cool. At least she wasn't one of those athletes who popped pills to sleep and other pills to wake. Dressed in white shorts and shirt, she felt remarkably relaxed despite her lack of rest. A note from Steve tacked to her door indicated that he was already at Glen Farm taking care of Navarro, but would return in time for early-afternoon lunch if she wanted. If she already had plans, he suggested they meet in the lobby at two and work Navarro over a few rails.

She took a long walk down Broadway and onto Thames Street, spinal cord of Newport's waterfront area. A few pre-yuppie remnants remained: one tattoo parlor, a couple of inexpensive bars with pool tables, and a store that sold uniforms to the large Navy population stationed a mile away. Diana found herself almost yearning for harbor days unprettified by latter-day graduates of the let's-make-everywhere-in-the-U.S.-look-like-everywhere-else-in-the-U.S. School of Design. Nonetheless, she felt her blood quicken when she caught sight of the exclusive row of shops on Bowen's Wharf. She entered the Narragansett's waterfront clothing store, lured by uncluttered and elegant window displays. Chopard watches from Geneva, Cole·Haan shoes, and Louis Vuitton luggage accessorizing a Ralph Lauren Polo collection provided the main bait that week. Inside, she walked over to the neckties, artfully displayed on racks of English pine. Her eye gravitated to the summer silks and pastels—turquoise and rose pinks. I think I'd know how to dress if I were a man, she thought; tastefully conservative with a streak of flair. Yes, she suddenly realized, I'd dress like Bill Stanford. Diana recalled the brief but exciting time she'd spent with the handsome and intelligent New York doctor and wondered—no, hoped—that she'd see him again.

"This is a nice one." Diana turned to see a tanned dark-haired man in his early forties pointing to a turquoise tie with embroidered coral-colored seahorses. His accent was French, his face attractive, almost pretty—features fine and close, cheekbones high. No fat. He dressed in white cotton slacks and shirt, under a meticulously cut brass-buttoned blazer. "And this Italian silk brocade. You don't see much of that in America. Wonderful texture."

"I'm just looking, thank you." Diana had never liked sales assistance, handsome and low-key as it might be, and especially unprefaced by "May I help?"

"Ah, well, so was I. I was just looking." He continued to stare deeply and appreciatively into her eyes, then picked a panama from the mannequin and tried it on. "What do you think? Too rakish, no?"

"You're not a salesman?" she queried, caught off-guard.

"Not here, anyway." He cocked the hat at an angle and glanced into a full-length triple mirror, allowing Diana to think he might work in one of the other shops. "Me, I sell wine. I have business—a few businesses. Know anything about wine?" His tone conveyed that he expected she did not.

"Not really, except that I like German wine generally more than French." Diana sensed that a criticism of American culture lay hidden in his question.

"Ah, German wines," he mused to himself. "They can be very good. Clear and crisp—like the people. I think, perhaps, like you." He had spent a dull and expensive evening gambling and could use something to lift his spirits. He moved in for an early-morning adventure.

"I did come in for a tie."

"For your father, I hope. May I suggest this one?" He pulled out a yellow silk, horrendously dotted with bright red whales spouting green water. "Is this style what you call 'Le Prep'?" Diana tried to stifle a laugh but failed.

"The tie is for a friend with good taste."

The Frenchman, undaunted by evidence of a possible contender, went on. In fact, it made the game more sporting. "Ah, lucky him. I can see he has taste. Alas for me, so do I." He sat down in a chair, assuming a posture of dramatic rejection. Diana ignored the languishing Frenchman, her eyes continuing to inventory the variety of material displayed in front of her. "If he's boring, you could get him this." The man reached up, arced his thin tan wrist in the air, and pointed to a green silk with little red points.

"He's not boring and I'm going to get him *this* if you don't mind." She pulled out a blue silk with discreet dark red anchors and walked to the counter, where a young salesman wrapped it in tissue before putting it in a white-

and-blue-beribboned box. As she stepped out onto the cobblestones, she still found herself accompanied.

"My name is Philippe DuChamps and I'm a stranger in your Newport." (He said New*port*.) "I think you should take pity on a foreigner and help me find a good place to breakfast. If you are truly nice, join me to see that I order the traditional things—you know, pancakes, grits, porridge. No, not porridge, that's Scotland." Diana couldn't help but feel engaged by this little scene performed for her benefit.

"But I'm a stranger in Newport too, so I can't be of any help." There, that should be clear and crisp enough, she thought.

After a few steps on the empty sidewalk in the opposite direction, Philippe DuChamps suddenly grabbed at his chest, reeled sideways, and fell on the grass. Pain contorted his face.

"My God, what is it!" Diana hadn't been there for her mother when her heart failed, and that memory haunted her as she rushed to the prone figure. She knelt and began unbuttoning his shirt, hearing his labored breathing.

Then he opened his eyes wide and looked up with little-boy glee. "Shouldn't we wait until after breakfast?" he asked wryly, restraining her wrists with friendly hands, all traces of pain gone.

"You lout! How dare you!" Diana shoved him back to the ground and stormed off.

"Miss, I am so sorry. That was, it's true, not very nice, but I was dejected and desperate." Philippe DuChamps could not remember a woman forcing him down on his back and taking off his shirt, only to walk away.

"You must be. You . . . Please leave me alone!"

"You forgot your man's necktie." He handed Diana the blue-and-white package she'd dropped at the scene of the rescue.

"Thank you," she said brusquely, her anger partially defused by having Steve's gift returned.

"Now, will you *please* join me for breakfast?" He saw by her face that the reticence had buckled, and seized the opportunity. "Please, as a way of accepting my apology. I am ashamed for myself. I behaved badly."

Diana could no longer resist the Frenchman's light-hearted—and appealing—drama. "But I hope you know where to go, because I sure don't."

"I know of one place only, but I think you'll like it. It is on—no, in—the harbor. I am always getting my English prepositions mixed up." Philippe DuChamps escorted Diana across Thames Street and onto the dock behind the Black Pearl. There was no restaurant.

"What did you have in mind?"

"There." Philippe indicated a large white ship anchored about a quarter-mile out, a hundred-and-forty-foot Benetti, perhaps the world's ultimate transoceanic vessel.

"Is that boat yours?" Diana asked, unable to conceal being impressed. DuChamps's delight soared. He'd pegged her right—she was not a member of his jet set or she'd certainly have been on board for one or two casino nights outside the twelve-mile territorial limit. He'd be able to introduce her to it all—the parties, discos, fashions, jewels, and perhaps occasionally, the drugs.

"It's a ship, actually. We do not say 'boat' for this size." His smile broke, broad and pleasing.

"Is that *ship* yours?" To Diana it floated midway on the waves like a beautiful sight within a sight—the streamlined white vessel flying all its flags and pennants in Newport Harbor.

"Yes, it is. Or rather, it's my family's. Let's breakfast."

"I thought you wanted to breakfast in Newport."

"I did, but as you had no recommendation to make . . . here, come have it *in* Newport harbor." She obediently followed him down steep steps and onto a small launch. He turned the ignition with a set of keys from his coat pocket. "I usually have the coxswain take me in, but I was up so early and the whole crew had a late night, so . . ." Considering his explanation finished, he opened up the motor and sprayed white water on a small boat of local fishermen just returning from sea. Their morning had started much earlier.

"Hey! You got those men wet," Diana commented.

"What?" DuChamps failed to hear over the roar.

"I said, you got those guys wet," she yelled.

"What guys?" Philippe glanced casually around the open harbor.

"Never mind," Diana whispered to herself. As the luxury launch sped through sailboats and inboard craft, moored and under way, she felt the remainder of the morning slip out of control like an anchor chain dropping fast to find a bottom that might be too deep.

"Welcome to the good ship *Bacchus*, best restaurant in or on Newport harbor," Philippe said as he hopped off the Jacob's ladder onto a spar-varnished mahogany deck. Diana followed him across the forecastle and into the luxurious interior. "How do you like?" He gestured expansively with his arms. "This is all Giorgio Vaiofilis—restored teak cabinetry taken from a Spanish galleon sunk in the Armada. Silk and suede make a nice combination, no?"

"Very nice, Mr. . . . ? I'm sorry, I've forgotten your name." She really had.

"I am wounded beyond recovery. You forgot the name Philippe DuChamps? I have not forgotten yours."

"But I haven't told you my name," Diana replied with a smile, charmed by his continental antics.

"You *are* Diana Winston—yes? I read your bank card." He was pleased with his detective work. Diana wasn't. She suspected he might have been trying to memorize her account number. Philippe also read her face.

"Oh, don't worry. I have no head for figures." He simultaneously admitted to himself that he did, indeed, have a head for figures, but those that offered greater variety and enticement than bank cards. Diana's, he imagined, were 36-24-35. These English measurements were not so difficult after all.

"I hope not," Diana said with mock sternness. "Who knows what sort of money this thing is built on?" She gestured at *Bacchus* all around her.

"Oh, you are so right to be cautious. Why, what I

could do with a credit line of two or three thousand!"
Philippe said with light sarcasm and a quizzical grin.

Diana's face flushed with irritation. Her line was fifteen hundred, but she paid each month's bill in full (if
there was one).

"I'm sorry. I didn't mean to insult. I had no intention
of using your card. I just wanted to know your name."
Philippe caught the eye of a passing crew member. *"Pierre,
nous voulons prendre du petit déjeuner. Faites Charles
savoir, s'il vous plaît. Et au dehors."*

"You might have asked," replied Diana.

Once again his face portrayed dramatic emotion exceeding what the moment called for. Diana couldn't help
but be amused by his ginned-up remorse. "I wanted to
have your name in case you walked away from me.
Which you did, by the way. Then I would have it to
search for you. Is that so very bad?"

She shook her head with exasperated amusement. "No,
I guess not—not so very bad."

"Good, very good. Now, come, let's breakfast." Taking Diana by the arm, he walked her out of the opulent
cabin and onto the sun-drenched stern. Behind a spacious swimming pool Diana saw the French tricolor snapping in cool breeze, now shifting onshore. Philippe followed
her gaze. "So, at least you know now I am honest. I told
you I was French."

"But you also told me through dramatized body language that you were having a heart attack." Diana now
enjoyed this repartee.

"Ah, yes, well, as you Americans like to say, 'touché.'
But I *was*, of sorts." He then gestured to white deck
furniture shaded by a pink umbrella. "Breakfast." A
steward put finishing touches on the table set with bri-
oches and croissants, scrambled eggs and sausage, a variety of jams, butter from Normandy, papaya with a slice
of lime and a sprinkle of coconut, Vichy water, Blue
Mountain coffee, and guava juice bubbling with added
champagne. It was intended as a feast for the eyes as
well—delicate English china service in rose and yellow,

crystal glasses, and bird-of-paradise flowers in a vase from the Amalfi coast.

Seated, Philippe DuChamps took Steve's tie from Diana's hand and put it with the launch key on the linen tablecloth. He gestured toward the flag. "You know, Diana, I have morning and evening colors every day on *Bacchus*. Ceremony must be kept up. Otherwise nothing is." She felt pleased that, playboy or not, he had a sense of tradition and aesthetic value. Noting her expression of approval, Philippe immediately went on to destroy it. "Yes, I can do without the symbol of 'La Belle France' flapping in my ear all day. Besides, flags don't tatter so quickly if you put them away at night. Just like you and me, yes?"

"Are you here for the boat show?" Diana asked, changing the subject. How quickly this man could give innuendo to a remark about flags. But she didn't wish the conversation to continue in that vein. It made her feel uncomfortable and nervous.

"Yes, of course." Philippe then addressed his serious attention to the food and sniffed the papaya. *"C'est bon"*— the comment to himself rather than his guest.

"Is it *really* that good?" she asked. "I mean, the boat show?" She took a sip of her laced guava juice, sweet, fresh, strange, but pleasing.

"But of course," he replied in a manner suggesting any imbecile would be aware of it. "Here you can see the newest in electronics, sails, rigging, and engines. More boats are introduced here than at any other show in the world."

"I suppose a lot of the newest and best are right here." She gestured at equipment jutting out from the mast.

"Oh, yes, the very best—special fuel-management system, computerized state-of-the-art navigation with digital readout, and Vigil radar." A shadow of disappointment crossed Philippe's face when he saw her interested but unimpressed expression. As for Diana, she realized she'd just been shown the sailing equivalent of Hermès tack, and that she resided on the fringe of only one of the number of worlds inhabited and controlled by the rich.

"Do you sail?" she asked, spreading more brandied peach conserve on her croissant.

"Yes, a Baltic 48DP. Do you know it?" Diana had to admit she did not. "A nice little boat. I call mine *Giselle*, and together we came first in the Virgin Islands Rolex Cup."

Through the remainder of breakfast Diana and Philippe traded personal histories. She struck him as a rare combination, an athlete and a beauty—a pleasant change from Monique, who spent hours lying in the sun and hours more applying expensive "institute" creams to save her skin. It also became delightfully clear Diana wasn't really impressed with his background and life-style. Nor was she the type who would try to ensnare him into a commitment. No, this girl seemed a free spirit, but she hadn't experienced his kind of life, and that put her at a delicious disadvantage. He would enjoy exposing her, so to speak. He stared at her breasts, his eyes concealed by the dark glasses he wore to ease the midmorning glint of bright water.

Diana *was* impressed by Philippe DuChamps and his surroundings—overwhelmed, in fact. As she bit into the succulent papaya, she stilled an impulse to shake her head—a shake intended to dislodge a dream. Here she was in the company of a very handsome man, son of a famous winemaker, on his spectacular transoceanic ship. The harbor panorama had no end—it circled all around her—sailing boats and motor launches, the graceful Newport Bridge and shoreline, Historic Hill, Trinity Church, and Fort Adams. She felt an ocean away from feed buckets, hoof picks, straw, and manure. Everything here seemed to come in an immaculate wrapping. But as she placed her napkin on the table, she knew she had to get back.

Philippe half-read her thoughts, which he didn't like at all. He stood up and asked her to excuse him a minute. Then he bent down and kissed her on the lips. Very brief, he designed it to lay the groundwork for passion. She just wished this had been any other day, for on any other she could have lingered, but not this one. She had to meet Steve, whom she hadn't so much as glimpsed since they parted yesterday afternoon. Steve had done it all—picked up her number, then fed, watered, and groomed Navarro. She felt more and more guilty, and glanced at her watch: eleven-thirty already. She absolutely had to leave.

Philippe had excused himself in order to prepare his stateroom for Diana's impending arrival. He jettisoned under his bed the *Hustler* he'd read the night before, but only after a quick glance at a nude lesbian couple that had caught his fancy. He grabbed the silver-framed photo of his fiancée and shut it in the bottom drawer of the bed table. *"Au revoir, Monique. A bientôt."* He blew her a hasty transatlantic kiss, then switched on the stereo. A glance in the mirror confirmed what he already knew—he saw one of Europe's most-sought-after eligible bachelors.

Diana was standing when he returned. "Philippe, I've got to go."

"No, Diana. Please stay. It is early," he protested. Monique had not been rudely shoved into dark seclusion for this.

"For you, maybe, but for me it's very late. I told you I was riding tomorrow; I've got to prepare my mount."

That's exactly what I've been doing, he told himself. And he wasn't about to be outdone by a horse. "Lovely Diana, please." It was now a simple and unaffected sincerity, hard to resist.

"No, really, I must go."

"Well, you will have to swim. I'll not take you back. Do you think I am a crazy man?" Philippe DuChamps, with folded arms, assumed the posture of a thwarted but determined schoolboy.

"Philippe, please." Diana's voice expressed exasperation not only at his threat but also at his unwillingness to take the commitment to her sport seriously.

"Absolutely not. Now, you told me you do not ride until Sunday. Stay here until then."

"Another time, yes, Philippe. But not now. Take me back." Diana started to walk forward to the brow.

He caught her, wrapping his arms around her waist from behind. He entreated her with kisses on the neck. "Please, Diana. Do not leave me alone, one man among many." He removed an arm from her waist long enough to gesture toward a passing crewman. Almost comic, he was a wonderful actor, but she felt flattered that he meant it all for her.

"I've got to go." Diana ignored the longing in her body as she moved to free herself from his grasp. Philippe felt a flash of impatience. He was not used to being rejected, not for horse, dog, or man. He turned her around, pressing her against the bulkhead. He closed his mouth over hers and thrust his tongue in deeply. She moaned as she felt the full weight of his body against hers. He put a hand under her shirt and stroked a breast with expert fingers.

"Okay, all right, I'll stay," she panted, pushing him off. These incredible advances, she thought: right out on the open deck with boats surrounding them. She felt conflicting feelings of desire, embarrassment, and determination to leave. "But couldn't we have a little after-breakfast drink?"

"Of course," he replied. It works every time, he congratulated himself. It's amazing what a good body rub will do. "I'll be right back." He gave Diana another of his quick, temporary good-bye kisses.

As soon as he was out of sight, Diana moved back to the table and grabbed the launch keys. Her escape, however, seemed thwarted by the appearance of a sailor sanding rough spots on the side deck. The Jacob's ladder stood just behind him.

"Excuse me, could you tell me where the ladies' room is?" The sailor looked up from his work, unable to conceal approval at the shapely pair of legs standing in front of him. "No, madame. I no English—English no."

"I see. Diana groped for her ninth-grade French. "Well, uh—*où est . . . où est le bain?* No, *où est la salle de bain?"*

*"En bas."* The sailor smiled, pointing to a ladder that would lead Diana in a direction she did not wish to go, down—and into the ship. *"La salle de bain est en bas."*

"Thank you. *Merci.*" This solved nothing. She had to get him away from the other ladder. *"Monsieur, pouvez-vous dire à Monsieur DuChamps que je suis dans la salle de bain?"*

*"Oui, mademoiselle."* The sailor smiled at being called *"monsieur"* in Diana's imperfect French. He put his scraper down and headed to find Philippe and inform him that his guest was temporarily inconvenienced. After two or three strides in the direction of the bathroom, Diana did an about-face to the ladder, quickly descended, and hopped onto the launch. She put the key in the ignition and throttled the boat forward. As she circled off the stern to try to get a feel for the craft before negotiating through the crowded harbor, she saw Philippe DuChamps, shocked, staring at her over the side, a Bloody Mary in each hand.

"So long, Philippe. See you later." Diana waved and turned the boat toward shore and the Derby.

Tricked, Philippe confessed to himself. She did not want this drink. And as he watched the launch speeding away, he poured the Bloody Marys over the side and vowed he would not leave Newport harbor without making love to this beautiful and elusive American girl.

As she climbed back onto the wharf, Diana realized she'd left Steve's tie on the *Bacchus.* And it had been right underneath the keys! Though she was late, the Narragansett was on her way, so she simply ran in and selected an identical one, leaving the salesmen to draw their own conclusions about her social life. She remembered that a salesgirl acquaintance at Shreve's had reported how a man once came in and ordered six pairs of identical one-carat diamond-stud earrings, then explained it by stating that this year he wasn't going to forget what he'd given to whom!

*    *    *

"So, do you like it?" Diana asked Steve as they turned down Glen Road onto the showgrounds.

"Yes, I like . . . I love it. Didn't I tell you?" He glanced over at Diana.

"Yes, but you took it so quietly. Why don't we go out to dinner someplace where you can wear it? I'd like to spend some time with you. We deserve to relax together, don't we?" Diana tried once again to get her strange relationship with Steve on a more conventional plane. She was afraid her slight irritation showed.

"Dinner would be nice, but I didn't bring anything except work clothes. Besides, you're going to the barbecue this evening." The mild grin hovering about the corner of his mouth revealed pleasure at having thwarted her once again. But still a part of Steve—the part that lay dormant since he had shouldered blame for the death of his wife and child—wanted to express love.

"Right, that western thing. I guess I ought to go to that. At least Jim will be there. And I can hardly wait to see Courtney again," Diana said sarcastically. Steve's old Ford backfired as they stopped in among the Land Rovers, Jaguar XJ-S's, and other fashionable sport vehicles.

When Diana first got on Navarro and showed him about the grounds, she was scared. He neighed challenges to every horse they passed. She had trouble sitting to his highly active gaits. He seemed too interested in establishing Glen Farm as his own territory. But after two circuits, the surroundings grew familiar and he began to relax and address himself to work. Over fences, he schooled so perfectly that Steve suggested he be hand-grazed and then walked back to his stall.

Diana concurred, but as she headed to remove Navarro's tack, she recognized the waving arm of Tony Russo. He was walking straight toward her. "Diana, hi! How're you doing?" She wondered where his cohort, Billy Jones, was lurking.

"Tony, where's your pal?"

"Back to Sand Dollar in disgrace. I decided to stay and watch the show. For a Californian, this is a good chance for a firsthand look at East Coast competition." She watched him scrutinize Navarro with a professional eye.

"Well, there's plenty of it. Too much," Diana said nervously, thinking about the next day.

"So this is the mystery horse," he observed as he felt Navarro's right pastern. "Suspensory problem?"

"Keep your hands off my horse, Tony. He might kick," Diana flashed out angrily.

"Yeah, right." Tony looked up at Diana, his insolent face conveying he knew the injury was the true reason she didn't want her horse touched. "You think he's going to make it around?" His eyes now fastened more on Diana's thigh, lying slender and muscular against the saddle, than on Navarro's damaged physique.

"If we're lucky, he'll make it," she replied, deciding it *really* was time to head back to the barn.

"Hey, Diana, how 'bout going to the Western Roundup together? Billy's gone and you don't have a date, do you?"

"How would you know?" Now *she* wanted to kick him.

"You weren't really with Jim Williams at Beechwood. I've done some checking up. Unless you date grooms, you're free. I've got a great car—a Corvette." Tony put an unwelcome hand on the toe of Diana's boot.

"I was at Beechwood. Jim was at Beechwood. Jim and I arrived and left in the same car. I'm curious—what makes you think we weren't really together?" Diana knew exactly what Tony meant. Jim was gay and therefore nothing sexual would happen between them. Unless there was the prospect of bed, it didn't count as a date in Tony's book.

"Maybe I'm opening a can of worms here, but that guy's a fag. Didn't you know?" Tony's pseudo-serious face assumed an air of patronizing consolation. He was all too willing to offer himself as the consolation prize.

She could contain herself no longer. "I see no reason to tell you everything I know and don't know. What I do know and don't mind repeating is that *you* are a worm. Now, just step back and let me through." Navarro's forward-moving body forced a surprised Tony several yards back. The horse seemed to hate him too.

"Diana! You didn't tell me about the barbecue. I'll pick you up at your hotel. Did I tell you I've got a Vette?" But Diana and Navarro trotted across the field to the stables. She looked straight ahead.

"What set her off?" Tony addressed the question to a portly man in a western Stetson. "Guess she didn't know the guy was a fag. God help him when he runs into her."

After putting up Navarro with fresh water and hay, Diana and Steve climbed into the bleachers to watch the Bollinger Speed Classic. A sort of abbreviated Derby, it entailed eighteen jumps, four to five feet high, with six-foot spreads maximum. The Derby required twenty-eight, averaging five feet each, all over a mile-long course. But by watching other riders now, Diana could get a feel for the terrain and an idea of the striding required between jumps.

"Hot dog?" Steve asked. He hadn't eaten anything since an early-morning cup of coffee and a Danish. It was already three o'clock.

"No, not for me, thanks. I had a late breakfast." No hot dog could compete with the memories of champagned guava juice and the open-sea breeze. Steve wove his way down the stand, taking care not to disturb or annoy any spectator. Diana smiled as she saw her friend, ever thoughtful, pick up a little coin purse and return it to its shy but grateful three-year-old owner. Loud applause immediately caused Diana to readdress her attention to the show. Hiro Tomizawa had just completed a flawless round on Don Carlos, his time now the one to beat.

Entering the ring came a young mare named Spindrift, ridden by the Virginian Barbara Doyle. The gray's easy pace startled Diana. This was a speed class—knockdowns and time counted. The horse seemed fit. If it were lame, Barbara would have pulled her short. No, there was no explanation. Then, to add to the puzzle, Barbara went off-course, missing the wall and the brush, two of the easier jumps. Instead, she went on to jump the Liverpool —a water combination with an in-and-out—then the sunken road, two of the fixed obstacles on the Derby course set for tomorrow. Spindrift disqualified and the whistle blew.

Mrs. Averill Harriman's Special Envoy appeared next, ridden by Katie Prudent. The pair took the course as Diana expected competitors would. They went for broke —no rails down, no time faults, but a bare thirteen-hundredths of a second slower than Ann Kursinski. But again, the following horse, Global Estate, ridden by Jay Meyer, took an easy ride too, and went off-course precisely where the gray mare had. Suddenly it became abundantly clear what kind of strategy operated. These slow riders, also listed in the Derby next day, were using this class as a warm-up session for other mounts while simultaneously getting a hands-on look at some of the Derby's more difficult jumps for themselves. Diana could scarcely believe it. Clearly, the haves had the advantage. It was all prepaid: those with a string of horses to compete could afford to expend one this way, as long as it enhanced their chance of winning the more prestigious and lucrative event.

"Steve!" Diana gestured to her tray-laden friend to accelerate his climb. "Steve, they're cheating. Sit down, hurry. Wait'll you see." While she spoke and waited, two more riders confirmed her report. Steve seemed disturbed, not so much at the "cheating"—people would try everything —as at how blatant it was.

"That's what I call creative competition," he commented. He shook his head at yet another example of how sport is simultaneously elevated and denigrated by the lure of money.

"You can call it that, Steve. I—and a lot of other people—would call it cheating."

"Excuse me, ma'am." Diana felt the press of stubby, hard, yet friendly fingers on her shoulder. "Do you mean to say them folks is cheatin'?" Diana turned to look at a big-barreled, genial man with a mustache. He then lifted his broad-brimmed Stetson and tipped it toward her.

"That's what I mean." Diana turned to Steve. "I'm going to find the show steward."

She started to get up, but Steve caught her wrist. "No, Diana, don't."

"Why not?"

"You'll make it harder on yourself. Sit down. Please." But she pulled free and ran down the bleachers, using the shoulders of strangers to assist her rapid descent. Steve shook his head. She would never learn to be politic. Her fiery spirit would either make or break her, and today he feared it would be the latter.

"Where've you been, friend?" asked the Texan, thumping Steve on the back with his hand. "I thought you were happy with me."

"I was. I wasn't happy with me," Steve replied. "It had nothing to do with you, Lee. I'm sorry. I just had to do it that way. I couldn't, I just couldn't . . ."

Heeding Steve's obvious desire not to talk, the Texan obliged. "I've been watching that little lady today. I wish I were thirty years younger. Now, that gal's one to ride the river with."

"Sir, I think she *is* the river," Steve wanly replied, caught between his admiration of Diana's indignant anger and his fear that she had charted a rough course with the show world.

The westerner took out his wallet and handed Steve a card: Lee Caudrey, owner of Silvervein Ranch, a top breeder of racing Quarter Horses in the United States. The most prestigious Quarter Horse race pays far more than the Kentucky Derby and takes about one-fifth the time. "Just didn't want you to forget my address, Steve."

Diana found the steward at the in-gate. Silver-haired and portly, he was a member of the Newport Chamber of Commerce and disinclined to take any action that might reflect negatively on the event's reputation.

"Sir, may I speak with you?"

"Certainly." Bob Foley turned to look at Diana only after he finished watching an entrant successfully negotiate the Derby Bank.

"My name is Diana Winston and I'd like to lodge a complaint. Those riders who are going off-course are doing so intentionally." She felt like adding that any idiot could see it, but made a tremendous effort to control her anger.

"You think so?" His voice conveyed skepticism and lack of interest.

"Yes, I do. By going off-course, they're getting a chance to school over the most difficult portion of tomorrow's competition." She was annoyed to see Foley's eyes return to the horse then jumping the course. Unfortunately for her, that horse sped along in earnest.

"Do you know for a *fact* that they're going astray in order to practice?" He was determined to put a stop to what he considered little more than a disruptive accusation.

"Sure, you just have to look and know something about show jumping. You can see that a percentage of them go off-course at precisely the same point, yet continue to go over the Liverpool and the Sunken Road— two of the Derby's most difficult jumps. They're figuring out the striding."

It became perfectly clear by Bob Foley's blank expression that he didn't know exactly what striding was. Diana groaned and took a deep breath to steady herself before continuing. "They're learning how many gallop strides their horses will need between jumps tomorrow. You saw Spindrift and Global Estate, didn't you?"

"Yes, but I don't think you can accuse world-class riders of dishonesty just because they go slow."

Diana bit her lip in aggravation. "Look, either the riders are incredibly dumb or very smart. And if they're dumb, why are they all dumb at exactly the same place?"

"I don't quite follow," replied Foley, his gaze once again turning to the ring. "Now, if you'll excuse me, I've got to keep an eye on things."

"Somebody's got to see what's going on. This isn't only

unfair to competitors who haven't the luxury of an expendable horse. It's unfair to the spectators. Why should they have to spend an afternoon watching competitors who aren't really competing?"

Bob Foley's first response to Diana's well-reasoned objection was a shrug. "Well, I'll take down your complaint and show it around, but I don't know that anyone'll do anything. After all, according to you, they're not competing so they're not going to win anyway. You're complaining against losers."

Diana slowly shook her head in exasperation. "Never mind, mister. Just never mind." She turned on her heel and walked off to rejoin Steve.

"So?" Steve inquired with icy patience.

"So nothing. I lodged and dislodged a complaint—all in sixty exasperating seconds."

"Fine, I'm glad you changed your mind." Steve felt surprised and pleased by Diana's politic move. He would have shivered a little more had he listened to her testy conversation.

"It wasn't going to do any good." She'd let him believe in a diplomatic gesture. "Steve, I'm scared to death. These people come here with the best horses, some school illegally or, at least, unethically. Don't you think we should just pack up and go home? Why should we be subjected to this kind of cutthroat competition?"

"You mean, why should you be subjected to this kind of cutthroat competition," he said gently. "Diana, don't go at things head-on. If you do, you'll be no good tomorrow. Why can't you just duck and let the wave pass? Want a sip of Coke?" He held out the red-and-white cup.

She smiled. Here was daddy consoling his little girl, deserted by friends. "I guess you're right, Steve, but it all makes me furious. I love this sport for its purity. You knock a rail down and you lose. You don't, you win. At least, I loved it until today. Those people will win more money tomorrow, not because of the quality of their ride but because they have more money today."

"It *is* hard to reconcile art or sport with money, but

most of us need them all. There's no shame in that. Look, let's go back to the motel. Take a hot shower and get ready for your party."

"Aren't you going with me?" Diana asked. She didn't want to leave Steve alone yet another night. *And* she needed him.

"No, Mr. Williams'll be there. If I go with you, it'll only give them something to talk about." He gently brushed a strand of Diana's hair off her forehead.

"I don't care about that. You know I—"

"And I'm busy," returned Steve.

"Need some more shirts from that Fall River mill outlet?" she asked with mild sarcasm. "No lame excuses. I want you with me."

A big voice suddenly boomed out. "Well, I'm not lame—at least, not yet, but I am the excuse, young lady. I'd like to borrow your friend here for an evening, if you don't mind," drawled Lee Caudrey. He'd just returned laden with two hamburgers and two large orders of fries, which looked minuscule next to his huge frame.

Diana glanced at Steve, who confirmed these plans with a nod of his head. "I see," responded Diana weakly. How odd, she thought to herself. For the two years I've known Steve, there's been nobody. Then all of a sudden he takes up with a strange cowboy in the bleachers.

"I'm sure you won't mind, Diana." Steve smiled, sensing her surprise and embarrassment.

"No, not at all," she replied quickly. "No."

"Of course, you can come—if you don't mind Quarter-Horse talk over beer and steak. You'd sure pretty up the table." Politeness compelled Lee Caudry to make the offer, but as interesting and attractive as he found Diana, he hoped she wouldn't take him up on it. He wanted to talk to Steve alone. They would dine at the Sheraton Islander on Goat Island, where he occupied the penthouse suite King Hussein had used when his son graduated from Brown. The view was worth twice the rent.

"No, thank you, I've got a barbecue I guess I really

should go to," Diana replied. "Just so long as Steve's not alone."

"You got a date or something?" asked the large Texan inoffensively. He wanted to make sure she wouldn't go unescorted.

"I guess I've got an 'or something.' " Diana recalled Tony Russo's crude comments. Somehow Lee Caudry posted twenty notches higher on the civility scale.

"Good. Well, you and that 'something' have a fun time. I promise to take good care of your friend."

"Please do that, sir. Because if you don't, you'll have me to contend with." Diana's tone was light and teasing, but the serious undercurrent wasn't lost on the Texan.

"Honey, contending with you would be an honor and a pleasure." His formal and chivalrous tone was quick, his doffed Stetson neutralizing any offense Diana would have normally taken.

The Derby Foundation expended a huge effort to ensure that the barbecue, despite its New England location, recreated the West. Held on the grounds of Glen Farm under a huge green-and-white-striped canopy, it was wonderfully staged. Piled-up bales of straw lined the tent. An authentic-looking "ghost town" from the 1984 Olympic three-day event course on Fairbanks Ranch served as backdrop. The lead singer of a famous western group acted as master of ceremonies. The musicians appeared in glittering cowboy attire—rhinestone red shirts, black bandanas, and black hats with sprays of eagle feathers. Virtually all the guests came in western gear as well. Only one or two refused to trade in their yellow pants punctuated with whales or sailboats. The buffet consisted of chicken off the grill, and varied chili strengths—one-, two-, or three-alarm. Then corn, different salads, and desserts completed the informal feast.

Diana wore jeans and a red silk shirt. In her back pocket she stuffed a bandana, which she felt discharged the "costume" obligation. Why English-style riders delighted in a western-getup party was beyond her.

As soon as Diana walked in, she realized that her pitiful bandana would never be noticed. She stood out like a city slicker walking down the streets of Laredo. Everyone seemed dressed to the hilt in ten-gallon hats, pearl-buttoned shirts, and leather (sometimes plastic) fringe. It was western in the new Grand Ole Opry style, like the new Opry building and "Opryland."

"Diana, what's going on? I haven't seen you since Lake Placid." Tim Craig, dressed in a cowboy hat, black-and-turquoise shirt with onyx buttons, jeans, and—incredibly—Top-Siders, greeted her. Diana smiled. She liked Tim and knew he was Jim's good friend. The foot gear was typical. He'll die with his Top-Siders on, she thought.

"I haven't been doing much, Tim. Keeping house and learning to ride"—she lowered her voice—"unconventionally and on an unconventional horse."

"So I've heard. I wish you the best. I'd like to see you in the rookie ranks again." Tim noticed she was empty-handed. "May I get you a drink?"

"I'd like to get something to eat, if that's okay with you. I haven't had anything to eat since breakfast." The harbor and *Bacchus* flashed in her mind's eye.

"Not since breakfast? Sure, let's get in line. How'd you manage on just breakfast?" he asked, knowing how much energy riding demanded. That people thought "just sitting" on a horse demanded little effort continually puzzled him.

"The breakfast was late and large," explained Diana, but didn't elaborate. They walked to a long row of tables decked out in red-and-white-checked cloth. About ten people stood waiting in line. New pans of chicken arrived.

"I noticed your groom up and about early. He drove his pickup in with private hay. Seems he doesn't like the quality distributed here."

"He's more of a trainer and friend actually. He's very fussy about food." Diana felt a little embarrassed by Tim's observation, but relieved that he assumed she had been around, when, in fact, she'd still been in bed. She also felt a twinge at Steve's having been referred to as her groom.

"Well, anyway, it was so good and green I had our groom ask where he got it and then ordered some myself. Great quality. Mostly first-cut timothy."

"Mind if I join you?" Jack O'Dell had come dressed as himself—chino pants and polo shirt. He wasn't going to play the game.

"Not at all, please do," replied Tim, making a space.

"Diana, I have a message, I almost forgot," O'Dell said, reaching for a set of plastic dinnerware. "Jim phoned and asked me to tell you he's not feeling quite up to speed, so he couldn't make it this evening."

"Will he be able to ride tomorrow?" Diana asked, concerned.

"I certainly hope so. I've got to sell Comrade. He's a great horse, but my summer's packed with students. I don't have the time to campaign him." O'Dell noted Diana's worried expression. "Jim says he'll be fine for tomorrow. Just that he needs a little rest."

"What exactly is it?" she asked softly, recalling Jim's dry cough.

"Says he picked up a cold. All that evening salt air, I guess. Here." He handed Diana a paper plate and napkin.

"I'm sure he'll be okay," Tim added. "Look how quickly he shook that pneumonia."

"I'm not sure it was shaken," Diana replied. Here I am without Jim, she thought, and soon among the piranha. Her scan of the room caught Courtney as she joined the line with Tony Russo hanging on her arm. Courtney had dressed outrageously: a purple-and-white cowgirl outfit (the skirt well above her shapely knees), complete with double holster, white boots with tassels and silver eagles on their fronts. Tony, more conservatively attired in a red-and-black pearl-buttoned shirt, yellow neckerchief, black hat and jeans, seemed glued to her. Courtney hadn't had a good lay in weeks and had at first set her sights on Billy Jones. But the party pooper O'Dell had prevented that. She wasn't wild about Tony. His score card at the shows and subsequently with women hadn't been high this season. He didn't have money or relatives of note, but it seemed he'd have to do. Still, if something or someone better showed up tonight, she'd drop Tony easily enough.

"Hi, Tim. Didn't you know it was a costume party, Diana? But I suppose you've never been to one of these," Courtney said, reaching across Jack O'Dell without so much as an "excuse me" to get at the three-bean salad.

"Hungry, Courtney?" Jack asked pointedly.

"Oh, Jack, how *are* you?"

"Fine, thanks. How's your mother? I understand she's not going to give up the farm." O'Dell helped himself to a cup of draft beer.

"Nope, she's not. Must be her way of dealing with the divorce. She's busier than ever, and driving our farm manager nuts. Here, Jack, let me get you some of this three-alarm."

Diana felt delight at the image of Bob Sloan pestered by Mrs. Snyder, who, nice as she was, didn't have the first idea how to run a large operation. And since the divorce, it had to make itself pay. Some attempts at putting together a breeding syndicate had failed. Courtney's mother had taken a huge loss on an imported champion German stallion who died of painfully twisted intestines. It seemed he had carried only partial insurance. Nonetheless, Hampstead jockeyed with Beacon Hill as the stable with the best show record that season.

Diana watched Courtney ladle out the flamethrowing chili. She noticed that O'Dell never extended himself beyond the minimally polite gesture to Courtney, and that only because of Hampstead's stature.

"Where's your doctor friend, Jack?" Courtney asked. Diana had just been wondering the same thing.

"You mean Bill Stanford?" Jack took the plate from Courtney. "He had an invitation to go up to the Shriners' Institute in Boston. One of his friends is a burn specialist who's doing a politically sensitive operation on a boy just flown in from El Salvador. Bill wanted to observe."

"Ugh! Burned children. Let's not hear any more about that." Courtney licked her lips as she set widening eyes on the end table, groaning under Viennese pastries and cakes. About to take one, she saw she wouldn't be able to fit it onto her chili-laden plate. "Oh, I'll just come back later."

"I thought Dr. Stanford came here to relax," commented Diana, ignoring Courtney's tasteless remark.

"Pleasure was his initial intent, anyway," said O'Dell, then paused, wondering why Diana pursued the doctor's itinerary with such eagerness. "But trying to distract Bill from medicine would be like pulling any of us away from horses—almost any of us." He speared Courtney with a glance. "Dr. Stanford's about the most dedicated doctor I've ever met."

"Why don't we all sit down together," said Courtney, turning around from the desserts as she looked for a table. "There! I see an empty one." Diana had been hoping that she and Tim could go off with Jack O'Dell *sans* Courtney and Tony. She observed Tim in eye dialogue with O'Dell, who gave a "what-the-hell—we're-trapped" shrug. "Now, Diana, you sit right here next to Jack. I'm sure it's quite an honor for you." Courtney pointed to a metal chair with the proprietary air of a hostess.

"The honor's all mine," said O'Dell, pulling out the chair for Diana.

"Thank you," she replied. The fresh aroma of chili made her realize how hungry she was. She looked around for Tim Craig, who had left to fetch a plate of rolls for the group.

"So, Diana, where's Sancho Panza?" asked Courtney, her eyes bright with malicious interest.

"Who?" Diana asked. She knew what Courtney was up to.

"Sancho. You know, your groom." Courtney turned to Tony. They both sniggered. "Squire to the female Quixote."

"I don't have a groom named Sancho Panza. I don't

have a groom at all. I have a trainer who advises me—
Steve Rodríguez." Diana glanced sideways at Courtney
with disdain.

"Yes, Steve. Hampstead's groom but *your* adviser.
Well, one woman's soup is another woman's meat, or
however that saying goes. Well, where is he? Grooms
and trainers *are* allowed here."

"Steve had a previous engagement," Diana replied
coldly.

"And what's he engaged with—fixing the suspensory
of the knight errant's nag or looking for a windmill?"
Diana glared at Tony, who looked away like a bad dog
scolded for the mess he'd left on the kitchen floor.

"Courtney, I always have difficulty trying to understand what you really mean. You talk in code. How
about plain, simple, unencrypted English?" Diana casually took a jalepeño from her salad and chewed it slowly
without flinching, at least outwardly.

"I'm talking about your sidekick and your mount. Or
is your sidekick your mount?" Tony jabbed Courtney in
the ribs, warning her she went too far.

Diana stood up, her face flushing red with anger. "I
see sitting here is going to interfere with my digestion.
Excuse me." She turned from the table and motioned the
approaching Tim to join her. They left an unhappy Jack
O'Dell, who would, no doubt, chow down quickly.

"Courtney's fangs out again?" Tim asked.

"Several pairs, it seems," Diana commented. They
walked to another table of riders, all of whom displayed
disinterested politeness toward her. And as their conversation regrouped and went on and on about the season's
circuit, Diana felt awkward and inadequate. She could
only be silent and try to appear as if she belonged. But
the strain of smiling and looking involved in what she
herself ached to be part of became too difficult. Once
again she felt as if she'd been left standing in the doorway of an exclusive club that had closed its membership
list to her. Besides, all the talk about refusals, spills, and

run-outs made her nervous. She hastily dispatched her dinner and got up.

"Tim, I'm going to get a drink to extinguish the smoldering chili fire in my mouth." But the lighthearted attempt at excusing herself fell on deaf ears. Craig was now in the middle, telling how he thought the American Event Team got screwed when one of its horses failed to pass the vetting at Badminton.

Diana wandered over to the bar, ordered a gin and tonic, and stepped out from under the tent into the silence of the salty night air, the black sky awash with stars. Fireflies sparked the darkness with beacons of yellow light. Suddenly she heard a neigh break the silence. It sounded like Navarro. Fearing an injury, she ran to the stable. But when she got there, Navarro was standing peacefully in his stall, also looking out into the darkness filled with specks of light.

"Hello, big fellow. Thanks for calling me out of that party. Thinking about tomorrow?" Diana stroked the arch of his white neck. He broke his gaze and shoved his muzzle into her hands. "You're far better company anyway. She didn't even know Rocinante's name." The white horse nuzzled Diana's pockets for a treat. "Sorry, no sugar. I forgot." Diana felt fear coming over her. She doubted tomorrow's outcome in the extreme, and wondered if she could manage to do better than not disgrace herself. Thought of the Derby Bank and Pulverman's Grob made her feet tingle and her stomach tighten. She felt isolated. It would have been better to have gone with the Texan and Steve. If she'd only known Jim was going to be ill. She recalled his thin face and cough. She knew pneumonia was difficult to shake and wondered if he really should ride the next day. He'd get into a sweat, maybe catch a chill. She also recalled the healthy boyish smile that had greeted her in the aisle the day of her first lesson. But just the night before—though in good spirits —he had seemed tired and unwell. She looked at her empty drink glass and the night stars it reflected. Diana decided she'd salvage the rest of the evening by returning to the motel and sleeping through it. She patted Navarro and headed back to the tent to return her glass.

During the time Diana ate at the other table and went to check Navarro, Courtney did, in fact, find a replacement for Tony Russo. She'd seen this other man around the circuit, often with a striking woman on his arm, a different one every time. But she'd never been introduced. Handsome, he walked with the casual air of a man who automatically got the things he wanted. And since he seemed to be the only game in town worth playing, Courtney decided she'd be one of his wants. As for Tony, she simply left him holding two margaritas.

"Hello, I don't believe we've ever been introduced. But I've seen you around a lot." Courtney spoke as if Glen Farm and all other shows were held on her own property.

"Hello, too. I don't believe I've seen you either, or I certainly would have noticed." His eyes fell to Courtney's pendulous breasts. Her nipples were erect against the purple cowgirl shirt, causing three or four of its fringes to stick out. As the man glanced at the short skirt and little white boots, he felt himself swell warmly against his inside thigh.

"Why don't you buy me a drink and I'll try to figure out why you've never seen me before?" At least tonight I'll get a real man between my legs, Courtney thought. Someone with hair and a good chest on him.

As Diana stepped out of the dark into the artificial light of the tent, she smiled at the group of East Coast equestrians trying to follow the emcee's instructions as he took them through square-dancing basics. "Then you go alaman left your corner, walk right by your own, three hands around and promenade, you promenade her home. You take her all the way home, home again." The floor broke up in laughter as the riders, completely at ease on the most difficult courses, had difficulty distinguishing left from right. "All right, all right, you noncowboy riders, let's give her another go."

Diana walked to the bar, chuckling, but as she passed her glass in front of a man seated at the bar, she gasped when he turned around. Hugh Simpson talking with Courtney—very with her.

"Diana!" Hugh exclaimed. He stood up as soon as he saw her. "How are you?"

"Hello, Hugh," Diana answered coolly.

"You two know each other?" Courtney asked. She immediately suspected Diana and Hugh not only knew each other but also had slept with each other. In that case Courtney would have to determine whether she should count Hugh Simpson as damaged goods or someone worthy of being snatched away from the competition. But to make the correct assessment, she'd have to observe them together. "Won't you join us for a drink?" she asked.

"Yes, do. What are you drinking?" Hugh thought it odd that Courtney would invite Diana to join them. Hadn't she somehow communicated that she intended to bed down with him that night?

Diana felt her throat tighten and her heart beat faster. "No, thanks, I've got to get some sleep." She put her empty glass down on the counter.

"Oh, yes, tomorrow's your day to shine—maybe," said Courtney sarcastically.

Not waiting for a further response, Hugh grabbed Diana's glass and waved it in the air. "Waiter!" he bellowed to a young sunburned blond in white shirt and black tie. "Another one of these."

"Sorry, Hugh, I can't stay with you—not this time." Diana glanced at Courtney to make sure she'd made her mark. She had—and Courtney looked pissed. He was damaged goods—big barrel or not. She wanted Diana out, Hugh out, and Tony back.

"That's right, Hugh," cut in Courtney. "Diana's riding only once at this show, so she's got to make it count. It's very important to her. So important, in fact, that she complained to the steward about having only one horse to ride. Naturally, the poor man got confused. What was he supposed to do—give Diana a loaner, or furnish her with her own string?"

Courtney's sudden hostility confused Hugh Simpson even more. Why had she invited Diana for a drink if she was going to have at her? Women, Hugh thought to himself. Give them to me one at a time. His old internal memo still seemed a good guide—the four F's: find 'em, feed 'em, fuck 'em, forget 'em. And here were *two* lovely sets of tits having a go at each other—obviously, thought Hugh in his talent for self-deception, over him.

Courtney seemed surprised that Diana didn't respond to her comments about the complaint she'd registered. Could it be she was actually going to stay to have another drink? "Diana, I thought you were going to run along and get your beauty sleep. Best do it now. I understand you're staying at a motel, and those walls can be so thin. I wouldn't want the three-o'clock moans and shrieks to keep you up. Unless Sancho and you plan some of your own."

"Sancho?" Hugh asked. Now he was bombarded. He didn't like the possibility of another contender.

The waiter arrived just in time with Diana's drink. She wouldn't have been able to hold her temper much longer.

"Here, my treat," Hugh offered with largesse as he lifted his half-empty Rusty Nail in the air and proclaimed, "To horse lovers everywhere, but especially to the three of us." Maybe that would draw some clarifying action.

"All right, Hugh," Diana said, apparently yielding. But as she reached for her glass, she saw to it that she accidentally knocked it over, drenching Courtney's suit and dribbling into her boots. "Courtney, I am *so* sorry! Here, let me get that mess." Diana took a napkin and swiped several ice cubes so they fell into the loosely buttoned shirt. One lodged near the front, making it look like Courtney had one perfectly square tit, wet and cold. Hugh now stared in bizarre delight.

"Bitch!" Courtney raged. She jumped off the bar stool and tried vainly to shake herself dry.

"That's exactly what you are, Courtney, and a perfect

match for Hugh." Diana delicately placed the empty glass on the bar and looked directly at Hugh. "I told you I didn't want a drink. You should have listened." She stalked out of the tent.

Hugh did his best to soothe a blubbering Courtney. "Let me get this lime out of your hair," he offered. The ridiculous scene had attracted attention.

"Don't touch me, don't touch me! I don't buy second-hand. God, how I hate that bitch." Courtney ran out of the bar area to look for a mirror in what would be a vain attempt to put herself back to rights. As for Hugh, the whole episode had left him confused and unhappy, at least temporarily. Later that evening, in the lounge of the Viking Hotel, he met a pretty nurse from the Naval Hospital and took her to bed, where she ministered to his wounded ego and other equally delicate parts.

# The Derby

Diana had intended to go back to the motel, but changed course and pointed her pickup in the direction of downtown Newport. The encounter with Hugh and Courtney had sent her adrenaline pumping and made an early night impossible. She'd only lie awake ensnared by anger, nervousness, and fear. Like an actress before the curtain rose, she needed to address herself to her lines—the next day's course—but felt too overwhelmed to be alone. She parked the truck at Bannister's Wharf and took a stool at the Black Pearl's small bar.

Her immediate reasons for not returning to the motel, however valid, weren't the only ones. She felt repelled at the thought of another night in the cheap surroundings—which on arrival had offered a choice of regular, water, or gel bed. The mattress, covered in protective vinyl, became hot and uncomfortable. The decor, epitomized by an orange-and-black-velour "painting" of junks in Hong Kong harbor, was junk indeed. And Courtney's comment about nocturnal sounds had been true. Through the night Diana had to suffer the unrhythmic squeaking of a couple making love in a "regular" bed.

"Gin and tonic, please. No, make that a bourbon and soda." Diana recalled the unpleasant circumstances of her last gin and tonic. Good, no horse people, she thought, looking around at the resort crowd: seagoing sunburns and tans—a pleasant change from riders with tans only on their arms and faces. On days when the mercury

climbed over ninety, rules permitted them to compete
without coats. But even then, sticklers kept them on,
their only concession a summer-weight wool. Diana looked
discreetly at the long, thick burnished legs of a handsome
man with a square jaw. He seemed to be listening intently and swaying to the background music of Stan Getz.
Tennis shorts and a Brown University T-shirt emphasized
rather than concealed a powerful waist and set of shoulders. A few minutes before, he'd been talking to a couple
of friends.

"I play tennis a lot," he now said amicably to her.
Diana felt mortified. She hadn't been as discreet as she
thought.

"I'm sorry, I was just—"

"Staring. That's cool. I stare at a lot of stems too. Can
I get you some suds or something?" Weighing the pros
and cons—perfect body against barbaric manner—Diana
quickly determined that companionship, of the kind she
needed anyway, wouldn't be forthcoming from this laid-
back blond Adonis.

"No, my drink's coming. But thanks anyway." Her
tone was slightly formal, not so much to offend as to
prevent.

"Okay, that's cool too. Each to his own, I say." She
dropped her eyelids in relief.

"Diana . . . oh, Diana!" She felt an odd combination
of dread and eager anticipation and turned in the direction of the happy excited voice. Philippe DuChamps was
reveling in the company of his obviously well-heeled peers.
He smiled broadly, apparently not bearing any ill-will
toward her solo exit aboard his launch. Clinging posses-
sively to the waist of her continental find, a gorgeous
leggy blond smiled up at him. She tossed Diana a smile,
then turned back to her drink. Philippe liked showing off
his new American ticket, yes, quite a billet-doux in the
flesh. He might still be upset, Diana thought.

But that wasn't true; the Frenchman had just found a
way to amuse himself for the evening. He'd tried to
contact Diana immediately after she left, calling several

hotels and asking to speak to her, only to find the name unregistered. He guessed she was staying at a private residence, but planned to go to the Derby the next day because he knew she'd be there.

"Excuse me, Muffin," Philippe apologized to his blond. "That girl there, she is my cousin, long lost." He nodded in Diana's direction.

"It's Muffy, not Muffin, Pierre," said the svelte young lady with some indignation. One look at Diana told her that her night with the Gallic millionaire had hit a roadblock. "Is she your first cousin?"

"Oh, yes, my first," replied Philippe, pleased she'd bought his story.

"Well, you can't have sex with your first cousin in the U.S. of A., monsieur." If she had to bail out, she'd at least let him see that she knew what was up.

"Oh, did I say *first* cousin? I thought you meant oldest. No, no, she's my very first second cousin, so sex is okay, is it not?" Philippe smiled charmingly at the infuriated Muffy.

"You're a real prick."

Philippe glanced down at the zipper on his cotton slacks. "I should hope so, Muffin. Now, if you'll excuse me . . ." He squeezed her affectionately on the arm, leaving her to drain a daiquiri before setting her sights several notches lower—a young Wall Street lawyer.

"Diana, my Diana, why did you leave me like that? It was really very naughty of you. I had to take the crew's launch to get mine back." His voice was bathos manufactured to seduce.

"I believe you were the cause of your own inconvenience. When I said I wanted to leave, you should have let me," she replied, neither contrite nor disinterested, but actually glad to see him again. He seemed frivolous and she needed frivolity now.

"Your departure, so abrupt, denied me the right to behave as a gentleman and to escort you back ashore properly."

"It seemed to me you had no intention of doing either." Diana felt herself succumbing to Philippe's theatrical flirtation once again.

"Oh, Diana," he said, taking her hand, "what man could? You ask too much of us."

"I asked to go so I could attend to my horse. I don't think that was too much." But now she smiled more brightly.

"Yes, you are right, perfectly right." Philippe dropped his head like a third-grader. He would try another tack. "What if we were to begin again, Diana?"

"Again?"

"Yes, come out to the *Bacchus*, and when you wish to leave, say the word. As soon as you do, I promise I shall take you back right away. Not a whimper or protest will you hear from Philippe DuChamps. *Tout de suite,* in the boat we shall go." He spoke evenly and his eyes searched hers steadily.

"Diana Winston?" She turned toward the deep, strangely familiar voice.

"Dr. Stanford—Bill!" Her face brightened at the sight of the large handsome man cutting sidewise through the bar crowd to get to her. Philippe assumed the erect posture of one about to be introduced. "Dr. Stanford, I'd like you to meet Philippe Du . . . Du . . ." Blushing, she quickly turned for assistance.

Philippe proudly and carefully pronounced the family name that had dominated the wine industry in his province for three centuries. "DuChamps."

"Bill Stanford." Bill held out his hand and quickly assessed the situation. Diana didn't know him well enough to remember his last name. Customary good manners, civility, and the fact of his marriage usually prevented Bill from intervening when another man was laying claim to a woman he found attractive. But his marriage was crumbling, and off the island of Manhattan he felt more free, almost entitled to pursue this beautiful and energetic young woman. Bill abandoned his usual restraint and put his hand on Diana's arm. "We got cut off from one another a little prematurely last night—before I had the chance to see if we could get together for a drink sometime this weekend."

Philippe stepped next to Diana and placed a proprietary hand on her back to underscore their couple status. "That is precisely what Diana is about to do with *me*," he injected.

"I didn't mean to interrupt your plans for this evening." Bill's tone was even and politely detached. He didn't particularly care for this man, who obviously had no wish for Diana to speak for herself. He addressed her again, his voice soft, almost intimate. "I understand you're engaged and—"

"I'd like to go with you, Bill. Now," Diana replied firmly. The prospect of a glittery continental evening aboard *Bacchus* had evaporated as soon as she saw Bill walking toward her. More than frivolity, a quiet drink with this thoughtful, handsome man was what she needed.

"But, Diana, you agreed that we should be together tonight." Philippe simultaneously lodged a complaint and a plea.

"I didn't agree to anything, Philippe." She smiled. "We were just reviewing your ability to keep your word. I hadn't given mine—yet." To close the conversation, which made her feel awkward and uncomfortable, she added, "I am glad that we met again. Will you be at the Derby?"

"Of course, Miss Diana Winston, I shall be there to cheer you on." Though miffed about the doctor's arrival —he struck Philippe as a bore—Philippe had no doubt about his own ability to get Diana into bed sooner or later. But this evening his task would be to regain Muffy. A glance at her new escort—wearing bright green suspenders —informed him that it would really be no task at all.

The ocean air felt cool and the diminishing wake of a passing boat lapped against the pier. Bill noticed Diana shiver. "Are you warm enough? Here, take my jacket."

"Thanks, I'm fine." She glanced down at her thin silk shirt and jeans. "I'm not very well-dressed, though—sorry."

"You'd be well-dressed no matter what you wore."

"I know I'm being flattered, but I'm not sure how," Diana said, hoping for an explanation.

But Bill did not go on. "Would you like a nightcap at the Sheraton Islander? I was there earlier this evening—quite quiet. I'll drive you back here later so you can pick up your car." He didn't want to add that the Islander was his hotel. That might lead to a real misunderstanding.

"I'd love to. The excitement of the last two days has been wonderful, but a rest would be nice, especially before tomorrow." As they walked along the harbor toward the Seamen's Church Institute on Market Square, where Bill had parked, Diana recalled her conversation at the western barbecue. "I thought you were going up to the Shriners'. That's what Jack said, anyway."

"He's right, but I decided to drive up at dawn's first light tomorrow. That way I could take in a little more of Newport."

"But you didn't want to come to the barbecue?"

"If I'd known that I could have spent some time with you, I would have been delighted to go."

"Well, if you had come, and if you had known, I would have been delighted too," she replied, sliding into the front seat of his black BMW. As they drove down Thames Street, Diana thought how much more fun she would have had if Bill *had* been there. They crossed Goat Island Bridge and Diana took in the harbor's night beauty. "See—there on the water."

He looked out into the light-studded darkness. "Skeins of flung necklaces—pearls on black velvet."

She felt captured by his sensitivity. "You sound more like a poet than a doctor."

"Can't be both?"

"Yes, of course," she replied hastily, not wanting to appear narrow-minded.

Pink and vermilion streaks lingered in the darkening west over Jamestown, and the last ferry to Block Island slid silently by.

The corner table at the Islander's Roger's Roost looked

out on Narragansett Bay and the ocean beyond. The sky and water were almost dark. "Lucky for me you not only stayed in Newport this evening but came to the Black Pearl. Philippe would have been too much company tonight."

"I'm less?" A smile hovered at the corner of Bill's mouth.

Diana immediately blushed. "No, no, I didn't mean that at all. I . . ."

"I know what you mean." His broad smile admitted the gentle teasing.

"I'm glad." She glanced at him, then picked up a cocktail napkin and began worrying it with her fingers.

Bill closed a hand over hers. "Nervous about tomorrow?" His tone indicated sympathetic understanding.

Diana straightened her back against her seat. "Very." She smiled and felt herself relax—though just a little— and sighed. "I'm not going to get much sleep tonight without a little help. Maybe you should prescribe something for me," she added half-jokingly.

"What's worrying you most?"

"Getting over all those jumps."

"When you return to your room, I want you to visualize the course completed. Imagine yourself leaving the ring—all jumps behind you."

"That will help?" she asked, her voice skeptical but interested. After all, what good could her imagination do when it was reality that counted?

"Anxiety's related to the things that people think may go wrong—like your jumps."

"Especially the Derby Bank," she stated quietly, fearfully.

"Then if you visualize the Derby Bank as a constructive completion rather than a destructive threat, it should help."

"Mind over matter?"

"Mind over what matters."

Diana stirred her drink thoughtfully, then glanced up. "Has this worked for you?" Her voice was light, but he could tell she was thinking seriously about what he had said.

"At times."

"In the operating room?"

"Yes, in the operating room—and other places."

"I'll give it a try—certainly can't hurt." She paused, brought her drink to her lips, then smiled. "I guess you're not going to prescribe a sedative."

He reached across the table and squeezed her hand. "I just did. Further instructions include one more drink, just one, followed by a warm bath and a distracting but superficial book."

"I know you need to leave early . . ." Diana thought Bill might be trying to end the evening tactfully.

"Not at all," he replied, glancing at his watch. "I could talk to you all night. Remember, I'm just an observer—in Boston tomorrow morning and back here in Newport tomorrow afternoon. I learned to get by routinely on four to six hours' sleep in medical school."

Over the second round of drinks she did relax—partly because of the alcohol but mostly because she felt that this man had her best interests at heart. He wasn't going to push her into bed, but wanted her to rest alone and to prepare mentally for the task ahead—the Derby. She thought this gentleness and consideration might explain why he was a physician—at least in part. So she asked. "Bill, why did you become a doctor?"

Her direct gaze and serious tone took him slightly aback. More than thirty years had passed since his boyhood accident, but he remembered the trauma with yesterday's clarity. "Why? Because I wanted to be a baseball player." He smiled at the accurate but confusing answer. "I guess I should elaborate."

"Please," she replied. Diana wanted to hear him talk about himself. When he did, he seemed like a shy little boy.

For the next half-hour he told her, beginning with the day he played right field on an abandoned farm in upstate New York near where he'd grown up. He was ten, and backing up to catch a fly ball, he tripped over a discarded window sash. Jagged shards of glass ripped deep into his right forearm. Emergency-room staff at Mohawk Valley Community Hospital stopped the bleeding, but he couldn't move his wrist or wiggle his fingers. His pinkie felt numb. A neurosurgeon from Utica tried to repair the severed tendons and nerves. And after six months Bill could move his wrist, but still not his fingers. Some numbness remained. His doctor had failed to restore the torn ulnar nerve, so the search for a surgeon willing to operate on the botched job of another began. After six months, his worn and distracted parents approached Dr. Felix Spiratos, chairman of neurosurgery at Mass General in Boston. The soft-spoken man with tired eyes candidly addressed the boy's fears. He promised to try his best. The next summer Bill was throwing strikes from right field.

"So how did a little baseball player turn into a doctor—exactly, I mean?" She wanted to know the precise moment of Bill's conversion.

"There's no 'exactly.' I think my subconscious registered the significance of Dr. Spiratos' rescue. I had no career in mind other than one in the major leagues—at least, consciously. But while I was memorizing those hundreds of batting averages and RBI's, I think I was really preparing myself for the demands of medical school. A psychiatrist might say I went into neurosurgery as a counterphobic—a way of dealing with the fear and pain I'd experienced with the accident. I wanted to help others because of the need to fix myself. Or he might say I have a compulsive urge to exercise the kind of power over others that Dr. Spiratos exercised over me. A limitation of psychiatry, of course, is lack of proof. Humans just don't lend themselves to it. The brain's too complicated to understand itself fully. I guess"—he paused—"that's why we have emotions." He ended his sentence with a lighthearted smile, which she returned.

As they walked back along the dock to Bill's car, Diana looked out at the harbor and the sea beyond. "See your flung necklaces now—the pearls have turned to diamonds."

She was right—the lights' iridescent hazy quality had grown sparkling and clear. "Why, Diana, you sound more like a poet than an equestrian." He put an arm around her shoulder and she laughed.

"Why diamonds now? Do nights make for sharper contrasts?" she asked.

"Usually. In the evening the air cools and can't carry as much moisture. The drops coalesce . . ."

"And become dew."

"Exactly." Bill walked over to a flowerbed and placed a large rose in Diana's hands. The pink petals were heavy and wet. "The moisture's here. That's why pearls to diamonds."

That night, after her bath, Diana lay in bed and thought about her evening. Bill had said she should visualize the jumps as completed, imagine leaving the course, and that would help allay her anxiety. But oddly enough, she felt no anxiety. Instead she recalled Bill—his face, his voice, and what he'd said about the harbor lights: pearls, diamonds, and dew. She'd never met a man who paid such attention to the details of life and nature. She turned out her lamp and tried to sleep. Light from the moon shone through the window and illuminated the single rose Diana had placed in a glass by her bed. She wouldn't sleep for hours, not because she was anxious but because she was in love. The Derby seemed light-years away.

Diana woke to raindrops pattering against windows. The forecast had been early-morning clouds giving way to partial sun. Rain would make the Derby still more difficult. She glanced at the clock—eight-fifteen. Plenty of time to clear. The Derby wasn't until two. She pulled back her sheets and walked to the window. In the downpour all she could see of Newport were browns and grays and the yellow outline of the McDonald's arches across the street. She flicked on the news. A warm front over

Virginia had hugged the coastline rather than turned out to sea as expected. It would rain heavily all day. Diana sat on the end of her bed and moaned. With so many horses competing, the ground would be chewed up and the course treacherous. She felt a sudden wave of anxiety and nausea—the Derby Bank, the Sunken Road, Pulverman's Grob—she couldn't do it. Her breath came in shallow gasps and she felt faint. As she put her head down, she caught the light fragrance and saw the flower Bill had given her, as fresh and pink as the night before. She recalled his advice: visualize the course, and all jumps it contained, as completed. This she did, and immediately began to feel better. She wondered if Bill was still on the road or already in Boston, and hoped he would return with good news about the little boy's operation.

After a warm shower Diana carefully packed her riding kit—white breeches, red Grand Prix coat, velvet hunt cap, boots, shirt, and stock pin—in a valet bag. She and Steve had a big job ahead—not only getting Navarro clean but also keeping him clean until his entrance. She went out the door dressed in jeans, Wellington boots, and slicker. A note in the main office left by Steve told her all was well and that he'd caught an early ride to the showgrounds with Tim Craig. She could come out anytime, but only after she'd had a good breakfast, which should include some protein. Diana smiled as she climbed into the front seat of her truck. What a thoughtful, beloved friend.

After stopping at a Greek diner—she picked up a full take-out breakfast for both of them—she drove down East Main Road, black and slippery with rain. Her inner excitement mounted in the slow traffic, crawling because of the Derby and the continuing downpour. Despite the weather, everyone seemed to be going. She wished she were already there, anything but trapped behind the wheel at a standstill with nothing to do but worry and fret. Finally turning down Glen Road, she followed the instructions of the yellow-shirted rain-soaked parking attendants. She pulled in the exhibitors' lot, put on her

poncho, and walked across the spectators' parking toward the barn.

An aging but superbly cared-for 1955 white Cadillac
convertible, driven by an elderly woman, slowly made its
way down the serene grass lane. Just as it began to turn
into the first available space, a red Corvette—seemingly
from nowhere—zipped in. The driver leapt out and Diana recognized Tony Russo. He smiled broadly at the
furious lady in the idling Cadillac. The rain made it look
like a great white boat.

"That's what you can do when you're young and vir-
ile," Russo said gleefully to the woman as he shut his car
door.

Without a word or a moment's hesitation, the old
woman crept back a few yards, then proceeded to drive
into the space as if the Corvette wasn't there at all.
Tony's face went bug-eyed as the sporty fiberglass body
splintered and split under the two bullet shapes of chrome
that gave the old bumper its characteristic heft. She backed
up and did it again.

"Lady, what the fuck are you doing!" Tony ran up to
her, but the woman pretended to be deaf. She backed up
and commenced a third assault. Tony Russo covered his
ears as a final sickening crunch filled the air. Little pieces
of Corvette fell to the ground. Backing out a last time,
the lady sent her window down and in an even, clear tone
said, "That's what you can do when you're old and rich."

The window went back up and the Cadillac slowly
lumbered away. "Well, Tony," Diana said, "I guess your
car is everything it's cracked up to be." Tony feebly
picked at the red fiberglass remnants that lay about on
the grass, streams of rain running down his distraught
face. Diana's anxiety had been allayed: she owed a debt
to the matron in the old classic. It was a completely
unexpected catharsis.

After sharing the breakfast and her glee over Tony
Russo's Cadillac encounter, Diana and Steve set to work
on Navarro. Shampooed, cream-rinsed, yellowed por-

tions of his mane and tail bleached with a special equine bluing agent, he looked whiter than Diana had ever seen him. Hooves glistening black and wet with newly applied polish, muzzle soft and dark with baby oil, he seemed a work of living art. "Well," said Diana, surveying the stallion, "if the worst happens, at least in failure he'll be an aesthetic sight."

"The worst isn't going to happen, Diana," Steve couldn't disguise his irritation. "I hope you got enough sleep last night."

"I did." She felt an accusation implicit in his question.

"Good." He busied himself with Navarro's tack. He wouldn't say any more. Diana hadn't returned to her room until well after midnight, and he felt sure she'd been out partying. Slight feelings of disgust and sadness underscored his irritation. In his milieu—the best of Mexican society—such unacceptable attitudes in a young lady signaled the beginning of her end.

"Steve, don't be cross. I got to bed at one. I just went out to clear my head." Her voice turned light and teasing. "I don't suppose you want to tell me about your evening with that Texan, Mr.—"

"Caudrey." Steve smiled. "No, that wouldn't be my first choice for a topic of conversation. I'm sorry if I was snappish. I've got your number here," he said softly, changing his tone. The double meaning hung in the air.

"I'm sorry. You've got a lot at stake here too, and I should have been more considerate." She took her riding coat out of the valet bag and laid it across a saddle rack. "Has Jim been by yet?"

"No, he hasn't," Steve replied a bit quickly. And Steve knew Jim wouldn't be. Just a half-hour earlier Jack O'Dell had stopped by asking for Diana. When Steve told him she hadn't arrived yet, O'Dell asked him to tell her that Jim Williams had been rushed to Newport Hospital in an ambulance the evening before—acute pneumonia. O'Dell was going to ask Bill Stanford to make arrangements to get Jim back to Briggs and DePrete that afternoon. But now Steve kept this to himself. Such information would likely affect her ride. It had already affected Steve. If this was the kind of pneumonia Steve thought it was, and if Diana had been to bed with Jim—and he thought it likely—there were possible life-threatening ramifications for her.

"Did we pack those cross-country studs?" she asked absentmindedly, going through the tack trunk. She was thinking about Jim's dry cough and his absence from the western barbecue.

"Flapgraft"—a fascinating procedure, reflected Bill Stanford as he stepped into the Sheraton Islander's elevator. Hideous third-degree burns covered the boy's scalp, but this new technique enabled skin from his back to be grafted onto his head without detaching the flap from its original blood vessels. Disfigurement would be minimal. He admired the skill of his friend who performed the operation at the Shriners' Burn Institute. That most "superficial" and "obvious" organ, skin, could be as delicate and demanding as complex recesses of the brain. But now, back in Newport, Bill anticipated the afternoon—perhaps even dinner?—with Diana Winston. The Derby started at two; first Jack O'Dell expected him at Glen Farm for a quick lunch at one. After placing his overnight bag on the bed, he noticed the telephone's flashing red message light. An operator relayed O'Dell's cryptic request: "Call showgrounds and ask the secretary to page me. Jim Williams in Newport Hospital."

A minute later O'Dell dismissed Bill's initial fear of a riding mishap. It was much worse. Jim himself had confirmed what O'Dell and others suspected—AIDS. Could Bill get Jim back to Briggs and DePrete in New York, where he'd received treatment before? Perhaps Newport Hospital could arrange a local ambulance. Also, Jim hadn't checked out—could Stanford do that for him as well?

Bill changed his three-piece suit for a sports coat and quickly started to pack. He might as well check out too. Acquired immune deficiency syndrome—AIDS; what a miserably ironic acronym. And now Jim Williams—like hundreds of thousands of Americans between the ages of twenty and forty—harbored the virus that didn't kill outright but invited other diseases in to do its dirty work. Diseases like the one Jim had carried into the ER the previous night—*Pneumocystis carinii*, a parasitic infection of the lung lying dormant in almost everyone. But in AIDS patients, short-circuited helper T-cells allowed the sleeping pathogen to wake. This rare pneumonia had coursed through orphanages and nurseries in postwar Germany, but confined itself to infants under one year, immunodepressed because of malnutrition. The walls between air sacs in their lungs thickened, skins turned blue, and the small victims died slowly. Now chiefly an AIDS-related disease, this pneumonia struck in the prime of life instead.

After a brief discussion at the hotel desk—Stanford, of course, did not reveal the famous guest's illness—the concierge unlocked Jim's room. Entering, Stanford was overcome by anxiety, then admonished himself. The fragile virus couldn't survive outside the body—he couldn't contract the disease from a man's clothes. One glance around the room suggested a careful occupant—sweaters neatly folded, shirts hung squarely and facing the same way, toilet items—brush, shaving bowl, and razor—laid out as if awaiting inspection. On the bedside table a copy of Ford Madox Ford's *Some Do Not* was centered precisely on top of *Sports Illustrated*.

Stanford opened Jim's valet bag and started to collect the belongings. First the bathroom—robe, slippers, shampoo, shaving kit. He unzipped the dark leather case, then hesitated just before his fingers closed on the razor. He'd read that the virus could survive outside the body in bloodstains, especially damp ones. Stanford tried to throttle back his fear, but yielded. Taking a hand towel from the chrome rack, he fashioned it into a mitten around his fingers. Then he picked up the razor firmly but gingerly, placing it deep, edge down, in the far corner of Jim's kit.

*        *        *

"I'm Dr. Bill Stanford. I called an hour ago to start arrangements for Jim William's release." An overweight nurse looked up from the chart she was annotating. Not satisfactory, Stanford thought as he glanced at the dangling spears of gray hair and buttons that strained to keep a prodigious bosom from bursting through.

"Oh, yes, Dr. Stanford. He'd in our isolation room at the end of the hall. I'm sorry, but we haven't been able to get him a ride. Both Narragansett and Newport Ambulance are completely booked."

Ambulance drivers—scum of the earth, thought Bill. He'd just bet they were booked.

"Did you tell them he has AIDS?" Stanford wanted confirmation of his suspicion.

"They asked and, of course, they have to know in order to treat the patient." She sensed Stanford was going to be one of "those" doctors—uncooperative, demanding, ill-tempered—who treated nurses as mere handmaidens.

"Right," he responded laconically, annoyed at her tone, hovering between defense and lecture. "Any other ambulance companies in the area?"

"You might get one from Providence. Boston would be the safe bet." She watched his fingers tap out an impatient code.

Safe bet. Sure, that's what the local boys thought too. "Never mind. I'll drive him myself. Just give me his face sheet, lab work, and nurse notes." Why not? he thought. He couldn't stand there all day trying to get an ambulance service. As for his own holiday, it was pouring rain—no one could see the Derby jumps, much less any horse going over them. And Diana—well, if she were the sort of person her eyes promised, she'd surely come to New York to see Jim.

"It's time to walk the course, Diana." Steve gently touched her shoulder.

She glanced out at the gray sheets of rain. "I think we'd better use the big studs," she said grimly. Much like track cleats for runners, cross-country studs screw into horses' shoes, giving them better leverage, particularly on turns. In the constant downpour, the ground at Newport looked more than bad—it was getting lethal.

"In this weather, don't give time a thought—just go for a clean round. The clock will take care of itself. Navarro's a handy horse, but don't even let him think about lighting his afterburner." Steve took out his comb and ran it through Diana's dark, wet locks.

"Yes, sir," she replied obediently. "I feel like your daughter in her first school play." She fondly touched Steve's shoulder with her hand. For a moment he said nothing.

"It's about as serious as that—very, and not at all." Steve adjusted her stock.

Abruptly a professional voice boomed over the loudspeaker. "Riders in the Mercedes International Jumping Derby may now walk the course, please."

"Steve, I've got to go. Will you walk it with me?" Her face flushed with excitement.

"Can't. I've got to tack up Navarro. Remember, you're first." He started out of the barn.

"First? Oh, no." All at once Diana realized she hadn't checked the order roster. To go as the initial rider meant a serious disadvantage. If she could watch one or two horses jump, she'd get an idea where to handle the patchy spots. In this rain there'd be a lot.

"Yes, first—primero. It'll be over before you know it. Go walk it now so we have time for one or two schooling fences before the real thing. Meet me behind the bleachers when you're through. I'll have Navarro out there."

Diana threw her poncho over her riding gear. The rain fell in torrents. As she passed the green-and-white-striped tent, steady streams splashed on the dirt, diluting it to slick mud. The bleachers now stood almost empty, except for a few diehards nestled under umbrellas. The well-off at the show appeared, as usual, well-off, dry and secure at banquet tables under large tents—a necessary luxury that day, costing fifteen hundred per table of twelve. Most tables were filled. And if the sun had been grilling down, the same would have been true. As a guest of Jack O'Dell, that's where Bill Stanford would be seated.

When Diana walked the course alone, though in the company of several other riders, it flashed through her mind just how few people experienced the real thing. Fields of cars, trailers, and rec vehicles dimly showed their colors through the hard rain, and many spectators had come in them—some quite far—and many sat under the big umbrellas and tents sipping coffee and wine and bottled water; and many tradesmen, specialty stores, and manufacturers vanned their displays here—and to all big shows; and crowds sat in the stands, some enthusiasts sporting cameras with long lenses, some with binoculars, a few studying the program; and even more curled up at home who flicked the cable remote to see horse jumping. But very few of this huge gathering would ever once in life feel alone on a fast horse, leaping in air, concentrating, timing, totally there. Yes, she wasn't here because they were; they were here because she was. Only one of those few would become known to everyone. And with this feeling came the most powerful electric shock of energy through her frame. And in that instant she put all thought aside and looked up past strange faces, and searched out Steve's. His hand held Navarro.

Standing in the rain, head high and proud, the horse seemed a gorgeous apparition. Diana noticed he was wearing a new white saddle pad with embroidered blue initials, DW. He whinnied to greet her approach.

"Steve, where did this come from?" she asked, pointing to the pad with friendly accusation.

"One of these new close-contact improvements. Let's not talk about it now. Take my word, they're very good." He gave her a leg up.

"I know they're good *and* expensive. I suppose since its initialed, you can't take it back." She recalled the reason Steve had refused to return the custom-painted jumps.

"That's right," he said, surveying Navarro with a professional eye before clipping the number to his outside browband.

"Thirty-four," commented Diana. "Not a remarkable number."

"Make it remarkable," Steve responded seriously. "You can do it because that's what you both are. Make everyone here remember you."

Diana held out her hand. "Steve, I don't know how to begin to thank you."

He drew her hand to his lips and looked up at her face. "It is I who must thank you. Off you go: you've got five minutes to school. It'll give him a feel for what's in the ring."

If we can *see* what's in the ring, Diana thought in grim silence.

"You'll be fine. But, please—no speeding tickets."

"No speeding tickets." She handed Steve her poncho, took up the reins, and as they walked off, called over her shoulder. "And, Steve, you're the one who's remarkable."

Steve took refuge under the stands as he watched Diana school over two perfectly timed jumps. The soaking rain picked up. "Santa María," he whispered. "They're going to be all right." But he had to hold Diana's raingear against his stomach to relieve a wave of excited nausea.

Navarro and his rider waited quietly in the in-gate while the downpour continued and the announcer introduced his audience to the art and spectacle of show jumping. Two thin, steady rivulets trickled off either side of Diana's hunt-cap visor and down her coat. She felt the saddle grow slick as water seeped under her breeches. When the announcer called her name, it seemed far away and dredged up from another time. She barely heard it. Everything now seemed distant—the crowd, the challenging course ahead, and all those months of training behind. Diana felt physically weak and unable to balance, her calf muscles quivering. In a panicky moment walking Navarro toward the judges' box, she wondered whether she would be able to stay on the horse, much less maneuver one of the most difficult courses in the world, made still more unnegotiable by soupy mud.

She came to a halt, took a deep breath, saluted, and began to circle at a slow canter. The rhythmical, confident gaits relieved her weakness and fear. Thought and feeling merged—a desire to get over each obstacle without a knockdown. As she expanded her circle, she felt Navarro's body charge with excitement. She sat into him and closed her legs in one half-halt, followed by a second. His eagerness mustn't take him beyond caution, particularly with bad footing. He responded by steadying his pace and concentrating his gaze on the first jump. It was no problem, a simple rail over a brush fence, deliberately easy—intended to encourage rather than challenge—it inspired a horse to continue rather than quit on the spot. There would be time for that, and not much later.

The second provided another confidence builder—a simple oxer that Navarro and Diana handled automatically. But the third jump elevated the stakes to a higher plane—a pair of gaping ditches two strides apart. Navarro slowed as he approached the first, almost coming to a stop, then freezing his eyes on it when he should have been looking ahead to the second. Diana squeezed him on. He responded by propelling himself as high and as far away from the ditch as he could. The crowd gasped as the white horse caught sight of the second ditch and in an extraordinary physical effort took off early, completing the combination in one huge stride rather than two. That day some horses took three.

Deaf to the thunder of applause, Diana shook her head in an effort to clear her rain-blurred vision. It was useless—the wind picked up and drove sheets of water directly in her eyes. The Vichy Double Banks—twin dirt mounds with facing verticals—came next. Navarro cantered strongly up the first bank, sprang handily to the second, but dithered on descending when he saw the rail to jump. Again Diana pressed him forward. And again he responded by an unstylish but spectacular physical effort. He cleared the vertical by two feet. The crowd roared approval. Jack O'Dell shook his head in a mixture of concern and wonder.

Across a brush fence with no difficulty; then the Sunken Road came next—an excavated rectangle with a single three-foot-six rail fence right in the middle. As Diana felt Navarro gather himself, she realized he was going to attempt the fence before getting down into the rectangle. No horse, no matter how athletic, could do that. She checked him forcefully with all her strength and he responded. He suddenly eased himself into the muddy pit, neatly hopped the fence, and took the final bank like a walk in the park.

Diana headed him toward the five-foot-six-inch "stone" wall, the approach and takeoff perfect. But as he went over, Navarro dropped a hind leg, almost dislodging one of the gray-painted units. He didn't like near-misses, and it showed. He picked up an incredible burst of speed and headed toward the difficult Liverpool—a ten-foot span over water, followed by one stride and then a five-foot vertical. Diana tried to half-halt but failed. She had all she could do to keep the slippery leather reins from sliding through her hands. Navarro catapulted himself forward like a cat clearing water, by four feet. But this put him too close to the vertical. When Navarro saw the rail, he tried to halt but ended skidding forward a yard in mud. Once again the powerful hindquarters propelled him straight up in the air. Despite a sharpened burst of rain, the audience stood and cheered.

Two relatively straightforward jumps brought them to the Derby Bank—three tiers rising to a height of nine feet, with seventy-five degrees sloping the downgrade, no exaggeration. Navarro ascended with agility an obstacle that had been the demise of many Grand Prix competitors. Diana gave the white horse his head on the steep descent and it proved the right move. Showing great intelligence, as if skiing cross-country, Navarro slid on all fours rather than cantering or trotting. Galloping to the final fences, he left two perfectly straight mud tracks in the rain-soaked grass.

Over an oxer, and now only one brush fence to go. Navarro sensed the end of the course and fought for his head. The reins tore through Diana's leather gloves as she strained equally hard to keep him under control. He raised his eyes and looked straight up at the sky. She pressed him forward into her hands and forced him to pay attention. When he dropped his head and caught sight of the last fence, Diana flapped the reins, demanding all-out. Navarro charged over the obstacle and sprinted past the finish line. No jumping faults and only one fault in time penalty for being four seconds over the limit. They would be hard to beat.

"Wonderful! Great ride," exclaimed Steve. He took Navarro's reins, and as Diana dismounted he saw the rain-drenched bottom of her white breeches, stained with Lexol and oil from the saddle. "You're soaked." Then he put his arm around her and kissed her for the first time in months. "But you were terrific!"

"This fellow wasn't so bad either," she said, stroking Navarro's shoulder, full of lather and rain. Steve's smile lit up, his face conveying unchecked pride. Navarro had borne out the faith placed in his ability. Diana had confirmed what Steve already knew: talent coupled with force of will may be derailed and delayed, but in the end will prevail.

"Where's Jim?" Diana asked, eager to celebrate with her friend. "He wasn't walking the course when I did. Maybe earlier."

"He'll be along. There are twenty-nine entries." Never comfortable with half-truths, Steve now winced inwardly when he lied outright. He looked away, afraid something in Diana's face would make him confess.

"That's right. I saw the list at the schooling jumps—he's twenty-third, after Melanie Smith." Her excitement diverted her usually acute ability to detect Steve's discomfort. "Steve, it's pouring. Do you think you could walk Navarro to the stall, towel him down, and dry off the tack? I need to see how the others go."

"Sure. But if there's a jump-off, make sure a runner announces it in the stables. Then I'll bring Navarro out again." Steve turned the big horse in the direction of his barn.

"There can't be a jump-off," Diana commented, more to herself than Steve. She hadn't thought there'd be one. Two riders with exactly four seconds in time penalties would be as common as a 4–4 score in football. She would be beaten by a faultless round with fewer or no time penalties, or else win.

"Well, a jump-off's not likely, but possible," Steve warned with the deliberation of experience, and started off.

Oh, no, Diana said to herself. If there's anything I don't want, it's going out on that course again. I'd rather be second or even third—almost. She held up her hands to look at the torn gloves. Thumbs and index fingers hung completely ragged and ripped away. Sliding down the Derby Bank again? No, there couldn't be a tie.

Under a tent reserved for owners and competitors, Diana watched with empathic disappointment—and increasing measures of hope—as top riders negotiated the course. Actually, the course dictated terms; there was little negotiating. Some gave up. After taking a single fence, Norman Dello Joio pulled up, saluted, and excused himself from the ring. He wasn't going to risk World Cup winner I Love You for a shot at a portion of the sixty-five-thousand-dollar purse. The horse was worth ten times that. Nine other riders followed suit, excusing themselves after—or even before—they cleared the first jump. Others racked up fault after fault. Horses and riders, singly or simultaneously, surrendered to the big obstacles and muddy course, carrying away patches of it on their respective coats. One or two spills provided spectacular entertainment. Fortunately, no one—and no animal—came away hurt.

The announcer passed Jim's slot, and Diana barely registered that he had scratched. After all, other sensible riders did the same. But then the worst happened to one of the last horses. Flying Ace—a Hanoverian import and the first jumper in U.S. history syndicated for over a million—stumbled and fell while descending the Derby Bank. For one horrifying split second he looked as if he'd land on his rider, Sue Breyer. But her momentum carried her out from under the falling stallion and she felt only the brush of his fate. Up in the air, the four legs of the chestnut quivered in spasms. A vet ran out, enough sodium pentathol in his syringe to give fatal rest. But by the time he knelt down, the nervous response had ended. One missed stride from glory, the great athlete lay dead in a heap at the base of that terrible jump. Her face contorted with tears, Sue Breyer pulled at the horse's bridle, imploring him to get up—a heartrending gesture to deny the worst—then hugged the warm, broken neck. The vet turned and held her close, saying nothing. There was nothing to say. Diana gazed at the ground immediately in front of her when she saw the yellow front-loader roll in. She didn't look up till the tractor left the stadium, the once splendid and graceful creature now resting alone in the metal bucket, quiet forever.

"Are you hiding?" inquired a softly accented voice. It was a slim, attractive man, impeccably dressed for inclement weather—trench coat and an umbrella with maroon and navy stripes, the tie with little red anchors she'd left on board *Bacchus* crisply knotted at his neck.

"Philippe." Diana, relieved for someone to distract her from—or to share—the tragedy, asked in a subdued voice, "Did you see?"

"I did—a horrible thing. Poor girl, and poor, poor horse. Such a magnificent animal." Philippe shook his head and glanced at the Derby Bank. "But you are finished, no? And you did well?"

"I did fairly well, but not well enough to know whether I'm done for the day. Two more riders are going after this one."

He observed Diana's clothes, so wet they could have been wrung out. "*Mon Dieu*, shouldn't you change?"

"This is all I have to wear. I don't have time to change. What would be the use anyway? I'd just get soaked again in a couple minutes." She completely forgot that Steve had her poncho.

"Surely you can wear some sort of 'horse' raincoat?" To Philippe, rain supplied an opportunity to show one more side of his perfect wardrobe—elegance under adversity. Hence the Burberry trench coat, a style available only in England. "In sailing one has the good sense to put on fashionable foul-weather gear. *This* seems a bit crazy—in fact, what dear Dr. Freud might call anal."

"I didn't know Freud went to horse shows," replied Diana a bit curtly. "Does he say anything about sidesaddle envy?" She now was distracted by him: no time to ponder equestrian dress codes and their cultural or sexual implications.

By the end of the last two rides no one had surpassed Diana's score. But, incredibly, one tied her. Mark Jacobs and the nine-year-old Canadian gelding Banff had no knockdowns but accrued one time penalty for their excess four seconds.

There would be a jump-off.

"Bravo, you ride again!" exclaimed Philippe. He gave Diana a congratulatory hug. Sure, congratulations, she thought to herself. Another chance at second-degree suicide.

"Look, Philippe, you don't know this sport. You've no idea how dangerous the course is. Please don't burden me with your uninformed optimism." Diana's tone came out sharper than she intended.

"I'm sorry, Diana. I, too, saw that horse go down. I have some small idea what you face. But I must tell you that you are not the only woman who has cursed my optimism. True, it is not always justified. But please forgive me." Philippe stroked her cheek with the back of his fingers, genuinely sorry to add to her distress.

"I'm the one who's sorry. I'm just nervous. I . . . Look! There's Steve and Navarro. Come on, I'll introduce you." Philippe offered a perfunctory greeting and Steve noticed the Frenchman's handsome tie.

"Nice tie, especially in this downpour." Steve glanced at Diana, who busied herself adjusting Navarro's girth. It was the first thing he said, not even hello. "It seems extremely popular in Newport."

"Well, it is an appropriate souvenir of this town," replied Philippe. "Also, an anchor symbolizes hope, and we hope the best for Diana."

"Yes. I've seen several such symbols since I've been here," he retorted, his remark meant for Diana's ears. "An anchor's on the state flag—and a snake."

"I am unfamiliar with horses." Philippe changed the subject by referring to Diana's earlier objection. "It is true. I don't know this sport. Our family owns a few thorougbreds that do the Deauville circuit—and a Selle-Français steeplechaser we keep in Ireland. My acquaintance is slight but, yes, this fellow seems special. Very proud. His marvelous eyes have the look of . . ." For once Philippe seemed at a loss for *le mot juste*.

". . . of eagles," finished Steve.

"Yes, well put, the look of eagles," agreed Philippe.

"Steve, did you see the fall?" Diana asked.

"I was spared, but Mr. O'Dell told me about it. Terrible. We didn't come here for that, did we? It makes our foolishness and vanity seem even smaller." Absentmindedly Steve stroked Navarro's neck with a protective gesture.

"I don't think I can do it again, Steve." Diana's voice shivered, weak with further tension and fear.

"You certainly can," Philippe urged.

"She *will*," Steve replied in a tone and indirect third person meant to convey greater authority about the problem at hand: Diana's shaky confidence. He didn't care for this interloper DuChamps. In the few minutes observing him, Steve deduced he was rich, spoiled, and that self-interest motivated his concern for Diana. Steve now suspected that Diana had made love to this man while he had worried, sitting up alone in his motel room.

Steve went on. "You'll have no trouble because you have had no trouble. You've been over it all. The first ride was rough, but that's expected. Navarro's smart.

He's careful. You watch—he'll be more consistent this go-round."

"But that bank, did you see how we slid down? I thought I was on the shoulders of a skier instead of a horse. Can't wait to see a video of that." Diana laughed to herself as she imagined how they must have looked.

"Navarro took that jump the best he knew, and you both got down it," Steve said. "He might get you down again—the same way."

"Yeah, another horse got down too—dead."

"Diana, stop it," he said sharply. "We didn't come this far to fall apart because we saw a fundamentally inexperienced horse pushed too far too fast. It was a tragedy, but don't make it *your* tragedy." Steve straightened her mud-spattered stock and brushed her coat.

Diana drew courage from learning that Flying Ace had been one of the jumping industry's wunderkind rush jobs. "Okay, I'm sorry."

"Good luck, Diana Winston. I'll be watching." To Steve's dismay, Philippe then blew her a kiss. She trotted to the warm-up ring and her men headed in opposite directions—Steve to the in-gate and Philippe to the bar.

In accordance with American Horse Show Association rules, Diana rode first in the jump-off. Mark Jacobs would have the opportunity of taking her fortunes into account. Her ride would determine his: she suffered a disadvantage.

As she cantered into the ring, she had difficulty holding Navarro in. One round in his first competition, and the Andalusian had caught on. He was going to do a repeat performance. Diana tried to halt him in order to render a salute, but Navarro would not stand still. He sidestepped, backed up, and bucked out in anticipatory excitement. In a final effort to bring him under control, Diana kicked him up into the bridle. It was the wrong move. To evade the bit, Navarro drew his head into his chest and reared up, white legs striking out in the down-pour. Diana leaned forward, grabbed his mane, and put her weight in her heels in an attempt, barely successful, to stay on.

Knowing she wouldn't be able to get Navarro under any control until he went forward to the first fence, Diana glanced at the judge. He responded as she had hoped, indicating he'd return her salute by standing and gesturing toward his hat. Diana saluted and he returned it. She started circling toward the first jump—four upright barrels with two rails—and told herself that her aching arms would have to hang on only five more times. Clean over the barrels, the wall next. Recalling the dislodged block of her previous round, Diana asked for an enormous effort and got it. Navarro propelled himself forward and up, clearing the wall with a foot of daylight.

As Diana directed him to the next—the Derby Bank—she paled. The three-tiered hill was now nothing more than an enormous muddy chute. All grass had been torn and sloughed off by round after round of cutting hooves. Diana felt powerless as Navarro stretched his body forward, ears laid flat against his head as if to cut wind resistance. A thought flashed in her mind: they would be killed too—crushed and broken in mud like the Hanoverian. She should pull out now, she *would*—now! But by the time any thought translated to her clenched fingers, it was too late. Navarro approached two strides away from the base of the bank. With tremendous concentration she overrode her fear and readied to confront the muddy mountain ahead.

Navarro leapt, but when he felt his forelegs sink in the deep and unsure footing, he pushed off from his hindquarters with incredible power. Diana pitched forward and lost a stirrup. No time to recover it. At the summit, rather than slide down as he'd done before, Navarro sprang off the top in an attempt to reach the base of the seventy-five-degree angle at least twenty feet away. He landed five feet short and stumbled to his knees. The momentum of the fall carried Diana forward and completely out of the saddle. She was coming off, but in that fraction of a second Navarro gathered himself up and lunged forward and down. The inertia landed Diana back in the saddle with a painful whack. The crowd leapt to its feet thundering and roaring in excitement.

Diana pointed him to the last two jumps. She vainly attempted to regain her iron. Over the oxer, they raced to the water jump. The horse opened himself up and headed for the twelve-foot stretch of gray, barely distinguishable from sheets of rain and sky. He slipped at the takeoff, where grass had once again been chewed to mud. A half-stride spent in recovery would ordinarily mean loss of propulsion to clear the water. But Navarro's strength drew on an unearthly reserve. He surged forward, barely clearing the white marker lath on the opposite side, but here a spare inch was as good as a yard.

Finished, Diana circled Navarro to a walk. Not one spectator remained seated. Applause and the sound of pounding feet on bleachers filled the air and even swamped the announcer's powerful PA system. For the first time Diana became aware of a sharp pain in her lower back. She could no longer bear touching the saddle, slid down, and limped out of the ring with her arm around Navarro's neck. When the applause subsided, the loudspeakers could be heard. In a move no one on the jumping circuit would debate, Mark Jacobs scratched. He walked up to shake her hand, the first of many riders to do so. Diana Winston had won the Mercedes Grand Prix Jumping Derby at Newport.

# Friends

Bill Stanford glanced nervously in the rearview mirror, tilted down to show his passenger in the back seat. Jim Williams' lips were purple, beads of perspiration on his forehead. He needed oxygen. The nurse at Newport Hospital had said he'd been getting enough—pO$_2$ at 73. But his increased fever now drove the requirement up to a level Jim's congested lungs couldn't handle. And BMW engineers hadn't included an oxygen tank on the list of special options Stanford purchased. Finding a drugstore in the maze of I-95 exits would be difficult. He startled when Jim coughed—a large phlegm-charged, openmouthed hack. Pouring rain prohibited use of the sun roof. Bill wondered how many thousand more *Pneuomocystis* germs now shared the ride.

A little pharmacy in Mystic stocked only one canister of "Lifogen," but that would last the trip.

"Dr. Stanford?" Jim's voice came weak and labored.

"How are you doing, Jim? You okay?" In the rearview Bill saw Jim's quivering fingers trace the bluish tubing from his nostrils to the green canister.

"I'll manage. Dr. Stanford . . ." Jim paused and caught his breath.

"Call me Bill, please."

"Thank you, I . . ." The chest heaved but a weak cough failed to bring up any mucus. Another cough. Bill's eyes darted around the car, looking for a receptacle. Nothing. Then he remembered the coffee mug under his seat.

"Jim? Here, use this." Bill stretched his arm back over the seat, and feeling the cold touch of Jim's hand take the cup, recoiled inwardly.

"Bill, thanks for taking me." Jim's tone conveyed how deeply he felt the generosity.

"No need to thank. I was going home anyway. Watching horses slog around in the mud isn't my idea of a good time."

"Diana." Jim stated the name softly and with concern.

Had this fellow been to bed with her? Bill thought that a possibility when he first saw them together at the Astor mansion, but the implications hadn't yet crossed his mind. Diana would have to be tested. He could call her. "She'll be fine." But Jim didn't hear. The brief exchange had sapped him, and he fell asleep.

New Haven—ugly city, Bill thought, glancing at huge storage tanks. On schedule—two more hours. He turned the radio on and fiddled with the tuning knob. With no classical music in range, he flicked off the heavy metal in disgust. Dante might have used the Connecticut Turnpike as a ghastly byway to the Inferno, complete with musical accompaniment. How could a route located just miles from access to one of the finest coastlines in the East epitomize urban sprawl? With rain coming down in diagonal sheets, Bill switched his wiper speed up one notch. A green-and-white sign loomed overhead: "Toll— One Mile." Bill fished in his pocket for a quarter. He wasn't about to stand in line with tractor-trailers spewing diesel exhaust over his flawless paint job—and into Jim Williams' lungs. Nothing left but dimes and pennies. He pulled on his ashtray, where a quarter stood out among the assorted bridge tokens.

"Slow—Toll Ahead." Suddenly a rusted Pontiac Bonneville with mag wheels and a huge air duct on the hood cut into his lane. Bill hit the brake, swerving to avoid certain collision. Angry horns sounded from behind as he struggled to hold his careening vehicle on the road. He caught sight of the Bonneville's driver six inches from his window. A crude adolescent male leered at the doctor, then hit the gas pedal. Little shit! That's all he needed—an accident with an AIDS patient bleeding all over the pavement. The thought of resuscitating Jim made the surgeon's palms break out in a sweat.

Outside Bridgeport, visibility improved, but not the view. Shipyards, railroad tracks, fenced-in lots of rusting cars and trucks combined with the gray sky and sea to form a metal, monochromatic wasteland. The aborted weekend and the stress of transporting Jim were exacting a price. Exhausted, he knew he should have grabbed a cup of coffee in Mystic. As a resident he'd lived on the stuff to help him through the thirty-six-hour shifts. Coffee, and his wife's flower arrangements. He remembered the first time he saw one—the centerpiece in a conference room. It was during a seminar on cryosurgery—an exciting subject made unconscionably dull by the neurosurgeon's mumble. The air was close and stale with too many people and cigarettes. Lack of sleep made matters worse. But then on the table he saw it, three delicate branches of pale pink cherry blossoms rising up from a rectangular bronze basin. The graceful lines formed an exquisite symmetry, and the airy space between gave unanticipated pleasure. He'd directed his now alert mind to neurosurgery performed with freezing probes, but continued to gaze at the flowers.

Soon he encountered more arrangements—outside the coffee shop, on the information desk, in the boardroom, or sometimes at a nurses' station. The variety of moods elicited by the creations was stunning: three sprays of pink cosmos in a jade ceramic vase, a pine branch flanked by camellias and narcissus, willow branches bent to appear as waves, tossing up azalea and gentian blossoms. When hospital fatigue, fluorescent lights, and OR scrubs dulled his senses, a serendipitous floral encounter splashed with vibrant color left an exhilarating air. On those terrible days of a failed procedure, perhaps the loss of a patient, when depression took hold of his bones, they were lifesavers pulling him through the waves back to shore.

The day he went into the Briggs and DePrete florist shop to wire flowers and an apology (late again) for his mother's birthday, he met Emily. With a smile as fresh as the flowers she was sorting, a pretty blond in her early twenties cheerfully informed him that the nonprofit flower shop served only the hospital. No FTD. Her name tag read Emily Rigg, a member of the Briggs and DePrete Register of Volunteers. Completely staffed by women, "The Register" transported patients in wheelchairs, ran the bookmobiles and coffee-shop cash registers, and staffed all fund-raising events. But there the similarity with volunteer groups at other hospitals ended. The ladies of the Register were mustered from New York's social register, the commanding generals of which had selected Briggs and DePrete for their primary staging ground. Various hospital drills—art shows, concerts, galas, and benefits, all managed with discreet and subtle manipulation by the Register patronage system—might result in spin-off invitations extended by New York Society denizens, Rockefellers, Annenbergs, or Laskers.

The young doctor from Longwood Avenue had only vaguely sensed the ramifications of a "Register" pedigree. Her bloodlines—Emily, daughter of Edgar Rigg, board member of Briggs and DePrete and former U.S. ambassador to Japan—escaped him. But he did notice her polished beauty—fine face with even features, eyes the color of blue delft blinking with the clarity of a porcelain doll. Not a strand of her wedge-cut hair out of place, nails perfectly manicured—the light pink polish reminded Bill of the inside gloss lining a seashell. Matching bracelet and earrings accented the simplicity of her navy-blue Chanel dress. And as she gave him directions to a Madison Avenue florist, her hands transformed the sorted double narcissus into one of those arrangements that had pleased him so much. This creature—herself a study in perfection—was the creator.

More than four hundred guests attended the June wedding at Our Lady of the Sea Episcopal Church in Southampton, the reception just three miles away at the Riggs' summer home. On the perfect day for the perfect union, under a cloudless blue sky, the salt air of a calm ocean combined with fragrant honeysuckle. The guests—New York stalwarts and the water walkers of modern medicine —danced to Peter Duchin while children rode plumed ponies and consumed plates of strawberries and cream. Everyone congratulated Bill on his fine bride—not only was she beautiful but her family (descendants of Dutch patroons on her mother's side, a nineteenth-century railway magnate on the father's) was rich and influential. The attractiveness of such a marriage had become especially clear to Bill the day he met Edgar Rigg at the Century Club to ask the older man's blessing. Emily had informed her father that Bill still owed thirty-two thousand in loans for his medical education. Mr. Rigg would happily pay these off. He did not want his daughter made anxious by personal debts. Also, would an apartment in the East Sixties be an acceptable gift to express his congratulations and best wishes? To be sprung, debt-free, from the sterile resident dorm couldn't be turned down. And although Bill was a promising neurosurgeon who worked at the nation's most prestigious and professionally challenging institution, his salary would peak at less than two hundred thousand—not much for Manhattan, damned little, in fact. He could have entered private practice and made ten times as much. So Bill viewed Mr. Rigg's gifts as compensation for an idealistic career choice. Later, he would realize that every compensation had its price.

At the wedding reception Bill relaxed completely, savoring the warm pulse of sun on his face. Friends, food, unending streams of champagne from Reims, and the prospect of a three-week honeymoon in the northern Italian countryside put his critical senses on hold. Otherwise, he would have noticed what objects had been individually wired to the trees at Mrs. Rigg's behest. It was family tradition to wed in May, with apple blossoms at the reception. But because of Bill's medical commitments, the schedule lagged a month. Mrs. Rigg's soul was overcome—abandoning tradition invited bad luck. At the very least there had to be apple blossoms. In the end they were found at their peak—in the St. Lawrence Valley of Ontario. Carefully plucked and packed in humidity-controlled crates, thousands of blossoms were flown to Kennedy, hand-carried to refrigerated trucks, and delivered to Southampton. While the happy couple exchanged vows, eleven gardeners and five florists wired the fragile blossoms to every available apple bough in the summer yard.

Only after their return from Italy did Bill begin to learn that the Rigg family affection for its members could impose itself in bizarre fashion and create disquieting trophies. Going through the wedding presents temporarily stored in the attic of the Long Island home, Bill found a cocker spaniel, mounted and alarmingly lifelike except for its unblinking glass eyes. Emily laughed dismissively. Nothing to be shocked about—it was Tray, her childhood companion and friend. His death had so upset young Emily that Mrs. Rigg sent the cold little fellow to a taxidermist. On the occasion of Emily's twelfth birthday, Tray returned with an added feature. You lifted his right ear and a music box deep within played "How Much Is That Doggie in the Window?"

Bill came out of his reverie and stared out at Long Island Sound through high-tension towers and a rusted overpass. It had all begun with Emily's "creations." How different now, he thought. Even in the middle of this concrete-and-steel hell, the last thing he wanted to see was one of Emily's flower arrangements.

When Diana returned to the motel, the desk clerk handed her a pink message slip from Bill Stanford. It explained what Steve couldn't—Jim Williams had scratched because of a sudden relapse. Stanford had personally driven him to New York City and to Jim's own physician there. Diana recalled her friend's gaunt face and the intense stare that Steve had given him when they met a few days ago. Jim shouldn't have taken O'Dell up on his offer. He shouldn't even have come to Newport. Then Diana stopped the uncharitable irritation and castigated herself. Jim Williams, her gentle friend and mentor, was sick—and here she was annoyed because he'd made her worry on the one evening she wanted to exult *and* have a chance to see Bill Stanford again. How could she regard herself as Jim's friend? As soon as she returned to Southfield, she'd get in touch with Stanford, find out what Jim's relapse meant, and where she could reach him. Of course, Diana could just as easily call Jim's parents. That was the address he used on personal correspondence and the number he'd given her. But she rationalized that it would be better to get information straight from a doctor. As she stepped into the bathtub, a sharp pain in her lower back instantly replayed the beating she'd taken in victory. Nothing's easy, she thought—there's a cost to everything. Right now I'm a celebrity. Alone. She turned the scalding water on full force.

At that evening's ball in the Sheraton Hotel on Goat Island, Diana had no free moments. She was the woman of the hour. Fashion-conscious Newport didn't notice that she wore the same dress she'd had on at Beechwood. Of course, no one then—except Bill Stanford—had even taken note of her. Now she felt miraculously born or, at the very least, born again and baptized in the sacred gold and glittering waters of success and celebrity acceptance. The mayor, the Auchinclosses, the Dukes and the Pells and the Browns all wanted to speak with her; her friends couldn't get hold—and the media wouldn't let go—of her. Before the music had started, Diana found she had a mental dance card full of exciting names. And she loved it. It seemed the payoff for long months in isolation, hours of riding on frozen ground and in broiling sun. And it offered the best revenge for her humiliation at Hampstead. She knew that somewhere on the fringe, the very fringe of this party of which she was epicenter, Courtney doubtless seethed with rage and envy. And Hugh Simpson would still be wondering, not what he'd done wrong, but what had "gone" wrong. Layers of gowns, jewels, dinner jackets, and breeding, both good and ill, buffered her from those malicious or foolish people who had once succeeded in bringing her down. She reveled.

Steve Rodríguez had prepared for Diana's victory but not for the celebration. At her entreaty, which verged on an order, he rented a tux from the Viking's Men Shop and stepped into new, stiff Florsheim shoes he bought at a local store. They looked a bit odd; most of the men wore black pumps. At a table heavy with cuisine minceur and hors d'oeuvres, he fell into casual conversation with Dr. Mark Jenson of the Dana-Farber Institute—one of the leading cancer research facilities in the United States. He and Dr. Jenson spoke of the Derby and the increased spectator interest in Grand Prix jumping. They were joined shortly by Dr. Jenson's colleagues, and the conversation flowed cordially until it turned to the subject of Steve's occupation. Then, like the stances of the men, it shifted, awkward and inhibited. What do you say to a foreign groom who moonlights as a trainer?

Sensing their discomfort, Steve politely mentioned veterinary practice. The doctors, with less tact, turned it again to medicine and people, quite willing to let the groom stand silent. But Steve, now back in his real element, wasn't silenced. For the first time in many months his wall of reserve crumbled. Like a green actor he jumped into their dialogue with a discourse on the interferon treatment of cancer. He spoke eloquently and accurately about DNA, messenger RNA, supressor and helper cells, and even cited a recent *Nature* article. Dr. Jenson and his colleagues stood mute as this strange man expressed knowledge that could only have been gained in a lab, coupled with extensive reading of specialized journals. Only when he summed up his views did he note their expressions, ranging from wonder to suspicion. He blushed and backed off, and then, sighting his old friend Lee Caudrey across the room, Steve excused himself. The perplexed trio deduced that this articulate stablehand might be some quack Latin doctor on the run from federal authorities. They could not fathom that Dr. Esteban Rodríguez was not only one of them, but the best of them.

As for Courtney, she sublimated her envy by devising two new modus operandi. She would initiate her long-term plan at Hampstead by boxing Bob Sloan's ears. After all, he had failed miserably by allowing Navarro to slip into Diana's hands. She was going to get the horse back: a Grand Prix jumper sells for hundreds of thousands plus. As usual, Courtney thought of horses, even this horse, as one more piece of property. The fact that Diana Winston had won the Newport Jumping Derby on a Hampstead horse—and one she was passing off as her own (that's what Courtney now told people)—galled the young heiress. She'd speak to the family lawyer and, if need be, to the special litigator Hampstead kept on retainer.

Philippe DuChamps was there too. For a short time he tried to pose as Diana's escort, but failed disgracefully. Diana was spirited away by the press, several East Coast dowagers, and members of both the United States Grand Prix Association and the New York Yacht Club.

Reveling in the attention, Diana danced through most of the night, but shortly after four, she excused herself— the ladies' room, obviously—and didn't return. Instead, she hailed a taxi, went back to her motel, and slept two hours before Steve knocked on the door. It was time to fetch Navarro and go home. Home: what was that, now that she'd won? And what would she do? These questions she really hadn't considered seriously. She was all dressed up and suddenly wondering where home really was. She'd won thirty-two thousand dollars (and a new Mercedes). Together with the money she had left from her mother, she now had forty thousand, enough to buy a quality brood mare, with Navarro as stud. Or she could renovate her own farm. And, of course, she had to pay back Steve for those jumps. Over coffee in the cab of the pickup, she put the question to Steve, who gave her a far more preferable option. They should go to Spain.

"Spain. What on earth for?" Diana asked, totally off-guard. They turned down Glen Road and onto the Derby grounds.

"I want you to have the Cría Caballar registration papers on this horse." Steve looked straight ahead, waiting for the predictable question.

"What's Cría . . . ?"

"The Spanish Registry for Andalusians. It's controlled by the military. The papers Sloan gave me on Navarro just seem to be missing a stamp—that's all. A personal visit would be the best way to clear things up. Sloan didn't have Navarro's true papers, but he should have— and we must." It became clear that Steve had done some independent planning.

"Why do we need them? He's an open jumper." Diana simply implied that jumping ability was the criterion for judgment, not conformation or bloodlines.

"He's got a suspensory tear. That connective tissue isn't going to stand the stress of show after show. If we're lucky, he's got a few left." Steve had waited to drop the bombshell. He hadn't wanted to demoralize Diana prior to her entering the Derby in-gate, but now they both needed to be realistic.

"A few shows?" Diana asked softly.

"Including the Puissance at Madison Square Garden this November."

"Puissance?" She shook her head, dazed. In that event, horses competed not only against each other but also against the world record for height, well over seven feet.

"Why must you repeat everything I say this morning?" Steve teased as he hopped out of the truck.

"I guess to see if I heard your morning's madness accurately. I can't jump a Puissance wall. Those horses and riders are crazy. You can't even see over the wall when you're mounted. I've watched the horses go over: they're not landing when they clear it, they're breaking the worst fall of their lives."

"It won't be a fall for Navarro. He's the perfect Puissance horse. You've just seen too many horses overfaced. They get to the wall, then crash and burn. A well-executed

Puissance is one perfect physical act with a marvelous crescendo. We haven't pushed Navarro near the limit of his abilities. He'll make seven-foot-four look like a walk in Central Park."

"Seven-foot-four!"

"That's the height in New York this year."

Navarro had passed a quiet night and stood patiently waiting for his morning hay. Steve bent to his pastern and felt its considerable heat. Diana followed suit. The Derby, not surprisingly, had aggravated the tissues. So Steve was right, after all. The foreleg couldn't tolerate the pounding of any jumper circuit. There was nothing to discuss. While Steve packed up, Diana led Navarro to a well tap and ran ice-cold water over his foreleg. "Anyway," Steve said as he rolled up the polo bandages the horse wore during warm-ups, "you can bet Navarro's original owner will try to get him back. And Sloan and Courtney will try to get him back too—even sue. They're not going to let you get away with this, though the sale, of course, was perfectly legitimate."

Diana hadn't considered this. A year or two ago she would have been stupefied that people could act so hideously, but not anymore. Courtney had flatly notified her that she was on a search-and-destroy mission. Now she would try to do it through Navarro, the horse Hampstead originally intended to ship to the killers at six cents a pound.

That evening, after a brief dinner at Anthony's, the only restaurant in Southfield, Diana unpacked. Derby excitement and lack of sleep had exhausted her. She tossed her red Grand Prix coat onto a kitchen chair, where it landed in a heap, stained with mud and still damp from the downpour. She'd take it to the dry cleaners in the morning. After going through the mail, nothing but vet and electric bills, she showered and poured herself a drink. Curled up in her favorite leather chair in the library, she felt protected. The coolest room in the house, a place of music and words, it had always been the Winston refuge from summer heat and sun.

On her way back from pouring herself a second light drink, Diana put on *Concierto de Aranjuez* because Jim had played it during their Ten Mile Drive. She glanced at the clock on the mantel. Eleven, too late for telephone calls. Tomorrow morning she'd ring Briggs and DePrete and get in touch with Jim. She wondered if he'd heard the news of her victory. As she sipped her drink, Diana recalled the day they'd met. She'd been nothing then, less than nothing—a mucker on the verge of getting fired. But he helped and encouraged her, even though he knew that horse-enamored teenagers seldom made it without heavy financing from Daddy and constant chauffeuring from Mommy. Jim had done more than that. He'd taught her more about sportsmanship and character than she'd ever have had the inclination to learn on her own. And what had she done to repay this unfailing man who assisted her unselfishly in the realization of her desires? Nothing other than fail to understand his. Well, Newport had changed that. Gay didn't matter. In fact, she wondered if, minus the double edge of sex in their friendship, it hadn't risen to a higher level of confidence and trust.

Only after the record had clicked off did Diana hear the kitchen phone. She put her glass on the butcher-block counter and picked up the receiver. "Diana, it's Jim." The voice sounded surprisingly clear and strong for someone with pneumonia.

"Jim, how are you? Did you hear?"

"Yes, sure did. Congratulations. I wish I'd been there." "Diana . . ."

"Thanks. *I* wish you'd been there too. Navarro's an absolute genius. But how about you—feeling better?"

"Still in the hospital." He paused a few seconds. "Diana, you may want to have a test . . ." His words were now soft and nervous. "I think you'd feel better—I'd feel better—if you had a test."

"A test? What do you mean—haven't I been tested enough this weekend?"

"Don't joke, please. I was going to tell you after the Derby so it wouldn't interfere. My doctor thinks you'll be fine, but . . ." She heard his voice catch and swallow, more like a sob, then regain itself. "Diana, I have AIDS."

Sun streamed through the blinds of the small examining room. As Dr. Edel, the Winston family physician for over thirty years, washed his hands, Diana recalled how as a child, like most children, she considered herself immortal. Dr. Edel, her father, and her fifth-grade teacher, Mr. Burke, became guardians of that immortality. The doctor set a broken arm (pony accident), removed stubborn splinters, and immunized her against childhood diseases. But this short bald man no longer could slay all the dragons. Myths had faded into the limitations of science. Everyone knew AIDS was communicated by body fluids, and that night along the Charles River, she and Jim had kissed.

As Edel toweled off his hands, he saw in the overwrought face a girl who thought she would die. "Here, Diana, take a seat—no need for an exam." He gestured to the black-and-chrome chair. "Now, you've not had intercourse with this man, but you say you've kissed."

"Just once, really."

"Deeply?"

She recalled the hard press of Jim's mouth and his searching tongue and nodded. "Yes, deeply."

"Well, saliva carries only a minuscule amount of the virus. Diana, do you floss regularly?" He took in her surprised expression and went on. "Flossing causes the gums to bleed. When injury meets injury . . ."

"The virus spreads," she finished bleakly. "Dr. Edel, I can't remember what I did that day, but I usually floss if I'm going out in the evening."

Her body tightened with increased anxiety. Edel put a hand on her shoulder. "I still don't think you have it. I'd put your chances at one in fifty thousand."

Diana allowed herself a feeling of slight relief. "I still want to have the test."

"We'll both feel better if you have it. The Elisa test checks for AIDS antibodies, but the time it takes them to develop varies—three months to seven years. The likelihood of a positive peaks at six months. You say it's about six months since your last exposure, so the result should be accurate. I'll call the moment the news comes in—one or two weeks. The wait can be difficult. Keep yourself occupied. Take a trip. See some good friends." He handed her a consent form turgid with legalese and a white lab slip with "HIV" handwritten across the top. The test, too new to be printed with the others, each beside its own little check box, had already created a long waiting list at Boston labs.

Diana started down the hall, but turned. "Dr. Edel, there's not going to be a medical breakthrough—I mean, a new vaccine or some drug?"

"Not for a while, I'm afraid. Again, just odds, but this time it's a hundred to one."

"My friend's going to die." The intonation simultaneously carried a realization and a question. She froze. He sympathetically clasped her hands between his two.

"Yes."

"Soon?"

"Not long. His second bout of *Pneumocystis* came hard on the heels of the first."

Diana didn't stop thinking about Jim until she found herself staring at a technician's latexed hands and the needle that drew ten milliliters of blood. As a child she'd always turned her eyes away.

Jim automatically tossed the Kleenex into the wheeled hamper with big red letters—"HAZARDOUS—INFECTIOUS WASTE." It contained everything he touched or that touched him. In addition, all his body excretions and fluid samples were labeled—blood, urine, feces. And the spectrum of fluorescent colored stickers seemed endless—"Isolation," "Contaminated," "Biohazard," "AIDS Precautions," "Blood Precautions," "Seizure Precautions." Weren't some of these measures excessive? A glass or plastic fork put to his lips wasn't contagious. Sheets he slept in and towels with which he dried himself provided the virus no shelter. Denise Barker, the social worker, Father Conti, the chaplain, and Dr. Lindemann, the infectious-disease specialist, agreed—excessive, but regrettably necessary. Irrational fear didn't disappear inside a hospital, but increased everywhere in proportion to ignorance and anxiety. Measures were needed to reassure the staff.

Jim no longer shook hands much—too many visitors interpreted it as a test or threat. Hugs and kisses? Nobody offered those except the staff members either trained or predisposed to overcome fear of AIDS. But who wanted to be hugged by a roving social worker coming around in a red sweatshirt advertising "Hug Therapist" in pink block letters? And who could bear his hand being held by a priest dutifully loving the sinner? And why should Jim have the burden of feeling sorry for his doctor, whose officious manner obviously masked a struggle to distance himself from a patient exactly his own age? Jim felt like a leper subjected to the modern equivalent of stoning, and it was killing him in a way the disease couldn't.

But after five days he packed his belongings to go home. Paroled—fever down, weight up—pentamidine had done its job once again, though vomiting had initally cost him a precious three and a half pounds. He drank two dozen Tiger's milkshakes to regain it. His mother phoned to inform him that Reynolds would pick him up at eleven. Could he manage to check himself out? As expected, minimal support.

His parents had never had any time for him. His father, Douglas Williams, headed a large New York publishing house, and his mother was a sought-after portrait painter of society stalwarts. Having no siblings, but a number of governesses, maids, and chauffeurs looking after him, Jim had been treated like the sole orchid in a luxury greenhouse. Other than birthdays and Christmases, his parents devoted little personal time to him. They sent him to St. Benedict's—a monastery and well-to-do prep school on the Hudson, sixty miles north of New York.

Children of upper-crust conservative Catholics attended. Jim preferred Manhattan, but his parents rationalized that a boy needed to get out of the city—and out of their hair. Jim had been on his own long before he entered college.

Mr. and Mrs. Douglas Williams received news of Jim's first bout of *Pneumocystis* while vacationing at Gstaad, so it was understood they could not be at his bedside. But this second time, Jim's primary nurse informed Dr. Lindemann that the parents were in town and had not once come to Briggs and DePrete. The doctor placed numerous calls to the Williams household. He needed to see them—their absence underscored something very wrong. The social worker registered another failed attempt at contact. The staff barely concealed their shock when they learned from Jim that the family chauffeur would take him home.

But this one time, parental duties could not be pawned off on surrogates. His mother and father drove the family Mercedes into the hospital underground parking lot because Reynolds had flatly refused. Belinda, the maid, learned that Jim had AIDS by inadvertently glancing at a letter from a friend of Jim's, which she found while cleaning his room. And she mentioned it to Reynolds. In any other circumstance, refusal to transport even a remote acquaintance of the family would have given Mr. Williams, in his inimitable autocratic fashion, sufficient reason to fire his chauffeur on the spot. Ironically, this refusal to drive the only son of the family, though now clearly not its heir, prompted Mr. Williams, in bizarre fashion, to "understand" Reynolds, though not, perhaps, to forgive him. In any case, including that of his own son, Mr. Williams had never been a forgiving man.

Diana's thoughts had traveled a difficult path before she knew she could face Jim, even embrace him. She read the information Dr. Edel sent her, and with his demystification of the virus, she gained a new, more rational perspective. Fear and accusing anger gave way to sympathy, but slowly. Feelings of friendship, compassion, and the need to communicate with someone who could understand her fears began to affect the habits of her heart. Friends called and influenced her course in subtle ways. Steve wanted them to leave for Seville from Kennedy Airport in ten days. He had some business in New York—could she meet him there, not Boston? Bill Stanford asked her to pick up Jim's Porsche in Newport and drive it to New York when she came to visit Jim. He'd mail the keys to her. Then, the night of those two calls, she caught sight of Jim's gift—the Grand Prix coat—muddy and ignored. She picked it up, clutched it to her chest, and cried. Going to see him had become inevitable.

The interior of the East Sixty-first Street brownstone revealed owners with eclectic, expensive, and superficial tastes. In the living room, blue and yellow tiles from Portugal framed an oversize stone fireplace, its crown a seventeenth-century mantel of English pine. Upon it rested a sculpture—the torso and thighs of an obscure Greek mortal, standing beside a Ming Dynasty bowl from the wheel of an overrated potter. Above all, where it could be beamed upon by both "Bickie" Williams and a recessed spotlight, hung last year's purchase from Christie's, a gilt-framed Stubbs of a young man riding to hounds. Oak bookshelves, which lined two walls, had sliding doors of glare-proof museum glass to protect incunabula and less rare volumes from dust and ultraviolet rays. In a dark corner on the top tier of a nine-foot mahogany étagère, sat a brass sextant. Retrieved from a Yankee clipper that broke apart on shoals off the coast of India, the instrument had fared better than the crew. An assortment of Fabergé *objets*, including an emerald-and-ruby-encrusted egg once belonging to the son of Nicholas, last Russian czar, graced an eighteenth-century rosewood writing table. An overstuffed Roche-Bobois sofa and chairs came in matching beige leather. The absence of flowers and plants—save one arrangement of artificial peonies—suggested owners too transient or too busy to care. "I never liked this room," said Jim.

He'd invited Diana to sit on the sofa, situating himself two feet away, considerate as always. But she slid over and closed the distance between them. "There are some nice things in it," she stated, but at the same time found the room oddly disquieting.

"Valued remnants of the dead," Jim said flatly. The truth and timing of the comment made Diana shiver, her bleak expression relaying to Jim the damage he'd done. He was infecting her with his morbidity just as he might have infected . . . He couldn't bear to finish the thought, and months of remorse overpowered him. "Diana, I'm sorry. How can you forgive me?"

"There's nothing to forgive." Relieved to be called away from her own worry, she put her arms around his frail body. "Besides, how could you have guessed? Nobody knew about this miserable disease. I haven't been a good friend—terrible, in fact. I'm the one who needs to be forgiven." In the arms of the first friend to hold him since he was told he would die, Jim sobbed with relief and fear. They held each other a long time, gently rocking back and forth in a comforting motion.

Then he drew himself up and asked without suspicion, "Aren't you afraid to touch me?"

"Hugs are risk-free," she replied lightheartedly, pulling him toward her again. "And you know it's highly unlikely that I could have become infected by one kiss."

"But I've caused you such terrible anxiety."

"I was well-acquainted with anxiety before I met you, Jim."

Diana's strength in the face of her own fears gave Jim the courage to ask another question: "When do your test results come in?"

"A week, maybe two."

"Better than New York. A couple of months here, sometimes longer. Of course, things are very bad—not just gays, but addicts, mothers . . . even infants."

"I know. I saw Mayor Koch on TV fuming about lack of federal support." The conversation stumbled. They both knew what they were remembering—Koch had presented Diana with her first Grand Prix blue ribbon. She pushed through the silence created by the past. "Anyway, I'll know about the test soon enough."

"I'm sorry, Diana. I always seem to be repeating myself these days."

"Let's wait for the results before we feel sorry. Anyway, I didn't come to talk about my health. I came to see you."

"I'm fine—better, that is. I gained three pounds." He smiled proudly.

Where? Diana wondered, looking at his gaunt frame. He appeared even thinner than at Newport. His skin was sallow and his red hair lay lifeless and dark against the skull. As Diana rubbed Jim's back, her hand could feel every rib and vertebra. A glance at his trousers revealed more bone. An odd, discomfiting smell emanated from the core of his body and hung in the air. She was swept by a sudden wave of nausea. Thoughts stopped and vision blurred as she felt a rush of heat and dizziness. "Jim, where's the bathroom? Just tell me." Her smile broke despite herself.

"Down the hall, second door on the right." He drew a blanket over his lap. The loss of Diana's touch had brought on a chill. She walked as quickly as she could without conveying a sense of urgency. Door closed and locked, faucets open and running, she bent over the toilet and retched. When the spasms had passed, she rinsed out her mouth, leaned against the tiled wall, and cried for her friend whose body she felt disappearing beneath her own fingers.

"Are you all right?" Jim inquired gently at the door. She came out smiling, but her eyes were red and there was the smell of vomit despite Bickie's bathroom deodorizers. "Maybe the travel upset your tummy. C'mon, Belinda's making us some tea." He moved to take her hand, but hesitated as their fingers touched. He knew perfectly well he was the cause of her distress.

He led Diana to separate quarters inside the apartment. A sitting room furnished with an applewood love

seat, chairs, and coffee table made by Jim's maternal
grandfather—a watchmaker from Poughkeepsie—filled less
than half the floor space of the interior. His gold medal,
a rectangular Princeton class banner, and two Dufy prints
hung on the wall between a four-poster oak bed and
matching bookcase, the comfortable place of a successful
young man—except for the hospital bed with its stark
metal frame. Centered in the middle, it dominated the
room. A white mattress and adjustable chromium side
bars underscored its Spartan mission—not a place to
dream or make love, but to recover or die.

"It doesn't match," Jim joked, walking over to the
bed.

"No, but it must be comfortable," Diana replied quickly,
averting a gaze she knew had lingered too long.

"This helps if you're having trouble breathing. See, it's
adjustable." He pushed a black button and the head of
the mattress rose to the accompaniment of a thin electronic hum.

"That's convenient." She hoped her voice conveyed
more enthusiasm than she felt. The piece of machinery
reminded her that the murderous virus held center stage
in the last act of Jim's life. He returned the bed to a less
conspicuous posture.

"Want to see something my mother did?" he asked,
savoring an opportunity to demonstrate a rare example
of maternal care. He took an unframed painting from the
closet. It was Jim jumping Calliope—a photo Diana had
once seen in *Time* had been the obvious inspiration. The
portrait conveyed Jim's force and determination—one
sensed the dynamism. But his artistic side—light touch
on the reins, beautiful form and balance—were completely lost to the artist. And Jim's face, intelligent and
sensitive, appeared hard, even ruthless.

"You certainly look a winner," Diana commented. It
was the best she could do.

"Mom's never seen me ride. She got this from a photograph. Pretty good for not being around horses much,
don't you think?"

Pretty bad for not being around her son, Diana thought. "She's very good at depicting muscle and power."

"That's probably why she's so popular with the hard chargers on Wall Street. I'm sorry you haven't met either of my parents yet. They had these reservations to stay at a medieval fortress in Lucerne and couldn't change them. Mom offered to stay, but there was no point. I was getting better and . . ." Jim's thoughts stalled. For the terminally ill, to get "better" merely presaged getting worse.

"Where's Calliope—still at Gladstone?"

"Slipped her second foal," he replied, smiling sympathetically at her poor but innocent change of topic.

"That's terrible." Diana was lamenting the fate of the two foals and of Calliope as well. A champion mare with arthritic hocks was useless unless she could be bred successfully. "What's going to happen to her?"

"The syndicate's trying to dump her, but I don't know where she can go. Her arthritis is worse, and you can't hide the fact that she's lost two foals." Diana shook her head at the familiar story.

"Here's your tea, Mr. Williams." A diminutive black woman carrying a tray laden with tea and pastries came into the room. She nodded a greeting to Diana.

Jim took the tray, set it on the coffee table, then put his arm around Belinda. "Diana, I'd like you to meet Belinda, one of the most important women in my life." Belinda waved her hand dismissively but her smile relayed pleasure.

"Ain't you the cake! He's always been like this. When he was just three and wanted some more dessert or candy or somethin' else he knew his mama would say no to, there he was telling Belinda how pretty, how important, how wonderful she was. Well, it's still the same old thing." She took an amiable swat at Jim's arm with the tea towel she was carrying.

"No, it's not," replied Jim. "I only asked for tea this time, and look what you brought—five, seven . . . no, nine pastries."

"Well, every now and again—not often, mind you—my eyes gets tired and I make mistakes. If I was you, I'd take advantage, 'cause it's not likely to happen again." Belinda poured two cups of tea.

Observing the warmth between them, Diana understood the sweet excess. Belinda's cakes were intended to stem the tide of Jim's weight loss. "I'll see that he eats at least six," Diana offered.

"You do that, miss, and you have one or two for yourself as well." And with a broad smile and a firm pat on Diana's arm, Belinda left the room.

"She's quite something," said Diana.

"She certainly is." He paused and looked off in the distance of the room. "Diana, I hope you don't mind, but I've got to lie down. Just for a bit." He eased himself onto the hospital bed and the head of it rose to the atonal whine. "Better. Could you hand me some tea?"

"Which pastry do you want?" she asked, passing Jim a cup. Like Belinda, she didn't want him to miss out on calories.

"Anything. You pick." His voice quivered with fatigue.

She took a napoleon. Butter-brushed and filled with custard, it had to be loaded. But as she slid the pastry onto a plate, she heard even breathing. After gently freeing the teacup from his fingers, Diana sat and watched her friend until he woke three hours later.

# Medicine

Bill Stanford poured himself a double Scotch, collapsed in his favorite chair, and picked up *The New York Times*. A pamphlet with "AWAKE" boldly printed on the cover slid out of the Arts and Leisure section onto his lap. His cleaning lady, a Jehovah's Witness, familiar with the surgeon's habits and vigilant in her commitment to spread the word, had once again invaded him with all the news *she* thought fit to print. With an exasperated sigh he tossed it onto a nearby table. Today he had failed to restore the severed radial nerve in the arm of a sixteen-year-old ballerina, condemning her to a wrist that would dangle like a broken marionette's. Her dream of joining the New York City Ballet had been severed as well. Bill closed his eyes and swallowed half his drink. The last thing he wanted to be was "awake."

"Bill, *darling*, I'm home. Aren't you ready yet?" Emily's voice, higher-pitched than usual, seared the silence. She was already getting into character for dinner with the Van Rheins and the Lewises—a dinner he'd completely forgotten. He glanced at the table—fresh flowers. Emily always "created" an arrangement on the days they entertained. He should have noticed it and taken the cue. His suit—an old Brooks Brothers—would meet her immediate opposition.

"Bill, that won't do. Please wear the dark gray with chalk stripes. And get that newspaper up off the floor. Honestly. They'll be here in a half-hour." Without inquiring about her husband's day, Emily Stanford disappeared into the bedroom to attend to her wardrobe and makeup. She must succeed tonight if she were to continue her rise in the Register. Jill Van Rhein was vice-president, and Maggie Lewis, Emily's immediate superior, ran the flower shop—a key position in the Register hierarchy. Emily had once slaved for her by scrubbing ceramic pots, refilling gift-wrap rollers, and setting up the ribbon. She even delivered flowers to patients' rooms, a task she loathed. All those sick people made her feel so uneasy. She understood that those errands had been a rite of passage, but did her best to eliminate them, employing her resources and skills—daughter of a board member, wife of the chief neurosurgeon—all combined with prowess in arranging people as well as flowers.

If only Bill had learned to perform half as well at social functions as he did in the OR. She groaned inwardly, recalling the manner in which he had expressed disappointment that the Register had invited Frank Sinatra to sing at the Briggs and DePrete annual benefit—not Luciano Pavarotti. Bill had remarked to Barbara Sinclair, the very Register person who'd engineered the Sinatra coup, that "Old Blue Eyes" would have been okay thirty years ago, but why waste an evening listening to a set of calcified vocal cords? He could at least acknowledge that Sinatra had raised over one billion dollars for a variety of worthy causes. But he didn't. And Bill was getting worse. Hardly a dinner party passed when he didn't make at least one snide remark. Perhaps she should have married that stock analyst at Kidder Peabody. Now, *he* understood that attendance at the right parties meant attendance at even more of the right parties. But the arbitrage specialist from Wall Street would have been of limited use anyway. Assigned to the Tokyo market, he virtually lived on East Asian time. He'd be more likely to get their names in the social column of *Japan Economic News* than the *Times* Style page.

It was sixteen years ago, when she was rejecting a role as "Japanese wife" at Kidder Peabody, that Bill first

walked into the flower shop. At first he seemed just one
more emotionally deprived resident (however handsome),
but her sources soon revealed him to be exceptional—
Harvard-educated, Hopkins-trained, six journal articles
already to his credit, one of laser surgery's *wunderkinder*.
His skill and reputation far exceeded his rank. Finally,
Suzie Carwin, the Register member who wheeled patients from the neurosurgical ward, reported that Bill
Stanford had saved the life of the Kuwaiti ambassador
to the United Nations and, in the bargain, the professional neck of Richard Elliman, Chief and Wilkinson
Professor of Neurosurgery. Admitted for observation following a concussion (the CAT-scan revealed some brain
contusions), the ambassador collapsed in the hallway at
three in the morning. Spätapoplexie, a crisis even for the
most experienced neurosurgeon. Dr. Elliman, overseeing
the case, was snowed in at his Rye colonial and couldn't
get to the hospital in time. Stanford, the resident on call,
with only an intern to assist him, evacuated the blood
clot, brilliantly putting an end to the nightmare. News of
the double rescue overrode all other gossip, crackling
through the hospital with record speed. But, thanks to
Suzie, by the time it hit the other misses of the Register,
Emily had already moved in for the kill.

Walking down Second Avenue, Bill savored his escape. Unable to bear the self-serving dinner-party blather
another minute, he had resorted to the one fail-safe
excuse—he set off his beeper halfway though the *medaillons
de veau*, initiating an imaginary phone call to an equally
imaginary emergency-room doctor. Hospital business, urgent, so very sorry. He knew beeper calls at social functions pleased Emily because they created a little flurry
that served to underscore her husband's importance and,
by association, hers. But she objected to calls that sounded
while they slept. If he turned the light on, she had to don
her eye mask; if he didn't, she had to endure his crashing
about the walk-in closet, with no one there to appreciate
her sacrifice. After a beeper escape he usually went to

the hospital in case his story needed corroboration. But this time, for the first time, he'd left his wife to meet another woman.

He sat at the bar of the little French restaurant, ordered a martini, and waited nervously. This was new territory for him. He'd had a couple of brief sexual encounters, that's all they were—or rather, all he intended. Recalling Sandy Markley, he shook his head. A fourth-year medical student from Columbia Presbyterian rotating through neurosurgery, she constantly turned up in his operating room. Medical students and residents often observed his techniques, but she came every time without fail. And whenever he stretched his back or turned to have the perspiration wiped from his forehead, he saw two eyes over the surgical mask distinctly inviting him to make love to her. One morning in the OR he had had a particularly nerve-racking time—a tumor embedded in the meninges had securely wrapped itself around the spinal cord. Under these conditions the $CO_2$ laser required a degree of skill that fewer than a dozen surgeons in the world could provide. Otherwise, it would cripple or kill the patient.

As he followed the laminar flow of sterile air currents and left the central rosette of operating rooms, Bill thought the operation had been a success, but stifled his satisfaction. Never rejoice in the operating room. He'd observed and assisted in too many procedures technically successful except for one item—the patient died—either in recovery or ICU. The cliché was true. But in the recovery room, in response to Bill's verbal commands, this patient could wiggle his toes and open and close his hands. The tumor had, indeed, been successfully removed. Bill had cheated death again, and when he turned to exult, Sandy was there, radiant and willing to celebrate life.

He immediately realized the implications of having taken a medical student to bed. So when she called or left messages, he didn't respond and hoped she'd go away. She did not. After a routine removal of a ruptured disk—Sandy was there, of course—he took her aside, admitted his indiscretion, apologized, then breathed a premature sigh of relief. The next afternoon Dr. Doug Schaller, his friend and chief of service, called him in. Sandy had filed a complaint for sexual harassment—the bare lies baldly and simply stated. Dr. Stanford had made sexual advances which Sandy rejected. Dr. Stanford then said he would not write her a recommendation for a residency program at Vanderbilt "unless she cooperated more with senior staff." Doug, of course, believed Bill—he just wasn't one of those surgeons. But if she pushed the charges, it could get messy—very. The simple solution, Sandy had spelled out herself: write her a stunning recommendation. Bill revolted at the blackmail but yielded to Doug's unpleasant bureaucratic reasoning. Hadn't he himself mentioned how Sandy Markley had impressed him with her attention to detail and her precocious grasp of laser techniques? Bill acceded but vowed to keep a vigilant eye on the future Dr. Markley, soon to join the élite ranks of the laser certified—ranks over which he exercised considerable power. Bill's memories were interrupted by the raised voices of a couple seated by the window. A glance at the well-heeled pair revealed anger and hurt. Why did "comfortable" life have to be so damned unhappy and complicated? He ordered another martini.

"Diana." Bill closed his hand on her elbow and kissed her cheek. She looked wonderful—trim, tan, vital. Her skirt, white blouse, and blazer looked refreshingly non-Manhattan. With all previous negative thoughts purged, he directed her to the dining room.

"Very nice. French Provincial?" she asked, taking the seat the maître d' held out.

"Yes. I feel comfortable here—pretty and unpretentious." His direct blue eyes cast about, then settled on her. Another time she might have responded with a joke to defuse the compliment, but tonight she broke from his gaze and bit her lower lip. He reached across the table and squeezed her hand. "Diana, I'm so very sorry about

Jim. I haven't seen him since he was discharged. How's he doing?"

"Physically he's awful—every bone . . ." Diana checked herself by turning to Jim's spirits. "Emotionally—and I don't understand this—he seems fine . . . too fine, in fact. He's facing death with such equanimity. Shouldn't he fight it? You know, the will to live. The only person he seems worried about is me."

Her observations came as no surprise to Bill. He'd seen the reaction time after time in relatives and friends of the terminally ill. Acceptance of the end was somehow viewed as selling out. "Diana, Jim is past anger. He's preparing himself for death by . . ."

". . . giving up." The tears in her eyes and the despair in her voice tore at the surgeon's heart.

"No, he's liberating himself. He's letting go. It's hard for anyone to understand that. And you, you experience life with all your sails unfurled. You're young, healthy—"

"Who says I'm healthy?"

Stupid, insensitive idiot, he thought to himself. How could he forget—he'd even intended to talk with her about it. She must have gone to bed with Jim. Was he unwilling to admit there was a chance, no matter how small, that he might lose this girl? "I know it must be doubly hard right now. You've had the blood test?"

"My doctor thought it was necessary, just so I could stop worrying. He doesn't seem to think one kiss is any cause for alarm, though. The report's due in a week or less. Dr. Edel said he'd call." She distracted herself by jabbing the plastic swizzle stick at the lime slice in her drink.

"I think your doctor is right on both counts—there's nothing to worry about but there's a need to deal with the anxiety as quickly as possible. No one should have to endure what you're enduring now—losing a good friend and the fear of having contracted the same disease from him."

"Bill, it's so unfair that love—the ultimate act which creates life—can destroy it too." She was crying, and he shifted his chair over, put an arm around her shoulders, and drew her near. Relieved that there had been only a kiss between them, Bill nonetheless worried too. He recalled how carefully he'd handled Jim's razor.

As dinner proceeded she slowly regained her spirits. He loved to see her laugh. She glanced at a matchbook bearing the restaurant's name. "But 'Les Sans Culottes' —doesn't it suggest a strip joint and not an uptown bistro? Or am I suggesting the limitation of my French?"

He laughed heartily and glanced at the match cover. "More of a history lesson. Les sans-culottes were revolutionaries too poor to wear knee breeches. My friends and I always used to come here." He looked as if he missed those days.

"Don't you anymore?" she asked.

"My schedule's wild—well, wildly structured." He continued to gaze around the restaurant with a nostalgic eye. They both paused.

"Why do you like show jumping?" Her voice was soft but her eyes were direct and earnest.

"It's beautiful and exciting." He paused, then went on. "Going to horse shows gets me out of the antiseptic, fluorescent-lit artificial environment of the hospital."

As she listened she became aware once again of what an extraordinary man sat before her. "And what do shows take you to?"

"With luck, blue sky and sun." Their reciprocal smiles acknowledged Newport's rain. Bill continued. "Also beauty and excitement. The elements of trust, talent, training, love, and danger make show jumping a thrilling and aesthetic experience. It's really the ultimate test of two nervous systems—the kinetic transfer of the rider's muscle to the horse's muscle enables them to clear those jumps. And there's nothing like it—horse and rider forming an arc of beauty, efficiency, and power, like a double helix."

"DNA," Diana said softly.

"Yes, DNA, the code to life."

\*     \*     \*

The clock in the bell jar read just after midnight when Bill walked in. Emily had left the caterer's invoice on the kitchen counter, the sole evidence of her work that evening. "Taste Buddies" and the maid had done the rest. He poured himself a Dewar's. What the hell? Tomorrow was Sunday, Emily's turn to operate—a champagne brunch and exhibit sponsored by the Register at the Museum of Modern Art. He sank into his chair in the dark living room and sighed. Wishing he hadn't come home, he imagined feeling Diana's face, her hair, her body, and— another hope—offering her the same release, if she wanted it. But to put it that way to her, even delicately, would have been callous and self-centered, an assault on her already besieged emotions. It would get much worse for her. Jim would deteriorate—mentally and physically. As the virus invaded his brain, she'd witness failing memory, time disorientation, outbursts of temper, hallucinations. So when their taxi pulled up to the Pickwick Hotel, Bill had simply squeezed her hand, then kissed her cheek and said he'd call.

He reviewed the advice he'd given, and berated himself for its inadequacy. Perhaps Diana should see a professional, someone intelligent and sympathetic but disinterested—better equipped to assist her emotionally. Gordon Farley, a psychiatrist and director of the Beekman Hospice, seemed ideal. But would Diana's own natural self-reliance consent to help, or would it retreat and defend? Bill decided he'd put his concerns to Gordon himself and see what he had to say.

He drained his glass and walked to the bedroom. Emily lay sound asleep under the silk sheets. He looked dispassionately at the slender figure and recalled the hopes and expectations he'd held. He rolled his belt and quietly placed it in the top bureau drawer. Removing his cufflinks, he noticed that his jewelry box was gone. In its place stood a little pine tree not more than four inches tall in a ceramic pot. Bonsai, he groaned. Emily had announced that Jill Van Rhein was taking lessons from a Japanese master. And now Emily obviously would follow the lead.

And why not? He asked himself. Dwarfing and cutting off roots was right up Emily's alley.

He went into the bathroom and turned the shower on full force. As mist filled the glass-enclosed space, he felt caught between belief and disbelief. Wiring, twisting, and breaking flowers hadn't been enough. After all, no matter how good the arrangement, cut flowers always cheated Emily—they died. Hadn't she once hurled an arrangement across a room because the petals of a hibiscus had dared turn brown under her care? No, trees would suit her better—live oaks, cypresses, and pines—boughs and roots pinched, pruned and potted, miniaturized and diminished, controlled, displayed.

He stepped onto the white rug and toweled off. He was supposed to dry his feet before getting out of the tub. Wet feet and water took the fluff out of the rug, making it look used. He opened the cabinet to take out toothpaste, and saw the baby powder—Johnson and Johnson, the white plastic trimmed with blue and capped with pink. Emily never let anything less than Germaine Monteil touch her skin. Must be for some project, he deduced. It certainly wasn't for a baby. As he closed the cabinet, a familiar sadness overcame him. No, there'd never be a baby in this house. After seven years of trying, he had convinced his wife to see an obstetrician specializing in infertility. The initial workup and postcoital tests were negative. Bill's sperm count and motility looked normal; Emily ovulated monthly—her pH normal as well. But then the Kubrick test at the Andrology Clinic revealed the cause—Emily's immune system attacked and killed his sperm. Adoption was the only alternative. Yet Emily couldn't conceive of that—just as she couldn't his child. He'd dreamt of holding a baby girl and playing ball with a son. But Emily's perverse and destructive nature—now scientifically demonstrated—had put an end to that.

He slid under the covers, turning his body and thoughts away from his wife. After brunch at the museum he'd call Diana, and if she needed him, he'd make excuses and go to her. And perhaps, sometime later on, she would turn to him, not out of pain, but love. Love with Diana; that would be wonderful—spontaneous, honest, and fresh. As he imagined covering her body with his . . .

"Bill," the sleepy voice intruded. "Did you see it?" Emily rolled over and stroked his chest.

"What?"

"My bonsai."

"Yes."

"Like it?" She kissed his neck and drew her thigh across his.

"Only God should look down on trees." His voice was cold and dismissive.

"I didn't know you believed in God," she retorted in a hard-edged, sarcastic tone. The manicured fingers withdrew and the kisses stopped.

"I have my moments." Bill rolled out from under her leg and tried to recreate the image of Diana. But Emily's sobs distracted him. He reached over, put a hand on her shoulder, and apologized. Not that he was really sorry. He just didn't want to pay a higher price for his behavior in the morning.

Bill met Gordon Farley at the Russian Tea Room two days later. Over blini, caviar, and smoked sturgeon, Bill outlined what he believed were the sources of Diana's stress. Gordon agreed she was off the charts even for what a robust psyche could endure. He'd be happy to see her if Bill liked, though recommending a shrink might induce even more stress. Whatever he wished. He went on to speak about AIDS itself—aggressive, incurable, messy, and agonizing—and what Diana might do to help Jim in the face of it. Giving her a sense of mission would mitigate her own feelings of helplessness and those of her friend. She could help Jim deal with the hassle-type correspondence of his hospital and health-insurance company, take him on brief excursions, rent videos, and—this was very important—get him to make decisions, any decisions, over the payment of bills, what to eat, which videos to watch, whatever, as long as he could demonstrate some control over his life. This would build his confidence and reduce misery considerably. Jim would want to ventilate about the disease and go into gruesome detail, and Diana would have to check the natural urge to change the subject. She should listen quietly and sympathetically. Urge her to tell him at every opportune time that his illness was not a punishment for his homosexual behavior, but a virus. This fact would help her deal with her own feelings of victimization too. Also, and Gordon averred that Bill knew this all too well, the female in Western society was brought up from infancy to despise silence. But the chronically ill tire very easily, so Diana should cultivate the habit of sitting quietly and holding her friend's hand. That would do more for his soul than a lot of talky stimulation.

Over coffee Gordon turned the conversation to the status of Bill's soul. He was concerned, and spoke frankly. Since medical school he'd known Bill, clearly a "Type A" personality then—always in competitive overdrive, overweening sense of time urgency, impatient, fast-talking, and fast-walking. Twenty years later this condition was clearly taking its toll. Whenever Gordon saw him, Bill looked tired and was drinking too much. Of course, Bill rationalized and protested. It was a busy time—an endless list of scheduled operations. You couldn't slow down when you had patients with glioblastomas waiting in the wings. And then, of course, emergencies cropped up. Gordon recommended farming out cases (he'd heard from one of Bill's colleagues that he always reserved the most exotic, most critical ones for himself). Bill asserted that he did, indeed, delegate—all the neurosurgeons' schedules were packed. Gordon asked why he couldn't take some of the bread-and-butter cases—give the subalterns an occasional tough one. Bill answered with a question: If Gordon came into Briggs and DePrete with an arteriovenous malformation, would he want the most competent guy in the place to bump him down to a "subaltern"?

As they walked out onto West Fifty-seventh, Gordon

made one last attempt. Bill had to slow down—faster didn't mean better. He was brilliant and talented—no need constantly to prove himself. He should pay a little attention to his body—join a health club, jog in the park, schedule one night a week to abstain from alcohol. Bill responded by joking. He held his liquor very well, didn't even get high. What better test of equilibrium than a scalpel or laser? In his downtown cab ride back to Beekman Place, Gordon reflected on the key issue he deliberately hadn't brought up. Bill was falling in love— the light in his eyes and the concern in his voice offered sure evidence. Gordon knew all about the Rigg family and the power they wielded. By degrees Bill had isolated himself emotionally from his wife and had channeled all energy, thoughts, and affections toward his patients and work. It seemed he had been willing to ante up to a bankrupt marriage, until today. Total change—a rupture— might be a godsend for Bill. But Gordon recalled the extent of the Rigg family's involvement with the hospital and worried. If Bill pursued this other woman seriously, the rupture would need to be complete.

"He's been asleep about an hour. But I expect he'll be up in a few minutes. Please sit down." Belinda gestured to the beige sofa. "May I get you some coffee?"

"Yes, please." The Roche-Bobois sucked Steve's seat and thighs into a suffocating softness. With a quick upward jerk he extricated himself, moving to a straight-backed chair next to the rosewood writing table. He glanced at the emerald-and-ruby Fabergé egg, now devoid of its Easter association with new life, and shook his head. The world starves and Americans lay out inedible jeweled eggs. A scan of the room confirmed what he'd deduced from Jim's occasional comments. The Williams family was old money gone bad—more money now, but callous, isolated from any tradition of philanthropy.

His stomach churned when Belinda motioned for him to follow her into Jim's bedroom. He hadn't come to terms with the complex emotions that brought him there.

A young man he respected lay dying of a disease that pummeled the victim's body, mind, and heart like none other. Steve's power of empathy welled up, but checked and inhibited by attitudes toward homosexuality he'd been exposed to most of his life. Machismo certainly wasn't his natural bent, but upper-class Mexican society and the Church weren't exactly hotbeds of gay rights. Besides, what Jim had done—Steve finally began admitting it to himself—struck too close to home. And though Diana had told him they had only kissed, he still felt Jim had taken the one woman Steve cared about, jeopardizing her life and filling her with fear. As he took the coffee cup from Belinda, Steve bit his lip and walked in to face the man who'd threatened Diana just at the time she—and he—were winning.

"Steve, glad to see you." A stranger shuffled over to the door, the atrophied frame heaving breathlessly. Stunned by what seemed an apparition of Jim, Steve hesitantly offered his hand. The thin fingers felt cold.

"Sorry, I know I look awful. Sit down. Can you stay a bit?" The soft hint, more of a plea, came from a lonely man accustomed to visitors leaving after a polite interval.

"Yes, but I'm the one who's sorry." While Jim got back on his bed, Steve's eyes took in the signs: neck pulse elevated; flaring nostrils—struggling for oxygen; pale nail beds—failing circulation. He couldn't last more than a few weeks.

Jim suddenly turned his face, but Steve didn't miss the tears he was blinking away. Jim had decided it would be either the first or the last thing he said to Steve, and now he knew it had to be the first. "If Diana . . . if by any chance Diana gets AIDS . . ."

"If she does or doesn't I'll take care of her."

"Steve, I didn't know I had it when . . ." Jim gulped through his sobs, then started to gasp.

Steve reflexively rushed to his side and put his arms around the frail man. "I know that. It's not your fault. The chances that she'll get the virus are very remote. Here, it's better if you don't cry," though Steve knew that if anyone were entitled to tears, it was Jim. "Look, can I do anything for you—write a letter, run an errand? Let's get some things done for you while I'm here." He took a handkerchief out of his pocket and wiped Jim's tears.

"Steve, you're Catholic?"

"Yes, it's fairly automatic with Mexicans." But Steve had no desire for a religious discourse.

"Go to church?"

"Not often enough." Since the mass at the cemetery after the earthquake, Steve hadn't gone once, but he didn't want to disappoint Jim.

"You know the Church's position on homosexuality?"

"I do."

"And what the Bible says about it?"

"Yes."

"Don't you think it reflects society's bias rather than what Jesus said?"

Steve nodded, not in affirmation but in consideration. Jim's earnest, gentle questioning conveyed a need for an ally of the same faith. But Steve felt he was being judged himself, and accurately too. Jim went on to speak about a friend who'd died of AIDS the previous year. The parents, prosperous fundamentalists, would scream for him to repent as he lay dying. Jim had rented an anonymous apartment in the Village and watched over him until an ambulance rushed the young man to New York Hospital, where he died two days later. Jim made the funeral arrangements—chose the coffin and gravesite—and paid all the bills.

"You were very good to him," said Steve after he heard the story.

"He was good to me." Jim paused, then looked at Steve directly. "You said you'd like to get something done for me? Think you could get me a crucifix? Small, one I could hold in my hand. There's a religious shop four blocks up, just off Lexington. Tell me what it costs."

An altar boy's bell placed over the door announced Steve's arrival at the Liturgical Apostolet Center. "I'd like to see some crucifixes, please." How odd that sounded, he reflected, following the gray-haired sister past chalices, vestments, and Humeral veils to a glass counter. A variety of crucifixes—gold, ivory, silver, and wood—lay on the velvet tray. "I'd like that one." He tapped on the counter to direct the sister's hand.

"The little mahogany one? Very nice—hand-carved. Those all come from a mission in Mexico. Personally I like them, but some people find them hard to take. Jesus does look a bit of a skeleton. And the head, a skull really. Is it for you, or would you like it wrapped?"

Steve played with the ribbon on the papered box as he walked past Lexington Avenue's fashionable boutiques. He wondered why, of all the errands to run, he had gotten this one? And then to pick a crucifix made in Mexico. His eyes had simply gravitated to the familiar, that was all, and he'd been in a rush to get out of there and back to Jim.

"Results negative—good show. Edel." Diana read the message three times, gave a whoop, kissed a startled bellboy, and bounded out the hotel door. She slid behind the wheel of the pickup and headed up Riverside Drive, over the George Washington Bridge. New York's skyline, the glint of the Hudson River, ocean liners, ferries, and sailboats—all appeared incredibly beautiful. Sea gulls whirled and spun in celebration. Rolling down the truck window, she inhaled the cool salt air and savored a fresh wind against her skin. Now she could get on with life and move ahead. And that afternoon, moving ahead meant driving out to Gladstone, New Jersey, to buy Calliope, the mare that Jim had ridden to win his medal. Earlier that week Diana had called the syndicate to price the horse: twenty thousand, but that meant they'd settle for fifteen. The first day she visited Jim in New York she'd thought about purchasing the mare, but dared not act until Edel contacted her. Even now, buying Calliope didn't rate as a wise investment—jumping days over, two miscarriages; the mare could wind up an expensive pet. Putting the money in CD's offered an infinitely superior return. But she didn't calculate this transaction for gain, and only cared what it would mean to Jim. She had the bank check for fifteen thousand in her purse.

"What's this?" Jim asked in anticipation, elevating his bed with the button.

Sensing he detected a ruse, Diana teased him. "A blue movie. Bet you haven't seen one in a while. In fact, this one's so blue it's black." Before the video reached its first frame, she needled him again. "Wait'll you get a look at the leading lady in this flick." The screen cleared to reveal a striking black mare cantering in an open field. Her stride catapulted her forward, brisk and elegant, with no indication of discomfort.

"Calliope!" he exclaimed, genuinely surprised. "She looks terrific. Just the slightest hitch in her right hind. Where'd you get this?"

"Gladstone—they shot it for me. I just got back. She's yours now—I bought her. No armchair syndicate and their heartless CPA's."

"Mine?" he asked with disbelief. "You bought her . . . for me? But—"

"But nothing. I'll keep her for you at my place if you like. I can afford some help now."

"I can't believe you did this. You know she's got problems." He hesitated. "*I've* got problems." Somehow he managed to laugh.

"Don't we all," she responded with a smile. "In a hundred years the only thing left of any of us will be your Olympic medal. They practically gave her away. I paid for her, and that's that. No complaints. Never look a gift horse in the mouth." She wanted to wait for a good moment. Now seemed right: "More news. My test came back negative."

His voice dissolved into tears of relief as they put their arms around each other. "Oh, Diana, I'm so glad." She unbuttoned the cuff of her sleeve and used it to dry his gaunt cheek.

"Your lips are so chapped." Weeks of fever and dehydration had cracked and split them.

"I have a solution." Glad to turn to a practical task, he applied a little black-and-white tube of Chapstick, then pressed his lips together. "Problem solved."

She smiled at his ability to buck himself up. "You're wonderful, Jim."

"You're the one who's wonderful. And you've made me unbelievably happy—the news about your test, and her." He nodded toward the screen. The mare galloped, striking out at imaginary foes with her forelegs.

"She's beautiful."

"So are you," he answered, looking clearly into her eyes.

They held each other close and talked. "I'm supposed to go to Spain in a week." Her voice conveyed unhappiness with the timing of the trip. "Navarro's got registration problems, but Steve's certain we can clear them up by making a personal appearance at the military stud in Madrid."

"I'm sure Steve knows what he's talking about. And Navarro is one fabulous horse. You'll be able to get a stud fee of three thousand for him now that he's won the Derby."

"But I really don't want to go to Spain so soon." She almost said, "I'll wait . . ." but shuddered at the implication and caught herself.

"Why not? You'll have a blast. I've always wanted to see Spain." He paused to catch his breath, and noticed how her body trembled. "Come on, you deserve a vacation. Bring me back a wineskin and I'll drink my medications from it." Her face was stricken with grief, and he rushed to comfort her. "Sorry. Sometimes joking's all I have."

"You have me. And I won't leave you. Steve can take care of the registration. Besides, I don't even speak Spanish. I wouldn't know what was going on—a miserable vacation."

"If you went, you'd be helping me. Your return would

give me something to wait for." Her eyes begged him not to talk about waiting for what they knew would be his death, but with an effort he hitched himself up in bed and continued. "Go to a bullfight, and when you come back, tell me all about it. I want to know if Hemingway had it right." He slipped the transparent green nose prongs into his flaring nostrils and flicked on the oxygen tank.

"Does it help right away?" she asked, straightening part of the tubing that had caught around the metal frame.

"Right away."

As she smiled, her eyes brimmed with tears. "I want you to get out of this bed and be all better." Her body shook and she couldn't hold back from crying.

Jim took her hand. "But that's not going to happen. Remember the day of your mother's funeral, when I told you that I believed a spirit connects us? It comes out of shared experience. And when I die, part of me will remain with you as that spirit. You must believe that, because we make it true. And my *spirit* is well. I'll feel guilty if you don't go to Spain. If you go, I'll be there too."

She realized that arguing only exhausted him, and that this wonderful man really did want her to take the trip for both of them. "I'll go, but not for long. As soon as Steve straightens out the registration papers, I jump back on a plane bound for Kennedy."

"Not until you see at least *one* bullfight." He held up a forefinger. The gesture reminded her of a photo she'd seen. It was after a competition, with a blue ribbon pinned on his horse's bridle. Jim was giving the "number-one" sign to friends.

"All right, one bullfight." She walked to the video and rewound the tape, wondering how Jim could be giving courage to her, when that was what she'd hoped to give him. And as they watched the mare gallop in the open field again, they held hands and talked about Spain, horses, friends, and music. In between their conversations, periods of silence went by comfortably, with no strain.

Diana followed the kimono-clad woman past the sushi bar to a table and waited. When she left Jim's apartment and returned to the hotel, a desk clerk handed her the note from Steve. He'd arrived that morning, and personal business would take up the rest of his afternoon, so could she meet him at the Edo restaurant at seven? She looked around the understated room with its sliding doors of wood and paper, blond bamboo furniture, and calligraphy scrolls. Koto music punctuated the air, giving the space an added dimension. Though almost every table was occupied, the atmosphere remained tranquil. Diana watched the man wearing the white headband with black characters behind the sushi bar. With speed, unerring accuracy, and artistic flourish he sliced, chopped, rolled, and presented little portions of raw fish on rice to the customers sitting on the other side of the refrigerated glass case. She heard a vaguely familiar belly laugh from the same direction and keyed on the incongruous light green western dress suit. Lee Caudrey, the Texan who'd taken an interest in Steve at the Newport Jumping Derby, sat at the bar—with Steve next to him.

"Diana, sorry. Last time I looked at my watch, it was a quarter to six. You remember Lee."

"Congratulations on your win, honey. I was glad to learn cheatin' didn't pay—'least not that time." As Diana shook hands, she recalled the hard, friendly fingers that had poked into her back at Newport. But now his large frame seemed larger still. Steve wore an off-white suit Diana had never seen. It set off his tan. Somehow Steve looked bigger too. Must be the small restaurant, or the Japanese, she thought, glancing at a diminutive waitress shuffling by. Diana led the two men to their table.

"How was the western barbecue of yours? Remember— the one you went to instead of dining on top of the Sheraton Islander with a real cowboy?"

As the recollection of Hugh and Courtney struck home, Diana inadvertently wrinkled her nose.

"That bad, huh? Well, you shoulda known better. When you told me easterners was holding a 'western-style' barbecue, I knew you'd've done better with us."

"The barbecue wasn't so bad, just the easterners." Diana stifled a smile as she recalled the enraged Courtney, her tit on ice—and Hugh, as confused as he was rich.

"But that's what I mean. It was bound to fail. Lookee here, when you come to Texas I'll put on a party you'll never forget. Won't be many easterners, neither. Jus' fun folk. We'll even invite Steve here. Now, he's a real southwesterner."

Steve put an arm around Diana's shoulder and kissed her cheek. "Where men of real taste live—no Tex-Mex. How have you been? Drive down okay?"

"Driving a Porsche's like riding a great horse—it responds to your thoughts before you translate your thoughts into actions."

Over tempura and bottles of warm sake, Lee Caudrey revealed himself to be far more sophisticated than his down-home manner initally had led Diana to believe. He handled chopsticks with skill, and displayed familiarity with Japanese etiquette. He got after Steve for supporting his rice bowl by putting his thumb on the inside rim. And when Diana left her chopsticks inside her bowl, sticking straight out of the rice, he picked them up and laid them across the little ceramic holder she'd overlooked. According to Buddhism, chopsticks sticking in a mound of rice symbolized death, he said. Two Japanese businessmen at the next table noisily slurped noodles from huge bowls. Before Diana's shock converted to irritation, Lee told her that was acceptable in their culture.

Eventually the conversation turned to Caudrey's business—Quarter horses. He'd found a two-year-old filly to syndicate and wanted Diana to buy in. "A Quarter horse?" she asked, her voice caught between laughter and incredulity.

"And a racin' horse. Her name's Ladybug. And, honey, she'll run the socks off the big boys. In ten months' time she'll win the Kindergarten Futurity."

"Kindergarten Futurity? Will your filly bring a rattle?" she asked with amusement.

"The purse is four-hundred-thousand-plus."

"My God, more than ten times the Newport Derby." Quarter horses raced at a very exclusive school, she thought to herself, glancing over at Steve, who merely shrugged.

"How much?"

"Ladybug's going for a million, with twenty holders."

"I haven't got fifty thousand dollars, Mr. Caudrey. I'm afraid that was only the *Newport* Derby I won, not Kentucky or the Kindergarten whatever-you-call-it."

"Futurity." Caudrey stood up, pushing his chair back with a loud scrape. " 'Scuse me, I've got to find the little boys' room."

As soon as the Texan was out of earshot, Diana pounced. "All right, Steve, you set this up, didn't you?"

He refilled her cup with sake. "I thought you might like to invest some of your winnings."

"I haven't got fifty thousand."

"I'll chip in. We'll use my name—or yours," he added quickly. "I've known Lee Caudrey for years—by reputation and personally. There's none better. He's an expert at picking out young horses and turning them into sure winners."

"And I don't have fifteen thousand," she said quietly. "I bought Calliope."

"Jim Williams' horse!" She nodded grimly. "Cheap for that level brood mare." He'd heard that she had retired.

"She's slipped two foals." Diana moved to preempt the next question. "I bought her for Jim. She's really his now. And I've still got to pay for Spain, the entry fee for Madison Square Garden, and there's board on Navarro and Calliope too." She shook her head as she mentally confronted her credit and debit ledger. Whatever financial security had come with Newport, she'd undermined in less than two weeks. Steve was taken aback. He'd been so instrumental in Diana's Derby win that he couldn't help but feel he should have a say in spending the money.

The purchase of Calliope offered no way to get ahead in the horse world. Again, it was Jim, his AIDS, and the feelings Diana had for him that complicated things. His irritation must have surfaced. Diana closed her hand over his. "Don't be angry. He needed me to do this, and I needed to do it for him."

He paused. "Well, I'm glad you did it. Generosity shouldn't depend on financial considerations. But now let me help you. Can you put up ten percent of one share for this filly from your savings? I'll underwrite the rest."

"Sure, but you haven't got any money." She studied his face and then realized how steady his resolve remained. "Do you?"

"Sorry to keep you waitin'. I needed to call Amarillo." Lee Caudrey pulled up his chair. "Well, young lady, what's your answer?" He did business at an amicable but brisk pace.

She glanced at Steve, who nodded a go-ahead. "I don't know you very well, Mr. Caudrey, but you seem very nice and Steve says it's a good bet, so I guess I'm in."

"Great. I'll have my secretary forward the contract to you as soon as I get back to Dallas."

After champagne to celebrate the transaction, Diana touched the Texan's elbow. "Mr. Caudrey, the show-jumping world's on the rise in the U.S. and I'm going with it. I intend to have the best show barn and want to offer you a chance to go in on it with me—soon."

He smiled broadly and doffed an imaginary hat. "I'll be waiting."

The phone started to ring as she walked into her hotel room. Bill Stanford had called late that morning and again in the afternoon, but she'd been out. He was leaving town the next day and wanted to get together to talk about Jim. Could she meet him at the Algonquin for a drink that evening—just a ten-minute walk from her hotel?

Empty, the main ground-floor room of the Algonquin looks inauspicious. It could be an older, well-maintained hotel in Bloomsburg, Pennsylvania, or Joplin, Missouri.

Just off to the right of the main entrance a small bar provides less light and a bit more privacy. Through a doorway, another function room extends to the left and rear. But in the main room all functions flow together: bell desk, reception, cashier, elevator, coatrack, lounge, and newsstand. At the rear, again not separated by any partition, the main dining room displays its predominantly red decor. Filled with guests and haunted by its legendary literary ghosts from Broadway, *The New Yorker*, publishers, and major magazines, the Algonquin becomes crowded and vital. Fifty conversations go on at once, people constantly but unobtrusively finding free chairs, greeting friends, or talking business with clients. The setting, unlike some of the conversations, is no-nonsense, utterly without pretension, and delightful.

Bill liked the Algonquin for two reasons: Emily disliked it and—as with the show-jumping world—it provided another milieu for rest and recreation away from Briggs and DePrete.

"And I thought I was busy," he said, kissing Diana's cheek as she walked in the door. He escorted her to a pair of wing chairs behind one of the square columns and rang the bell for service.

"Cointreau would be fine," she said to the white-jacketed waiter while straightening the pleats of her navy skirt and looking at Bill. His ruggedly handsome face now appeared to her sensitive, almost vulnerable. She couldn't identify the after-shave, but loved its scent—fresh, woodsy, and subtle.

"I'll have a Dewar's on the rocks." The waiter nodded and turned on his heel. "So, how's Jim, and how have you been doing?"

"Under the circumstances, he's fine, I guess. And for me, some good news: I don't have AIDS. At least, I'm HIV negative." At that moment, the waiter who was placing their drinks paused for a split second, looked at his customers—and the glasses—then continued.

"Wonderful, you must be so relieved." It was too early for him to tell her how relieved *he* felt.

"Jim seemed so happy when I told him."

"I'm sure it was a terrible burden for him to bear. Now he can concentrate on himself. And you can concentrate on yourself too. This trip to Spain comes at a good time. I only wish I could go too." As he spoke, Bill averted his gaze to the ice still settling in his glass, afraid that looking in her eyes would reveal the true motivation behind his wish.

"Work getting a bit much?" she asked sympathetically.

"Not just work," he replied. Rather than elaborate, he dug his fingers into the dish of nuts.

Their conversation paused momentarily, but she tried again. "You take exquisite care of your hands, don't you?" It was the first time she'd really looked at them. They were large and strongly veined, the fingers long and tapered. He kept his nails impeccably manicured—uniform and round at the edges, no cuticles.

"I have to." His voice combined pride and embarrassment as she examined them. "Instruments I work with— surgical clips, for example—can be very small. I need to pick them up easily, and a ragged nail can tear surgical gloves."

"What a great excuse to be vain," she teased. "They're certainly in better shape than mine." She glanced at her own.

Impulsively seizing the chance to touch her, even surprising himself, he took her hand. "Nails of various lengths, ragged too. You'd tear any glove, even a Rawlings." With nothing more to say, he gently released her. His hands had been warm and dry.

"What would you like from Spain?" she asked, filling in the blank left by his retracted gesture. "It's got to be small, something I can fit in my suitcase."

He remembered a rainy night driving back from Newark airport and the music he'd listened to on WQXR. "A record by a Spaniard named Turina. I don't know anything else about him except that I heard a piece of his over the car radio and liked it. Unfortunately, when they announced the title, I was stranded in the Lincoln Tunnel."

"Turina," she repeated to herself, sure she'd remember. "You wouldn't prefer some dark-eyed beauty peering over an ivory fan?"

"Your eyes are dark enough. Besides, you said it had to fit in your suitcase."

She smiled, pleased at the compliment and the feelings it revealed.

And that night, alone in bed, Diana thought about those feelings. And Bill Stanford. She'd been in love with him ever since that night in Newport. Bill—a married man—so it was hopeless. Or was it? How much did his attention simply echo sympathy for the situation with Jim? And if Bill loved her, would he be willing to leave his wife? Diana could never be the "other woman." Maybe he only saw her as an affair, an attractive antidote to some mid-life crisis. Why, then, the warm touch of his smooth soft hands holding hers, and his kiss when he said good night after walking her back to her hotel? If only things were different and he could have asked to come up to her room. As sleep overcame her, she imagined how they would have made love and what she would do to please him.

# Andalusia

"There." Steve tapped Diana's shoulder and gestured to the window of their Iberia 737. Great black-green mountains, the Sierra Nevadas, gave way to citrus groves, vineyards, and colored fields where white horses and black bulls grazed. At ten thousand feet, the world below suddenly proffered a mysterious invitation. An almost mythic land was swelling up to meet them.

"And you've never been here?" she asked, sitting up to look beyond the aircraft's banking wing.

"No, never."

A tone sounded and the cabin seat-belt lights flashed on. Diana closed the metal buckle, recalling how easily she'd let Steve talk her into seeing a bullfight in Seville. Within two hours of their arrival in Madrid, while she slept at the Ritz Plaza de la Lealtad, he'd visited the Cría Caballar and straightened out Navarro's registration problem. The papers suffered from an incorrect stamp—that was all—according to the colonel responsible for stallion records. A negligible administrative fee and Navarro became legitimate.

That first evening in Madrid, over plates of cold shrimp and a bottle of white Chacoli at the Café Gijón, Steve proposed catching a plane to Seville—the place to see a bullfight. At first Diana objected. Couldn't they go to the Ventas ring just a few miles away? But no, that wouldn't be good enough. They'd come too far to stop at Madrid, he explained. In pre-Christian times bull cults flourished throughout Andalusia. The Catholic Church tried to put an end to the province's pagan fascination with taurus by prohibiting a Christian burial to anyone killed in the ring. Church authorities even portrayed Satan as a bull. But the Andalusian people resisted and won. And since the horses and bulls that fought most heroically were bred in Andalusia, Steve added, it only made sense to see them there. After dinner they walked to the Prado Museum and viewed the paintings of Velázquez, a native of Seville. In many he portrayed Spanish royalty on the backs of powerful Andalusian horses, rider and mount ennobling one another. Never had Diana seen such majestic bearing, something foreign to a world that called itself postmodern.

Over cognac at the Nicandra, Steve told her about flamenco, Andalusia's native dance, and the post-Easter *féria*, where people sported the best in traditional Andalusian dress—velvet jacket, chaps, and Córdoba hat. Riding between tents and pavilions set up for the occasion, they stop to chat with friends and drink glasses of sherry without dismounting. Steve remarked how the Spanish philosopher Ortega y Gasset spoke of the collective but fascinating narcissism of the Andalusian people, which manifests itself in songs, dances, festivals, and spectacles such as the bullfight. The underside of this, however, was a profound awareness and self-knowledge.

Still on eastern daylight time, Diana and Steve quickly fell into the late rhythms of Madrid. At midnight they found themselves at the Puerta del Sol, Gate of the Sun, the intimate crescent-shaped plaza from which all road distances in Spain are measured. As Steve spoke, Diana wondered how many kilometers away Seville lay—and began to succumb to the allure of Andalusia. Later that night, before they went to their separate rooms, she told him she wanted to go.

They circled now over an azure sea, with giant Africa spread just to the south and east, while the sun shot through a blue sky, leaving it almost incandescent. Land again, white buildings and a shimmering harbor. "Must be Cádiz," observed Steve. "It's called 'cupful of silver' because mica dust in the atmosphere makes the air sparkle. Pretty, isn't it?"

" 'Pretty' doesn't describe it," Diana replied softly, her eyes moving between harbor, sea, and coasts. This, she thought, must be what the ancient writers meant about a poet seeing the world from the vantage of an eagle. When the plane began its final approach and miniatures turned true to scale, she felt her senses heighten in anticipation and was glad Steve had persuaded her so easily.

As the cab sped down Seville's Paseo de las Delicias, lined with palms and acacias, Steve pointed to a broad green river. "The Guadalquivir. Centuries ago merchant ships coming for silver and gold returned to their home ports with refined bullion. Magellan set sail from here too." His voice grew animated and his face lit up with excitement. "Sorry. I sound like a tour guide."

"Are you sure you've never been here before?" Both in the air and on the ground he evinced a remarkable familiarity with the province.

"No, but I've heard a lot about it." He ended his sentence with a smile, and Diana knew it meant that this part of the conversation had finished. Then he thrust his head out the window to savor the sights and smells that his father had detailed to him so many times. The white stucco homes offered to the streets their black grillwork and their balconies overflowing with bougainvillea, spice pinks, hibiscus, and lilies-of-the-Nile. Down San Fernando into the Plaza Triunfo, dominated by two remarkable buildings—the Alcázar, a great Moorish palace where Queen Isabella received Columbus, and the Gothic Cathedral of Seville with its honey-colored walls. An uncharacteristically square minaret topped by a belfry formed a tall, curious ensemble: the cathedral bell tower—the Giralda. After defeating the Moors, the Catholic victors had razed most mosques, but with this minaret, aesthetic sentiment overrode religious zeal.

In the residential areas, the city seemed nothing but

endless white walls and narrow streets. The sky remained blue-white, the sun beating down in a dry, antiseptic wash, its heat strong with the scent of oranges. At one intersection Steve looked through the iron grille gate of a private home. Four children were playing on a patio amid ceramic pots filled with red geraniums. Water splashed down three tiers of a marble fountain, giving sonorous relief to the sun's white glare. The glimpse made his lips move spontaneously.

> This light of Seville . . . The great house once again
> Where I was born, filled with fountain sounds.

How often his father had recited that sonnet. Like the poet Machado, Gregorio Nováles Rodríguez had professed Republican sentiments. After Franco had confiscated all his property and holdings, he emigrated to Mexico City, where he married Linda Ramírez, Steve's mother, and swore he'd outlive Franco to return with his family to Spain. But just months before the dictator's funeral, a fatal auto accident on the Paseo de la Reforma put an end to that dream. It had been 1974, November 2, the Day of the Dead.

"Steve . . ." Diana's young, energetic voice pulled him back to the world of the living. He quickly brushed the tears from his eyes. She removed her sunglasses, looked at him directly, and took his hand. "You're crying."

"My father. My father was from Seville."

As Diana hung up her clothes in the small but tastefully furnished room, she thought only about Steve. Something was happening with him. Her thoughts backtracked, searching for clues. Yes, at the ball following the Derby, she'd seen him talk to strangers, no longer a reticent shadow but a full partner in conversation. Then that cosmopolitan night in New York with Lee Caudrey, he'd dressed in a stylish beige tropical-weight suit and seemed so tall, even in the Texan's company. At first she thought

Steve gave that impression because of the Japanese restaurant, or maybe it was because she'd spent so much time with Jim, whose miserable health and shrunken frame made everyone else appear vigorous and big. But that theory didn't explain it. And Steve no longer kept his remarks confined to horses and routine events. In the plane he spoke about Andalusia with the happy authority of a tourist returning to some beloved location. Yet, it was more—his father came from Seville. She didn't ask for details, but held his hand until the cab pulled up at the hotel. Now she knew the real reason for their trip, and it wasn't a bullfight.

Also, Steve had money. By going in with her on that Quarter horse, he'd become a player in Lee Caudrey's syndicate. Derby winnings covered their air tickets, but Steve insisted on paying for hotels and made all the arrangements. Diana had anticipated some inexpensive pension, but no—in Madrid he chose the super-deluxe Ritz Plaza, and in Seville the ornate Alfonso XIII. Bars and restaurants they visited clearly catered to the upper class. And now he dressed well too. Several new articles— sports coats, shirts, ties (conservative but uncommon) —had made their debut in his previously shabby wardrobe. She'd learned not to quiz or confront Steve about his past. The discomfort became obvious. If only he would confide in her. She still didn't know anything about him—really—except that he was no groom. In Seville perhaps she would learn what he was, or had been.

After a quick shower she met Steve in the hotel's inner courtyard by the pool. They'd agreed on a walk before dinner and so strolled down San Fernando past the Tobacco Factory—more famous for *Carmen* than its current status as part of the University of Seville—then onto the Paseo de Cristobal Colón. "So we go to a bullfight tomorrow?" she asked.

"Yes." He paused. "But I think instead of a regular *corrida* you would prefer to see a *rejoneo*, where all fighting against the bull is done from horseback. It's more exciting and you'll see advanced dressage put to a practical, as well as artistic, purpose."

"It sounds terrific. But I promised Jim I'd go to a bullfight, and neither of us knew about *re* . . ."

"*Rejoneo*. Well, then, let's go to both—a *rejoneo* tomorrow afternoon, a regular bullfight the day after." Steve's voice conveyed good-humored resignation.

Church bells pealed across the river. Diana scanned the white stucco buildings for a tower but saw none. She walked over to the stone wall that ran parallel to the clay embankment and stopped. "Soon I have to get back to New York."

He came up and put an arm around her shoulders. "Yes, Jim needs you, I know. There's a plane departing Seville in two days. We could leave the day before and catch a flight from Madrid, but we'd get to New York only eight hours earlier. It's up to you. Think about it and let me know tonight." The end of their walk took them to the Bridge of Isabella II. Steve pointed to the low white buildings across the river. "That's Triana, the old Gypsy quarter. Matadors and flamenco dancers live there. Also, its kilns produce the best pottery in Europe. My father . . ." He hesitated.

"Yes . . ." she gently urged.

"He had some pieces shipped to my mother once. See how the river changes color," he said, changing the subject.

Diana allowed the diversion. "This morning green, but now it's the color of the sky, which is no color at all."

"No deep New England blues here."

As they turned onto the Circo and walked past the ornate Plaza de Toros, Diana slipped her arm under Steve's. And this time, rather than stiffening against her touch, she felt his body soften, and he affectionately pressed her arm against his side.

They took seats at a sidewalk bar in Calle Alemanes, looking across to the wall of Patio de los Naranjos, the inner court of the cathedral. Thirsty from their walk, Steve ordered *sangría* as well as servings of thinly sliced ham *serrano*. It arrived in a few minutes.

"This ham's delicious," Diana commented.

"While curing, it's laid out on the snow of the Sierras so it doesn't spoil in the sun."

"Dr. Rodríguez? . . . Steve!" A friendly voice emanated from a large figure obscured in the late sun. Using his hand as a visor, Steve looked up. As the man moved into the shade of the bar's veranda, Steve's heart pounded in his ears.

"Marshall Simpkins. You were my chief resident in eighty or eighty-one." The balding man, in an Izod shirt and chino pants, held his hand outstretched, his eyes conveying that he hardly believed what he saw.

"Eighty-one." With a supreme effort Steve pushed through the immobilizing shock, stood up, and clasped the hand of the chief of pediatrics at Stanford Medical School. "Please, take a chair. Diana, I'd like you to meet Dr. Marshall Simpkins."

"Marshall, please. Or Marsh, if you like."

"Pleased to meet you." As Diana shook hands, her thoughts flashed back to the fall from Navarro, the concussion, and Steve's expert first aid. Yes, Dr. Rodríguez—despite his denial. She fell into stunned silence.

"You look well—trim and tan," commented Simpkins, his unblinking eyes driving into Steve's.

"Why shouldn't I?" he asked blithely, pouring *sangría* into a third glass.

"Because I was told you were dead." Steve's stunned face demanded explanation. "The earthquake. Joe Malvezzi called you as soon as phone lines were patched again. Beat me to it, in fact. But the command post at the Military Hospital said you'd been buried under Juárez."

"They got it wrong. My . . ." Steve's voice faltered, then regained itself. "My wife and child died in Juárez." He quickly drained his glass. The short but painful sentence had rasped his throat. "Of course, there was tremendous confusion then."

Diana reached over and squeezed his hand. Now she knew the pain that he'd lived with alone.

"I'm very sorry. We should've double-checked," Simpkins said softly.

"A triple-check might have yielded the same response. Months passed before things got back on track." Odd, he thought to himself, that Malvezzi would be first on the phone. He'd never struck him as the caring type. Self-promotion seemed more his game.

"Well, I'm very glad to see you. You've made my vacation." Simpkins turned to Diana. "So, how did you get hooked up with this guy?"

"I . . . uh . . ." She fumbled her words. Newly complicated feelings for Steve prevented her from trading revelations. "We met in Boston."

"Boston!" he boomed jovially. "Great town. So you decided to move to the U.S. after all." He turned to Diana. "We wanted Steve to stay at Stanford but he had this unshakable notion about duty and obligations to Mexico. We used every argument in the book, but he was adamant. I think it's terrific he practices in Boston."

"I don't practice," Steve said starkly. But both Diana's and Simpkins' silence created a blank that Steve had to fill. He poured himself another glass of *sangría*. "I couldn't practice . . . The loss, it came . . . I just couldn't. Not for a long time. And finally, when I thought I could, if only I left Mexico, the American Board of Pediatrics turned me down."

"No!" thundered Simpkins. The idea of his selfless chief resident—the most talented he'd known in two decades—being denied certification was ludicrous. A resident of Steve's caliber wouldn't need to crack a book to excel.

"I passed my oral and written exams with distinction. The recommendations—if you could call them that—did me in."

"Whose?" Simpkins demanded, ready for action. "I certainly didn't have the opportunity to write one."

"Don't know. The letter only said that the rejection stemmed from evaluations made by 'preceptors and peers.' And, Marshall, I did write to you for a reference."

"No such letter came to me, Steve. When was it?" All business now, Diana could see Simpkins scrolling through his mental files.

"October, eighty-five."

"That explains it. I was fishing—here in Spain, in fact—recovering from a frontal meningioma. Malvezzi was acting chairman. Your letter must have gone to him. Strange, he didn't mention it."

Steve passed up the chance for critical speculation and asked about Simpkins' health instead. "Marsh, I'm so sorry about the tumor. Everything go okay?" Though a meningioma was usually benign and slow-growing, any brain tumor triggered great concern.

"Couldn't have gone smoother. Taken out by a crackerjack neurosurgeon at Briggs and DePrete."

Bill Stanford. It must have been Bill, but this was no time for coincidences, so Diana remained silent.

"Steve," Simpkins continued, "this mix-up shouldn't have happened. There's obviously been a major mistake. I want you to reapply." Both Diana and Simpkins read Steve's impassive face as a refusal.

"Steve!" Simpkins' voice verged on exasperation. "Pride has nothing to do with it."

"Pride has everything to do with it," Steve snapped suddenly.

"You've been screwed. I don't know how, but I'm going to find out. You should've called me. I could have . . ."

". . . told me you wrote a 'confidential' letter?"

"I see," replied Simpkins softly, catching Steve's logic. "But I thought you knew me better than that."

"I'm sorry, Marsh. I couldn't be sure. My life had taken so many bad turns."

Marshall Simpkins put his hand on Steve's shoulder. "I'd go to the ends of the earth to help you. Now, tell me you'll reapply. Please."

Steve glanced down at his lap to break off the torture of Simpkins' uncompromising gaze. Maybe his rejection had been a "screw-up." He'd have every reason to expect that a new application would be looked on favorably. And yet, the thought of a carbon copy . . . He just couldn't take another loss, another failure. As he stared at the cathedral wall hiding the orchard of orange trees from his view, he felt Diana take his hand.

"I'll give it another try." But his voice carried only enough energy to convince Simpkins.

"Terrific! Scratch down your address on this card. You've got mine, I know. And we'll be in touch."

"Can't you join us for supper?" Diana asked, offering to refill his glass, eager for more conversation about Steve.

"No, I'm meeting a friend in Granada later this evening. We're going fishing, so I've got to scurry off. My bus leaves in an hour." He backed out his chair and stood up.

"Good fishing here?" Steve asked.

"Excellent. Trout."

"Hope you catch some big ones," commented Diana, offering her hand.

He waved Steve's address up in the air. "I already have—and no one, believe me, no one's going to throw him back this time."

As Steve watched Simpkins disappear behind the corner of the cathedral, he felt the pounding of his heart slow and his eyes brim with tears. He moved his hand to the side of his face to catch any if they fell. Diana slid her chair next to his.

"You *are* a doctor?" she asked quietly.

"I was."

"Will you reapply?"

"I don't know."

"I'm sorry about your family."

Steve's shrug conveyed a distant, fatalistic acceptance. "You just learned about it. It really was a long time ago."

"Sometimes, to me it seems as if my mother died yesterday."

"You were young and still needed a mother."

"But didn't you need your wife and child?" Diana tried to put the question as gently as she could. "Steve?"

He stared at the table for a moment, then looked up. "Yes, I did. Of course I did."

That evening Steve and Diana hardly spoke as they dined in the Burladero restaurant at the Hotel Colón. The meeting with Simpkins added a new dimension—a shared intimacy—and their silence conveyed unspoken understanding. Any words, when they came, only involved planning the next few days.

Next morning, over *tortas de aceite* and dark coffee at La Campana on Calle de Sierpes, Steve told Diana about the *rejoneo*—fighting the bull from horseback. "In *rejoneo* the horse acts as the cape that taunts the bull into charging so the *rejoneador* can implant darts—the *banderillas*—in the bull's neck. The nobility practiced it centuries ago, so it predates the *corridas* in which a matador fights from the ground."

"Maybe we should skip the *rejoneo*. Jim just wanted me to see the . . . well, the kind of bullfight most Americans see." The thought of witnessing an enraged bull stampede, then gore a brave horse repelled her.

"Don't worry, a *rejoneador*'s mount is highly trained and it's a great disgrace for him if the bull's horns so much as graze a flank or leg."

"And the bull?" asked Diana.

"He will die, of course. With all the darts in place, he carries his neck low, allowing the final act. The *rejoneador* again taunts the bull into charging, and when the horns come just parallel to the stirrup, he plunges the Valencia sword into the bull's muscle and heart, killing him immediately."

Diana struggled with her contradictory feelings of fascination and horror. "Sounds gruesome."

"It is—if you feel for the bull. It is a ritual of terrible beauty and death because it pits animal against animal, but it's far more elevated and controlled than the mongoose and cobra. *Rejoneo* is an art. The horses—they're totally unafraid—actually enjoy the fight." Steve glanced at his watch. "We should head over to La Maestranza to pick up our tickets."

As they cut through the Plaza de Triunfo, Diana looked

up at the Giralda and its great weather vane on the top. A strong south wind blew. "Do they allow people to climb the tower?"

"I think so. Want to have a look?" They entered through the Puerta de los Palos at the southeast corner of the cathedral and strolled up the inclined plane. "No steps," commented Steve. "The Moors rode their horses up here."

The panorama was limitless—the medieval Alcázar, the Gold Tower, unending white walls, and the Guadalquivir's seductive curve. Steve looked to the west, expecting to see the green canopy of a residential neighborhood, but instead saw distant marsh and olive groves. He laughed to himself.

"What is it?"

"A sort of déjà vu. When I was a boy, my father took me up in the belfry of the Cathedral of Mexico. Just to the west, I could see Chapultepec, where I grew up. Somehow, I expected to see it here in the west too."

"But your father came from Seville, so I don't think it's odd at all." She closed the distance between them. And as their shoulders touched, Steve put his arm about her waist. "Tell me about your father. Please." Her voice urged him to come still closer.

"He—Gregorio Rodríguez—he lived and worked in Seville as assistant director of the General Archives of the Indies. See that rather severe Renaissance-style building there? It contains thousands of original documents relating to the old discoveries and conquests."

"So your father was a scholar."

"Yes."

"And he walked by here every day."

"Almost every day—at least until Franco." Steve's face darkened with loathing at the thought of the dictator his parents had taught him to despise. "My father fought for the Republican cause. At the end of the Civil War, Franco's government confiscated all his property and holdings. He emigrated to Mexico and joined the faculty of the Colegio de Mexico, where he taught Spanish colonial history. He met my mother there—her father served as dean of the faculty. And later, I attended the Colegio Madrid, a school established for the children of Republican exiles. My father always wanted to take us back to Seville, but he died before Franco's regime ended. I was fifteen."

"Sounds like he was wonderful," offered Diana, aware how painful this touching on the past could be for him.

"People said he had extraordinary character, but . . ."

"But what?" she asked. Her own father paled beside Steve's description.

"Distant, a distant man. He didn't know me, *really* know me. He operated on models—what one ought to do rather than following one's gifts or talents. Each Saturday during my years in secondary school he had me do volunteer work at the Sanatorio Español—a free hospital serving the poor. All those patients, so needy, so destitute—a brutal experience. I didn't want to go there Saturdays—I wanted to play soccer. But my father insisted that I develop a sense of civic duty and moral responsibility for those less fortunate than I. And that I do it his way."

"Don't you think it was a good thing? After all, you became a doctor."

"But every Saturday for six years? Too much of a good thing. I read to a boy with terminal cancer, an orphan exactly my age. His doctor and nurses told me not to discuss death. We were to delude him. That would be best for his spirits. So every week I lied and constructed false dreams with him. I even invited him to our house." Steve laughed ironically. "My mother would have killed me if he had come to our gate. But there wasn't a chance—he was so sick. Anyway, on that white wrought-iron bed we charted his life. He wanted to be a baker, so I loaned him my mother's cookbooks. We discussed prestigious bakeries where he could apprentice, and how I would send business his way when we were both grown men. You must understand, the hospital staff didn't lie to make him feel better, but to make themselves feel better."

"But you didn't feel better?"

"Sure I did. At least when we were together. I didn't want him to cry, be angry, or talk about death in front of me."

"You did what you were told to do. I'm sure you made him happier."

"No, he made us happy. He didn't want us to feel badly. I see now, of course, that he knew he was going to die. It was in his face at odd moments—I'd walk by and glance in his room or catch him between medications as the pain flared up. Whenever I returned home to our house with its marble patio, palm trees, and swimming pool, my parents told me how proud they felt about my service. But I cringed. When that boy died, I actually felt relieved—glad I'd never have to sit with him again."

"It was better that his suffering ended." She regretted at once her awkward effort to comfort him.

"Better for me too. I'd never felt so responsible, so powerless, and so guilty."

"But you were just a boy. No one expected you to do more."

"*I* did. I expected it."

"But you couldn't."

"No."

She brushed a lock of hair back off his forehead. "I'm sorry your father died when you were so young."

"Good, in a way, don't you think? I mean, he remains an ideal man for me, a god even. If he'd lived longer, I would have learned all his faults."

"Maybe that's why you're so hard on yourself." Her voice was low as she recalled the night she had read the consequences of her own father's weakness, printed in stark black and white at the Southfield Library, and circulated to thousands of homes. Idealizing her father had ceased at age thirteen.

"Diana, do you think we could stop in the Archives before going to the ring? Everything's in Spanish, so you might be bored, but—"

"I'm never bored."

\*    \*    \*

*"Buenos días."* A tall thin man in a blue open-collared shirt and white slacks beckoned them forward. His face, long with dark eyes, gained added distinction from its fine aquiline nose. His expression was cordial but not devoid of formality. He rose from behind a desk piled high with folders and books—more like an emeritus professor than a duke, thought Diana, moving forward to take his outstretched hand. Over tea and biscuits she sat mute as the two men spoke in animated Spanish about Gregorio Rodríguez, his life in Spain and Mexico. For the first time in her life she couldn't participate, and felt frustrated. Of course, when Steve or the duke translated, she understood, but that was hardly enough. Without language, the more subtle interpretations—gestures, smiles, and frowns—eluded her. In the middle of the conversation the duke phoned someone he apparently knew very well. Not until a full five minutes after the call did she find out that they'd been invited by a friend of the duke's to see some Andalusians at a riding school. Only after they left the Archives did she learn how rare the invitation was.

"Álvaro Domecq is a good friend of the duke's. His father knew my father. You probably recognize the Domecqs as producers of sherry. You must have seen a bottle with their label at the liquor store in Southfield."

"We had Harvey's Bristol Cream at home."

"Yes, well, that's popular with Americans. But there are many different kinds." He refrained from adding that Bristol Cream was the only sherry for those who knew nothing about sherry. "When you order a *fino*, or dry sherry, it should always be a Domecq. But in addition to the family *bodegas*—or sherry cellars—Domecq is the founder and head of the Andalusian School of Equestrian Art. Like the Riding School in Vienna, they do classic dressage, but with a Spanish flair. It's in Jerez de la Frontera, a three-hour drive. He has asked us to a training session. Unfortunately, performances take place only on Thursday. I thought we could go tonight after the *rejoneo*, return tomorrow evening, stay at the Alfonso again, then catch our flight next morning."

"What about Jim's bullfight?" Much as she wanted to see the Andalusians, she wouldn't break her promise.

"According to Domecq, the school's performance ends early enough for us to make the *corrida* scheduled at the Jerez ring. Also, he's invited us to see his sherry cellars."

"It all sounds wonderful, as long as I can get to that bullfight. If it were just for me, it—"

"—I promise."

As they walked along the Avenida Dos de Mayo, Diana told Steve how she wished she knew Spanish, and mentioned the isolation she had felt when the duke spoke with him.

"But I translated for you."

She gave his arm a reassuring squeeze. "You were very considerate—and happier and more animated that I've ever seen you. But I want to know what it was all about—the feelings, your feelings—not just the words."

He hadn't spoken Spanish in years, and it made him feel alive and happy, even joyful. But he hadn't quite realized it until she told him. For the first time since the quake he felt at home with his language and could express himself more completely and freely than in English. "I was glad to be talking to someone I'd heard so much about. Decades fell away, as if my family were still living—my father, my mother . . . my wife and daughter."

Diana took Steve by the shoulder and kissed his cheek. "Thank you for interpreting."

As they walked in and out of blue shadows cast by unending white stucco walls, they heard the refreshing sound of someone watering a garden hidden from their view. In the brightness again, as the water sounds receded, the trill of a pet canary filled the sun-washed air. When they arrived at the box office of the Maestranza bullring, Steve found that two tickets bearing his name had already been set aside. He deduced—quite correctly—that after he and Diana had left, the duke called some-one, perhaps one of the blue-blooded members of the ring's board of directors. As a result, their seats offered the best location, at least from his point of view—a box in the *sombra*, or shaded side of the ring—affording a wide visual sweep yet distancing them from the blood and smells of the fight. Though he knew a great deal about the two schools of bullfighting, Steve was no aficionado of either. The first *corridas* he'd attended were with his father. They went only three times because Gregorio Rodríguez found Mexican bulls inferior to the *toros bravos* of Andalusia, the bullfighters less skilled and inclined to trick the uneducated and unruly crowd with optical illusions of danger and death. But after Steve returned to Mexico from California, courtesy compelled him to attend more frequently. Whenever colleagues from Stanford visited, they insisted on seeing a *corrida*. He tried to persuade them of the merits of the *rejoneo*, but they wanted the *de rigueur* tourist attraction.

Intellectually Steve could understand the mythic symbolism and tragic aspect of the fight. In the *corrida* he could cope with the sticking of a bull's neck and the emplacement of *banderillas*—even the bull's death—but not the goring of the picadors' horses, pathetic, miserable nags that absorbed the bull's horns while the rider thrust his pic into the bull. Often killed, they were hastily covered by canvas sheets, then dragged out of the ring by mules at the end of the fight. However, since the bullring management leased these horses, every effort was made to prolong their lives, no matter how grave the injury. Once, when Steve was eight and with his father at the Plaza Mexico, a picador's horse became so badly gored that the crowd demanded an immediate end to its suffering. Instead, an economically minded crew member beat the horse to its feet. Unable to bear the sight, Steve hid his face in his hands and turned to bury himself in his father's side. But Gregorio Rodríguez didn't wish his son to grow up unable to confront life's tragedies, so he straightened him in his seat, then pried the little fingers away from the eight-year-old face, forcing him to watch the horse crumple to the ground as the spectators rose to their feet in unison and shouted *"Matalo"*—kill it. The wet earth was stained with blood as the horse stretched its neck in a hopeless effort to obey the man tugging so cruelly at the reins. In the end, a dagger was driven into the skull—too late for the horse, which already lay dead, but not too late for the management to lay a specious claim to humanity. And now Steve would attend a *corrida* once again, because of the promise Diana had made to Jim. He couldn't bear the thought of witnessing those horses, or of watching her witness them, if she could.

After lunching on splendid hors d'oeuvres, *tapas*, at the entrance bar of the restaurant Mesón Don Raimundo, a former convent redone in festive Sevillian decor, they caught a cab to the bullring.

At the sound of trumpets, six *rejoneadors* attired in *traje corto*—Córdoba hat, short velvet jacket, and leather chaps—entered the ring astride six of the most gorgeous horses Diana had ever seen. Fiery and proud, Velásquez' models, they arched their noble heads like a strong wave, rippling white muscles reflecting the sun, manes and tails streaming like banners. With an almost haughty bearing they lifted their glistening black hooves in a highly cadenced, airy yet energetic trot—the passage. Then they approached the *sombra* side and Diana watched for the physical commands by which a rider communicates—closing the leg, a touch of the spur, shifts of weight—but there were none. Pure anticipation of the fight was eliciting these brilliant and difficult movements. Approaching the presidential box, the *rejoneadors* slowly, and in rhythm with the gaits of their mounts, removed their hats to salute the mayor of Seville, *el presidente* of that day's fight. Circling the ring, they acknowledged the public and exited.

The first *rejoneador* to fight remained in the ring and commenced an exhibition in dressage exceeding anything Diana had ever seen—half-passes and pirouettes at the trot and canter, flying changes of lead at every stride, then passage again, and finally the arrogant Spanish walk.

The crowd roared its approval and returned this greeting with a shower of roses and carnations. Now centered in the ring on his mount, the *rejoneador*—a colorful *banderilla* in his right hand—stood like a porcelain statue and waited for the first bull to be admitted. The silence was the kind that presages a fierce thunderstorm—eerie and charged with electricity. Suddenly the sound of a heavy gallop filled the vacant air and the bull appeared. Massive and black, horns catching the sun, he charged straight at horse and rider. Diana stifled her scream in Steve's side.

"No, they're safe. Try to look if you can." He put a protective arm around her shoulder. She turned just in time to see rider and horse standing unhurt to face the bull again—a *banderilla* now implanted in the thick hump of muscle behind his neck. He charged a second time, and she held her gaze long enough to see the *rejoneador* and his mount gallop headlong at the oncoming bull, second *banderilla* poised in hand, the horse's ears flat against its head as if laid back by a storm wind. A fraction of a second before the two opposing forces met, Diana averted her head again. Steve stroked her paling cheek with the back of his fingers, gently urging her to watch. "You hear that applause? The horse has turned in time. They have years of training. Remember, the rider is dishonored if the bull so much as touches his horse." With the next charge she took a breath and held it as she watched. Again the bull streaked toward his enemies, and horse and rider countercharged. Diana clenched her teeth and watched as black met white. A half-yard from impact, the horse pirouetted on his hindquarters, turning away from the bull, and the *rejoneador* thrust a third colorful harpoon into the gristly muscle. Now Diana looked on as the bull chased horse and rider. Barely out of range of sharp horns, the horse did not panic, but cantered strongly on. The *rejoneador* glanced back to gauge the bull's distance. The horse's silver tail waved like a victory banner just inches above the head of its enemy.

"The *rejoneador* has implanted his six *banderillas*. See how much lower the bull carries his head. Now comes the *estoque*—the sword."

A full fifty yards downwind stood the bull—still majestic, dangerous, enraged. At his rider's command the horse commenced a highly cadenced trot in place, the piaffe, with neck proudly arched, eyes never leaving its enemy.

"The rider uses this to bait the bull, as the matador uses a cape."

The bull pawed at the yellow sand in response. Sifting the air with his black, wet muzzle, he shook his head, furious and disgusted by the smells of his tormentors. With an angry thrust of his horns, he gored the air, then charged, faster this time. Horse and rider rushed forward— charge meeting charge, horns and sword glinting in the late-afternoon sun. Diana gasped as the rider suddenly and completely dropped his reins. Once more the horse pirouetted, placing the bull's head parallel to the stirrup. And at that moment the rider swiftly turned in the saddle, raised his sword to shoulder height, then with one thrust plunged it through muscle, between bones, and into the heart. The momentum of the bull carried him several strides forward as he dropped one shoulder, then stumbled and fell motionless. But death had been instantaneous.

Of the five bulls that followed, none was as fierce and consistently aggressive as the first. But that came as no disappointment to either Steve or Diana, whose main interest was not the bull or its death, but the horsemanship. Diana's initial fear for the horse gave way to admiration of the classic movements executed in mortal combat.

"And Jerez. The word, of course, means 'sherry.' During the reign of Henry VII, the British imported our white wines, naming them sherry—a corruption of 'Sherish,' the city's name under the Moors. These casks contain fermenting wine called must, made three weeks ago from small white grapes. At the vineyard they are crushed by foot, still the best method, then transferred to wooden presses. It will take two months before all the sugar from the grapes has changed to alcohol."

Steve and Diana followed the short and swarthy *capataz*,

foreman of the Pedro Domecq Company. He held his glass and *venencia*, a silver-and-whalebone instrument for extracting wine from the wooden casks, rows of which spread over several acres. "I feel as if I'm in church," Diana commented, looking up past the white-washed walls to tall pillars and lofty arches supported by dark beams.

*"Exacto,"* replied the *capataz*, turning as he walked, a broad smile indicating pleasure at her observation. "Jerez *bodegas* are known as the 'cathedrals of wine.' To age correctly, sherry requires even temperature, day and night, year-round. This architecture creates such an environment. Did you know that Jerez stores enough wine to intoxicate every man, woman, and child on earth? We are not a member of the nuclear club, but our equivalent of overkill seems far more pleasant and civilized."

They strolled under an arch and out into row upon row of wine butts. "Keep in mind, in one *bodega* alone six thousand butts each hold over a hundred gallons. This area we call the 'University of Sherry'—here the drink is educated. We produce thirty types, not including our brandies. Sherry can take ten years before achieving a state fit for consumption. After two months the new wine will be moved here, either to mature in its own *bodegas* or to refresh the *soleras*, mother wines used in blends. To make a blend may require ten casks. That means up to one hundred *bodegas* will have been handled, and that's why Sherry is comparatively expensive. We never know how many barrels will become *finos* and how many *amontillados*—even if the grapes come from the same harvest and are handled exactly the same way. A few will stop maturing and turn to vinegar. So we call the sherry production *la crianza*—bringing up baby. You can't force or mold a child to your will, but must love, support, and help it along."

Diana gave Steve's back a supportive pat at the unintended irony of the foreman's remark. But Steve's easy smile denied the relevance to his own childhood.

"Señorita, taste this." He handed her a *copita*. In the

bottom glistened a few drops of clear liquid extracted from a *solera*.

"Ugh, vinegar—this must be one of those immature characters." She winced at the acrid taste.

"Not at all. A most treasured mother wine—over a century old. One drop of this added to a younger wine can rival Jove's nectar. Wait." He climbed a ladder and tapped into a *bodega* with his *venencia*, then siphoned its contents into her glass. "Now taste."

To the palate this amber-colored sherry was crisp, dry, but unremarkable. "Nothing special, right?" He added a single drop of the sherry that made her grimace. "But with this . . ."

"Incredible." She marveled at the change. Blended with a young wine, the sherry attained a subtle but robust character. "Steve, here, try it."

"He needs to appreciate the contrasts," interrupted the foreman politely, and handed Steve another *copita* after adding a few drops from the *solera*.

"For the gods," responded Steve, savoring the blend's exquisite numbness on his lips.

"Bacchus grew his own." They all turned in the direction of the unexpected voice. A small-framed man energetically stepped forward from the shadows to place his hands on Diana's waist and kiss her warmly.

"Philippe!"

Much to Diana's delight—Steve could barely hide his anger at the coincidence—Philippe DuChamps had come to Jerez on business, first attending the annual Harvest Festival, a pageant for the blessing of the grapes that provided informal opportunities to meet owners and managers of local vineyards. He also wanted to arrange for the importation of *flor*, a tiny yellowish-white plant that grows only in those casks destined to become *finos*. Arnaud DuChamps, Philippe's father, intent on duplicating—if not improving—the character of Spanish sherry, had sent him on this mission, hoping his son's relaxed business attitudes would approximate those of the Andalusian sherry producers. And, as usual, Philippe was intent on combining business with pleasure. He invited his fiancée, Monique De LaPlace, for a prenuptial sail aboard the *Bacchus*, and anchored the yacht in Cádiz, an hour's drive away. When not tasting wines or engaging in incredible lunches with his father's Spanish counterparts, he passed the hours with Monique in settings he affectionately referred to, in English, as the "three b's"—beach, bar, and, of course, bed. These places took up most of his time. Neither Monique nor Diana knew of the other's existence, but that would end in ten minutes. The *capataz*, delighted that respective guests of Pedro and Álvaro Domecq should already know one another, invited everyone into the "boardroom" for a formal wine tasting. Monique was en route with Yolanda Ramón, a Geneva-finishing-school friend and daughter of the mayor of Jerez.

This turn of social events caused Philippe concern. First of all, here was this alleged groom again. Morever, Newport had meant, he thought, the beginning of an affair with Diana, not a short good-bye. He'd copied her address from the exhibitors' list in the Derby program and just two weeks ago had sent her, through his U.S. agent, a case of the best DuChamps Médoc. The primary motive of his gift was not to celebrate her Newport victory (as the card purported), but to pave the way for his November visit to Boston's Meridien Hotel, where he and other wine producers planned to meet with American distributors and importers. By that time he would be married. But some women, he knew, considered a new wife a challenge rather than an obstacle.

As the group proceeded to an alcove between the rows of *soleras*, Philippe recalled a recent discussion with his father, who'd kept a number of mistresses—most with success. Father and son agreed on the necessity of outside feminine companionship. It kept one young, relaxed, and made for a better father *and* husband. However, discretion, proper management, and good luck were essential elements. Now, as Monique entered the alcove and saw Philippe, she rushed forward to smother him with the possessive kisses of new love. He glanced at Diana and smiled weakly. This time, with discretion and proper management taken out of his hands, good luck eluded him.

"Monique, I'd like to introduce Miss Diana Winston. Diana, Miss Monique De LaPlace, ah . . ." He hesitated, unwilling to serve as his own executioner.

"His fiancée," the chic strawberry blond finished in flawless English, annoyed at Philippe's uncharacteristic reticence.

"Congratulations. When did you become engaged?" Diana shot Philippe a barbed glance, intercepted by Monique.

"July."

"I see." Newport was August.

"And how do you know my future husband?" Monique's inquiry was falsely pleasant.

Philippe stepped in to take the helm of this conversation before he found himself in stormier seas. "Miss Winston rides horses. We were introduced at a show in America. Diana Winston and Steve . . ." Philippe gave an apologetic shrug.

"Steve Roderíguez." Though relieved that the Frenchman's stock with Diana had fallen and that Monique had cornered the market, at least temporarily, Steve couldn't hide his uneasiness.

"*Damas y caballeros*, please come this way." The *capataz* reappeared, motioning them into the boardroom. He sensed some tension among the guests, but felt confident that his wines would soon take care of that.

For the next hour he instructed them in tasting *amontillados, palos cortados, olorosos, finos,* and *manzanillas.* He filled ten *copitas,* holding them all in one hand, with a three-foot stream directed by the *veneciador* held in his other. Not showmanship, he noted modestly, but to aerate the wine quickly and bring out its flavor. Before passing a glass to Steve, he poured a third of its contents on the earthen floor.

"I gave you too much. It should never be more than

two-thirds, otherwise no bouquet. Sprinkling some on the earth satisfies our local gods and brings good fortune." The *capataz* then turned to Philippe, his eyes twinkling mischievously. "Monsieur DuChamps, how many wines can you recognize from bouquet alone?"

"Twenty, maybe twenty-five."

"Any Spanish Wines?"

"No—French, of course, German, a few Californian, one or two Chilean, perhaps."

A young man wheeled in a linen-covered cart carrying thirty *copitas* of sherry. The *capataz* handed Diana a typed list corresponding to a number engraved on each glass.

"You must take my word that the order changes every time. Sherry comes in seven distinct colors, a very agreeable rainbow, so my eyes will narrow the choices for my nose." He picked up the first *copita*, glanced at the color, then inhaled deeply. "You will see, number one is an *oloroso*."

"He's right." Diana smiled, amused with her role as game host.

Quickly and accurately the *capataz* tested each glass. In less than ten minutes he'd identified Domecq's thirty sherries without error. He blushed and beamed at the unanimous applause, then excused himself briefly and left the room.

As Diana returned to her seat, she felt a rush of heat and dizziness. "Sherry sneaks up on you, doesn't it?" she whispered to Steve, steadying herself with a hand on his shoulder. They'd all sampled numerous varieties, and on an empty late-morning stomach it added up.

"Twenty percent alcohol and a long time since breakfast." He felt the effect too.

"One gets accustomed to *les tours des grands ducs*— what you Americans refer to, rather inelegantly, as pub crawls," Philippe interrupted. "A good lunch and you'll be fine."

"The voice of experience." Annoyed at the condescension, Diana directed her remark to Steve, but hoped Philippe would overhear. "And we say 'bar hopping.' We're American, not English."

"Experience? I'd like to think so," Philippe replied with boyish charm, ignoring the critical edge in her voice.

Emboldened by almost two hours of sherry, she continued. "Monique, you asked where I met Philippe, but *I* didn't get a chance to tell you." Everyone felt a bit drunk, and everyone knew it.

Monique ceased her chat with Yolanda, her voice indicating only slight interest. "Let me guess. The beach. Perhaps in a bar. Or bed?"

The detachment and deadpan tone of the remark left Diana speechless. Adept at quick damage control, Philippe stepped in. "Actually, we met in a men's shop. She was buying her man here"—he nodded at Steve—"a tie, and I merely offered some advice on its selection."

"Philippe's good at giving advice." Monique turned to Steve. "I hope you received a nice tie."

"Very nice," Steve replied, hoping a short answer would dilute the conversation.

Had Steve been absent, Monique would have pursued an aggressive line of questioning. But they were guests of the Domecqs and she had no desire to upset the Mexican, who seemed decent enough and obviously had a romantic connection with Diana. Nor did she wish to appear shrewish.

Her voice back, Diana chose not to expand on the odyssey of the two Narrangansett neckties. "Yes, thank you, Philippe. You're right. I'd almost forgotten. Lovely neckwear."

"Álvaro Domecq," announced the *capataz*. The head of the Andalusian School of Equestrian Art walked through the door, hand outstretched. Short and heavyset, but with distinctly aristocratic bearing, Domecq projected enormous energy and vision. Once Spain's greatest *rejoneador*, he and his magnificent horse Opus were legend. Retired from the bullring, Domecq now concentrated on his quadrille of Andalusians and their dressage performed at the school. Scanning his guests, he walked to Steve first.

"Gregorio Rodríguez' son. No one need tell me. Welcome to Jerez and the Domecq *bodegas*." Philippe recalled that his own arrival had required a formal introduction. Who was this Mexican?

Over coffee Domecq invited everyone to the luncheon followed by a rehearsal at his school. Philippe declined because of a noontime engagement with Yolanda's father. Afterward he and Monique had tickets to the bullfight. Domecq turned to Diana. "I forgot, you are going to the *corrida* also. We could have ridden across the countryside following your visit."

"I'd love to, but I promised a friend I'd attend a *corrida* for him. He couldn't come with us." Steve endorsed her words with a nod, but he wanted to ride again. Turning down a Domecq horse to see others gored made little sense to him.

"Then Diana shall come with us." Philippe smiled, proud to hit on a solution. With Steve sheared off, he could ascertain any harm caused by the news of his engagement. The only hitch was Monique, but, as proper escort, he'd sit in between. And good manners required he divide his attention equally.

Monique's eyes flashed involuntarily at her fiancé. "Yes, Diana, do come. It would be so much fun." Her tone was thin and insincere.

"Sure, why don't you go and let me take Señor Domecq up on his offer? I've seen bullfights, but I haven't ridden for a long time." Steve now sealed the arrangement.

Diana was stunned. Treated badly by Philippe, she had no desire to accompany him *and* Monique. Surely Steve knew this. And yet she couldn't protest. He'd been unflagging in his friendship, and during this trip he'd seen to everything. If he wanted to stay behind, he had a reason. With *pro forma* expressions of warmth, the two couples separated. After observing the training and equitation methods of the Andalusian School of Equestrian Art—Diana had never seen such rapport between man and horse—she rejoined the French forces at city hall, and Steve headed for the Domecq stables.

\*     \*     \*

At the trumpet's flourish, two mounted bailiffs galloped across the arena to the president's box and received his order for the *corrida* to commence.

"Five o'clock—exactly. A bullfight must be the only event in this country to start on time," Philippe observed dryly.

Three matadors in magnificent brocade and satin entered, hips swinging, bodies erect, eyes directly on the president. Their respective *cuadrillas*, or crews, the *banderilleros* and mounted picadors, followed. Diana's eyes instinctively focused on the horses—bony and badly conformed, sides covered with thin mattresses and eyes blindfolded. Their walk—hesitant, shaky, confused—tore at her heart. The scene provided her with an advance summary. "They're going to be gored."

Philippe didn't move his eyes from the colorful pageantry as he spoke. "Don't feel sorry for those creatures. They're en route to the abattoir."

"Abattoir?"

"Glue factory."

The first bull seemed oblivious to the picador's lance as his horns ripped into the horse and lifted it in the air before dumping it on the sand, soon darkened by a pool of blood. Members of the *cuadrilla*, sticks waving, tried to force the animal to its feet. No response. Within seconds one had removed the saddle and covered the dead horse with a canvas sheet.

"Please don't cry. The horse is a comic figure in all this, the bull the tragic." Philippe took his handkerchief to wipe Diana's tears. "Haven't you read your man Hemingway? These are shadows of horses—parodies. That's why they're called Rocinantes."

"Then someone has missed the point of *Don Quixote*," she replied.

As Steve had predicted, the goring of the horses in the first act prejudiced her reactions to the second and third—implanting the *banderillas* and the bull's death. The grace and skill of various passes—*veronicas, mariposas, mule- tazos*—were lost on her. She regarded the fight as a brutal contest instead of a tragedy and catharsis. And no matter what the danger, man had the upper hand. First, he set the bull against pathetic blindfolded nags. Philippe tried to calm her by explaining the rationale. Lifting or knocking over the horse fatigued the bull. Then the picador's lance forced the bull to lower his head, making him less dangerous for the matador. But because of her natural inclination to root for the disadvantaged, the man with his yellow-and-magenta cape became the enemy. She cheered the bull silently at each charge.

During the next two hours, twelve horses were gored—four killed—and six bulls met death by sword. Philippe felt nothing for the poor picador horses. Yet Diana recalled his sorrow at the death of Flying Ace in Newport. The difference for him seemed to lie in expense and vitality. The loss of a strapping million-dollar money winner was tragic, but not that of an exploited creature whose protracted death came more horribly. Like most of the spectators she observed, Philippe sided with the haves, not the have-nots. Now she knew that nothing long-term could ever have worked with this man. And she felt no anger at his Newport deception, only the opposite of love—indifference.

But Philippe interpreted Diana's lack of hostility in an optimistic light. She had succumbed to the DuChamps charm once again. She would see him in Boston, if not that very evening in Jerez. She would surely be staying at the Hotel Los Cisnes. He'd tell Monique about an impromptu meeting of the General Agreement on Tariffs and Trade relating to wine. So when Monique excused herself to find a ladies' room, he attempted to set up the late-night rendezvous.

"Sorry," Diana said flatly. "We return to Seville this evening." Yet she no longer felt sorry. To no avail, Philippe implored her to delay the departure. They'd have to meet in November in Boston. But this tack failed too.

"I don't go out with men who are engaged." She thought about Bill with a pang and wouldn't say "married."

Before Philippe could launch another assault on her resolve, Monique's return silenced him. Miffed and out of sorts, the *corrida* no longer holding his attention, he excused himself, only to return ten minutes later, spirits buoyant. As the audience showered the last matador with flowers, and as the last dead horse and bull were dragged from the ring, Diana saw a trace of white powder near Philippe's nostril. The bulls hadn't been the only ones snorting.

Just after midnight, Steve and Diana returned to their separate rooms at the Alfonso. Steve slept poorly, swept from consciousness to sleep back to wakefulness again. The trip to Andalusia had opened the gate of repressed memories that now surged and eddied around him. He woke to the hard ping of rain on the window and glanced at his watch—six o'clock. To the northwest he saw the wet blurred lines of the Giralda, its amber-colored stone now a gray wash. Dressing slowly, he decided to go down to breakfast.

The headwaiter politely informed him that he was too early, but offered to bring coffee and pastries to the lobby. Steve took a look around the lobby, empty except for a tall man in a dark suit who sat under a portrait of the hotel's namesake. The tall man read *El Diario*, a Mexico City daily. Steve heard a soothing rush of water and turned to see the bellboy switching on the fountain. "Fountain sounds"—now he understood his father's love of homeland and the pain of forced emigration to Mexico. He'd almost forgotten those stories and special bedtimes as a boy: this Andalusia—where myth, legend, and history fused, this edge of Atlantis, place of the Elysian Fields and Solomon's mines, home of Pegasus and Geryon's bulls, this source of unlimited silver and gold, crossroads of the pre-Christian world, where Greeks, Cypriots, Phoenicians, Hebrews, Carthaginians, and Celts could trade in the open market of Tartessos, lost capital of the Ancient Kingdom of Andalusia.

The man seated under the portrait had gone, but left

his newspaper. Steve hadn't seen *El Diario* since he left Mexico, and walked over to pick it up. Turning the pages gave the impression that nothing had changed—the PRI still in power, corruption identified but unsolved, Mexico offended by the United States. Suddenly he stopped glancing at news columns and fixed on one picture, a familiar face in the center section, Miguel Quintero. A brief headline announced his death at the age of seventy-four. Steve's eyes scanned the article four times before his mind could absorb the news. Dr. Quintero had died in his sleep two nights before. The details of his eminent career—graduate of the National University of Medicine, chief resident of pediatrics at Juárez, chief of medicine at Military Hospital—Steve knew them all. But then he saw the last line: Miguel Quintero had bequeathed two million, five hundred thousand pesos—virtually his life savings—to the construction of a new pediatric wing at the Sanatorio Español, the hospital where Steve had served as a young volunteer. He felt overtaken by panic and began to hyperventilate. Faint, he shuffled to the privacy of the gentlemen's lounge, turned on the cold tap, and stooped down to let water stream over his head.

The immediate shock over, but still feeling shaky, Steve decided to get some air. The rain had stopped but the sky persisted in its gray overcast. Miguel Quintero. It didn't seem possible he was dead, the man who'd played a key part in his life. And now Steve had lost forever the chance to tell him how grateful he was. He walked down San Fernando, where strong and varied smells—garbage, flowers, dog excrement, coffee roasting—assailed him and banished the last trace of sleep from his head. Rain began to fall again, first lightly, then in torrents. He looked for a shop or restaurant to dash into, but it was too early. The massive but airy proportions of the cathedral and its lofty bell tower loomed directly ahead. He'd take shelter there until the shower abated.

Down the Calle de Alemanes onto the Patio of Oranges, then through the Puerta del Perdón: the great bronze doors closed behind him and all light vanished. He could see nothing. As his eyes adjusted, interior details slowly detached themselves from the darkness. On either side of a wide aisle, marble Doric columns and reliefs rose up. Chapels and altars, rich in silver and gold, and paintings and carvings lined the walls. Stained-glass windows and votive candles provided the only illumination. He walked further down the aisle, the surrounding space multiplying the sound of his footfalls, and came to an immense shrine adorned with gold and wood—the sarcophagus of Christopher Columbus borne by four allegorical bronze figures.

Andalusia linked ancient world to old, and old world to new. In the Alcázar, oldest royal seat of Spain, Columbus had won Queen Isabella's backing for his voyage. Vespucci and Magellan had sailed down the Guadalquivir to uncharted seas. The discoveries opened the way for conquistadors and soldiers of fortune seeking to serve God and Mammon. Steve's father had told him he studied colonial history because it reflected both the brutality and the refinement of civilizations. In Mexico the conquistador Cortés, with four hundred men and Indian allies, accomplished the downfall of Cuautemoc and the whole Aztec nation. The Rodríguez house in Chapultepec had been constructed on the grounds of a former Aztec summer palace. How many memories he'd left behind there, how much happiness as a boy and man. Now it was empty, furniture covered, pictures stored. He recalled the garden that Carmen had lavished so much attention on—the bougainvilleas, the roses so profuse and arresting—now surely ragged and overgrown.

His thoughts returned to the earthquake. But this time, for the first time, he didn't stumble into the internal and habitual traps of anger and self-pity. He found himself overtaken by excitement and, above all, strange relief. This time, as he pulled on the great bronze doors of the Puerta del Perdón, darkness yielded to light. The rain had stopped and he blinked in the early-morning rays like a blind man regaining vision. Through the Patio of

Oranges and onto the Calle de Alemanes, he ran back to the hotel without stopping. Steve had turned the final corner in the labyrinth of his solitude.

Hearing the soft sounds of *cante jondo* music, he paused at Diana's door, then took a deep breath and knocked.

"The sign says 'Do not Disturb,' " a sleepy voice complained.

"I'm not a maid."

Diana undid the brass chain and opened the door. "Are we late? Did I oversleep?" She took his wrist in her hand and looked anxiously at his watch. "Seven-thirty. I thought we were going to sleep late. The flight's not until two."

"May I come in?"

They made love several times that morning—gentle, easy, warm, and exciting. The strain that had burdened their deep but hardly easy friendship now vanished with their physical closeness. Each had waited so long to express affection for the other this way, that they hardly spoke as they kissed and caressed. She knew that in some way Steve had come to terms with his past and that he needed her. And he knew that she knew, and that was enough.

# Briggs and DePrete

At the precise moment Diana and Steve were returning the rental car they had driven from Jerez to Seville, Bill Stanford pointed his BMW in the direction of Chemical Bank, just down the block from Rockefeller Center. Site for the kickoff stage of the Briggs and DePrete annual Gala fund-raiser, the bank represented another coup for Emily Stanford. Chemical's president had traded after-hours use of the art-deco building for a warm thank-you from the B&D chairman of the board, a thank-you printed in black script on a full gold page of the gala's program, a space which this year cost other sponsors fifty thousand a crack. Nevertheless, gold pages outnumbered the thirty-thousand-dollar silver ones. Emily had already asked the printer if he could approximate a platinum shade that wouldn't be mistaken for silver.

"Not giving a damn about your clothing will have to come later, darling. You can do what you like at Daddy's age, but right now, please look like the man with the laser." How could he pull out that tartan cummerbund? she asked herself, flicking open the lighted visor mirror for a final check. She'd worked hard, not only on the gala committee, but getting on the gala committee in the first place, and didn't want her husband's disinterest or social ineptitude—she didn't know which would surface faster—to spoil things.

The course Emily had charted for herself fifteen years ago as the most junior member of the Briggs and DePrete

Register of Volunteers had gone well. She no longer scrubbed pots, changed gift-wrap rollers, or pushed flower carts. Her four afternoons a week she devoted completely to flower arrangements, found throughout the hospital in waiting rooms and admission, registration, and other offices, including, naturally, the boardroom. And because Emily worked "like a little Trojan"—Register Vice-President Jill Van Rhein's exact words—she soon found herself on the committees for Christmas Decorating, the Patient Art Show, and Staff Night on the Town. Now, a decade and a half later, for the fifth time running, she'd been appointed to the benefit committee. If she played her cards carefully, Emily knew she'd eventually replace Jill Van Rhein. After all, as head of the decorating committee—one of the benefit's numerous subcommittees—the year before, she'd done the impossible and made the tiresome Waldorf Astoria, venerable host to cause-oriented society events, look different. How she swelled with pride at the compliments and congratulations, especially when Jean Schelling, wife of B&D President Dr. Howard Schelling, told her the apple blossoms she had flown in were a very Annenberg thing to do. And the trampoline act—well, that had been just plain original.

Of course, Emily did not owe her success to merely working like a little Trojan. Shrewdly recognizing that the greatest power in the Register derived from pure political patronage, she avoided stepping even near influential toes. Gossip had proved the downfall of several in her junior cohort, so she never wagged her tongue, save the brilliant and strategically placed "slip." Emily's connections were fully understood—daughter of a board member, wife of the already renowned neurosurgeon—so she never mentioned them, letting silent understatement do the trick. But when it came time to augment the flower shop's budget or purchase a gold page in that year's benefit program, she always came up with some quiet money from Daddy.

Also, she'd learned to follow religiously her mother's

doctrine for successful dressing: "Never outglitz." In order to determine how dazzling she could (or dare not) be, Emily would obtain an advance copy of the seating arrangements for the concert as well as for the supper that followed. She'd do herself in if she used her tight sheath, figure, and relative youth to "outyoung" the senior Register lionessess. For example, if she found herself at a table with Mary Rockefeller, who wore what her grandmother wore—never a fashionable dress, but always a very good dress and very, *very* good jewels—she'd have to hold her sartorial impulse in check. Rockefellers, with the exception of Nelson, never glitzed. But if she were seated near Brooke Astor, well, that was Emily's ticket to cut loose. And since Emily had been one of the selected few to arrange the seating—negotiations this year occupied two working days and evening phone calls—she'd placed Bill and herself with those who mixed rich with glitz. If she could do all this at thirty-eight, what maneuvers might be accomplished at fifty? As Larry Gregson, public-relations chief, had said, any one of these Register ladies could run the United States with one arm tied behind her back. They were State, Defense, CIA, and Treasury rolled into one.

But Bill had become a wild card in her deck. He just wouldn't recognize that the Register was the hospital's backbone. Without it, the well of funds would dry up. These events and others—annual golf tournament, fashion show and bazaar—primed the pump and kept the money flowing. Bill could at least make a pretense of caring about these functions and about the women on the committees that drove them. Still, since their marriage he'd made some concessions. Though it took five persistent years, he finally retired his secondhand tux, picked up at Keezer's while he was an undergraduate at Harvard, for a tailored model from F. R. Tripler. Tonight, for the first time, she'd gotten him into black patent pumps, which was very good, since it would underscore their Briggs and DePrete establishment image. But tuxes and pumps would all be for naught unless Bill helped her "work" the gala. She carried a rather longish mental list of people she needed to be seen with, and it would be much easier if her illustrious husband were at her side. She couldn't depend on Daddy for everything.

True enough, subtle and seasonal fashion rotations that occurred in society circles eluded Bill—the good plain white shirt, not pleated, with evening wear, a somewhat large black bow tie rather than a small straight one—but to say he did not care how he presented himself was false. He generally liked styles that he associated either with field sports or with sailing—tweeds, shooting pants with leather-edged pockets, blazers, white cotton slacks—comfortable, unpretentious, and masculine attire. But he cared most about ties simply because at work his white lab coat hid everything except his shoes. He had the usual rep stripes, polka dots, and solids of varying weights of silk. However, he grew particularly devoted to those Emily condescendingly referred to as his "National Geographics," ties he picked up while traveling. In Peru he found a beautifully woven wool with a llama; in Ireland, jockey racing silks; and in Tokyo, one with little white cranes. But his absolute favorite became the red silk with T. S. Eliot cats he'd purchased in England. This he wore on days he anticipated reading a lot of CAT scans or seeing children.

Bill placed his drink order at the ballooned and beflowered teller's window, an old-fashioned for Emily and club soda for himself. He'd operate next morning, and while one or two drinks would do no harm, he knew they'd turn into six or eight as the protracted evening wore on. This was the worst place for a bar, he thought to himself impatiently while the young man opened a new bottle of white wine. He abhorred standing in line at the bank, yet here he was again after-hours. He spotted Emily on the other side of the room with Vince Marchetti, vice-president for Briggs and DePrete development. Not one of her usual targets, he reflected, and cut through the crowd.

"Bill, good to see you. I was just congratulating Emily

on this evening's seating arrangements. She placed all the important donors exactly right. How she keeps all those names in her head, I'll never know."

"My wife has a talent for names," Bill replied, handing Emily her drink. He wanted to say: She picks them up and then she drops them. "Where did the Register send the hoi polloi this year, dear?" he continued, making reference to the "other" party thrown for guests who purchased less-expensive tickets. Only those who knew Bill well—and they numbered but three or four—would recognize the inherent irony. His tone certainly didn't give him away, yet he entertained himself constantly with this double-edged verbal game, which made Emily understandably nervous.

"People who bought the two-hundred-and-fifty-dollar tickets went to Rockefeller Center's downstairs lobby."

"And the heavy rollers who shelled out a thousand now get to line up at bank windows again."

The Sinatra concert at the Metropolitan Opera proved a quick sellout, relieving Emily no end. One evening's rent cost sixty thousand, plus orchestra and stagehands. The PA system worked well, Frank seemed happy with the logistical support, and his audience was warm and responsive. As the evening wore on, even Bill made the most of it, at least according to his own tastes, by catnapping during the performance and, at intermission, taking a close look at the magnificent Chagall murals in the lobby. Aware that he had some obligation to mingle, he escorted his wife to various members of the ranking power structure—Laurance Rockefeller, Henry Ford, Armand Hammer, Grant Tinker. Emily had wanted to chat with Barbara Bush but found her conferencing with her husband, the Kissingers, and William F. Buckley. Politics (of the global or national varieties, anyway) did not interest her.

The final curtain call for grand entrances came at the post-gala supper, one hundred and seven stories atop the World Trade Center at Windows on the World. The

fifty-mile skyline view and, no doubt, the menu prices
prompted its acronym WOW. As the Stanfords made
their way toward the center of the multitiered mirrored
dining room, Emily communicated to Bill *sotto voce* at
which strategic points to pause for her last chance to be
seen with the heaviest of heavy rollers. Bill, spotting his
friend Nick Rizzo, head of transplantation biology, off in
the distance, suddenly realized that he was not going to
sit with colleagues. His relation to Edgar Rigg—not his
own standing as one of the world's top neurosurgeons—
had determined his social echelon that evening. All the
other doctors, with the exception of the president, chan-
cellor, and chief medical officer, found themselves in left
field, or the bleachers.

Seating arrangements flashing in her head like an internal neon sign, Emily directed her husband to the table
adjacent to the head one. Thirty minutes of rubbing the
right elbows elapsed before Laurance Rockefeller entered and escorted "the Voice" to his seat. Bill glanced
at his watch and groaned inwardly—just past midnight:
he wouldn't get out until after two. If only coffee didn't
make his hands tremble the next morning. Diuretic, too.
If it wasn't damned uncomfortable, it was damned in-
convenient. He hated breaking scrub to use the urinal.
Bill wondered whether he wouldn't be better off going
directly to the hospital at the evening's late conclusion. It
might be less painful than rousting himself from bed with
only two hours' sleep. Then he peered out at the New
York night, its rivers and harbor, sky, its ships, planes,
stars, and thought about Diana.

"That's the *real* view here," commented Register member Liesel Taubman, noting Bill's gaze. After raising five
children with Briggs and DePrete Vice-Chairman Larry
Taubman, Liesel had started a successful business im-
porting hydro-massage units from Munich, her native
city, and sold them to resorts—Gurney's Inn, the Golden
Door, Rancho del Puerto. "I came here just two weeks
ago for a MOMA benefit and saw the Goodyear blimp

floating about, except I was looking down on it. Strange sensation, seemed almost immoral."

"I can understand that." Bill smiled. Now, here was someone he could talk to, someone with a bifocal perspective. Liesel was one of the Register members with an ability to distinguish between a doctor who was doing exceptional research and who should therefore be funded, and one who simply played the violin very well. Since no money raised by Register events went anywhere without its approval, women of Liesel's skill became essential. The administration could ask, cajole, stamp its feet, but not order. If the Register walked—taking its connections, skill, and influence with it—Briggs and DePrete would be hurt. And everyone, from the chairman down to the candy stripers, knew it. Two years ago Bill had put in a request for new furniture to improve the neurosurgical residents' dour lounge. His plea seemed permanently back-burnered until he talked with Liesel. Within a week dirty yellow walls turned soft blue and the torn black vinyl sofa and chairs gave way to a comfortable leather-and-chrome set from Scandinavian Design. A urine-stained patient bed, the only place his residents could grab some sleep, had been replaced by a new bunk bed. He didn't even need to explain to Liesel that his people couldn't use the rooms reserved for other residents: they must be right on the neurosurgery floor. A fraction of a second could determine whether a patient lived or died or, if he lived, whether he would walk, talk, or have the same personality before and after the OR. Liesel, a volunteer for more than thirty years, knew all this. Besides, she cared.

On his right, good fortune did not hold. Fanchon Nugent also pulled Register purse strings, yet the one time he had felt compelled to seek her out, Bill met a brick wall. The preceding spring he'd needed his counterpart at the Briggs and DePrete Research Institute to run some special neuropathologic studies. His own department lacked funds, so he approached Lou Ramsey, vice-president of finance, and asked about getting his hands on some money gener-

ated by the patient art show. But no, Briggs and DePrete
had finally managed to woo Peter MacKenzie, incoming
head of molecular biology and genetics from McGill, and
all proceeds from the patient art show were slated to
fund his promised lab. Reluctantly Bill went to Fanchon.
She headed the art show and could exert considerable
influence over where profits went. Fanchon flatly declined any interest in research, and Bill soon knew why.
She and superstar MacKenzie were in the throes of an
affair, and neither she nor Peter had been enjoying the
New York–Montreal commute. End of request.

For the next two hours Fanchon compulsively expressed
her views on every subject that came her way, whether
she knew anything about it or not. Bill didn't mind if
someone suffered from *culte de moi*—he could excuse
entertaining conceit—but this lady was dull, infantile,
frivolous, and fundamentally inhumane. She'd exploited
the hospital to serve her own purposes, to the detriment
of his colleagues and his patients. Tonight she paraded
the absolute latest in fashion—hair henna-dyed and
crimped, toothpick arms—dressed in one of Oscar's short-
hemmed, puff-sleeved, polka-dot numbers. Bill looked at
the women of the head table. Brooke Astor and Mary
Lasker also appeared henna-dyed and crimped, their
dresses cut along the same lines—up for knees, down for
breasts.

"Very pretty blue, Liesel," commented Bill, turning to
Mrs. Taubman. The airy and elegant silk camouflaged
her stout frame.

"I've had it for years," she replied with a dismissive
wave of her hand. "It's one of my three charity-ball
uniforms."

"It's a Halston, isn't it?" Emily asked from across the
table. Her grating tone sounded as if she were being
presented a used car.

"A very old Halston, as you no doubt know, my dear,"
answered Liesel, addressing her spoon to the boula-boula
soup, apparently oblivious of the ripple effect caused by

her reply. Bill felt a rush of anger directed at Emily, who now exchanged knowing winks with Fanchon.

"Bill? *Bill*." Cannon to the right of him. "Did Emily tell you about the *blanquette de veau*?" Fanchon whispered harshly.

"No."

"Well, she sent a trio of us over here to sample main courses. I won—we got the veal. But only after I *insisted* they lighten up the sauce," she added with satisfaction. Ignoring Bill's silence, Fanchon went on. "You still think research is where it's at for Briggs and DePrete?" Without waiting for a response, she turned to Emily. "Bill wanted some of my patient-art-show money. Can you *imagine* trading Peter for statistics?" Emily and Fanchon dissolved into boarding-school giggles.

"Statistics alerted people to Thalidomide," Liesel declared with irritation.

"Yes, those unfortunate babies." Fanchon felt obligated to put on a sympathetic face.

"Dear, yes. I remember." Emily also adjusted her tone. "I'm glad in a way that Bill and I decided not to have any. For nine months I'd be a wreck, wondering if the thing had all its fingers and toes."

"How do you think the gala's going?" Liesel asked, changing the subject. She'd learned through the Register grapevine why the Stanfords were childless.

"Too bad Hogarth's dead. He would've liked it," replied Bill.

As Liesel chuckled at his allusion to the eighteenth-century satiric artist, Fanchon mentally flipped through names of board members, benefit underwriters, benefactors, and patrons, but failed to come up with a Hogarth. "Was he on the medical staff?" she asked, baffled. But no one seemed to hear.

At the moment that Chairman of the Board Laurance Rockefeller got up to the mike to pronounce the gala an unqualified success, and to thank the other "chairman of the board," Bill's beeper went off. Emily glanced angrily at her husband, fumbling at his waist to locate the switch.

An interruption at this level and at this moment did not enhance status. The chartreuse figures 7-9-4-7-2-5-2 materialized on his readout: infectious disease. Why on earth would they . . . ? Jim Williams. Bill had written a note on his chart requesting notification—immediately—if anything significant developed.

"Dr. Lindemann?" The doctor carrying a clipboard and petri dish nodded. "What happened?"

"Seizure. The maid called an ambulance, found him on the floor. Must have hit something on the way down. Black eye."

"How's he now?" Bill asked. A bruise was the least of Jim's problems.

"Not good. Pulse 124, respiration 36, axillary temp 103.6. We've got him on diazepam and DPH to control seizures. Oxygen, of course. It looks like the *Pneumocystis* is out of control. CAT scan indicates no tumors or abscesses, but the lumbar puncture shows elevated protein and cells."

Bill acknowledged the duty physician's grim news with a nod. The AIDS virus had penetrated Jim's brain. "Is he conscious?"

"He can follow one-step commands. Speech is slurred, but that's the medication. He bit his tongue too."

"What does your attending think about this?"

"We're considering taking him off the pentamidine."

"Was Mr. Williams alert enough to have this discussed with him?"

"No. That's why I said we were only considering it." The physician, realizing he'd overstepped, began to backpedal.

"Will he make it through the night?"

"I think so."

"Please, tell him I'll see him later in the day, but call me in the OR if any changes occur. If I'm not there, have me paged. His chart says Diana Winston should be notified, but I can take care of that."

"Thank you, sir."

Oblivious to the stares from the staff that his tux provoked, Bill walked down the corridors—tripping over the cord of a floor waxer—to the head neurosurgical resident's office. Close by, its key in his case, he'd call Diana from there. Besides, he didn't want to register the overseas charge to his own office phone. Rose Pitzer, his snoopy "personal" secretary, went over long-distance calls like a hawk after baby rabbits.

Bill took out the Algonquin matchbook cover from the inner pocket of his wallet where he'd kept it since they'd met for drinks. That night, over her second Cointreau, Diana had written the phone number of the Ritz Real on the inside cover. He stared at her clear feminine script, picked up the phone, then paused. How could he tell her that Jim had come to Briggs and DePrete for the last time? While the switchboard downstairs placed the call, he undid his tie and cummerbund, then waited anxiously. The hotel desk four thousand miles away in Madrid told him that Diana Winston had checked out three days ago. Thinking she might have returned early, he called the Pickwick. No, she hadn't arrived but had reconfirmed her reservation for that day. So Diana must be en route. He left word for her to call him immediately. At three-thirty A.M. he took the elevator to his seventh-floor office in the Erikson Pavilion and reviewed the morning's procedure—a subdural hematoma. But before taking a look at the departmental budget and fellowship requests, he crossed his arms on his desk and laid down his head. Two and a half hours later, rays of early sun woke him.

Exactly six hours after that, he took a large gulp of coffee and sighed with exhausted relief. Everything had gone well. The patient's brain had reexpanded to fill the void created by the evacuated blood clot, and the resident, reasonably skillful, hadn't gotten in his way.

An OR nurse appeared at the door of the lounge. "Dr. Stanford, Diana Winston's on four."

"Put her through, please." As the phone gave a loud half-ring, Bill felt anticipation mixed with dread.

"Hello! How are you? Your trip—yes, I'm looking

forward to all the details. Diana, listen, we readmitted Jim last night. He's on medication and conscious, but I don't think"—he hesitated—"I don't think he's going to be with us much longer."

"What's a seizure?" Diana asked. "Bill Stanford said he had a seizure." She and Steve walked quickly down the black-and-white diamond-tile floors and through the swinging doors to Infectious Disease.

"The body arches backward as the limbs extend, the face contorts, and—"

"I know what happens during a seizure, but what *is* it?"

"No one really knows—only that under normal circumstances the brain sends out orderly messages in a rhythmic sequence, but during a seizure they become scrambled, probably causing the terrible contortions. Jim's fever apparently triggered it, though we don't know the real causes."

As they approached the nurses' station, Steve wondered if, in Jim's case, fever had been the real agent provocateur. Several conditions were associated with seizures, all bad.

"We're here to see Jim Williams." Diana leaned across the top of the white counter. The head nurse nodded but kept her eyes fixed on a Chinese takeout menu. Diana looked down the cold shiny hall, wondering in which room they'd find Jim.

"He's right this way. I'm afraid you can stay only a short time. He needs to rest." The first door led to an anteroom, where they all stopped. "Please put these on." She gestured to a pile of bilious green cloth and paper.

"Is this necessary?" Steve inquired, doubting it was.

"Yes, for protection. And please read these instructions." She handed them a printed white sheet covered in transparent plastic. "When you're done, the gowns go in here," she said, pointing to a cloth hamper marked

"Infectious Hospital Waste" in large stenciled red letters. "If you have any questions, ring his buzzer."

The door closed behind the nurse with a pneumatic click, and Diana turned to Steve. "All this?" She nodded toward the array of gowns, gloves, booties, goggles, and masks.

"AIDS depresses the immune system. These protect Jim from what we're carrying," Steve lied, knowing that the measures afforded psychological protection for visitors and staff, not physical protection for the sick. "Here, let me help you. Arms through the sleeves first, then the gloves." Assisting her, he recalled the last time he'd worn the gear. A little boy with tuberculosis—on the same day Miguel Quintero suspended his privileges.

Despite herself, Diana couldn't help laughing at the sight of Steve masked and goggled. "You look like a sanitary bug."

"Then you're a ladybug." He gestured for her to open the door to Jim's room, glad she could reduce her stress through humor. It helped him too.

" 'Universal Precautions'—what are they?" Diana asked, reading the notice on the door.

"You're wearing them." He pulled on the metal door handle.

Jim's eyes stared blankly as Diana approached him. "Jim, it's Diana and Steve." He only grunted each time he exhaled. "Jim, it's Diana. I'm back from Spain. I'm here. Jim? It's me, Diana." Her slightly raised voice grew edged with despair. "He doesn't recognize me." She turned to Steve, then immediately back to Jim, and spoke more softly. "Jim. Please."

Steve intervened by touching her elbow. "He recognizes you. Didn't you see his eyes widen when you came in? He can't speak—he needs his energy to breathe. Let's sit next to him and not talk." Steve placed a chair on either side of the bed.

Diana traced the outline of the swollen brow with her forefinger. Bill had told her about the black eye. "And his hand's so cold. How can I warm it, wearing these gloves? Can't I take them off?"

"I wouldn't. If you get us in trouble, nurses will reappear every two minutes." So she took Jim's hand and held it between two gloved ones, hoping her warmth would penetrate the latex.

Jim's body thinner still, his skin of a loathsome sallowness, hair lusterless, temples hollow: these signs Steve took in, and counted a pulse of 132. Muscle cords in Jim's neck stood out thick and pronounced. Failing circulation caused the cold hands. His nostrils flared in an effort to draw the oxygen. On Jim's other hand, the one Diana wasn't holding, his fingers opened and closed softly for several minutes, then lay extended on the sheet. Steve wondered if this was the start of "picking at the bedcovers," the gesture of seeking the linens with restless fingers. No medical explanation for the reflex, but every doctor knew it presaged death.

Five minutes passed. "He needs to get some rest now." The nurse held the door half-open.

"We just got here." Diana looked to Steve for support.

"We're only sitting—quietly. No talking. She's holding his hand." The nurse peered over to make sure gloves were on.

"A bit longer, then. No more." She left.

Steve got up, walked to the closet, and found a blanket. "Here, help me spread this. There." Jim suddenly gasped and his chest heaved. He struggled to get up but failed. Steve glanced at the monitor—heart rate up.

"What *is* it?" Diana asked with panic.

Loud tones of an electronic bell sounded at short intervals. Steve glanced at the clear tubing that ran from Jim's nose to the oxygen valve in the wall. Kinked. He straightened it quickly, the bell stopped, but Jim still gasped.

"Steve, you're a doctor. Help him! I'm scared."

"I just did. He'll be okay. Watch." In a matter of seconds, Jim's breathing returned, labored but regular.

The nurse rushed in to check the tubing. Must have

straightened on its own, she thought, before turning to the visitors. "I'm afraid you must leave now."

"Why?" asked Diana.

The nurse's eyes flashed, but she drew a measured breath. "The respiratory team's coming to administer his medication." Noting Diana's unconvinced expression, she added, "And he really does need to rest."

On their way out of the hospital, Steve and Diana stopped in the coffee shop for a late lunch. Neither one had eaten anything since breakfast on the plane. "Did Jim know I came to see him?"

"Yes."

"Or did he only know that somebody was there?" No response. "Did he know it was *me*?"

Steve pulled the straw from its wrapper and pushed it down through the crushed ice floating in his Coca-Cola. "I don't know." He recalled Jim's cold fingers opening and closing, and wondered if he'd make it through the night.

Tavern on the Green—Diana would like that, Bill thought as he walked into the Pickwick lobby. The view of Central Park, alive with red and gold colors of the changing season, would be beautiful, and he'd reserved the one table that looked out on the bridle paths. But when Bill rang Diana's room she protested that she wasn't ready and asked him to come up, her voice sounding distant and strained.

"I can't go." Tears streamed down her face before she could close the door behind him. She wore a terry-cloth bathrobe and had just stepped out of the shower, dark hair hanging in wet straight lines. Her eyes looked puffy and red.

"We can go another time." He took her in his arms and held her close against his chest. "It's Jim. You saw Jim." She nodded, trying to compose herself to speak, but failed. Instead, she dissolved into shudders of tears.

"You don't have to talk about it. Just sit with me for a while." He caught the light clean fragrance of her hair and looked around the room but saw only two hardback chairs and a bed. No sofa. So he turned down the bed-covers, propped up the pillows against the headboard, and helped her get in.

"Thanks." Diana smiled.

He left and returned with a towel from the bathroom, slipped off his shoes, got on the bed too, and gently positioned her in front of him. "You didn't do a very good job drying your hair. You'll catch cold." He began to press her head softly with the towel.

"I'm sorry about this evening."

"No reason you should be."

"I never break promises."

"I'm a doctor, remember? Flexibility."

"When I was with Jim, I felt okay. Even with Steve afterward. But here, by myself, every horrible piece came crumbling together."

Bill felt her rib cage expand when she inhaled to main-tain self-control. "It's perfectly fine to cry."

"Crying can't help Jim."

"It'll help you. I spoke today with the head of infec-tious disease. They're going to make breathing a little easier for him by using a special nasal cannula. He'll get more oxygen. A tube is placed high up in the nostril. It won't change anything, ultimately, but he'll rest more easily."

He felt her body relax, then immediately tense up again. "I won't be able to see Jim until tomorrow after-noon. I've got to drive up to Bedford to ride Navarro. He's at Montdale—you know, John Oakley's place. They give lessons all afternoon, so I'll go in the morning. Steve's checking on him now. The Puissance is coming up, I haven't ridden in over two weeks and, . . ."

"Of course, it's important for you to ride. Jim's getting superb care. Camping out with him wouldn't do either of you any good. Be his link to the world outside. Make him part of it and he'll feel less lonely."

"How?"

"Think about it for a while. You know him better than any of us."

"I'll think now." She laid her head back against Bill's chest.

He moved up against the headboard to offer her more support, continuing to pat her head with the towel until he heard the soft regular sounds of breathing, sleeping. How could he have expected her to go out after the shock of seeing her dearest friend semicomatose? He'd stopped by Jim's room himself that afternoon, and though accustomed to sickness and death, the sight of the emaciated Olympic athlete had been a blow. Dr. Lindemann's clinical brief on the hopelessness of Jim's condition had weighed on Bill's bruised heart like a stone.

Careful not to waken Diana, he leaned slightly forward and slid off his coat, letting it drop to the floor. As she turned on her side, he felt the damp weight of her warmth against his groin. So young, he thought, looking at her forehead and neck—not a line or crease. In the folds of the bathrobe he could see the soft outline of her breast. He moved his legs further apart to make her more comfortable, and she continued to sleep soundly—eight o'clock, but one A.M. in Spain. He stroked her face with his fingers. Twenty-one, beautiful, a champion, but with both parents dead, and going through death one more time. He recalled himself at her age, a Harvard senior with stellar grades and worried only about making an oar on the varsity crew. How different now, he thought, and reached over to turn out the light.

Seven hours later he woke with a start. The luminous dial of the clock radio read three-ten. Diana still lay asleep, but her body had shifted down so that her face lay cradled against the inside of his thigh. He touched her head.

"Diana." Nothing. "I've got to go."

"Umm, is it morning?"

"Just after three." Bill lifted her shoulder and slid his leg from under her. "Close your eyes. I'm going to turn on the light for a second." As soon as he spotted his shoes he clicked the lamp back off.

"Do you have to leave?"

"I fell asleep too. My wife doesn't know where I am."

"Are you going to tell her?"

"No. Now, go back to sleep," he half-scolded, and drew the cover around her shoulders. "I'll call soon."

When he turned to leave, Diana caught and kissed his hand. "Thank you."

How different from the pink satin apathy of Emily's sleeping mask, he reflected. The elevator took him down to the lobby and the outside world.

"Where have you been?" Emily Stanford could tolerate being excluded from her husband's professional schedule, but not from knowing what it included.

"A case. I told you that this afternoon on the phone. I spent the night at the hospital. Didn't make sense to come home." He slid under the sheets and squeezed her hand, hoping some token affection would settle the matter.

"That was last night. I mean tonight. It's nearly four."

"Same case. I'll tell you about it tomorrow."

With that Emily withdrew and returned to sleep. Acceptance of her husband's involvement with "cases" —however grudging—had been part of the marital bargain.

In bright late-morning sun, and in air charged with the crisp invigorating smells of autumn, Diana guided Navarro across the field to the outdoor ring. His bold carriage lifted her spirits and filled her with excitement. After a brief warm-up and a series of suppling exercises, Steve set up a gymnastic line, no fence higher than three-foot-nine, none less than three-six, the horse taking them all like a gazelle.

"Not a bit stiff." She smiled at Steve, who perched on the top rail of the ring. His dark eyes shifted from Navarro to Diana. The horse, no; but her stiffness revealed itself in tense arms and transferred through the reins, which lacked her usual sensitivity. It worried him. She hadn't ridden for a while, and the stress of Jim's situation made it worse. And the Puissance was in three weeks.

"Lungeing without a rider helped him. His back muscles look fine and I like the way he's seeking the bit. I'll set up an oxer at three-nine and the wall at four feet. Let's see what he does with that. If Navarro's going to have a problem, it'll be mental, not physical."

"He's very brave," Diana countered, misinterpreting his last remark.

"And that's his liability. You could barely hold him in at Newport. He sees each jump as an enemy to be defeated. The higher the fence, the fiercer the enemy. When his excitement increases, so will the chance that he'll rush into a mistake. And he's never shown or jumped in an indoor arena the size of the Garden. Nonstop commotion. The usual idiots will be flashing their cameras in his face. A drunk yelling, maybe a balloon or two. So we've got to work on his concentration to keep him calm. No jumps over four-six, except a few times before the real thing. Maybe."

"Four-six, that's even lower than the Derby." Diana felt certain that she and Navarro would jump the height set for New York, seven-foot-four, at least once.

"The U.S. Equestrian Team rarely schools over four and a half."

"I'm entering Madison Square Garden in front of thousands of people to clear a height I've never even taken before?"

"You both are. And you both will. If a rider can jump five feet, he can jump seven. You don't practice for Puissance as if it were the human high jump."

For the next twenty minutes Steve directed her through a variety of gymnastics designed to help Navarro round his back and use his muscles efficiently. Not until Steve said they should quit did she notice a small crowd in the bleachers. They'd come to watch her. From the top row a man in jacket and tie sprinted down to her side. "Ron Lasky, *Sports Illustrated*. I've been trying to reach you for two weeks. We'd like to run a story on you."

When they drove up the ramp onto 684, she asked Steve, "Am I a good rider now?" The spectators and the prospective *SI* feature mixed more stress with her excitement.

"Always were. Now others know it too."

"But I haven't done a full season on the show circuit. Who ever won the Newport Derby without pounding the dirt for years?"

"You."

"A fluke?"

"You're a great rider. You couldn't even finish Newport, much less win it, with as little experience as you had unless you were great. You must know that . . . you've got to feel that. Von Engerson thought so. He told me at Hampstead—more than once. I believed him then, and I believe him now."

"Did you believe you were a great doctor?"

Steve hesitated before answering. "Yes."

"And now?"

He turned to her with a look of lighthearted chagrin. Caught in his own trap.

Marshall Simpkins *knew* Steve was a great doctor, so immediately on his return from Spain he set out to learn why the American Board of Pediatrics had turned down the certification. He tried to reach Joe Malvezzi, who'd served as acting chairman during his own illness. Steve's request for a recommendation would have gone to him. But Joe couldn't be reached—white-water rafting on the Snake River in Idaho. Simpkins instructed his secretary to pull the folder, but found no recommendation at all. Perhaps someone had inadvertently placed it in Malvezzi's personal file, yet he felt reluctant to go through that folder in Joe's absence. Calling Grant Fisher, chairman of the American Board of Pediatrics, provided the first awful clue. Joe had indeed written a letter about Steve, but hardly a glowing recommendation. The paragraph which praised his tissue-culture findings simultaneously impugned Steve's character by stating he'd violated university research ethics on "more than one" occasion.

Simpkins took Steve's file home that night, read every paper his younger colleague had written while at Stanford, and was struck by the commercial applicability of the findings, more obvious now than three years before. Yet he knew Steve to be idealistic, more interested in finding cures than striking contracts with pharmaceutical companies or looking for backers to form his own. Ironically, deals with the big drug boys would be more Malvezzi's style. Then it clicked. He recalled one night, more than a year before, stopping at the lab to check some data. Packing a bottle of tissue medium in his briefcase, Joe had joked in response to Simpkins' query that the liquid dramatically increased the growth of his Transvaal daisies. Feeling, with this connection, that a reasonable doubt had been established, he went into Malvezzi's personal file and found extended correspondence with Ranco, a leading manufacturer of vaccines. Joe had represented Steve's formula as his own and seemed embroiled in the last stage of negotiation over royalties. Simpkins immediately called Grant Fisher again, who assured him that he would reopen the case. He then wrote the Stanford general counsel to lay the groundwork for a hearing and subsequent censure of Malvezzi. It would be messy. After the detective work and reporting, he pulled out the phone number Steve had written down when they met in Spain. But he didn't call until the next morning, after determining the best strategy to draw Steve back into the world that had betrayed him.

Steve was about to leave his room to meet Diana in the lobby—they'd returned to change before going on to Briggs and DePrete—when his phone rang. Because Diana was anxious to see Jim, he almost ignored it, but then realized it might be the hospital. If Jim's condition had slid, he'd want to prepare Diana. But it wasn't the hospital, at least not Jim's hospital. Marshall Simpkins had tracked him down via his landlady in Eastford, and enthusiastically relayed that although the mix-up over his

rejection needed more work, a reapplication to the Board
of Pediatrics would meet with success.

Simpkins then requested a favor, almost offhandedly.
That same afternoon a symposium at the New York
Academy of Sciences had invited Claude Bouchet from
the Institut Pasteur to discuss his research on virus recep-
tors in cell membranes, work which might have an impact
on Simpkins' own lab. He'd planned to attend, even
booked a ticket, but a pending and heated tenure vote on
someone he didn't like had now intervened. Since Steve
was in New York, could he drop in, take a few notes,
and mail them off? If he needed to track down a reference, Simpkins could arrange visiting-scholar status at
Rockefeller University. Steve assented for two reasons:
he'd been caught off-guard, and he always felt disposed
to help friends.

Diana grew uneasy as she stepped off the elevator onto
the infectious-diseases floor. She wished Steve had been
able to come, but understood the significance of Simpkins'
request. Seeing no nurses at the station, she continued
down the hall, where she knew to find the gowns and
gloves. Gowns and gloves—she shook her head at the
ironic echo of cotillions and children's romantic tales.
Outside Jim's room, uneasiness gave way to panic. A
sign—"Room Sealed, Do Not Enter"—hung on the door.
White paper stripping with "ROOM SEALED" printed in
black repeatedly on its length covered over the spaces
between door, wall, and floor. She surveyed the door,
trying to make sense of its prohibition, and suddenly
understood. Jim was dead. Devastated and overwhelmed,
she crumpled against a wall.

"May I help you?" Reading the trauma in Diana's
face, the rotund little nurse with black hair went on.
"Are you Diana Winston?" She nodded. "We've moved
Mr. Williams to the hospice wing."

"Hospice?" she repeated softly, now unsure whether
Jim was dead or not.

"It's homier there." She touched Diana's arm. "He's

waiting for you. Anderson Hall, seventeenth floor." Relieved and energized, she could barely keep her feet to the floor as she ran to the elevator, crossed through a glass arcade, and into another elevator.

"Diana Winston?" A tall black man in a camel-hair blazer stepped out as she burst through the double doors. "Jim's fine. I'll take you to his room in a minute. Just let me bring you up-to-date."

"Who are you?"

"David Jackson. I'm a social worker." He noticed Diana's eyes widen and smiled. "I know. Social workers tend to be women *and* Jewish."

Tactfully and professionally he determined the depth and nature of her friendship with Jim, that she knew AIDS caused his pneumonia, and foresaw the inevitable outcome. They walked down the hall and paused outside a door with the sign "Seizure Precaution" and one small fluorescent orange circle the size of a quarter. He asked Diana if she knew anything about the Williams family.

"Only that the best one's in here," she replied grimly, turning to Jim's door.

David Jackson nodded in acknowledgment. He'd been briefed on the family just before Jim moved, and that same afternoon Mrs. Williams had visited but stayed barely fifteen minutes. Mr. Jackson had been unable to direct her attention to the gravity of her son's condition. She denied that he had AIDS—*her* son (she eyed David Jackson suspiciously) was certainly no "homosexual," pronounced in five deliberately cold and distinct syllables. After all, Jim was a practicing Catholic. And, she added, he'd always been susceptible to lung infections. But what saddened David most was how Jim's mother had positioned herself next to the ventilator the entire time she spent with her son.

"No gowns here, but you'll need this." He took a mask from the stainless-steel canister that rested on the wooden table. "You'll see that he's looking and feeling better. If you have any questions, ask one of the nurses to track me down." Not yet recovered from the shock of the sealed door, Diana pushed on the curved handle and steeled herself.

"Diana, hi!" His voice, weak but animated, encouraged her to come in. The nasal cannula Bill had told her about had helped.

"Jim." She rushed forward and kissed his hollow cheek despite the scratchy interference of the paper mask. "Am I glad to see you!"

"Me too." He coughed hard, then swallowed. "Sorry I missed you and Steve last night."

"You didn't know we were here?" she asked, recalling what Steve had said about his eyes widening.

"I felt so sick, and my concentration's so bad I can't remember anything clearly except the ambulance doors closing in front of my apartment. Later, someone took my hand, maybe a medic checking my pulse."

"Last night I held your hand." She reached over the aluminum bar and took his thin fingers again.

"So, how was Spain? Did Hemingway get it right?"

Diana's eyes welled up with tears and admiration for this indomitable spirit in its deteriorating frame. "No, he didn't, not really."

"Why not?" Jim stroked her head with his fingers.

"He doesn't understand courage and nobility the way we do."

"No, I guess he wouldn't."


Days fell into a pattern. Diana would drive up to Bedford with Steve, ride Navarro, then return to the city. After lunch she'd visit Jim—and it didn't disturb her that Steve never wanted to come. She understood the significance of the paper he was now preparing for Simpkins and the afternoons and evenings he devoted to it. The foundation of his life was shifting, and she sensed a profound change. She'd already seen the portents—shedding his silent groom image, the chance meeting with Simpkins, Steve's subsequent willingness to talk about a troubled childhood, the return to his father's birthplace of Seville, capital of both his myth and his reality. Earlier signals that she'd missed came forward—the gift of Navarro, the custom jumps, his care, attention, and friendship. And then that wonderful sun-filled morning in Seville when they became one: a troubled, introverted doctor with wounds he couldn't heal by himself, and the outgoing, hard-driving equestrian with fundamental doubts about her ability to win.

On one of Diana's afternoon visits to Jim, his face brightened as she placed a large brown shopping bag on the chair next to his bed. "What's this?"

"Sustenance." She unrolled the poster, blown up from a picture that O'Dell had sent.

"Calliope!" Jim's arms lifted himself up triumphantly.

"*And* Jim Williams." She glanced around the room. "Well, where should I hang it?"

"There." He pointed to the wall directly opposite the foot of his bed.

"Need some help?" Sue Amory, Jim's primary day-shift nurse—and a horse lover herself—appeared in the doorway at the precise moment the poster rolled up in Diana's hands like a disobedient window shade. Sue fetched a chair to serve as stepladder and helped Diana tape the poster to the wall. "There, it looks spectacular," Sue commented. Both women stepped back to admire the arc of power and grace formed in the air as Jim and his mare cleared an enormous wall.

Jim boosted himself up with shaky arms once again to get a better look. "Our first Grand Prix—we won it. Diana, thank you, you really are—" But he started to aspirate on his own tears.

Diana rushed to the bedside, catching the moisture with a tissue. "Please. I didn't want to upset you."

"I'm not. I feel happier, in a way, than I've ever felt in my life." He searched out her free hand through the bars of the bed railing.

For the first time Diana noticed the machine next to Jim's bed, with "Lifepak" boldly printed across its face. "Is this a heart monitor?"

"My doctor's keeping tabs on nighttime heart rhythms,"

Jim replied. He didn't elaborate, hoping to make her feel confident about the quality of his care.

Diana looked to Sue, who nodded in agreement. "Yes, when it's lights-out, we still want to know what Jim's up to." But Sue didn't elaborate either. Jim was monitored only because his intern wanted to show students the EKG's of failing hearts. Neither Sue nor the hospice supervisor was happy about it, but Jim had already said yes, and at least Dr. O'Malley understood that the alarm switch had to be kept off.

"Well, now you can see Jim a few years ago, and in motion too. The Olympics." Sue Amory took the video from Diana's other hand and busied herself inserting it in the recorder she'd wheeled into his room earlier.

"You can stay, can't you?" Diana turned to her as she pulled another chair out of the corner.

Sue glanced at her watch. She had to do some charting before the next shift at three, but there was time. "I'd love to."

Jim Williams and Calliope completed the preliminary-round fences with control and agility, rising to heights and speeds that most others failed to sustain. In the jump-off, where others crashed, refused, or racked up faults, they soared to victory. Then, at the awards ceremony, James Francis Williams, face handsome and tan, gold medal ribboned around his neck, held his velvet helmet across his heart as the flag rose to "The Star-Spangled Banner." Just to the left of the podium a groom held Calliope, prancing in place. But now the last bars of the anthem gave way to sounds of labored breathing. Fatigued by the excitement, Jim had fallen asleep before the final images faded from the screen.

Diana stayed with him while he slept, read one of the magazines in the room, then stopped at the nurses' station on her way to the coffee shop. A tall dark-haired woman Diana had never seen looked up.

"Is Sue Amory still here?"

"Gone for the day. She'll be in tomorrow at seven. May I help you?"

"I'm curious about that little orange sticker on Mr. Williams' door, the kind most of the other rooms on the floor have too. What does it mean?"

"I'm sorry, I don't know." Her initial hesitation and peremptory tone indicated to Diana the opposite.

"But you work here."

"It's between the patient and his doctor," she replied with a more dismissive irritation.

"You can't discuss it with me?"

"No, I really can't. It's technical."

Now determined to learn the sticker's significance, Diana decided to call Bill that evening—he'd been flown to Johns Hopkins in Baltimore, but should be back. After tea and a muffin, she returned to Jim's floor. If he were awake, she'd offer to read him the article in *Equus* about the newest method of branding horses, encoded microchips implanted under the skin. He'd like that. But an intern and two medical students preceded Diana down the corridor. When the trio stopped outside Jim's room, she closed to within earshot.

"Jim Williams, thirty, male, Cauc., *Pneumocystis carinii*. Forget him. He's circling the drain." The red-haired intern waved his hand dismissively at Jim's closed door. One student laughed through his nose, and they moved on.

Diana stopped dead in her tracks, unable to believe what she'd heard. She replayed the monologue three or four times in her mind. "Circling the drain"—that's what this doctor thought about Jim. He saw his patient—her beloved friend, this suffering man—as dirty bathwater. Heart pounding furiously, she caught up with the group at another door.

"Excuse me."

"Yes?" Dick O'Malley glanced up from his clipboard, his interest stirring as he took in the beauty of the woman who addressed him. "Is there something I can do for you?"

"Did I just hear you say that Jim Williams was 'circling the drain'?"

O'Malley's face muscles froze, and the two students at his side stood motionless. "No, certainly not, you must have misunderstood. I was talking about a surgical drain." The weak, patronizing smile failed to soothe her.

"He hasn't had surgery."

"Of course not. A different patient—my reference was to another patient."

Diana walked away confused and unconvinced, reviewing again what she'd heard: "circling the drain," a dismissive wave of the hand, and the medical student's laugh. He was lying.

"Yes?" The plump, bespectacled secretary in the jersey dress looked surprised.

"Is Bill Stanford in?"

"Yes, but *Dr.* Stanford's extremely busy." She glanced at Bill's calendar to confirm that this attractive woman had no part in it. "Right now he's in a staff meeting."

"I'll wait, then." Diana sat in the corner chair and aimlessly picked up a *Newsweek*.

"I don't think that's a very good idea. He has *other* appointments." Like many jealous secretaries, Rose Pitzer derived considerable self-importance as well as sublimated sexual gratification from her powerful and handsome boss. This girl, who'd just blown in here—Rose certainly hadn't heard one word about her from Dr. Stanford—she'd have to follow proper channels if she expected to see the chairman of neurosurgery, and proper channels meant Rose Pitzer.

"Just mention I'm here. I'm sure he'll see me. My name's Diana Winston."

But Rose Pitzer would not interrupt a staff meeting. If this presumptuous girl wanted her name relayed to the doctor, she'd have to wait. And Diana did, for an hour and a half, before his office door opened. The moment he saw her, his tired face lit up.

"Diana! Glenn," he said, turning to his chief resident, "I need to talk to this lady. I'll see you tonight. And, Rose, would you call Vince Marchetti? Tell him I'm running late and that I'll catch him tomorrow. Diana, c'mon in, tell me what's going on." As she strode into the office, Diana couldn't resist arching a "so-there" eyebrow at the furious secretary.

"Maybe he did mean a surgical drain," Bill offered, though he suspected her indignant report was accurate.

"Do patients 'circle' surgical drains?"

"No," he had to admit, they did not.

"And do you dismiss a dying patient with a wave of your hand while you're talking about someone else?"

"It's possible. Interns and residents are overloaded with work, on the edge of burnout all the time. He obviously misspoke. I'll take care of it."

"I'd call that more than misspeaking. If that's what he thinks about patients, maybe he ought to go to work for the Sewer Authority."

"Did you catch his name?" he asked, trying to direct her anger.

"I don't remember. O'something-or-other. Bright red hair and a weak face the color of milk."

"I'll see to 'Dr. O'something-or-other.' Look, this is a difficult time for Jim *and* you. Don't let an insensitive blunder by a staff member rile you. Let's be as positive as we can for Jim's sake." He gave her arm a supportive squeeze. "Tell me what you've been up to this past week."

"I almost forgot," she said, ignoring his attempt to divert her thoughts to a happier course. "Jim's door has a round orange sticker. I asked a nurse what it meant, but she got defensive and refused to tell me."

Bill groaned inwardly. A nurse assigned to hospice, of all places, should be able to handle that one. "It means that Jim and his doctor have agreed that no one should jump all over his chest when his body gives out." Her expression remained puzzled. "The sticker means 'do not resuscitate.' There'll be no bells, no rush of staff, no adrenaline or equipment to keep him alive against his wishes."

"And those *are* Jim's wishes?" she asked softly.

"Yes." He put his arm around her. "It's hard to understand, but there comes a point of no return, when the dying need—they want—to let go."

"I understand." She hesitated, then drew a deep breath before continuing. "I mean, if that's what Jim wants. It's just that . . . it's just that I'll miss him so much." Her voice trembled, but Bill's arm gave her strength to continue. "You know, that sticker is international orange, the universal call for assistance. But when Jim's dying, it means the opposite—no one is to come."

Bill nodded at the grim irony. In the end Jim would drown in his own fluids. The DNR sticker, the color of all life jackets, meant he'd get none.

After seeing Bill, Diana returned to Jim's room to find him still asleep. A vase brimming with roses stood on his dresser. Diana opened the small envelope secured in the prongs of the transparent plastic stick. "Come home soon. Love, Mother." Diana shook her head in sorrow and disgust. She'd return the next day.

"What are you feeding this boy? Look at him!" Diana turned in the direction of the accusing whisper.

"Shhh, Mrs. Hamilton, he's asleep." Sue Amory tried to escort the Williams' maid Belinda out the door.

"Belinda? Is that Belinda?" Jim's sleepy voice asked.

"Yes, honey, it's your Belinda. I brought you some good things to eat. They don't seem to know how to cook round here. You're way too thin. I have a mind to go to the kitchen and straighten them out." She turned her fierce gaze on Sue. "If the food's this bad, honey, why don't you put one of those needles in his arm and shoot him some?"

"Now, you stop harassing people, Belinda. They're doing what they can. The food's fine but my body doesn't want to make proper use of it, that's all. Now, I hope you brought something for me." The intervention winded him and he fell back against the elevated mattress.

"Let me help." Diana took the heavy picnic basket

and swung it onto the table. "This weighs a ton." Belinda removed her coat, rolled up her sleeves, and began to take out an unending number of jars, boxes, tins, and small beribboned packages. "Ham made the way you like it—with cider and cornmeal. Then there's hotcakes, French doughnuts, pralines, pecan pie, and Mardi Gras squares and peach sauce. I didn't bring you ice cream for the sauce. Fancy place like this can come up with some plain vanilla ice cream." She turned to Sue for confirmation.

"Ice cream we have lots of," replied Sue, touched by the commanding devotion of this woman, who'd known Jim since he was a baby.

"Thanks, Belinda. You're terrific." Jim turned to Sue and smiled weakly. He couldn't get anything solid down; he just didn't want it. They were force-feeding him liquids now.

"I don't want no thanks. Just you tell that body of yours to start'n make proper use of this food. I've got to be off, honey. My little ones have little ones now, and they need me at home."

Belinda started to close the lid of her basket, but stopped. "Oh, I almost forgot—you might want these." She took out Jim's gold medal and a little wooden crucifix. "This bleeding Jesus that nice quiet man gave you was under your bed. I found it the day after you took the fit." Placing the two items on his bed table, she turned to Sue. "You see he gets some flesh back on his bones, miss."

"I'll try." Sue smiled at the woman's energetic kindness.

"She's used to taking care of me," commented Jim after Belinda left.

"I'll say." She pointed at the dozens of tins and boxes. "What would you like me to do with this?"

"Throw them out, I guess." He shrugged. "But not right away. I'll look at it for a while. It's the nicest 'get-well' card I've ever received."

"I'll be back in a bit to take your temp."

Jim turned to Diana. "I hate to throw out this food, but I suppose no one would want it."

"Why not?"

"Contaminated."

"With what?"

"Me."

"Jim." Diana's voice crossed between scolding and imploring. "If you're not going to 'make proper use' of these pralines, I certainly will." She cradled a metal tin protectively in her arms. "Is Steve the 'nice quiet man'?" she asked, glancing at the crucifix.

"I asked him to get it for me." He picked up the small cross and traced the body with his fingers.

"Want to see your video again?" she inquired softly.

"What video?"

Diana had become accustomed to his increasingly frequent lapses. "Your Olympic video. Yesterday Sue and I . . ."

"Oh, I remember. I can see that anytime. Why don't we talk about your next show?"

Diana was delighted, hoping Jim could help her gain confidence. "If you don't mind."

"Your first Grand Prix's very important. Too bad you're stuck with Aden. Ben Adams had him on the jumper circuit a long time, so he's had lots of experience, but he *is* a steamhead—gives new meaning to the word 'jock.' "

"Jim," Diana interrupted, "I'm not riding Aden. It's Navarro—my first Puissance."

"Navarro—that dressage horse owned by the Spanish ambassador?" He paused and closed his eyes momentarily. "Diana, Aden is Ben Adams' horse. Now, you've got to get this guy placed three strides before each fence. For the triple combination it's critical to start correctly."

"It's Puissance with Navarro that's next." But Jim paid no heed as the invading virus made his brain replay verbatim an earlier scene. "When he tries to have it his way, hold him with your legs and seat. You don't want him so excited he puts in extra strides. Keep him going forward so his antics won't throw you. Force him to move on or he won't concentrate. The reason he's a thriller to watch is he's hell to ride. And remember—

jump precisely. Six inches off means more than six feet down."

Stricken, Diana looked to the door, where her tear-filled eyes met Sue's. She'd come to take Jim's temperature but found she'd also come to grieve. The day Diana had won the I Love New York Grand Prix, Sue Amory had stood in the stands applauding.

For three days while at Johns Hopkins, Bill had looked forward to seeing Diana on his return, but not under such painful circumstances. She'd shouldered a lot during Jim's illness, and now he felt angry that some staff members had added to her burden. Late the next evening he walked to hospice and found a redheaded doctor—his name tag read "O'Malley"—measuring electrocardiograms.

"Are you taking care of Mr. Williams?"

"Yes, sir, I am." A glance at Bill's ID commanded the young man to alter his bearing. He'd never even seen the chief of neurosurgery, who ranked just below Jesus Christ on the Briggs and DePrete organizational chart.

"How's he doing?" Bill asked matter-of-factly, politely. He wanted to be sure he had the right redhead.

"Not good."

"So I've heard. Tell me, how long has he been in your care?"

"I just came on service two days ago." O'Malley's pale eyelashes fluttered nervously as the focus of conversation now turned to him. He put down his calipers and stood even straighter.

"You have students on the floor?"

"Yes, two."

This was the man. Bill's voice turned cold and sarcastic. "A friend of Mr. Williams' heard you refer to him as 'circling the drain.' We all talk tough in this business, but saying *that* in a public corridor gets you the most-insensitive-boy-doctor-of-the-year award. And *you* have students?" Before the intern could reply, Bill turned his back, leaving him to speculate whether his nascent medical career wasn't itself now circling the drain.

\*    \*    \*

The next day Diana skipped lunch after her morning ride and drove straight to the hospital. Though intellectually she understood about dementia, delirium, and hallucinations, having to witness them in this brave man she'd loved and still loved exacted a terrible emotional toll. She needed a reprieve, but there would be none.

"Why haven't you come to see me?" Jim's angry and accusing voice took her by surprise. His face taut, mouth drawn, eyes flashing—no trace of the teasing she hoped to find.

"I got here as soon as I could. I was here yesterday, remember?" she asked, trying a light and cheerful tone.

"No, you weren't. Nobody's been here since winter started. My lips have turned blue with the cold."

The force of the false accusation chilled her heart even as her eyes acknowledged the blue of his cracked lips. To Jim, perhaps a whole season had passed since she'd last visited, though the watch on her healthy arm—still tanned from summer—confirmed that it had been less than a day. "You and Sue and I watched a video together. Remember—the Olympics, your Olympics? Then Belinda brought you all that food yesterday."

"Do you see any food? I don't. And I don't remember seeing anybody in a long, long time. I said nobody's been here since winter started and that means you too." His voice grew inflexible, and his eyes, usually gentle and kind, burned with sharp, accusing fury.

"It's fall." Stunned, overwhelmed, and gripped with fear, Diana could feel her hands tremble as she spoke. "October. It's October," she urged gently. "The leaves are crimson and yellow and orange."

"Oh, yes, dying leaves. You know why leaves fall off the trees? I learned it at St. Benedict's from the monks, those dear moral monks who take such Christian care of little boys like me." His voice, raised and sarcastic, didn't wait for her to reply. "The trees withdraw their life-support systems." Then the quavering pitch of his voice dissolved into strangled laughter. "Isn't that the funniest thing? All those fantastic colors, from deprivation."

Diana felt horrified and powerless in the face of his distorted and pained laughter. "Jim . . ." she pleaded, placing one hand on an emaciated thigh, the other seeking out his hand. "I've been with you. Sue and I hung up that poster over there. Two days ago," she added timidly. "Look." As Jim's eyes glanced at the poster, confusion crossed his haggard face, then anger returned. "But how could you leave me for so long?"

"I won't leave again. I promise."

"It's winter."

"I know."

"I'm so cold."

"I'll warm you." She drew up the covers and squeezed his hand.

"Stay with me." His anger had suddenly turned to despair.

"I'm here, Jim."

"Till winter's over?"

"Till winter's over."


While he slept, Diana went to the cafeteria, but ate little, managing only tea and the crackers that came with her soup. When she returned to the room, another vase of flowers—red, white, and blue carnations—had arrived. "Another bouquet." No response from Jim. She turned to see his angry eyes staring straight ahead, body motionless. "Where did they come from? They're beautiful." No response. David Jackson had said depression would come, but it tortured her to find him so angry he couldn't speak, not even to her. "I'll just sit here for a little while, if that's okay." She pulled up a chair next to his bed. "We don't have to talk." Diana turned her thoughts to Navarro, hoping to cancel the anguish of sitting with her isolated friend. But the Puissance filled her with fear and brought her right back to him. Alone and upset, she finally broke the silence. "Can you help me?" No response. She buried her face in her hands, hoping to lock out Jim's impending death and the wall that loomed ahead of her.

"What is it?" he asked gruffly. A terrible minute of silence had elapsed.

"I'm afraid of the wall."

The fear in her voice rallied his overworked heart. "Puissance? Here, give me your hand." She pushed her arm through the railing and felt his fingers—now surprisingly strong—take hold of hers. "You can do it. It's a height you've never done, but you *can* do it. Navarro and you have the talent for it. You place Navarro correctly, at the base of the jump . . ."

"I'll feel so alone, and with thousands of people watching."

"Forget about being alone and forget about anybody else. You place Navarro square at the wall like it's any other vertical, and he'll get you over. But trust him to do that for you." He'd grown perfectly lucid and his eyes looked at her with remarkable concentration. "They can say all they want about right dynamics, ability, good approach, impulsion. We know you've got all that. For you it boils down to trust: if you can't trust him, he can't trust you. Your fingers are stiff. I feel them—rigid. You're afraid, and unless you do something with that fear, it'll go right through you to the horse, and the wall will be his fear too. If he knows the wall frightens you, he'll be afraid. And he'll have reason to be."

"But I can't ride to a jump that's so high I can't even see over it."

"Yes, you can. You've been over hundreds of fences just a couple of feet lower. For this one you trust your horse and the knowledge that there's level ground on the other side. Then you'll land in stride. Believe me, the wall is not the obstacle, but your fear." She took his hand and kissed it with her lips through the paper mask. Her comfort gave him the courage to confront his own worst fear. "But I don't know what's on the other side of this wall that's closing in on me now. How do I trust? Who do I trust?" He struggled not to cry.

"Me. You trust me. When my mother died, you told me that a spirit connects us all. I believe that." She supported his back as he now cried and started to gasp for breath. "Should I call a nurse?"

"No, hold me."

Diana slipped off her shoes, let down the railing, and climbed up on the bed. She held Jim until his crying subsided and he could breathe again. She rubbed his back and held a glass of water to his parched lips. As she returned the glass to the table, she felt a soreness around her mouth and undid her mask. Soaking wet. The salt from trapped tears had chafed her skin. She stared at the darkened green paper and let it drop to the floor.

"You need another mask." Jim fingered her skin.

"No, no more masks." When she drew the blanket up around them both, she felt the brush of the diaper Jim now needed to wear. "You warm?"

He nodded and took her hand in his. "Diana, aren't you afraid?"

"Not anymore."

That evening Steve walked through the glass arcade at Briggs and DePrete and took the elevator to hospice. He hadn't seen Jim since the day he and Diana returned from Spain, and he really didn't want to see him now. There was nothing he could do for him. Even without the earthquake's destruction of his own work in virology, no research he might have contributed would ever have been in time for Jim. His thoughts turned to the manuscript that Marshall Simpkins had sent, Federal Express, on the subject of T4 receptor kinetics, already accepted by Stanford University Press. In the accompanying letter Simpkins solicited his opinion before final submission to the press's board of syndics. A quick thumb-through indicated to Steve that some of the findings should be realigned, and he recognized the need for an added paragraph on topics for related future research.

Typical hospice, he reflected, stepping out onto the seventeenth floor of Anderson Hall—converted nurses' dorm, hard to disinfect, and beds filled with medicine's outcasts and incurables. He walked down the musty corridor and felt himself recoil as a gay couple approached. Ostentatious and defiant—tight jeans, cropped hair, leather jackets, no distance between the two men as they nudged each other. Steve breathed a sigh of relief when they disappeared through a doorway. He wouldn't have to cross paths with them, but glanced in the room they entered—hot-pink bedspread with matching curtains and flounces.

A few doors down he spotted a priest leaving Jim's room. The purple stole and little black box that the old man carried said it all—Jim Williams had just received last rites from a man who emphasized sin and repentance. As a result of Vatican II, priests administering last rites were instructed to wear white stoles, a change in color that emphasized life everlasting over corruption. Conservative priests, however, often continued to wear the purple. Steve halted abruptly and pretended to look for something in his wallet until the priest's footfalls faded. He had no desire for this man to know he was Jim's friend.

Semicomatose again, he observed, and quietly approached Jim's side. Increased temporal wasting, sunken cheeks, cadaverous—even a heavy dose of Lysol failed to conceal the putrid odor. Suddenly Jim's leg jerked involuntarily, throwing back the green corded bedspread to expose his emaciated frame. When Steve retrieved and straightened the covers, taking care not to dislodge the wires attached to Jim's chest, he saw the purple kneecaps— failing peripheral circulation. He wouldn't last the night. Light from the October moon—the hunter's moon—shone through the window on Jim's face, but his jaundiced eyes couldn't respond to the silver shafts. In that cold illumination the oils of extreme unction glistened on his forehead. He'd been unconscious, so the priest would have granted him only conditional absolution—forgiveness would be a matter between Jim and his God. All the better, thought Steve, realizing that if he had arrived during the rites, the priest would have encouraged him to respond to the prayers offered on Jim's behalf. And to that Steve would have said no. He walked over to the heart monitor and watched the failing heart rhythms on the screen. Luminescent upside down V's—each representing one heartbeat—crossed the window from right to left.

"I'm sorry, I'll come back." Bill Stanford started to close the door.

"No, please. Dr. Stanford? We met briefly in Newport. You drove Jim back here." Steve felt an urgent need for company.

With a glance, Bill took in the signs of Jim's decline, then walked over to the monitor. Sinus tachycardia; he guessed the heart rate at 150. Jim wouldn't last much longer. "Are you familiar with this machine?" His voice was barely above a whisper.

"Not really," replied Steve, inwardly wincing at his deception.

"It tells the nurses how his heart is doing without their disturbing him. You're Diana's trainer, aren't you?" Steve nodded, still staring at the monitor, his eyes glued to the armies of stick figures marching across the screen. "How's she doing? She seems worried about Puissance."

"She'll do it if . . ."

"If what?"

"If she can get over this," Steve said, turning back to Jim. "Look."

They saw Jim's hand slowly opening and closing on the bedsheet. Though Bill remained silent, Steve read his thoughts. "Dr. Stanford, it's not that, it's not exactly what you think. More like a butterfly resting before a long flight." Bill had to agree. He'd never seen picking at the bedclothes that resembled this.

"What is it, Jim? What do you need?" Steve asked softly.

Though he knew any attempt to communicate with Jim was useless—he would register no more than a five on the Glasgow test for measuring comas—Bill said nothing.

The opening and closing continued, but Bill saw that Jim's forehead was now furrowed and strained.

"What do you need?" Steve repeated. Suddenly Jim flipped his hand over. The opening and closing continued, but this time his fingers dug into the sheet as if each gesture repeated the same demand. Steve searched the room without knowing what he was looking for. Then he saw it lying on the floor next to the bed, the crucifix from Mexico. He picked up the small dark object and placed it in Jim's hand. And as the bluish fingers closed around the wood, Jim relaxed his brow.

Both men were about to part without a word when Steve noticed on the door a small orange sticker the size of a quarter and, next to it, a white one the size of a dime.

"Dr. Stanford, what do these mean?"

"The orange sticker means Jim isn't to be kept alive against his will. The white one means that he's received last rites."

"Well, at least someone got that color right," Steve observed, then turned and walked away.

Jim's fever had started to climb at five o'clock despite Tylenol suppositories. It was a hundred and four when Bill and Steve visited. Alveoli—the lung's air sacs—continued to fill with fluid, and his heart and respiration rates rose to meet the impossible challenges of the corrupting virus. After the two men left, Jim's swallow and cough reflexes began to fail him. A gurgling sound—breath struggling to get through a trachea constricted by accumulating mucus—escaped his throat. As arrhythmic nerve impulses caused his muscles to twitch involuntarily, sleep transported him back to the books and stories of his troubled childhood.

He was in India, crossing an arid plain on a white horse. He needed to get home but had lost his compass. For miles he saw nothing but unending desert under a relentless sun, which, now at its zenith, offered no direction. His horse, angry at keeping a halt, reared and lashed out at the hot air with black hooves. In the distance Jim saw storm clouds gathering. Within minutes darkness buried the sun, and the air crackled and whistled as a wind came up. At first he thought he heard thunder, but no lightning flashed. Again, closer now, not thunder, but many hooves striking earth at a gallop, but he could still see nothing except the approaching storm.

Jim spurred his horse forward, away from the impending darkness. The white mane whipped his face, and sand kicked up by the horse's legs stung his eyes. The wind increased and carried with it the sound of approaching horses. Jim looked backward, seeing only dark, then commanded his mount to greater speed, but the wind swallowed his words. Blood from his horse's overworked lungs spattered his arms. As the galloping thunder struck his ears like a hundred hammers, his heart filled with fear and he gasped for breath. This time when he turned in the saddle he saw assailants—four mounted figures cloaked in the darkness. Three horses had coats that glistened white, red, and black, but the fourth one that he beheld had no color. Jim choked as he inhaled sharp bits of the sand that now engulfed him. Suddenly, out of the brown swirl, loomed a mountain whose steep summit rose above the storm, and he knew that if he reached the top he'd be safe.

Again the exhausted horse struggled to obey his rider's commands and lunged up the rocky slope, flanks heaving as blood continued to spray from his nostrils. Jim lifted his face to the sky and to the sun at the pinnacle—almost there—then instinctively buried his face in his horse's mane to keep from choking. But his horse stumbled and almost buckled to its knees—then, propelling them forward with its hindquarters, managed to regain good footing. But the sudden momentum threw Jim backward and he fell to the ground, and his horse, now unhampered by the weight of a rider, fled. Jim sheltered his face in his arms and waited for his private apocalypse. But no horseman came, the storm soon abated, and he could breathe again. No longer afraid, he turned on his back and felt the rhythms of his pounding heart begin to slow as the gentle afternoon sun bathed him in warmth. He heard sounds of running water but felt too exhausted to respond. He was dying of thirst, but had to rest. He closed his eyes and sighed. Tomorrow, yes—he would drink tomorrow.

While Jim slept, the luminescent stick figures on the monitor screen grew shorter and shorter, until they evened out to a single line. A half-hour later he was found by a nurse, who quietly summoned the duty doctor. The certificate listed cause one of death as *Pneumocystis carinii* pneumonia. Cause two: acquired immune deficiency syndrome. No one would know about Jim's dream, or that the fall from his horse had killed him.

# Behold a White Horse

The funeral mass was celebrated three days later at St. Catherine's on East Sixty-eighth street, the Williamses' local parish, where Dominican fathers had built a small red brick church at the turn of the century. The two-hundred people in attendance included Jim's parents, an aunt and uncle, family friends, classmates from St. Benedict's and Princeton, and two members of the United States Show Jumping Team. Diana and Steve shared a pew with Belinda and Sue Amory. Steve felt immediate relief that the celebrant, who wore white vestments, was not the priest he'd seen in the hospital. Father Gendron had taught Jim his catechism before the parents packed him off to St. Benedict's. The morning that the old priest—now retired—learned of Jim's death, he called Douglas and Bickie Williams and offered to give the mass, and the service revealed that he knew Jim well. After the introductory rites, during which he prayed for forgiveness for those who had failed Jim in his hour of need, Father Gendron described Jim's life and death in phrases from the life and death of another young man.

In his last weeks, as he lay dying, "he had not form or comeliness that we should look at him, and no beauty that we should desire him. He was despised and rejected by men; a man of sorrows, and acquainted with grief; as one from whom men hide their faces, he was despised and we esteemed him not. Yet it was the will of God to bruise him." And we are deeply troubled by this, he continued. "Why *did*—how *could*—God bruise this young athlete so terribly—a young man at the pinnacle of glory? Why did he set such a terrible and protracted death upon him? A vile disease that causes many to turn their backs in revulsion and judgment? We would have preferred if he had been called quickly—an accident, perhaps a fall from his horse—a sort of divine solution that could almost make sense to us. It certainly would have been easier on Jim, on his friends and family. But the ways of the Lord are not always, or even usually, as we would have them. So again we are faced with the terrible why." The answer, Father Gendron suggested, could be found in Timothy. "For the time is coming when people will not endure sound teaching, but having itching ears, they will accumulate for themselves teachers to suit their likings, and will turn away from listening to the truth and wander into myths. As for you, always be steady, endure suffering, do the work of an evangelist, fulfill your mystery. For I am already on the point of being sacrificed; the time of my departure has come. I have fought the good fight, I have finished the race, I have kept the faith. Henceforth there is laid up for me the crown of righteousness, which the Lord, the righteous judge, will award to me on that day."

The elderly man then remarked that Jim Williams' final race did not take place in a public arena filled with adoring fans, but in a private room on the seventeenth floor amidst a small cadre of dedicated friends. Less than a week ago, he noted, a nurse had spoken to him of Jim's extraordinary ability to maintain cheerful interest in friends and with the hospital staff he'd come to know. "From his bed, he inquired how St. Catherine's would celebrate its ninetieth anniversary. Though none of us at the parish had seen him for many years, his thoughts had remained with us, generous and undiluted by distance and time. He spoke lovingly of those few who had stayed with him, and asked to be forgiven his doubts and anger. In the end, no one was there except the small wooden crucifix he held in his hand. But that was enough. Jim Williams died as he lived, a champion and a hero, an example to Christians. He won the race and kept the faith, and then the time for his departure came. As we commend his spirit to the Lord, let us rejoice in our knowing that the Lord will award him that crown of righteousness. At the same time, let us call to mind what, in accordance with The Book of Revelation, waits for us all on Judgment Day." Father Gendron concluded the sermon with a final reading from the Scriptures. "And I saw heaven opened, and behold a white horse; and he that sat upon him was called Faithful and True."

The rich, hopeful chords of Bach, the sermon, and the precise rites of the mass—the Eucharist, bells, incense, and the sprinkling of holy water on the urn containing the ashes—provided a soothing yet mysterious conclusion to Jim's life. Somewhere, underneath the grief, Diana knew she'd been liberated. Jim wasn't her responsibility anymore. Moving ahead with her own life would take time, of course. The death of her first real friend had been like a hurricane leaving terrible debris in its wake. Recovery would be slow.

Attending the mass at St. Catherine's—Steve's first since the one given for the unidentifiable corpses found in Juárez Hospital—affected him differently. He experienced an unsettling series of coincidences and convergences involving the church, its location, and mission. Jim's parish stood directly across from the Faulkner Laboratory, research arm of Briggs and DePrete, and in the forefront of virological research. This would not be so unusual if the church had been built after the hospital, since Dominican friars have a tradition of caring for the sick, but the architecture of St. Catherine's told Steve that the church had been there decades before. From his pew he caught sight of a small shrine—a statue and a row of red votive candles casting flickers of light on the shadowed floor. He approached it at the conclusion of the mass—St. Jude, patron saint of hopeless cases. He pushed a folded dollar bill into the offering-box slot and lit a candle, as yet unaware of the gesture's significance. For the first time he'd relinquished ultimate responsibility for life and death to God and his intermediaries.

Just as he and Diana turned up Sixty-eighth Street, dark cumulus clouds yielded to bright sunlight, but it was cold for November. The tall buildings acted as a tunnel for the north wind and sent curled dead leaves rattling down the streets and sidewalks like paper skeletons. In need of food and warmth, they ran into the first restaurant they came to. Steve held open the steamy glass door, and the spicy, hearty smells of familiar dishes filled his nostrils. Restaurant Chapultepec was jammed—the majority of customers drawn from the laboratory across the street. English conversations mingled with Spanish. When the bean soup and *quesadillas* arrived, the waiter placed on the table a loaf of bread baked in the form of a skull. Steve glanced at the calendar on his watch—November 2, the Day of the Dead.

He read the question in Diana's face. "All Souls' Day. It's an important fiesta in Mexico."

"Why?" she asked earnestly.

"To pray for the souls in purgatory."

"But why so important? In most Catholic countries they just pray at mass or at home. No parties."

"I don't know, really. Mexicans look for any excuse to cut loose." Hoping she'd be satisfied with that, Steve busied himself by twisting a piece of bread off the skull. But a glance at her intense, unblinking eyes told him she wasn't. "Mexicans are in love with death." He shrugged.

"Then I think they must be in love with life as well."

"What makes you say that? It's a Catholic country. Guilt and repression don't inspire love of life." He was at once amused and annoyed by her untutored generalization. "You've never even been to Mexico."

"No, but I've been to Spain, also Catholic and conservative, and it dominated Mexico for almost three centuries. Most of the Spanish settlers in the New World came from Andalusia. There are similarities, Steve, and you know it." She reached across the table and took his hand. "That's why we went to Andalusia in the first place. If it had just been to see a bullfight, we could've gone to the ring in Madrid. But you needed to find what your father had left behind, and to see if any of it was yours."

"Like what?" he asked softly. Diana's observations had cut to his core. He felt afraid, yet oddly comforted. How well she knew him.

"The *corrida*—your father liked it but you didn't. Remember you told me that he thought the ones in Andalusia superior to those in Mexico? How could you like bullfighting? Your father forced you to look at something horrible on the pretext that it would make you brave. On our drive back from Jerez you told me that he pried your fingers away from your eyes and compelled you to watch the death of a picador's horse—so you'd be able to face life's tragedies. To do that to a boy was inexcusable, sadistic. So you hate *corridas,* and who could blame you? Your father made you feel powerless, just as he did when he forced you to visit the boy dying of cancer. But while you reject the *corrida,* you love *rejoneo*. I saw it in your face each time I turned to you to hide mine. And in the end, when you helped me lose my fear by letting me see it for what it really was, I loved it too. The black bull and the white horse challenging each other in an arena—a beautiful celebration of life over death. You told me that yourself when you said that the *rejoneador* is disgraced if the bull gores his horse. The rider and horse have a vigorous love of life and a healthy fear of death. It's how they live; it's how they win."

Steve fingered the crust of his bread thoughtfully. No, he didn't like the *corrida* with its unmounted matadors and final emphasis on death—a contrived and unnecessary tragedy. But in Andalusia he came to appreciate the *rejoneo* for the first time. Not once did he turn away. Diana was right: those who averted their eyes were condemned to live in a cocoon. Life belongs to those who dare to pick up the lance.

"And, Steve . . ." She now held both his hands in hers. "You love life and fear death too."

"Because I like the *rejoneo?*" He seemed puzzled.

"Because you're a doctor." They sat in silence for a few minutes.

Over lunch they discussed Navarro and his training. Steve suggested she keep him in Bedford. The Garden was just three weeks away so it seemed the most practical solution. But Diana had no wish to stay in the New York area—now that Jim was gone, there was nothing to keep her.

"Bill Stanford made a donation to the memorial fund established in Jim's name at USET headquarters in Gladstone."

"He did? When did you hear about that?" she asked, at the same time wondering why Steve had changed the subject and mentioned Bill just at the moment she'd told herself that New York had nothing left to keep her there.

"He called me yesterday. Jack O'Dell told him about the fund but Bill needed the address of team headquarters."

"I see." He could have called me, Diana reflected, wondering why he hadn't. She hadn't seen or heard a word from Bill since he had phoned her at the Pickwick the evening following Jim's death. And then he only said how sorry he was—no offer to see her and no explanation why not. She must have been wrong about his feelings for her. She was overcome by a wave of sadness and loss. He had to know that she'd be leaving soon. Well, fine, she would. "Steve, tomorrow I'll go to Bedford, attach the trailer, and drive Navarro home to Southfield. I'll take him over to Brookfield Farm in Concord and use their indoor ring. Now that the nights are freezing, the ground's pretty hard, and I'm worried about the suspensory."

"What about Calliope?" Steve asked.

"I've thought about her. I can't trailer her side by side with Navarro, so I'll leave her in New Jersey till after the Garden. Then I'll have a professional shipping company van her up. What do you think?"

"I think you must have made Jim very glad when you bought her."

*     *     *

"How about a carriage ride?" Steve asked, pointing to the row of horses and hansoms in front of the Plaza Hotel across from Central Park.

After Diana and Steve were seated comfortably, the teenage driver released the brake and carefully guided her chestnut mare across the noisy press of late-afternoon traffic and through an arbor of trees. Though it was cold and near the end of the afternoon, Central Park was busy, the air alive with smells of pine, earth, and roasted chestnuts. Kites soared against the sky, toy sailboats charted courses on Conservatory Pond, jugglers juggled, lovers embraced, musicians and magicians made music and magic. Children took turns diving headlong into piles of leaves, near where a solitary man on a rock read a book of poetry, wearing sunglasses so he could see the lines through the sun's glare.

"We're right by the mall here. That's why it's so crowded. I'll take you to the lake, then up the west side of the park toward the reservoir." As soon as the driver negotiated Duchess past two slightly overweight, slightly out-of-control women on roller skates and onto a wider pavement, she urged the horse into a trot. Walkers, joggers, cyclists, baby carriages, purebred dogs and mutts, horses with riders astride, horses drawing carriages, and a pet ocelot on the end of a rhinestone leash shared their road.

"Quite a celebration," Diana observed, returning the solemn wave of a little girl who stood on a corner with her father. "It's so cold you'd think more people would stay home and snuggle up to their fireplaces. And there's such a wind."

"But the sun's strong. Look over there." Steve pointed south and east, across the acres of woodlands and rocky outcroppings, and up to the skyscrapers—Gulf and Western, Time-Life, Black Rock—where plate-glass windows converted fading sunlight into thousands of shining golden ingots. He drew the plaid wool lap blanket up around her waist, then held her hand. There were no sounds except the occasional whoosh of a passing bicycle and the chestnut's steady hoofbeats. By the time they returned to Fifty-ninth Street, twilight had descended and the sun was gone. They decided to go to Rumpelmayer's in the St. Moritz—neither felt very hungry, but wanted a warm place to sit and have something sweet.

Afterward, as they walked arm in arm down the street, Steve spotted a mailbox.

"I almost forgot." He took an envelope from his inside pocket, walked to the metal box, then dropped it down the chute. Diana saw the happiness and relief in his face when he linked his arm with hers again. Out of nowhere she felt a flicker of jealousy and fear. When he stepped forward, she remained. "What is it?" he asked.

"You tell me." She nodded gravely toward the mailbox. "Please."

"Oh, that." A smile played at the corners of his mouth. "A letter to the American Board of Pediatrics requesting that they reconsider my application."

"Steve!" She threw her arms around his shoulders and pulled him close. "I'm so happy. That's wonderful."

"I hope it's wonderful. They haven't said yes yet."

"But they will, won't they?" she asked, rocking him in her arms. "Won't they?"

He paused to wipe his tears with the sleeve of his overcoat, then gently took her face between his hands. "Yes—yes, they will. I'm going to be a doctor again."

It was in the Briggs and DePrete coffee shop, while having breakfast, that Bill Stanford had learned of Jim Williams' death. Two medical students at the cash register complained about having to attend the autopsy of an AIDS victim who'd died the night before. When Bill went to his office, a handwritten message left by Dr. Lindemann confirmed it. Though initially inclined to attend the funeral, in the end he decided not to go—his primary motive would be to see Diana, to comfort her and draw her closer to him. But perhaps she'd know that and think him opportunistic and hypocritical, which he couldn't bear. So Bill kept to his operating schedule. And at the precise moment Father Gendron committed Jim's soul to God, Bill removed, from a thirteen-year-old girl, the last pieces of a tumor that had been pressing on her pituitary gland, preventing growth and normal development.

That evening, after rounds, he took a cab to Les Sans Culottes—the restaurant where he'd met Diana her first evening in New York—out of an acute longing to recreate it. He sipped a martini at the bar and recalled how she looked, spoke, laughed, and cried. Then he thought about that night in Newport—their conversation had taken him back to the time he was a little-boy baseball player, injured but full of hope. It seemed as if she cared about that part of his life more than any other—and he loved her for it. She didn't appear at all impressed that he was one of the world's top neurosurgeons. Women he encountered, either professionally or socially, often altered their bearing markedly when he entered the room. And while he had enjoyed this feeding of his ego, he now acknowledged a real loneliness that came with celebrity status and stardom. Maybe Diana just didn't care about medicine. Emily certainly didn't. Then he immediately berated himself for comparing Diana with his wife—they were as different as spring and fall. Recalling Diana's precocious yet sometimes delightfully ingenuous questions about medicine, he had to admit that she did care, very much. But what Bill really needed to know, and didn't yet, was whether she cared for him.

And of that he couldn't be certain. In Newport she had struck him as an intelligent, beautiful athlete who seemed interested in him. He certainly guessed that she'd had affairs and might have a boyfriend, but he hadn't given it much thought until the night he accidentally ran into Steve Rodríguez visiting Jim. Steve had said that he had no knowledge of heart monitors, but he did. Bill could see his eyes trying to count the heartbeats. And as Jim's hand opened and closed, Steve knew it wasn't the death gesture but understood a physician thought it might be.

"Dr. Stanford, it's not that, it's not exactly what you think. More like a butterfly resting before a long flight." Steve also knew that the semicomatose man was seeking the crucifix that had fallen under his bed. And then Bill saw a Rockefeller University stack pass in Steve's shirt pocket when he stooped down to retrieve the cross. This man from Mexico knew something about medicine, but his knowledge went beyond physical ailments to the needs of the psyche. From that evening on he knew that Steve, not Jim, had been the major contender for Diana's affections. This man had given her Navarro, coached her to victory in Newport, taken her to Spain, and was about to help her jump the highest obstacle in her life. And he was a gentle man.

Another martini only underscored Diana's absence and intensified his feelings of loneliness and confusion, so Bill paid and asked for his overcoat. Just as he pulled on the glass door, a small gray-and-white cat darted in and ran through the bar to the dining room. *"Encore, le chat!"* The maître d' passed the alarm back to his headwaiter, who signaled a busboy. A brief skirmish ensued, with the busboy finally holding the cat triumphantly by the scruff of its neck.

"Sorry," Bill offered to the maître d' while holding the door open for the feline bouncer.

*"Non, non, monsieur,* there is no need to apologize. That cat has been invading my restaurant since lunch. If she's still here tomorrow, off she goes to an animal shelter. The Board of Health and my customers would not savor the thought of a stray cat in my kitchen—a foreign kitchen. Americans have xenophobic notions about foreign-cuisine trickery." He turned to the busboy. *"Arnaud, n'oubliez pas laver les mains."*

The cat sat in the middle of the sidewalk, looking directly at Bill. Barely more than a kitten, he thought, and so thin. Yet such a pretty face—capped in gray but with white forehead and pink nose. He bent over and beckoned her forward with his outstretched hand, but after having been chased all day by enraged Frenchmen, she kept her ground, body motionless but for her bright green eyes following Bill's every move. After several attempts to get her to trust him, he returned to the restaurant and asked the maître d' for some scraps of meat, quickly assuring him that he'd take the cat home if he could catch her. Relieved and delighted, the man immediately produced three succulent strips of filet mignon.

This time the kitten came quickly forward to extract the two-inch piece of meat Bill held between his fingers. "Poor thing, you must be starving." Not only did she allow Bill to touch her as she ate, but raised her back and purred like a little machine when his hand stroked her. "Why don't you come home with me? It's a nice apartment, and I'm sure my wife's got all sorts of exotic things in the refrigerator to fit your taste." Bill picked up the light, unresisting creature and placed her just inside the opening of his coat. "The question, I guess, is whether you'll fit hers."

"Late night?" Emily asked without looking up from the Chinese juniper, the roots of which she was teasing out, then cutting off to ensure that the tree would remain dwarfed but healthy. Her long-handled twig cutter flashed out in the kitchen light like a switchblade. "What do you think? Over seventy years old and only ten inches tall. Of course, it's been in training with me only four weeks, but I've done nothing to ruin it. Sato San says I'm a natural at root pruning. See the texture of the bark? As healthy as can be."

"This isn't, I'm afraid." Bill placed the cat on the counter beside the bonsai.

"A cat!" Emily's shrill disapproval sent the animal fleeing. "It'll tear this house apart."

"If you scream like that, she just might," he said softly, with controlled patience. Determined to keep this cat, but without the burden of going through a scene, Bill walked over to the silk camelback sofa, got down on his hands and knees, and coaxed the cat back into his arms.

"You don't mean to keep it? Look, it's filthy." Emily

pointed to the cat's dirty underbelly, the sand, grit, and dirt she'd left on the kitchen counter.

"I'm taking her to a pet place to get her groomed." He turned to address the cat, purring and butting her face affectionately against his jaw. "Bet you won't like that much."

"And what will you do about it tonight? We don't have any cat litter." Initial shock over, Emily returned her little tree to a pot, then proceeded to wrap wire up the seventy-year-old curve of its main trunk line.

"I could use a baking pan and some of your bonsai dirt."

"My imported Oregon soil for cat poop? Utensils from which we eat—for cat pee?" She returned to finish her trunk wiring, then stepped back for a complete view. "Wonderful—not so loose that it can't be shaped, not so tight that there'll be scars. I couldn't bear to be judged down at a show for visible scars. What do you think, darling? It's a Chinese juniper."

"I think I'm going to keep this cat, and since all the stores are closed, except that Korean all-night grocery ten blocks away, I'd like some of that 'imported' Oregon dirt, if you don't mind." His voice was icy and firm.

With an insolent, childish shrug, Emily walked out to the balcony and returned with a plastic bag of soil and a tray used for seedlings. She certainly didn't want a cat, she thought to herself, and Bill didn't either. But, like so many other things, he'd simply have to find that out for himself. He could be so stubborn. "Where do you intend to set up this kitty outhouse?"

"The yellow bathroom." It was the only place that could meet her approval.

"I suppose there's no other possibility except the balcony, but no doubt it might turn kamikaze and self-destruct thirty stories down. So I won't set myself up to take the blame for *that*." She glanced at the kitchen clock. "Bill, it's almost eleven. Are you going to bed?" she asked, cradling the wired bonsai in her arms.

"After I see to this cat and unwind a bit—I've had a hell of day."

Emily started down the hall to the bedroom but halted when she realized that Bill had been referring to the cat as "she." "It's a female?"

"She is." Bill watched the kitten as it lapped up the milk he'd poured in a saucer, the ambitious pink tongue flicking small white drops onto its whiskers.

"Spayed?"

"Too young, I think. But I'll look for a scar after she finishes her milk."

"Good, because if she isn't fixed, she will be. I certainly agree with the Humane Society on that one."

Emily didn't wear her mask after turning out the light because she knew he wouldn't come to bed that night. These days, "unwind" for Bill meant "drink," not one but several, and inevitably falling asleep in his chair or on the couch.

The next morning Bill dropped the bombshell just as John Palmer came on the screen with *Today*'s news. "How would you like to go to Nevis next week?"

"Nevis? Bill, do you mean it? What about your schedule?" Emily's face lit up with the prospect of fashionable beaches, calypso music, moonlit tropical dining, and endless boutiques overflowing with folkcraft and native fashions. "I've never been to Nevis."

Bill intercepted the cat just as she commenced tentatively batting the fronds of one of Emily's arrangements with her paw. "We haven't been on a trip together—just the two of us—for years. I need a break and so do you. Gordon and Marla Farley rented a bungalow at the Nisbet Plantation but they'll have to cancel because his father's taken a turn for the worse. He asked if we were interested and I said no, but he told me to sleep on it. Well, I have, and I think I'll say yes, but only if it's something you'd like to do."

"It certainly is, but what about your operations?" In the sixteen years of their marriage Bill had never canceled an operation except the day his father died.

"They can be rescheduled, except for one, and Tom Norris and my chief resident can take care of that." Tom's been itching to solo on an anterior communicating aneurysm, Bill reflected.

"What about that?" Emily pointed to the cat nestled in the crook of his elbow.

" 'That' is why I've got to run." He transferred the cat from one arm to the other and slipped on his blazer. "I doubt a kennel would take her without proof of shots, but I know someone who might—if she's still in town. The cat's name is Gritti, by the way, after the Gritti Palace—where we stayed in Venice on our honeymoon. I'll call you this morning to confirm." Bill kissed Emily on the cheek and rushed out the door, the little creature purring madly in the arms of her new owner.

Bill had decided to take Emily on a Caribbean holiday, not based on a sudden joyous urge to be with his wife, but because of what had happened the night before. After Emily had closed the door to the bedroom, he poured himself a strong Scotch and settled down to read the newspaper. If a story on the federal deficit couldn't put him to sleep, he intended to review his own budget. But the next thing he remembered, he woke up on the living-room floor with the cat nestled between his shoulder and chin, his empty glass ten feet away. He couldn't remember anything except sitting down to read the newspaper, though the television was on and neatly stacked departmental papers lay out on the coffee table. Bill flicked off the TV, sat down, looked at his watch, and shook his head—3:45—God only knew how long he'd been lying there. The little cat jumped on his lap, then climbed up his shoulders and started to lick his ear. Unable to bear the tickling, Bill lightly restrained her in one hand and stroked her head with the other. Though he tried hard—mentally reviewing everything he did from the time he came in the front door—he couldn't reconstruct what happened after he sat down with the newspaper. Then came the diagnosis—from a doctor who'd failed to face up to his own symptoms. He'd blacked out—probably on his way to the kitchen to get another drink. Nothing else could explain it. He put the coffee on and for the next two hours—the first time ever—he took a cold, sober look at his life, what it had been, what it had become, and where it was going. He finally acknowledged the desperate pain of his loneliness, and that unless he took radical steps to change, he would hurt not only himself but also his own patients. Yet to take these steps he'd have to see things clearly—no more gauze curtains. Alcohol would have to go, for a while, at least. He needed to spend some time alone with Emily, away from Briggs and DePrete. He had to determine what in his marriage, if anything, retained value, and if it could be salvaged. And so the Nevis option occurred to him.

"She's lovely!" Diana exclaimed, taking the cat in her arms and wrinkling her nose. "Even if she is a bit smelly."

"I'm sorry. Gritti—that's her name—should have made a trip to 'pet pamperer' or whatever it's called on Park Avenue, but then we might have missed you. I'm leaving town for a few days, and since she had such a hard little start in life, I was wondering if you'd look after her till I got back. I don't want to leave her caged in a kennel just when she's beginning to trust me. I know she'd be well-fed, but—"

"She'd hear the dogs barking," Diana replied lightly, but with the immediate empathy of someone who'd had years of caring for animals. "Sure, she can stay with me, but she'll have to come today. I'm taking Navarro back home to Southfield after Steve and I have breakfast." She bit her lip to keep it from trembling.

"Wanting to get home is natural after all you've been through," he said sympathetically. But her confirmation of what he'd thought she'd do after Jim's death pained him.

Diana nodded. "Why Gritti?" she asked, inviting the little white paws to attack her wiggling forefinger.

"When I visited Venice I stayed in the Gritti Palace. Have you ever been to Venice?"

"No place in Europe till Andalusia."

"You must see the rest of Europe." He immediately imagined how wonderful it would be to travel with her— France, Germany, Spain—it wouldn't matter where. "Anyway, Venice is overrun with sick, homeless cats. The only way to avoid them is to keep your eyes glued to the Veneto-Byzantine and Palladian architecture. So 'Gritti' is out of tribute to them. Besides, she's a tough little creature, and her coat had a pound of dirt and sand in it when I found her, so she's triply suited to her name. Don't you think?"

"She certainly is," Diana replied, touched by the care he'd taken in naming a little stray. "Where did you find her?"

"A restaurant." But Bill's eyes revealed more than his remarks intended, and when he saw the questioning look in hers, he almost told her everything—that he loved her, wanted to be with her all the time, and had gone back to Les Sans Culottes to think only about her.

"Not Tavern on the Green?" she asked, deliberately defusing the charged air.

"No, but that's a rain check you can cash when you're back to compete at the Garden. I estimate I owe you three dinners."

"Three!" she exclaimed.

"The one we missed in Newport, one for taking care of Gritti, and, finally, one when you win the Puissance."

"Bill." A wave of anxiety swept over her. "You do know something about the sport, but—please—keep your optimism to yourself."

Alarmed, he rushed to put things right. "I'm sorry, I didn't mean to diminish the obstacle ahead of you. It's just that I have so much faith in you."

"Well, don't," she snapped. "Then you won't be disappointed."

"You'd never disappoint me, Diana. I've already seen more skill, maturity, and heroism from you in Briggs and DePrete than you could ever demonstrate on the back of a horse." He put an arm around her shoulder. "That's your character—sterling—and it won't change even if you and Navarro knock a few wooden blocks off that wall."

"I'm sorry. Bill, you're the last person I . . ." She didn't finish her sentence, but brushed the tears from her face.

"No, I'm the one who's sorry. You'd think a surgeon would be less clumsy."

His genuine distress and self-deprecating humor touched her deeply. "I promise to treat Gritti as if she were mine. No rhinestone collars, but at least a warm New England fireplace."

"I'll call you as soon as I'm back. If she's a nuisance, I'll drive up and collect her. If not, maybe you could keep her until you return to New York."

"Why don't we do that, then? But I'm sure she'll miss you."

"I hope so—very much." His honest and direct gaze indicated an unspoken depth of feeling.

"Two weeks will pass quickly. Where are you going, anyway?" she asked.

"Nevis."

"The British Leewards. My parents went there once. A conference?" She regretted the intrusion at once, and almost tried to retract the question.

"A vacation. We need to get away." He stopped looking at her, and hated to mention Emily, even indirectly, when all he wanted was to be with Diana.

"I saw your wife once when I walked by the hospital flower shop. She's very beautiful—polished." Diana felt her heart breaking. The man she loved—who she thought might love her—was flying off to a quiet island to make love to his wife.

Bill nodded. Emily was very beautiful. If only he could tell Diana what she wasn't. "I should go. Trips—they require so many arrangements that you wonder in the end if they're worth making. Take care, Diana." As soon as he closed his arms around her shoulders and held her to his chest, he released her. He had to—if he'd held her a fraction of a second longer, he could never have let go.

*      *      *

As Gritti slept on Diana's lap, driving along I-84, Steve told her that a former colleague of his from Stanford, Bob Jorgenson, now at Boston University, had called him that morning. Mold kept growing on his tissue cultures, and out of desperation he'd called Marshall Simpkins, his former teacher, who referred him to Steve for help.

"Will you be able to?" Diana asked.

"I don't know. Mold's a common problem. Should be able to figure it out if I spend a day at his lab—could be as simple as the air conditioning, or what other researchers on his floor are doing. Or his procedures might be sloppy."

"You're very well-thought-of, aren't you?"

"That depends whom you're talking to," he replied with casual indifference.

"I'm talking to you."

He groaned inwardly. "Yes, I'm well-thought-of—very well, in fact. There, does that please you?" he asked half-teasingly.

"Only if it pleases you."

"Well, it does. All that reading at the Rockefeller Library—lots of gaps to fill—mine and others'." He already had in mind qualifying the findings of two papers he'd read.

"Steve, you're going to leave me, aren't you?" Her tone, now subdued and sad, conveyed a hard inevitability.

He turned to look at her, his eyes moist with tears. "Not until after Puissance."

"California?"

He nodded.

At Diana's, they turned Navarro out in the field. His energy pent up from the four-and-a-half-hour trailer ride, the white horse exploded as soon as Diana unhooked the lead shank from his halter—he galloped, charged, bucked, and reared, forelegs pawing the sky. Then he ran the fence line to check the limits of his territory. "He's glad to be home," Steve said. The solitary stallion now stood in the middle of the field sifting the cold November air, his breath white vapor.

"So am I. The New England country seems to put things in perspective. New York is so hyped-up. Even Boston seems pastoral by comparison." She turned to him directly. "Steve, thank you for spending so much time with me in New York. You didn't have to, but—"

"I *had* to be there. You shouldn't go through anything like that alone."

"You made it easier, and I thank you deeply. I know your feelings about Jim—all the complications—your feeling about me and my relationship with him."

"My complications, well, they're not the best part of me." Steve saw the sun's rays—now hidden by a purple cloud—blaze out behind the gold-lined darkness. "Jim helped me too. His death helped free me from the guilt that had paralyzed me ever since my wife and daughter died. You and Jim forced me to approach death and life again. I was your friend and couldn't stay behind. There was nothing I could have done to save Jim or others in his situation, but now at least I'll return to virology and do what I can."

Diana took him by the arm as they walked back to the pickup, but when he reached for the door handle, she held him. "Steve, I feel so alone—Jim's dead, my parents too, you're going to the West Coast, and Bill Stanford . . ." She couldn't admit how she felt about him.

"Bill Stanford wants to see you again soon. That's why he gave you this cat." Steve opened the door of the cab and placed Gritti in her arms. "And I'll call tomorrow first thing." He kissed her, got into the truck, then rolled down the window. "And don't forget him—he won't let you down." Steve pointed to Navarro—tall, proud, charged with life, low November sun burnishing his white coat gold.

As soon as she brought in her luggage, Diana turned up the thermostat. She was unused to coming into a cold house—her mother had always risen first in the morning and was the last to go to bed at night. She poured milk into a saucer and closed Gritti in the library—always the warmest room in winter—then drove to the post office and picked up the mail they'd held for her the past four weeks. Returning home, she turned on the kettle for tea, joined Gritti—now perched at the top of a bookcase— and began to sort through the cardboard box of envelopes, catalogs, and circulars the postal clerk had carried out to her car. A number of friends had written notes congratulating her on the Newport victory, but a fine, old-Boston Spencerian handwriting caught her attention first—the return address "Louis Winston, Mount Vernon Street"—Diana's uncle.

October 20

Dear Diana,

Not only did I hear of your victory in Newport, I actually saw it on the evening news.

Congratulations—please be as proud of yourself as I am. Had I known of your entry, I should have driven down to cheer you on in person. My retirement from the show ring came early, at the age of five: during a short stirrup class, my pony kicked at a deer fly and sent me flying. But, for myself, even a novice knows that Navarro is magnificent and that you're one devil of a rider.

I do have some sad news. Four weeks ago your Aunt Mildred died of complications following gallbladder surgery. She fought bravely for three days, spoke kindly about you, and died peacefully in her sleep. In two weeks I leave for Hawaii. It seems precipitate, but I may have mentioned a niece and her husband who run a cattle ranch on the Big Island (there really are cowboys in the fiftieth state!).

My only regret is that I leave Boston just when we might have known one another better. During the few months you spent with us, I learned—I confirmed— that I've missed not having children of my own. I neglected you during your childhood, not only out of respect for Mildred's feelings but also because of my bruised pride concerning your mother—weak and inadequate reasons—and for that I apologize. I shall not ask your forgiveness, because none is merited. When your father failed you, I should have stepped in. Now it's appropriate that your family give you some of that support—paternal and financial—that you lacked growing up. It's long overdue.

To discuss this, could you, perhaps, find time to meet me for lunch or dinner before November 10? Since my flight leaves on the eleventh, we could also say a temporary good-bye. Please call when you return (555-2307). I hope to hear from you soon. Again, congratulations to Navarro, and most of all to you.

Love,
Uncle Louis

Their table in the dining room on the second floor of the Union Club provided an unobstructed view of Boston Common. Leafless branches bent with the wind, as did pedestrians who walked briskly down paths that took them to Tremont, Park, and Beacon streets. In the distance Diana could see the old Hancock Building. Louis Winston looked older than she'd remembered—his chalk-pink face seemed puffy, and he no longer carried his body in the erect and deliberate posture suggesting a man in control. His wife's death had cut some strings, and the release had induced a general, though mild, bewilderment. But as soon as he started to speak, his face came alive—cheeks pinker, eyes blue and smiling. "The Common looks stark, but soon the Christmas decorations will cheer everything up. Have you ever seen how they do the trees? See it this year—it's worth remembering. Thousands of white lights tossed all through the branches, simple and beautiful."

"I will. I'm planning a long rest after the Garden."

"You've entered the National Horse Show?" he asked, his voice conveying interest but no genuine surprise. During her stay in Boston he'd come to know her so well that nothing she undertook now could cause astonishment.

"Just one event—Puissance."

He nodded. "The power jump."

"A solid wall as high as seven-foot-six. The current indoor record is seven-four. Of course, we could get eliminated in the first round at five feet."

"You might, but you know very well that you probably won't, barring the unexpected. And I've never cared much for the unexpected. That's what's so nice about Boston—nothing changes. At least nothing used to change."

The waiter took their orders—shrimp and avocado salad for Diana, broiled haddock for her uncle, who also ordered a bottle of muscadet. Tables were filling up—mostly with men.

"The Union Club now takes women," he commented with a smile.

She laughed but, feeling her face flush, added, "My thoughts must print out on my forehead like the news ticker in Times Square."

"Don't forget, I had some time to get to know you." He chuckled at her analogy and busied himself with the formality of approving the wine. Louis organized his thoughts. "Diana, our family's quite small, but dear to me, perhaps for that very reason. It helps explain why I've decided to live with Anne's family in Hawaii. Mildred and I visited them every February, and my grandnieces and nephews are like grandchildren. I hope to see you when I'm back in Boston—I do have friends here—and that you'll fly out occasionally. You'll like Anne and Rob, and they'll like you. They're different from the children of those old fuddy-dud would-be aristocrats you run into out there."

"Perhaps if I get a real horse business going, I will," she said politely, knowing a trip to the Hawaiian Islands would be beyond her financial horizon for years.

"This is what we need to talk about, Diana. Finances. That is, yours."

"Uncle Louis, don't worry about me. I've got the farm, two cars—one's a Mercedes—and some investments."

"That tells me you've got property taxes, excise taxes, insurance, a show horse that requires training, entry, and stabling fees, emergency and preventive veterinary care, equine mortality insurance, and promotional expenses. All this with no discernible income, other than what your mother left you—I know it couldn't be much—and what remains of your Newport purse."

"Uncle Louis, that really is not your concern." She felt mortified at the disheartening accuracy of his financial rundown. And he didn't even know about Calliope.

Reaching across the table, he pressed her hand. "Diana, it *is* my concern. You're barely into your twenties—don't be so tough. Don't feel you have to do everything by yourself because your father let both you and your mother down. You have family—I'm your family—and I'd like to help. Now, promise to listen for a few minutes. You can talk all you choose afterward, but for the moment, please, listen. Promise?"

Diana folded her arms and nodded, surprised at how she liked being spoken to in this avuncular, friendly manner.

"Unlike your father, I had good fortune in financial dealings. Now that Mildred's gone, I must shift some investments, and give you what you've long deserved as a Winston. Two hundred and fifty thousand dollars, which now belongs to you, is being individually managed by the Boston Private Bank and Trust Company. Fifty percent is in fixed-income securities and notes, thirty-five percent in blue-chip stocks, and the remaining fifteen percent rests in Chinese Panda gold coins. I've also rented the Mount Vernon Street town house, which today I shall put in your name. The tenth of every month, Beacon Hill Realty will forward to you the rental check less management and maintenance fees. You may wish to have the net sum of twenty-eight hundred dollars deposited directly to your own bank."

Louis now took a thick packet of documents from a legal folder he'd discreetly slipped under his chair. "The house is yours when you sign these. But, Diana, there is one stipulation. The house has been in the Winston family since 1791. You must promise me you won't sell it. The promise holds no legal force, but I'd value your word. Rent it, live in it, leave it empty, but don't sell. Someday you'll have children, and I'd like it to become their house too. You also must understand that this is no great fortune, but simply provides a good yearly income—security, a base that permits you to do what you want, to pursue your sport and your dreams." He moved his chair closer to Diana. "Here's a pen."

"I can't take all this, Uncle Louis. It wouldn't be right."

"Why not, Diana?" The gentle financier was hurt by her reticence.

"I just can't. I've come so far on my own, I've been so self-reliant . . ."

"And my admiration for your Emersonian ideals is boundless, but make sure these ideals don't obscure certain weaknesses."

"Weaknesses!" she exclaimed in astonishment. In twenty years she'd never heard this.

"Yes, an inability to trust." He raised his hand to postpone her immediate and stunned objection. "That became quite clear to me while you stayed with us. Your father let you down, he let your mother down, and in a way, they both let you down. You became a virtual orphan with an unpleasant—and unfair—paternal legacy to bear. Small wonder you don't want anything from your family: in the end, it shortchanged you—financially, of course, but emotionally as well. Take it from an old self-reliant Yankee who's fought many wars. By the grace of God, however, in the end I wasn't too old or too self-reliant to learn."

Even though Diana knew her father's defects, it pained

her to hear them from his successful brother. And her distrust, her inability to learn? She'd have to think about that later. "Uncle Louis, I don't hold you responsible for what my father did."

"I know that, and I didn't mean to imply it or to distress you. You're my closest living relative and mean the world to me. When I die you will inherit the bulk of my estate—about ten million dollars." The sentence hung in the air, no ruffles or flourishes. Writing the last chapter of his life, Louis valued candor and frankness. "What I offer you now is comparatively little, and you'll have to continue to demonstrate that great self-reliance of yours to make a success of it. So, please, don't deprive me of the pleasure of watching you soar under your own power. It's an old man's prerogative."

Diana now recognized Louis Winston's offer—direct, loving, and honest—and felt overwhelmed. Her eyes brimmed with tears; she struggled for control and looked out at the broad Common to steady herself.

Louis took out his handkerchief, leaned over, and dabbed at her eyes. "There, Diana, I had no intention of making you cry—the opposite. I didn't mean to make you feel sorry for me."

She shook her head. "No, you made me feel sorry for myself. I've been feeling sorry for myself all along but couldn't admit it. I didn't want anyone to know how alone I've been. *I* didn't want to know how alone I've been. And your offer . . ."

"My decision should tell you you're not alone anymore."

They sat quietly as the waiter removed their luncheon plates, returned with apple pie and coffee, then left. Diana picked up her uncle's hand and pressed it to her lips. "Uncle Louis, may I borrow your pen?" she asked, her voice subdued, almost apologetic. She wrote, her signature emerging clear, distinct, and feminine on the title of one of the most-sought-after properties in Boston, and she felt both chastened and empowered. Almost as quickly and deftly as Louis hailed him, an elderly gentleman rose from an adjacent table, approached, introduced himself, and quietly signed as witness. Then with good wishes for the Hawaiian move, Attorney Jackson R. Gray returned to his own lunch, glad to serve the trust of an old friend without superfluous ceremony.

The signing over, Louis handed her the title in a blue portfolio. "Put this in your safe-deposit box, Diana."

She nodded. "Uncle Louis, I'll never sell your house— our house, the family house. It's part of me now, what my family was and is. I'll love it and take care of it until I pass it on. It's what I love and can't be taken from me. Thank you for giving it back."

They cut across the Common and behind the State House to Mount Vernon Street. "The loveliest street in the world," observed Diana, recalling her aunt's quotation of Henry James.

"And I trust you'll live on it someday soon." Louis held open the door to Diana's car while she slid in.

"I don't know when, or how soon, only that I want to and that I will."

As the small charter plane transported Bill and his wife over the warm shimmering waters of the Caribbean, he felt his spinal muscles relax and his heart fill with hope. You had to work at a marriage to ensure its survival, but other than scrupulous attention to birthdays and wedding anniversaries, he hadn't worked on his at all—as much to blame as Emily, perhaps more: after all, he'd taken "Family Medicine" in medical school. He glanced at her, asleep, her blond head resting on a pillow. Though she'd pulled the shade, sunlight from the windows ahead fell across her face. Not bad for thirty-eight, he reflected, noting the negligible downward lines at the corners of her mouth and the slight creases in her neck. Ever since he'd been with her—Cannes, Easthampton, or even their balcony at home—she'd carefully sheltered her skin. Oversize dark glasses concealed other minor soft-tissue erosions and reflected strong twin images of the sun. Across the aisle, through another window, Bill glimpsed Mount Nevis rising from the center of the thirty-five-square-mile island. He'd read that clouds at the volcanic summit reminded Christopher Columbus of the snow-capped Sierra Nevadas in Spain, so he named the island "Nieves" —snows. But a lush rain forest, with temperate air seldom lower than sixty degrees, clad much of the island. Poor Columbus must have been homesick indeed. As the wheels of the twin-engine de Havilland Otter touched down on the miniature tarmac, Bill wondered how cold it was in Boston and if the sky were clear there too.

At Nisbet Plantation tropical flowers grew in profusion— flame-red royal poincianas, star-shaped plumerias in pinks and reds, vermilion bell-shaped jacarandas, and the crimson-and-gold African tulip trees. Never had Bill seen such a wild array of intense color. "I don't recall these flowers in any of your arrangements," he observed.

"They're wild, Bill, not for arranging. Once cut, they quickly die—especially those little plumerias. They make them into leis in Hawaii—beautiful, certainly—but they brown right away and their sweet fragrance turns fetid." Emily's tone dismissed him; such flowers were of little use to her and her art.

"Then we're fortunate to have a chance to see them thriving in such healthy abandon in their native soil." He immediately regretted the implicit sarcasm and hoped it escaped her. It hadn't, but she ignored it.

After registering at the Plantation House, they followed a path lined with sentinel palms and macadamia-nut trees to their cottage, itself half-concealed by a *Cassia fistula*, or "shower-of-gold" tree, more than forty feet high. Its bright yellow buds and blossoms cascaded over the roof and side like a brilliant golden waterfall. They changed clothes—Bill hadn't worn shorts in years, and felt rather odd—then walked along the lovely strand of beach, the sky powder blue, the water translucent turquoise. With two hours free before dinner, Bill left Emily lounging contentedly in a macrame hammock—guidebook in hand, Singapore Sling at her side—to return to the beach for a run and swim.

On the windward Atlantic side of the island waves broke

over distant coral reefs, then formed again and rolled straight to shore, breaking with a crash into deep white foam. There seemed to be little undertow. The hot sand tickled and massaged Bill's feet as he walked down to the water. He hadn't run in years—other than the short sprints that Briggs and DePrete emergencies required— and knew he must be careful. Laying shirt, shorts, and towel across a large trunk of driftwood, he started to jog along the hard, wet sand, but his body felt uncooperative and heavy—as if gravity took him for a three-hundred-pound man. Annoyed, he increased his pace to shorten the unpleasant warm-up, but soon his breath came in gulps. In little under a half-mile, Bill pulled up, soaked with perspiration, lungs inhaling the warm island air in gasps. He didn't dare count his pulse. Exercise over, he waded out past the breakers and let the swells cradle and cool him. The water held his now weightless body up to the sun then let it slide backward to be lifted again. About fifteen feet down he saw the white sandy bottom, the only shadow cast by his own body. He looked at his torso, at the outstretched arms and legs reflecting the powerful rays that illuminated a starfish below in the clear undulating blue. Twenty minutes later, picking up his clothes and walking back to the cottage, he felt pleasantly exhausted and looked forward to a large, cold Perrier with a twist of lime.

"Have a nice swim, dear?" Emily opened her eyes just long enough to verify that the footsteps belonged to her husband. The guidebook lay on the table next to her sunglasses.

"Wonderful—water's perfect. Let's go down tomorrow morning first thing before breakfast and see the sunrise together."

"Absolutely not." Emily laughed at the absurdity. "I've seen far too many sunrises—usually at the end of a long night of entertaining. I'm looking forward to getting some sleep here."

"Then you must sleep." He kissed her forehead, sat down on a wicker chair, and started to towel the sand off his feet. "Would you like to go into Charlestown tomorrow? I want to see the Alexander Hamilton museum. And I know there're some shops."

"I've already narrowed them to two—Caribbee Clothes has the quality resort wear."

"Gordon says Nevisian pottery is charming."

"Probably too naive, then, especially if Gordon recommended it. But let's have a look anyway." Emily pulled herself upright in the hammock and flipped through the guide. "For that we go to the Arcade, near Memorial Square." Her eyes then suddenly widened with delight. "Bill, we must dine at Croney's Old Manor Estate. According to this, some Texans poured millions into it—the al-fresco dining room's spectacular. And guess what? Not only was it a sugar and sea-island-cotton plantation, but a stud farm for slave breeding! Do you believe it? Wait'll I tell Jill."

"Most inns on the island developed from former plantations that relied on the slave system in some way or other." Bill picked up his towel and shorts. "I'm going to take a shower. Then we can go over to the Plantation House for a drink before dinner if you like."

"Sounds fine to me, darling. I'm about lounged-out. Time to get a look at the other guests." Emily stood up, plucked one of the gold blossoms, and twirled it between her fingers. "Can I fix you a drink? While you were gone I had them stock the refrigerator with your favorites. Outrageous prices—especially the Chivas—but at least they had it."

"Thanks, but I'll toss something together after my shower." He slipped off his trunks and stepped into the warm stream of water. A slave stud farm—of all places to dine, why did she hit on that one? And to regard its unfortunate history as quaint—something to be shrieked over with school chums.

Lathering his body with soap, he saw the faint pink lines left by afternoon sun across his waist and thighs, and felt the slight pull of exercised muscles. He'd been so happy walking back to Emily, but her conversation ended that. After he dressed for dinner, he opened the small refrigerator—Chivas, Napoleon, Beefeater's—the regular size and one-shot bottles all neatly lined up. She certainly knew what he liked to drink. Perhaps he should just wait until he got back home to detox—at least he was exercising. Besides, he craved a drink desperately. As his eyes lingered on the deep amber Chivas, a sudden flash of anger shot through his body. He slammed the door of the refrigerator, then immediately opened it again, quickly snatching the clear green bottle of Perrier.

That night, almost immediately after he started to make love to Emily, Bill came—he couldn't help it. He joked that making love to her on a Caribbean island sent him over the edge right away, and she'd now get at least forty-five minutes of foreplay while he recharged. But inwardly he felt mortified and castigated himself for his failure. The premature ejaculation didn't seem to bother Emily, but why should it? To compensate, Bill lavished her with attention. Three orgasms later (hers), just as his penis started to harden, Emily fell into an exhausted, satisfied sleep. With a groan Bill rolled onto his back.

Just before dawn, returning from the bathroom, Emily saw that her husband had an erection. Back in bed, she started to caress his chest and abdomen—after all, there was no Register work, no entertaining—she could stay in bed as late as she liked. Half-asleep, a smile on his face, he moaned with pleasure as she took his penis in her hand. But then he turned to embrace his lover and saw his wife. Erection dead, his penis slipped from Emily's grasp. With an angry flounce she turned her back.

"I'm sorry," he said, gently touching her rigid shoulder. "I must have been dreaming."

"Of whom?" she asked accusingly.

"No one. Just sex, I think."

"But put that together with your wife and that's the end of it." Her voice was bitter and sarcastic.

"No, not at all." He rushed to reassure and soothe her. "I told you at dinner, I'm not drinking—I'm sure that has something to do with this."

"Of all times to dry out, why now? It'll ruin our vacation. Why didn't you just make reservations at the Betty Ford Center?"

"Emily, you and I needed to go away together—to get reacquainted. And I needed to stop drinking." As her insensitivity continued to sink in, his voice turned cold and distant. "I guess my first mistake was thinking you might care."

They lay in the predawn hush and Bill listened to the sound of trade winds blowing through the palms. Here he was in Nevis, one foot from his wife, and more alone than ever. Damn Gordon and damn Gordon's father for dying.

"You know what I think?" Emily's voice cut the tropical quiet like a machete. "I think you ought to drive over to that slave stud farm and get some inspiration."

As he ran along the path to the beach, Bill didn't notice the wildflowers illuminated by patio lights or the fragrant air changing to the smell of sea salt. Head throbbing, he could only concentrate on getting away from Emily—as far and as fast as possible. But her face intruded on his thoughts and he started to gasp as he ran harder still. Her polished beauty, a hideous irony, concealed a destructive and hateful soul. In the blue dark he found the driftwood trunk where he'd left his belongings the previous afternoon. Out of breath and heart pounding, he sat down on the grainless wood and faced the ocean. Off in the distance soundless waves broke over submerged reefs, rolled forward over the blackness, then vanished. Nearer to shore another wave formed, black and powerful, ominously outlined against the inky sky, then tumbled toward the beach. A hundred yards from Bill, it curled and broke, white water rushing forward onto the sand. By the time it reached him, all force was spent—three inches of gentle salt water swirled around his feet before withdrawing to become part of another, smaller wave. He sat in the darkness, looking north past the reefs, and a terrible loneliness overtook him. His marriage had broken apart long ago, but he hadn't been willing to face it.

Here on this island, with its tropical splendor and crashing waves, he realized the full force of Emily's ugliness and that he could tolerate it no longer. As he watched the white waves and the black ocean, he felt a tear slide down his cheek, then another and another. In disbelief he wiped his face and saw his wet palm glisten in the night. Then Bill buried his face in his hands and cried in the darkness, unaware of the faint streaks of color in the east.

Emily poured a glass of guava juice, sat in the chair next to the hammock, and congratulated herself for having insulted Bill so effectively that he had had to leave—his usual procedure was to stay and ignore her, underscoring his invulnerability. Men—Wall Street brokers, construction workers, garbage collectors, or neurosurgeons, it didn't matter—they all fell apart when you socked them in the prowess department. Besides, Bill deserved it for thinking he could conceal his affair with that little equestrienne from Massachusetts. She took a long swallow of guava and recalled her sleuthing with pride. First, while going through the pockets of Bill's tux before sending it to the cleaners, she had found a matchbook cover from Les Sans Culottes—Bill's favorite bachelor haunt—with "Diana" and an overseas phone number (the directory revealed it to be Madrid) written across it in *her* handwriting. One week later he didn't get home till four in the morning, then said it was the same case that had dragged him out of the Frank Sinatra gala—a man with AIDS. A Register check run through Infectious Disease indicated Bill's interests lay in Jim Williams, a member of the United States Equestrian Team who was dying of *Pneumocystis carinii*. And then Bill left the sports page draped across the arm of his chair with a five-by-seven photograph of a woman jumping a white horse, captioned: "Diana Winston, winner of Newport Jumping Derby" —which Bill had attended with Jack O'Dell—"and her Spanish Andalusian stallion Navarro will be one of nine entrants in the Puissance event at the 105th National

Horse Show at Madison Square Garden." Another check in hospice indicated that Diana Winston—by all accounts very beautiful—regularly visited Jim Williams. And then she found a ticket to the National Horse Show for Thursday night in Bill's jewelry case. A call to the Madison Square Garden box office established the major event of that evening as the Puissance. Coupled with Bill's growing cynical impatience, the evidence, though not conclusive, she found highly suggestive. Also, she had to consider that at forty-two Bill was a prime candidate for male mid-life crisis. She wouldn't have so much minded an affair with a woman her own age—even a younger volunteer at Briggs and DePrete. She had at her fingertips an in-house arsenal ready to handle that one. But a little girl athlete, apparently self-employed to the point of owning the horse she showed, presented quite a challenge. Nevertheless, Emily had already picked up the gauntlet. At a "Patrons of MOMA" reception she approached the critic Ben Adams—he had show jumpers—and it turned out that Diana Winston had ridden one of his most difficult horses to victory at the I Love New York Grand Prix two years ago. But if she wanted more information, Ben Adams went on, she should call one Hugh Simpson, an acquaintance of his—bit of a lothario—who followed the Grand Prix circuit and seemed to have been a friend of hers at one point. Adams' emphasis on "friend" and his slightly raised eyebrows told Emily she was on the right track. She tried to contact Simpson before leaving for Nevis, but he'd gone to Buenos Aires on business and wouldn't be back for ten days. No matter, Emily thought, draining her glass—inviting the proper mix of guests to dinner parties took time as well as scrupulous attention to detail, especially when the guest of honor was to be her husband's lover.

As night yielded to the pinks and golds of a muted dawn, Bill reviewed his life and grieved. He'd focused all energy and emotion on neurosurgery and his patients. Virtually every event or function he attended was hospital-

related—art shows, concerts, galas—and he had to go;
his wife knocked herself dead arranging them, he was
chief of neurosurgery, and it yielded big bucks for Briggs
and DePrete. He couldn't attend a Yo-Yo Ma concert
at Avery Fisher Hall because it coincided with a B&D
benefit performance of some inferior Broadway musical.
And that hadn't been the first time he'd given up what he
really wanted to do. Horse shows, he reflected, had
offered singular pleasures, but how seldom he got away
to those—three, sometimes four times a year. You just
didn't get the sense of show jumping—the power, the
precision, the artistry—by watching it on a twenty-eight-
inch television screen. Panoramas couldn't be reduced.
He recalled Newport—the pouring rain and Jim Williams—
and how he'd missed the chance to see Diana ride to
victory.

A yellow sun rose above the pastels of the horizon,
becoming partially hidden in a narrow band of cirrus
clouds. Bill felt the salt tracks of evaporated tears on his
face. Never had he felt so powerless, so desolate—and
couldn't bear it any longer. He'd ask for a divorce, hoping Emily would accept incompatibility as the grounds.
She knew about the Sandra Markley episode—Register
gossip lines found a medical student particularly juicy—
and would probably insist on infidelity. But that was fine
with Bill—at this point he only wanted out, not just from
Emily, but from Briggs and DePrete, from the entire
scene. He'd establish himself at another hospital where
there were no Riggs, no Register, and no flower arrangements. San Francisco, Stanford, Hopkins, Baylor—any
number of places would be delighted to have him. In
fact, he'd been serving on the ad hoc committee that was
searching for someone to head up the neurosurgery department at Mass General Hospital, and they'd come to
an impasse. Boston was no longer the great medical
mecca and suffered a terrible malpractice climate because
of surplus lawyers—in the race for a bite of million-dollar
settlements, it was a photo finish between neurosurgery
and obstetrics. Baylor whiz kid Norm Harwood simply

laughed when Bob Loftus, Dean of Harvard Medical School and head of the search committee, put out an initial feeler. And at the close of their last meeting—at the Colonial Inn in Concord—Loftus turned to Bill and asked what it would take to get him to accept the position. Rather than laugh dismissively, Bill only said that he always kept an open mind.

But now on Nevis he gave the matter serious thought. Boston—he'd spent eight wonderful years there, four as a Harvard undergraduate in Cambridge and four downtown at the medical school. His love affair with medicine had started there—he didn't care whether it was a mecca, and, as for the malpractice climate, New York certainly had its share of lawyers too. The idea of this maverick move tantalized him (no department chairman would accept a lateral transfer except to a better institution, yet MGH was on a par with Briggs and DePrete). He'd call Bob as soon as he got back, throw his hat in the ring, and resign from the ad hoc committee, saying nothing to Emily about separation until they'd returned home and he talked to a good divorce lawyer. For the five remaining days on Nevis, he planned to get in shape—run, swim, snorkel, even play a little tennis if he could find a partner. He'd coexist with Emily—go shopping, dine, speak with her, walk on the beach. He would cope because of his decision to leave her—time spent with her was now finite.

He walked along the shore, seawater cooling his feet while the sun, strong in a cloudless sky, warmed his face. As he watched black-and-white terns spin and glide above the breakers, an exciting sense of freedom overtook him and he felt young, alive. Yes, he'd go home to Boston, where it had all started—not as a Harvard freshman taking advanced inorganic chemistry, but as the ten-year-old boy with a torn ulnar nerve. He'd almost forgotten that the boy's operation had been at Mass General, where his physician, Dr. Felix Spiratos, had been chief of neurosurgery.

\*    \*    \*

The rusty pickup and horse trailer turned off Route 2 and followed signs to the Mass Pike. Diana stroked Gritti and reflected on Steve's comments about her riding—more fluid, softer contact with the reins—much better. "Is it because I've got money in the bank and can relax?"

"No, I think you're happier."

"Money buys happiness?" she asked, her voice light and teasing.

Steve replied, interpreting her uncle's financial gesture, "Love and families buy happiness."

"If you'd said that a year ago, I would've called you a sentimental fool."

"A year ago I wouldn't have said it."

Steve was right. She still felt the pressure, but it wasn't so terrible, so consuming, as before. She wanted to win the Puissance more than anything else, but now knew that her life—professional and otherwise—wouldn't end if she and Navarro toppled the gray wooden blocks. She could accept the possibility of failure without its dragging her down, and sensed that, ironically, she'd become stronger and more likely to succeed because of that acceptance.

Navarro trailered well—always did—but then got his first look at New York City on the icy black pavement of Thirty-ninth Street. Surrounded by lighted skyscrapers in the late-autumn darkness and dozens of off-loading horses, he pranced, bucked, and pulled against the lead shank—flared nostrils and pitched ears taking in the conflicting smells and sounds of the city. At the sound of squealing brakes he reared straight up, forelegs lashing out at the hostile air. Steve pulled Diana quickly to the side as he came down—black hooves barely missing her head—then they struck the concrete like rifle shots.

"Don't tug on him! He'll only go up again," Steve said quickly. "Don't look back at him. I'll stand behind and urge him on."

The white horse surged ahead, impatient with Diana's short stride. She felt the angry pull of the lead shank and started to run to prevent him from rearing again. She heard Steve speaking Spanish—soft and encouraging. Again Narvarro went forward too quickly, absorbing the slack. But this time, rather than rear, he started the light, highly cadenced passage, and passersby stopped to marvel at the half-ton animal who strode past concrete and steel, then up the ramp and into Madison Square Garden.

# Puissance

Diana bolted the latch and leaned against the stall door. The prospect of Navarro galloping down Broadway in rush-hour traffic had made her feel weak.

"Pretty scary," Steve said, and heaved a sigh of relief. She took a Kleenex and wiped the perspiration from his forehead.

"Still trying to join the club?" interrupted a haughty and familiar female voice. They turned to see Courtney Snyder on the arm of none other than Hugh Simpson, arrogant in his colored suspenders and raw silk jacket.

Ignoring the taunt, Diana asked Steve to hand her two bucket hooks. "I want to make sure Navarro's water will last the night." Recalling that Courtney had left the Newport western barbecue fuming at Hugh, Diana speculated that the aviator must have launched another—and obviously successful—heat-seeking missile.

"Nice to see you're finally considerate to your equine charges. But I forgot, this one is yours. Or at least that's what you think." Courtney's down parka displayed the yellow ticket of an owner, authorized to walk in the stabling area.

"I'm sorry, Miss Snyder," cut in Steve. "Your friend without a pass will have to leave."

"No, he doesn't have one—but he's with me," Courtney replied petulantly.

"You're no exception—read the regulations—your name's not in them." Diana swung to face Hugh. "If you

427

don't get off this aisle immediately, I'll call security." She looked over his shoulder and located the nearest guard.

"We're going, but only to make a dinner engagement at B. Smith's on Broadway. You wouldn't know it—*the* place this season—publishers, agents, critics, actors."

Diana couldn't help laughing at Courtney's pathetic attempt to ruffle her. "You're amusing, but I want you and this man out—now." Steve started down the aisle to signal the guard.

"No need. We daren't be late. See you later, then, Diana." Courtney glanced at Navarro's right fore. "That leg's no good, and you know what'll happen if you get caught 'medicating' your horse."

"Steve, get security." But after her parting shot, Courtney left with Hugh. "She threatened to drug my horse." Diana's body shook with fury.

"She certainly did. I'll get a sleeping bag and spend nights next to the stall. During the day we can divide the guard shifts."

"No, we'll alternate nights too. Navarro's my responsibility and you're my friend. We'll share. Let's cancel my reservation at the Algonquin and just use the room you've got there." Diana looked at Navarro, now calm and nosing his hay. "Do you really think she'd do that?"

"She set him up for his first injury in order to fire you. Of course she'd do it. Look, why don't you check in at the hotel and return Gritti to Bill Stanford? Grab dinner, come back, and then I'll go get a bite. We shouldn't take any chances."

She glanced at her watch. "I'll be back about six. Do you want me to unpack any of your things and bring them here?"

"Please—my shaving kit, a clean shirt, a pair of underpants." He couldn't help blush—personal belongings were handled by himself, the maid, or, when he was a little boy, by his mother.

"I'll brown-bag them so no one will see how intimate we are." Her tone was sympathetic but touched with irony. The last morning in Seville had been the first and only time they'd made love.

"You look wonderful," Diana said, quite startled, when she opened the door. Bill's tanned face set off his deep blue eyes.

"And so do you." He kissed her and she enjoyed the feel of his rough cheek against hers, the smell of his cologne strange and inviting.

"New scent?"

"Found it on Nevis—Jamaican Khus Khus—odd name isn't it?" Bill found this attention to his toilette embarrassing but pleasant.

"Nice name," she modified his adjective. "And it's so warm and rich. That's how your trip was, I hope."

"In many ways. I got some sun and exercise, the island's absolutely beautiful and the beaches unspoiled. There's an incredible lushness—flowers, mangoes, coconut and macadamia trees. And yet it's so clean and pure with its blue water and sky, and its steady trade winds."

"Nevis seems to have agreed with you. I thought you were handsome before, but . . ." She let her eyes finish the sentence.

Afraid of telling Diana everything—Emily, pending divorce, new job—he reached into his pocket and handed her a white paper bag. "I brought you a souvenir."

"A sea gull, how beautiful!" Diana admired the streamlined white body and black wings formed from clay.

"A tern, actually. They were all over the place. You should see how they dart in and out of the waves and manage never to get hit. Anyway, it's not much."

"It's perfect, and you were very nice to think of me. I missed you, Bill." When she saw that her lowered voice and direct gaze caused discomfort, she went to the closet and brought out a cat carrier. "Someone else missed you too."

"I was wondering where you were," said Bill, opening the latch. Impatient meows gave way to loud purrs as Bill held the gray-and-white kitten against his chest and stroked her head.

"I had to keep her in the closet. She's not allowed here, and if I didn't have her in my arms every second, she'd scream bloody murder. Besides, Steve and I—we're sharing this room."

How could he miss the male effects—brown luggage, shoes by the bed, and three ties draped across the doorknob? He quickly glanced in the closet—a suit and two jackets. He'd been right: Steve was the contender.

Diana felt mortified. "I'm afraid I've confused you. Steve and I each had rooms, but someone threatened to drug Navarro—to get him disqualified—so we've got to watch him twenty-four hours a day. Steve's sleeping next to the stall tonight, and tomorrow's my turn."

"Who would do that to you? And why? It's incredible."

Quite suddenly, and in a detailed flood of information, Diana told Bill about her past—her father, Southfield, Courtney, how she had acquired Navarro—and was surprised how the telling relieved her. All the time she had thought her life had been something to be ashamed of, but relaying it to this man, whom she loved deeply, she understood for the first time that she'd been extraordinarily successful. She'd taken nothing—family dishonor, no money, no horse—and, with Steve's help, turned it into ribbons and trophies.

"Shouldn't you tell security about the threat?" he asked.

"No witnesses, and it was only implied. But believe me, Bill, nobody's going to touch this horse—not after we've gotten this far."

"You're remarkable." He squeezed her hand.

"It's been hard and it's been lonely—too lonely." Tears rose in her eyes as she felt his complete support.

"But you've had Steve," he added, his voice tentative, aware he was prying.

"Yes. Without him I would have been lost. He helped me push ahead despite the pain. But . . ." The tears streamed down her cheeks and she struggled to regain control. "But he's going back to California after the Puissance. That's where he comes from—I mean where he went to school. I don't want him to leave, but he needs to go. Everything's better for him now too."

Bill took Diana's hands in his and wondered, if Steve meant so much to her, why she wasn't going with him. Though he hated to see her in pain, he couldn't help feeling relieved that they were splitting up. "I spent some time with him in Jim's room—the night Jim died. Steve's an extraordinary man. Acutely, almost eerily, he tuned into Jim's needs despite the coma. And he's familiar with medicine, even carried a pass to the library at Rockefeller University."

"Steve's a doctor—a pediatrician and virologist." She hesitated but went on. "He's waiting to be certified by the American Board of Pediatrics so he can return to Stanford Medical School. I think you operated on a doctor who was head of his department once—Marshall Simpkins."

"Marshall Simpkins! I remember very well." Bill mentally replayed the procedure, an easy one, but he never forgot when he operated on another physician—it underscored his own mortality.

"Quite a coincidence, isn't it? We met him in Spain, accidentally." She recalled how upset Steve had been. "Bill, I shouldn't tell you any more—it's Steve's story, not mine."

"I don't want to pry."

"I needed to tell someone *something* about us. I've been so alone with Steve—he's done a lot for me—but it's been difficult."

"There's no need to explain. I know how lonely it can be in the company of someone else."

Bill gently placed Gritti back in the carrier, but as he turned to leave, Diana caught his arm. "Are you attending the Puissance?"

"I bought my ticket the day they went on sale."

She smiled and freed his arm. "I'm glad you'll be there."

"I wouldn't miss it for the world."

*      *      *

"This is the best takeout chicken I've ever had," Steve said, reaching for another piece across the horse blanket Diana had spread on the floor. "And the *papas fritas*— delicious—much better than the mass-produced, precut, lard-smeared fries Americans thrive on."

"Bill's recommendation. I told him about our guard setup, and that we'd be eating chez Navarro, so he suggested I stop at this Brazilian place—Restaurant Carioca."

"That was nice of him. And how was Nevis?" Steve asked.

"He loved it and looks so tan and fit. He said he and his wife needed to get away."

"I'm sure he did. He must have a grueling schedule. I ran into him in the hospital one evening—it was after nine."

"I told him you were a doctor," she said softly. "I know I violated a confidence. I'm sorry."

"I think he knew anyway." Steve recalled Jim's fingers opening and closing on the bedspread and on the cross. "It's all right, Diana. I am a doctor and that's what I should be called."

Diana put her arm around Steve and hugged him. "Thanks for everything, Steve—Navarro, your help, Spain, and most of all your friendship."

"It's mutual, believe me."


When Diana had stepped out of the cab she'd taken from the Brazilian restaurant, she got her first real look at Madison Square Garden. It reminded her of a latter-day Colosseum, some vast elliptical space devoted to the games of a rich, exciting, and increasingly decadent city, itself the heart of a large empire. The arches at Rome, built to last millennia, had decayed mostly from quarrying in the Middle Ages, when the large stones helped build the hovels of a small population. Would the American Garden last as long? Its predecessor, however carefully planned by Stanford White, certainly hadn't. If Rome and its monuments were eternal, New York seemed eternally transient.

Diana cringed when she found the small warm-up area just inside the gate leading to the arena floor. Less that three hundred feet in length, it was jammed with small ponies pulling spoke-wheeled carts and five-gaited saddlebreds, with their arched necks and luxuriant artificial tails, racking around like mad. Puissance, with only nine entrants, was the last event of the evening, so it wouldn't be as wild as this. From the in-gate she got her first look at the arena. In the modern space, high-stepping ponies, the best in the United States, drew bikelike sulkies at jog trot, road gait, and speed in the Open Single Roadster class, causing Diana to reflect on the hugely varied specialization in equestrian sports. In six days, sixty-four classes would be judged at the National Horse Show. Later the huge arena would host a multitude of games and shows—hockey, tennis, basketball, the Ringling Brothers Circus, the Moscow Circus, the Spanish Riding School, concerts, boat and car shows. Diana even imagined it flooded with water—like the old Colosseum—to recreate sea battles. But the modern space ultimately conveyed a dull, sealed symmetry, a directionlessness without natural light or natural markers. One, and perhaps the only, advantage of this was to place all attention on the event itself, not on its functional and undistinguished environment—which offered a space, and space only. Unlike the incandescent spots and klieg lights of the circus, the fluorescent and mercury vapor lamps cast a surreal effect on the ponies and their drivers, as if caught in a time warp sealed inside the throbbing city—inside one bubble of intense action, apart from the air, the sun, the moon.

After schooling Navarro, Diana returned to the Algonquin to find a phone message from Jack O'Dell requesting she call him at his hotel. Since it was after midnight, she decided to wait till the next morning. She hadn't seen O'Dell since Newport—an international judging commitment compelled him to miss Jim's funeral—and she wondered if it concerned the USET fund established in

Jim's name, or maybe O'Dell had a horse he wanted her to ride in another event. Early next morning he responded to her call with customary vigor. "So, how's Navarro doing under the bright lights of Broadway?"

"Absolutely terrific, Mr. O'Dell. I schooled him in the arena last night—he jumped as if he'd been raised there. The only thing that spooked him was a woman on our way back to the stabling area. She wore a full-length gold lamé gown that looked like medieval chain mail."

O'Dell laughed so hard that Diana had to hold the receiver away from her ear until he finished. "Diana, remember Bill Stanford—you met him in Newport? Well, his wife, Emily, has invited me to dinner the evening after next and wants you to come along as well. She would have contacted you herself, but didn't know where you were staying. I know it's the night before Puissance, but it might help you relax."

"I didn't know Mrs. Stanford was interested in horses."

"She's not, but Bill is, and she knows he and I are friends."

"How did she come up with me?" Diana asked, wondering if Bill had prompted the invitation—and, if he had, why.

"I don't know—women are always trying to match me up. Maybe Bill asked Emily to suggest you. Anyway, would you like to go? I hate to press you, but it'll be tough to reach me the next forty-eight hours."

In the space of a few seconds Diana faced a decision which could only be based on speculation. How did Emily Stanford know about her? Had Bill told her anything, and if so, what? Or did she suspect something between them? The only way Diana could find out—without calling Bill at his office and putting him on the spot—would be to accept. "I'd be delighted. I'll have to leave by ten to school Navarro, though. Do you think that'll be a problem?"

"You might lose your second cup of coffee, but everyone will understand. The evening begins at seven, so why

don't I meet you in the Algonquin lobby at a quarter
of?"

"That would be very nice of you. I'll be there. What's
the attire?"

"Informal. See you at six-forty-five."

"Thank you, Mr. O'Dell."

"Jack—please call me Jack. If riders are over eighteen
and competing in the Garden, they may use my Christian name."

As Bill slid the brass stays into his shirt collar, he
wondered why Emily had invited Jack O'Dell to one of
her dinners. She never had before, and surely didn't
expect him to enjoy the sort of in-house chatter that
would result from a Briggs and DePrete bunch. And
Fanchon Nugent? Bill couldn't help smiling at the prospect of Jack's dilemma. Because he was *the* force to be
reckoned with in the world of show jumping, he could
squelch spoiled students—was known for it, in fact—who
didn't give the sport, the horse, or him proper regard.
But Fanchon Nugent—Jack would just have to grit his
teeth as her insipid self-centered character announced
itself in grating tones of "Larchmont Lockjaw." Peter
MacKenzie would be all right as long as he refrained
from comparing McGill to Briggs and DePrete. Still,
pretty boring. Bill glanced in the bathroom door to see
Emily outlining her lips with a pencil, then filling them in
with lipstick. "Whom else did you say you invited?"

Emily picked up the pencil again and fine-tuned a
point of her lip. "Hugh Simpson—Wall Street broker—
and a friend of his, Courtney Snyder."

Bill shook his head and tried to remember. Hugh Simpson didn't ring any bells, but Courtney Snyder sounded
familiar. "How do we know them?"

" 'We' don't but *I* do. I decided that I'm going to learn
about horses. God knows you've sat through enough
dinners about flowers and now bonsai. The least I can do
is occasionally have a few people here who might be of
some interest to you. I met Hugh Simpson at an afternoon

'do' the day after we returned from Nevis. He follows the show circuit and is friends with Ben Adams. Anyway, he's bringing his girl of the moment, who actually shows some of these creatures. I think you'll find Jack knows her, she certainly knows him."

"Maybe that's where I've heard her name," Bill said, walking over to his closet to finish dressing. After giving instructions to the bartender, he noticed that there were eight—not seven—place settings. "Who's Jack's partner?" he asked when Emily emerged from the bedroom, a vision in black crepe silk and strands of seed pearls.

"Well, it rankles me to have an odd number, so I asked Jack to invite a lady friend. Diana Winston, do you know her?" Her eyes discreetly locked onto Bill for his reaction. And there it was: a muscle in his cheek twitched.

He cleared his throat and busied himself setting out the cocktail condiments. "She was the friend of a patient who died just a few weeks ago. I know her through him." What an extraordinary coincidence, Bill reflected—that is, if it were a coincidence. If Emily had asked Jack to bring someone, it would be perfectly natural for him to ask Diana. But all this about getting to know horses— could Emily be making a last-ditch effort to save what she'd already lost? Certainly she had to notice that she couldn't irritate him anymore. But what she didn't know was that this ability had come with his decision to divorce.

"Fanny, what a beautiful suit! Hand Bill your stole, let me see it all. My, canary yellow at night. How daring and how like you!" Emily bussed Fanchon Nugent on the cheek and shot a side glance at Peter MacKenzie to ensure he appreciated her display of female collegiality. But Peter recognized it as a temporary strategic alliance— one Emily would break if it suited her. To set about proving his political theory, he kissed Emily and let a forefinger delay just a fraction of a second too long on her arm.

"Fanchon, you didn't tell me Peter's such a good kisser! With all the bed-hopping and instant gratification of the eighties, they say it's become a lost art. Let's see, a martini for you each. Am I right?"

Just as Bill was about to respond to her cue to fetch them drinks, the bell rang. Heart pounding, he altered his course and turned to the door. "Diana, Jack, so glad you could join us this evening. You look lovely, Diana." She did indeed. Wearing a sky-blue silk dress, silver necklace and matching earrings—her shining dark hair held softly off her forehead with a silver filigree clip—Diana was more beautiful than ever, but Bill had to cap his emotions while he escorted the woman he loved to his wife.

"Diana, *so* glad you could come. Here, let me take your cape. I love the ermine trim. Was it your mother's?" And without waiting for Diana innocently to reply that the cape had indeed belonged to her mother, Emily cheerfully instructed Diana to give her drink order to Bill and spun on her heel to put the cape with the other coats in the bedroom. Before leaving, Emily checked her husband's jewel case. The ticket was still there, though he'd concealed it in a velvet pocket. Closing the lid, she smiled perversely at the prospect of publicly cutting Bill's little girlfriend right out from under him.

But then, unable to control her fury at seeing Diana's beauty confirmed, Emily stalked into the bathroom and locked the door to pop a Valium. How dare Bill even look at anyone else after all the care she'd taken with her appearance? It wasn't fair. Tossing her chin up to catch the little yellow pill, she saw the creases in her white neck, then looked dead-on in the mirror—the lines, wrinkles, and roots of her now tinted and artificially enlivened blond hair. Why on earth hadn't she had it highlighted that day? She brushed it back, concealing the roots as best she could.

It was a mistake to come, Diana told herself as Bill handed her a glass of white wine. She'd been wrong to accept a dinner invitation to the home of the man she loved. And it didn't matter that her initial reaction to his wife registered dislike: this was Emily's home, and Bill her husband. This evening would bring her to the core of Bill's life, and she felt afraid the hours ahead would reveal that it held no place for her.

"Are you getting in much schooling?" Bill's tone and expression indicated only polite interest.

"I am, thank you," she replied with automatic courtesy. She felt a flash of anger. Why did he have her invited, anyway? If he had no feelings for her, surely he knew she had feelings for him. Did he think he could have the best of both worlds—a younger single woman on the side, and a wife catering to his Upper East Side aspirations? She took in the interior's beige and black tones accented by chrome and glass. As cold as a surgical tray, she reflected.

Bill didn't know what was wrong, but he felt her distance. "Jack says he thinks you've got a good chance."

"Navarro's jumping well," she answered evenly.

"That's a fact," O'Dell chimed in. "I was coaching some of my kids late last night and saw him take a few. That horse is a powerhouse—a real straight-up-in-the-air kind of guy."

Diana couldn't help but beam at the master's compliment. "And you're not so bad yourself," O'Dell added; then, turning to Bill *sotto voce*, "I hardly ever say anything remotely nice about riders I haven't trained."

At that precise moment Diana felt something soft brush against her leg. "Gritti," she exclaimed, picking up Bill's cat.

"Well! I see you two know each other." Though Emily wore a smile, her face was dead serious with its unblinking china-blue eyes fixed on Diana, temporarily silenced by her slip.

"Diana offered to board Gritti while we were in Nevis," Bill stated. If damage was coming, better let it be caused by fact rather than fiction.

"How nice of you. Keeping pets—of any kind—can be such an imposition on a household." Emily shifted her gaze to Bill, who refused to flinch, though he now sensed she knew something about Diana, but couldn't tell how much. "Well, let's not bore ourselves with the stray kittens Bill picks up." Brass chimes announced the final guests. "Take the cat away, Bill. I especially want Diana to meet this couple—also horse people."

His worried eyes following Diana and his wife, Bill suddenly remembered—Courtney Snyder was Diana's enemy and the woman who'd threatened Navarro. He watched Emily festively open the door, and suddenly felt sick—Emily had orchestrated the entire evening to punish him. All hell would break loose, but, given the sadistic nature of his wife, it would be a controlled hell specifically designed to inflict maximum pain.

"Why, Emily, you didn't tell me Diana Winston would be here," exclaimed Courtney, shooting Hugh a side glance to convey their good fortune. "And hello, Diana. I suppose with a horse in the Garden you might expect to find yourself at a dinner or two."

"Good evening, Courtney, Hugh," Diana replied reflexively, too stunned to evaluate Emily's destructive social genius.

"Let me take your coat, Courtney," interrupted Jack O'Dell, feeling Diana's distress, not to mention his own. The Fanchon woman was bad enough, but Courtney Snyder too! Of all evenings for Bill's wife to try to turn horsey.

"Mr. O'Dell, I'm Hugh Simpson, we've never met. I'm a great admirer of yours." Hugh offered a power-driven handshake.

"Good." Jack didn't crack a smile, turned and walked off with Courtney's coat. Seeing that Diana was now completely without protectors, Bill disengaged himself from Peter and Fanchon and moved in.

"Darling, I'd like you to meet Courtney Snyder and Hugh Simpson. They're old friends of Diana's."

"How do you do?" Bill's tone lacked warmth. He glanced at Diana, aching to convey to her that the evening was a malicious plot designed by his wife, but Diana's eyes avoided his.

"Yes, Diana used to work at my stable. She could

muck out a stall faster than anybody, except one groom from Mexico. By the way, where is Steve tonight? He and Diana had—and still have, unless I've got it wrong—a very close working relationship."

"He's watching Navarro," Diana replied evenly.

"Oh, dear, I hope I didn't make a mistake by excluding your beau." Emily applied hand to cheek in feigned distress.

"I think we'd better get Courtney and Hugh a drink," remarked Bill, glancing at his watch. Seven-fifty. Emily always insisted dinner be served at precisely eight o'clock.

For the last ten minutes of cocktails Bill played diligent host to Courtney and Hugh, intentionally dragging them into conversation with Fanchon and Peter. The former Blue Angel was so taken with Fanchon—he'd occasionally make room in his black book for these older predatory types—that he failed to notice Courtney starting to seethe. This was a working dinner—Hugh knew that from the moment they stepped in the door and saw Diana—its mission to reveal Miss Winston as a usurping bitch, horse thief, and pretentious hypocrite. She'd hung her hat at Hampstead just long enough to get a reputation that could survive her getting fired for negligence. And then, incredibly, through that conniving inarticulate Mexican, she got the very horse everyone thought she'd ruined. Though Courtney had tried to retrieve the animal, she'd failed. Hampstead's lawyer, Judd Hanson, upon reviewing the circumstances and documents of the transaction presented by Sloan, could only conclude that the sale had been legal and futile to contest. Next, Courtney called Washington and tried to get hold of Luis Marqués Galván, the Spanish ambassador. But she only got as far as his personal secretary, who politely but firmly recommended she put the details in writing. The brief reply—with copies to stable manager Bob Sloan and Courtney's mother—arrived within a week from the embassy lawyer. The ambassador, having been informed of the gravity of Navarro's condition by Mr. Robert Sloan, had agreed to have him put down. However, he had not consented to nor had any knowledge of the sale. He had certainly not signed the transfer of ownership on the registration, nor had it been returned to him. It therefore was his client's intent to sue Hampstead for misappropriation unless he received eighty thousand dollars—the value of the animal prior to his injury. Courtney now raged in silence as she watched Diana engrossed in conversation with Jack O'Dell. Before this dinner was over he'd see—they all would see—Diana Winston for what she was.

At the last moment, just after the servant Emily had borrowed from her mother informed her that dinner could be served, she decided to revise the seating arrangement. Originally, Diana was to have sat on Peter's right, but that could not be. Emily was not about to distract him with this beautiful young woman. So she quickly switched place cards—Jack O'Dell would be on Diana's right, Hugh Simpson on her left. Observing his wife's momentary preoccupation, Bill walked over to Diana and whispered, "I didn't know anything about this evening until shortly before you came. I apologize for my wife's behavior."

"Shall we take our seats, please." Emily gestured to the dining room.

Polished silver, complex Waterford, napkins folded in the shape of fans perfectly laid out next to blue-and-white Mikasa plates—these, all set on the gleaming cherrywood table, provided an ornate frame for a Chinese juniper, the bonsai Emily had been wiring and pruning the night Bill came home with Gritti.

"So this is one of your bonsai," commented Hugh, holding out a chair for Diana. "You really *are* good. I deployed to Japan once with an F-14 squadron, and this is as good as any I saw there."

"Thank you, Hugh. I'm glad you appreciate it," replied Emily with as much genuine feeling as she could muster. She recognized Simpson as one of those "nouveaus" who somehow hadn't learned not to talk with his mouth full. What could he know about bonsai? Hers were infinitely better than any of the little twigs he would have come across. Japanese deployment, indeed.

"You know, one of these would look great in my office. Knock the socks off the Tokyo stock-exchange types I've got to see—show I understand and appreciate their culture. I bet they don't need much care and feeding."

Emily visibly paled at the thought of a neglected bonsai. "Oh, yes, they do, a lot of care of a very particular kind." Bill cleared his throat to catch her attention. "I did promise this would be an evening about horses. I love my little trees and flowers so much that I got carried away. Hugh, before you leave, I'll give you the number of an exquisite place to shop."

Halfway through the escargots, Emily placed her silver spring-handled snail-shell holder on her plate with a clink and turned to Diana. "I caught the photo of you and your horse in the *Times*—but it only said that you'd won the Newport Derby and were entered in the Puissance event. Puissance," Emily repeated, lifting a haughty nose as she pushed the second syllable through it in an attempt to get her accent right. "Everyone knows that's French for 'power,' but what does it mean in your world, I mean the horse world?"

"The same. It tests a horse's strength—his ability to clear large obstacles. In other jumping competitions—Grand Prix, for instance—different skills are tested more completely."

"Such as?" asked Fanchon, bored out of her wits but aware and concerned that Peter, on the contrary, was not. His face was riveted on the folds of Diana's dress, and Fanchon was sure he imagined the youthful body it concealed.

"The horse's ability to jump a variety of objects—wide fences, fences placed close together, and water. Course design can increase the difficulty. It's psychologically challenging for a horse to clear a five-foot-three vertical, then immediately go to a water jump thirteen feet wide."

Fanchon glanced at Peter's enraptured eyes and decided: enough—time for a little wing clipping. "Diana, did you know that a Saint-Gaudens statue of Diana the Huntress adorned the top of the old Madison Square Garden? She was totally nude, except for a bow and bannerlike sash, and illuminated at night by electric spotlights. Brought *sex* to American sculpture."

"I forgot you'd been a fine-arts major, Fanny. Do go on," Emily pressed her friend, heartened that another member of the alliance recognized the threat.

"Actually, my interest in sculpture extended beyond Bennington," Fanchon replied coolly before turning back to Diana. "It was said the model was his mistress, and you know, of course, that Diana—at least, the Greek Diana—was a virgin. So this gorgeous woman at the Garden caused a nasty little scandal. Some groups demanded her removal."

"But where is she now?" asked Hugh, titillated that talk about a work of art could turn him on.

"Some park or other."

"Put out to pasture rather than destroyed," observed Courtney, arching her brow and glancing at Hugh. Fanchon's metaphor had whetted her own destructive appetites.

"Exactly," replied Emily. "The moral stewards of old New York took the humane route."

Diana's expression tore at Bill's heart as she struggled to rise above the invidious onslaught. He intervened. "Well, tomorrow night this Diana will illuminate the Garden's interior with her own electricity. What do you think, Jack?"

"Without a doubt," O'Dell replied, aware of the nastiness taking place.

"But there can be only one winner." Courtney moved to deflate their supportive maneuver.

"No need to state the obvious." O'Dell turned on her as if she were an ill-behaved student. "You know as well as anyone here, Courtney, that some riders and horses— win or lose—are born crowd pleasers, natural stars. And that's what Diana and her Andalusian are. But some riders, despite their superb mounts"—he eyed Courtney even more deliberately—"are not."

"Peter, tell me how your new lab's setting up," Bill said, annoyed that he had to resort to the egocentric MacKenzie to divert attention from Diana. Fortunately, the main course arrived before his new colleague bored everyone completely.

"Beef Wellington—one of my favorites," Diana commented.

Peter turned to Diana, his rodent eyes widening. "My favorite too." The hard, intimate gaze irritated her. If this awful man thought the stars dictated love because of some culinary coincidence, he had another think coming.

"*I* requested it," added Bill. "Lately I've been fished and fowled to death."

"Yes, my concession to Bill," said Emily, ignoring the innuendo. "With this pastry and bordelaise, two bites and I'm full. And the cholesterol!"

"I think it's perfect," chimed in Fanchon. "Good for the soul not to yield to every trend."

"And the appetite," added Jack. "Take it from an old reactionary."

"Jack, do you think I might enjoy Puissance?" Emily asked.

"Yes, I do—very much." Respect for Bill, rather than good manners, compelled O'Dell to refrain from adding that one of the reasons the Puissance always sold out was its simplicity. The public didn't have to tax itself with time-clock fractions. "It's exciting—there's a steady crescendo and climax—but in the end it's one perfect physical act."

"Sounds very sexual," injected Fanchon.

"Not at all," O'Dell replied tersely. "It's a test of power and confidence. In the first round, most riders will clear the six fences without a problem. In the second, there are four. The purpose is to decrease the horses' anxiety—keep them from getting so cranked up they can't do the final big wall, which is what it's all about."

"And how high is this wall?" asked Peter, his tone

indicating he considered himself in a position to evaluate the true importance of a sport he knew nothing about.

"This year, by the second jump-off, I expect it'll reach six-foot-ten. By the third—and I think there will be a third, because some good Puissance horses are around— seven-two."

"What if only one rider makes it over?" asked Emily.

"Then that rider wins the class and has the option to try for the alleged 'world' indoor record—now at seven-foot-*seven* and three-quarters. It's not a true record, since the competition isn't standardized. Every Puissance event has a different-style wall. But it's good PR."

"My, that is high, but if it's not a true record, why do the riders go on?" asked Fanchon.

O'Dell remained silent now, out of respect for Diana —he frowned on this aspect of show jumping: it wasn't true sport—and was surprised to hear Diana herself frankly explain, "While the wall's being raised, the rider and show management negotiate. If enough money is offered, the rider will probably go out and give it a try."

"Some sport," Peter cynically observed.

"Still, for a horse to clear that height is a triumph, record or not," added O'Dell. "It takes courage and skill—nothing can detract from that."

"It's completely mercenary," said Courtney, looking sharply at Diana. "Jumpers break down quickly enough without the stress of non-world-records."

Fanchon turned to Diana. "But you're going to give it a shot?"

"I'm going to try. We're going to try," she added, her thoughts with Navarro. She glanced at her watch—eight-thirty. As O'Dell talked on about the history of the high jump, Diana suddenly felt far away, caught in the middle of a dimly lit tunnel. She couldn't follow him, but his words "confidence," "ability," "risk," "anxiety," "power," and "trust" filled her with fear and she began to feel ill. It was as if a giant vacuum had sucked all air out of the room. She started to perspire and took quick shallow breaths.

"Are you all right, Diana?" Bill's voice sounded distant but caring. She shook her head, pushed back her chair, and rushed to the bathroom.

"Oh, dear, I hope it wasn't the food. I'll see how she is." Emily folded her napkin and put it down carefully.

"No, you won't." Bill's voice grew angry and abrupt as he stood up from the table.

"But it's the least I can do."

"You've done quite enough already," he said sarcastically, then turned and walked after Diana.

"I'll go too," blurted out MacKenzie, eagerly pushing out his chair.

"No, you won't, Peter." Fanchon placed a restraining hand on her lover's arm. "One doctor is sufficient. Don't you agree, Emily?" Emily made no reply, but signaled for the table to be cleared. Yes, indeed, she thought, one doctor for this woman was more than sufficient, particularly when it was her doctor.

Bill heard water running and rapped softly on the door. "Diana, are you ill?"

She opened the door and smiled weakly. Beads of perspiration had formed on her forehead, yet she looked beautiful, but pale. "I'm fine—just dizzy all of a sudden—then I did get sick," she said almost apologetically. "My lips and fingers feel numb."

Bill pulled the lid of the toilet seat down. "Here, I want you to sit for a while. I think you're having an anxiety attack. Try to breathe through this for a couple of minutes." He unfolded his handkerchief, held it to her face, and took a seat on the edge of the bathtub.

Diana placed her hand on his wrist and backed away from the white linen. "What will this do? I don't need this. I feel like I'm suffocating."

"You were hyperventilating and took in too much oxygen. This will get carbon dioxide back in your system and take away the numbness."

"I'm sorry. I didn't mean not to trust you—it just feels

like I need air more than ever now." She turned her face back into the handkerchief and breathed.

"You must breathe your own breath." Within minutes the numbness disappeared and she felt better. He filled a paper cup at the faucet and handed it to her. "I'm so sorry about this evening."

"Bill, every one of those people—except Jack and you, and maybe that lech MacKenzie—hates me." Diana's dark eyes filled with tears as she drank the cool water.

"I think the real truth is that they hate themselves. They see in you what they aren't—never can be—and they attack it. I'm not excusing them, just trying to explain."

"But your wife . . ."

"My wife's the worst of them. She set this whole evening up to get at me. But let's not talk about my problems. You need to look after yourself. I'll fix some weak tea, and after a little rest I want you to let Jack take you home."

"I need to school this evening."

"That's not what the doctor would like to order. Can you keep it light?"

"I have to—for Navarro's sake."

"And yours, as well." He gave her cheek the gentlest of caresses, then took the cup from her hand and escorted her to a living-room sofa. He signaled the servant to put a kettle on.

"How are you, poor dear?" asked Emily, walking over from the table.

"She's fine," replied Bill. "Going home after some rest and tea."

O'Dell placed a hand lightly on Diana's shoulder. "Anything I can do?"

"Just nerves, I think, Jack. I'll be fine."

"Diana's got to ride Navarro this evening, Jack. Could you take her back to the Garden, then see her home afterward?"

"You're stealing my chivalrous thunder, Bill. That's exactly what I had in mind."

"I think we should all have dessert in the living room to keep Diana company," said Emily, glancing over her shoulder to ensure that those remaining at the table heard.

"Let's just go easy the rest of the evening." Bill's steely look carried a serious warning.

"Tomorrow night starting to get to you?" Courtney plunked down on the sofa next to Diana. "You simply haven't been on the circuit long enough—takes getting used to."

"Diana, I'm so—" The muffled sound of his own voice convinced Hugh that his mouth was indeed too full of pears in kirsch to go on until he'd masticated a bit more. "Excuse me, Emily, but this is delicious."

"Just something light to complement the beef," she replied, repulsed at seeing her instincts about this man's table manners confirmed.

Hugh held another forkful of dessert as he turned to Diana. "As I was saying, I'm so sorry to hear about Jim Williams' death. They say it was AIDS. Aren't you worried?"

Before Diana could speak, Bill shot his wife an angry look, but she just shrugged. How could Bill expect her to control a barbaric sort like this?

"No, Hugh. I'm not. Aren't you?"

"And why should Diana be afraid?" asked O'Dell, before Hugh could consider the implications of Diana's retort. "People are so frightened by this disease they can't separate truth from rumor."

"My, yes, even in Briggs and DePrete there are terrible misconceptions," stated Fanchon, eager to appear enlightened. At that instant Bill understood the only way to protect Diana—and himself—was to end the evening immediately. He stepped into the kitchen and looked under the pantry. Cognac—that would work—but then changed his mind. Not polite to force cognac on women. Then he remembered the magnum of champagne in the refrigerator. Perfect. He opened the cupboard and took out eight tulip-shaped glasses, filled one with ginger ale, then handed out the others.

"What do we have here?" Fanchon asked, examining the crystal for spots.

"Someone's birthday, I'll bet," Courtney surmised.

"An anniversary?" guessed Peter.

As he went around filling the glasses, Bill's only words were to Diana, pouring just enough champagne to cover the bottom of her glass. "For medicinal purposes." Then he touched her shoulder with his hand.

"This is so unlike you, Bill," observed Emily, her party tone failing to conceal uneasiness.

Bill moved to the center of the room, assumed a formal posture, and began to speak. "I now would like to propose a toast. Jim Williams was one of the finest sportsmen who ever lived. And he was a friend of mine." He paused to let the words sink in. "All great sport—sport at the level he exercised it—is an art. I think it's what people like Jim, Diana, and Jack do to recreate the world as a fair challenge. And that's why there are spectators—those who recognize this re-creation. Jim understood that. He had deep sympathies, a strong heart—and courage to face the worst. His success came from grace, a rare mix of skill and intelligence, and from that dedication to seek something larger than himself. He feared risks but took them. And he never felt above helping the person on the lowest rung. Everyone could learn from him—how to live, how . . . well"—Bill paused—"he was an extraordinary man. I still feel his presence, and can't imagine anyone criticizing him. Ladies and gentlemen, I propose a toast to Jim Williams." Bill checked to see that everyone's glass was ready, and lifted his own. "To Jim Williams." As that name echoed through the room, Bill remained standing while everyone drank, then spoke again. "I suggest that at this juncture we call it an evening and all go home."

"Bill!" Emily exclaimed with horror.

"I'm sorry, dear, but Jack and Diana are leaving and I really don't wish to spend time with anybody else. Now, if you'll help me fetch coats."

"Bill!" Emily repeated, surprise turning rapidly to rage.

"Control yourself, dear," he stage-whispered. "You know, grace under fire. The Register will admire you for it."

When she felt enough time had elapsed for her guests to be in the elevator, Emily faced Bill, now seated and finishing his ginger ale. "How dare you do this to me!" Her cheeks flushed scarlet and her nostrils flared.

He drained his glass slowly, placed it on the table, stood up, and walked over to her. "How dare I do *what* to you?" His tone was even and deliberate.

"Terminate my dinner."

"Your dinner?" He shook his head, then repeated more loudly, "*Your* dinner? You said, 'The least I can do is have a few people here who might be of interest to you.' Have you forgotten your largess?"

"No, I thought the guests would please you." Her words bristled, at once defensive and combative.

"Two hits—four errors."

"And why don't I think Diana Winston was one of the errors?" Feeling morally in the ascendant, she half-smiled.

Bill turned to the servant. "Thank you for this evening. We'll finish cleaning up."

The young man started down the hall, but halted at the sound of Emily's voice. "*You* don't excuse my mother's help. Look at this mess." She pointed to the dishes, wine and champagne glasses stacked on the anthracite counter. "I'm not touching them."

"Suit yourself, but I don't think you want someone employed by your parents to carry home tales."

Emily paused and reviewed the evening—little out of the ordinary. "Nothing happened that they shouldn't know about."

"Why am I not surprised?" Bill replied caustically. Again he addressed the young man. "Sorry things are so confusing. You may go." While the servant fetched his coat, Bill placed scraps of beef in a bowl, then opened the door to the yellow bathroom to release Gritti. The gray-and-white cat butted her head gratefully against his leg, then charged after the enticing scents in the kitchen. When Bill heard the front door click shut he turned his gaze to his wife. "I want a divorce."

Emily turned off the tap and placed the miniature watering can on the counter. Her bonsai could wait. "What?"

"I want a divorce," he repeated evenly, coldly.

She knew the root of this terrible surprise. He wanted to discard her for a twenty-year old—and that wasn't going to happen. "Well, you're not getting one," she replied tartly. "Many men go through this sort of thing. It'll pass. Perhaps you should seek out a professional who can help you. Our marriage is not going to be sacrificed because some younger woman catches your attention."

"I don't want a divorce because of some younger woman. I want a divorce because of you."

Taken aback, Emily picked up the watering can and walked to the Chinese juniper, now the sole object on the dining table. Don't take it personally—she told herself—he's just too controlling to admit male mid-life crisis. "As I said, I think it would be a good idea to see a professional."

"I already have—a lawyer."

Emily concentrated on ensuring the thin stream of water didn't splash the trunk. "I'm not going to give you a divorce, Bill."

"Then I'll sue." He moved to the table, unwilling to let her put distance between them.

"For infidelity?" she queried sarcastically. Her face was contorted with viciousness and pain.

"For anything that works. Now, if you'll excuse me, I've got to pack."

"You're leaving?" she asked, astonished.

"I was going to leave in a day or two, but there seems no time like the present."

At the prospect of Bill walking out, Emily's insecurities surfaced. Panic and desperation overrode her pride and anger. "I'm sorry the dinner got out of hand. Who wouldn't be jealous of such a beautiful girl? You just mean so much to me that the prospect of a younger woman taking my place drove me to extremes—that's all."

"No woman in the world could take your place, Emily. You're one of a kind." Bill pulled a suitcase and valet bag out of the hall closet and walked to the bedroom. As he closed the door firmly behind him, Emily collapsed onto the sofa, and the realization of her plight began to sink in. Twenty minutes later she turned her overwrought face to Bill, who reappeared with luggage in hand. He placed it by the door, then walked into the kitchen and poured the last of the champagne into a glass. "Finish this off. I'm sure you'll feel better. I'll be back for some other things—including my cat—in the morning," he said, placing the glass on an end table. "That's Thursday, so I expect you'll be at Briggs and DePrete twisting and snapping flowers."

"So, you really are leaving—how dramatic." Effective, anyway, he reflected, taking his overcoat out of the closet. Again desperation cut through her anger. "Don't you think it'll be difficult—the two of us at Briggs and DePrete? There'll be a lot of talk, and Daddy—"

"I'm leaving New York—going to a different hospital."

"I don't believe it! People in your position don't leave."

"That's what the chief of surgery thought until he learned otherwise. I submitted my letter of resignation the day after we returned from Nevis. So you see, it wasn't your vicious little dinner party, Emily—just vicious little you. My lawyer will be in touch." Bill walked through the door, but then turned. "Should the correspondence be sent here, or will you be going home?"

"You bastard!" Emily picked up her champagne glass and threw it full force at the closing door. Moët and shattered Waterford rained over the room. She glanced at the dirty dishes stacked on the counter, shuddered in disgust, then began to cry. A sudden odd scratching sound interrupted her tears, but she failed to locate its source. Surely there couldn't be mice thirty stories up? Again the sound, but this time she tracked it successfully.

To her horror, there on the dining-room table, Gritti was using her champion Chinese juniper as a scratching post.

"You little bitch!" Unable to control her rage, Emily hurled a book at the cat, but hit her bonsai instead. Shards of Chinese stoneware and little red leaves went flying. She rushed to the tree, now lying on its side, dwarfed roots exposed, and quickly examined the trunk. Small white gashes marred the once flawless bark. Glancing about, she locked onto the small feline face staring at her from under the sofa. But when she stepped forward, the cat disappeared. "I'll take care of you later." First things first, Emily thought as she lovingly took the wounded tree in her hands and placed it on a sofa pillow. "There, no need to lose more leaves." Returning from the balcony—imported soil, ceramic dish, and long-handled twig cutter in hand—she sat at the table and started restoring the damaged juniper. While she worked, fragments of roots, branches, and leaves fell onto her black silk dress. Ignoring the mess, she finished and stepped back, evaluating the little tree: though the loss of leaves and terrible gashes in the trunk saddened her, Emily was pleased at the sight of the repotted prize. And as she placed it on a side table—it would be a while before it could serve as an appropriate centerpiece again—a warm sweet smile, almost maternal, formed on her lips.

"We should've walked," observed O'Dell, closing the taxi door. "Glad I don't live in this city. I wonder how many men are found frozen to death each morning, arms extended up and out in 'cab-hailing position'? A perfect end to this evening, though." During the twenty-five minutes he'd spent at the Madison Avenue curbside trying to catch a cab, O'Dell tried to salvage the evening—and keep them both warm—by telling funny anecdotes about former "Courtneyesque" students.

But once out of the wind and in the warmth of the cab, Diana found she could no longer laugh. "Tonight was a disaster, Jack," she stated flatly.

"I guess joking can only soothe the pain so long," he

replied, squeezing her hand. "How the hell did we get stuck with that crew? One reason I enjoyed Bill's company so much is I knew I'd never run into any Courtney clones, but tonight I get the real thing. His wife—first time I've met her—beautiful and accomplished, but her friends! Can't imagine Bill putting up with them a whole hell of a lot of times."

"I think tonight was particularly unusual." Diana's lips trembled and her voice broke.

"Don't pay fools any mind. You won't have to see those people again. I'm sorry, I had no idea, or I would never have asked you. How are you feeling?"

"A little queasy—maybe I'm coming down with the flu."

"Before you do any riding, we'll get you a large Coca-Cola. It'll help settle your tummy and give you some sugar." When O'Dell spoke again, his voice was less instructive. "Diana, you have your own trainer, and you've both done a super job with Navarro, but I could watch you school and make some suggestions that might help tomorrow—that is, if you think it'd be beneficial, and if Mr. Rodríguez wouldn't mind."

Diana felt elated at the prospect of being advised by the nation's top hunter-jumper trainer. "Steve respects you enormously. I'm sure he wouldn't mind. As for me, I'd be honored. Jack, how can I thank you?"

"You just did."

Diana then turned her thoughts to the apartment they'd left. During the evening it had become clear that Emily viewed her as a threat and that she suspected—or knew—something was going on between her and her husband. "My wife's the worst of them. She set this whole evening up to get at me." That's what Bill had said in the bathroom. She had been invited, with O'Dell as the innocent catalyst, so Emily could humiliate and expose her, with Courtney and Hugh acting as co-conspirators in the dirty work. She shuddered as she recalled Hugh's remark about Jim. And then to ask her if she wasn't worried! She thought about Bill, how he'd taken command of the evening, said true and marvelous things about Jim and sports, how Jim—and she and Jack—engaged in sports to "recreate the world as a fair challenge." It was then she fully understood the depth of Bill's character. And after pointing out to those nasty people everything they were not, and never could be, he sent them packing. What a brilliant, powerful, and marvelous man. The cab pulled up in front of the Garden and she wondered if, after they'd all left the party, Bill had taken steps to "recreate his own world as a fair challenge," and if so, what place it might hold for her.

Bill put his suitcase on the bedspread and started to unpack. Though he'd attended a number of functions at the Harvard Club since he came to interview at Briggs and DePrete over sixteen years ago, he'd never stayed there. The simple furniture—writing desk, bed, dresser, and Hitchcock Harvard chair; and the crimson accents— bedspread, towels, and carpeting, pleased him. Though initially inclined to call the Algonquin, he didn't want Diana to misunderstand. And he needed to be alone—to think, to organize the steps he'd take now, and how he'd cope at Briggs and DePrete. His patient obligations extended through May, and he'd be working in a hostile world that would judge him as disloyal to the institution and to his wife. He smiled and wondered what ingenious explanations would be spread by Emily and by the Register—doubtless with some disparities—concerning the divorce.

After a quick Perrier in the bar, he showered and got into bed, wondering if Diana was still schooling or had returned to the Algonquin. He recalled how beautiful she looked that evening, and how she comported herself with extraordinary dignity in the face of the unanticipated assault. He wouldn't tell her about the divorce, about his hope of moving to Mass General—at least, not until things were further along. He wondered about her feelings for him and if his divorce would make a difference. He wouldn't want her to regard him as needy—so many divorced men were—simply because he no longer had a wife. He picked up his wallet from the bedside table and opened it to ensure he had his ticket for the National Horse Show. Bought the day tickets went on sale, it was the most expensive and, according to the diagram the man showed him, provided the closest, most central view. The Puissance wouldn't start till about nine, but he'd arrive early, grab a bite at the snack bar, and watch the other classes.

Almost asleep, the sound of scuffling feet and the hollow muffled sound of a ball being struck woke him—squash courts, on the fifth floor, one story up. The directory said so, but he'd forgotten. He recalled Dunster House, where he'd lived as an undergraduate at Harvard. There'd been squash courts there too, but those were in the basement. As he pulled the covers up around his shoulders, he felt relaxed, and a warm happiness came over him. The Harvard Club had been the right choice.

# A Wall Great and High

Diana woke numerous times during the night to check her clock—the time, and especially the stem—to ensure she hadn't inadvertently pushed it in. She got up at a quarter past six—the alarm would ring at six-thirty anyway—and walked to the window. The pulse of early-morning crosstown traffic had already started as headlights beamed on the wet black pavement—rain, just as in Newport. At least this time the competition would be indoors. She smiled, recalling Philippe DuChamps decked out in a fashionable Burberry trench coat, while she stood chilled and soaked to the bone in her riding kit, waiting to see if there would be a jump-off. Perhaps she should view inclement weather as a good omen. Still too early for breakfast, she examined what she'd wear that evening—black boots, Grand Prix coat, breeches and cotton blouse—both white—silk stock, gold stock pin, and velvet helmet. Navarro would look stunning in his German bridle and saddle and the white-and-blue-trimmed saddle pad Steve gave her at Newport. She hung some of the items in a valet bag and thought about the evening to come, still more than half a day away. She imagined entering the lighted arena on Navarro—the audience darkened—cantering to a wall she couldn't see over, and she began to feel dizzy. Better after a glass of water, she stepped in the shower. "Puissance," she thought: "power," "strength," "influential person"—that's what the *Dictionnaire Larousse* said in the library at home.

Navarro, she knew, had the power to clear more than seven feet. He'd jumped five-foot-seven at home the week before with barely a grunt. And she would be the "influential person" to place him at the jump so his power would be used most efficiently. But could she do that? She had a rapport with Navarro that she'd never had with any other horse, and more extensive training too. The night before, O'Dell had suggested she not take the jump with great speed. Navarro was a natural Puissance horse—he had the ability; placing him correctly would be more important. Sure, he was handy—Jack had seen him negotiate the Derby Bank at Newport—but a Puissance wall demanded absolute precision. An inch off on the ground meant fatal inches off in the air. If his striding faltered and they found themselves too close to the wall to take it straight on without knocking down blocks, O'Dell suggested they jump at an angle. That had its own drawbacks, but if they nudged a block it would be less likely to fall.

She stepped out of the tub, toweled off, and turned on her hair dryer. The hot wind felt good on her shoulders and neck. She'd placed Navarro correctly a hundred times; why couldn't she do it again? "The USET seldom schools over five-foot-four," is what Steve had said. "Trust yourself and you'll land in stride." She recalled Jim's final words of advice and then addressed her own image in the mirror. All right, I can do that—I can trust: Navarro, myself, and my friends Jim, Steve, Uncle Louis, Lee Caudrey, Jack, Bill. If I lose, I won't disappear—I'll still be the same person, I'll have Navarro and my friends.

Heading to the dining room for breakfast, Diana saw Steve approach from across the lobby. He wouldn't have left Navarro alone unless there'd been an emergency. "What's wrong? Is Navarro all right?"

"He's fine. Jack O'Dell sent one of his grooms to watch over him so we could spend some time together."

"You told him about Courtney?" she asked incredulously.

"No, I didn't. He was just being generous. Anyone who went by our stall could see we practically had Navarro under armed guard. Don't worry, I told the girl no one was to come near and that all she had to do was sit in front of his stall and turn away visitors."

"Did she seem responsible?"

"Very. Anyway, I thought we could breakfast together, then go for a walk if the rain lets up." Diana felt herself begin to relax in her friend's company. She was hungry, and a slow hot breakfast was just what she needed.

After the waiter poured coffee and took their orders, Diana and Steve discussed whether Navarro should take the vertical before the wall if he qualified for the second jump-off. It was optional—if it came down, no faults were accrued—and served as a schooling fence. Some riders liked to take it in order to calm their mounts. The night before, O'Dell had suggested that Diana consider bringing Navarro into it tight, forcing him to knock it down. That would make him particularly attentive and careful when he approached the wall. "Before becoming a coach, O'Dell competed in—and won—many Puissance classes himself. What do you think?" Steve asked.

"Maybe it would work for another horse, but not ours. We've spent near a year and a half not only developing and refining his physical abilities but also building up his confidence and trust in me. I couldn't make him hit a fence. He hates hitting fences. It would completely shatter his faith in me."

"Mr. O'Dell only intended it as a suggestion," Steve said. "We know Navarro. He's just too good a horse to have a fence down."

"Courtney and Hugh Simpson showed up as dinner guests last night. I thought of calling so you could have a few hours off, but then realized they might hire someone."

"I think you were right. I wouldn't have left him—no sense taking any risk. But how did Courtney and Hugh wind up at the Stanfords'?" Steve had liked Bill from the first—he seemed sensitive, hardworking, and honest—but if being an aficionado of Grand Prix brought those awful people to his dinner table, then he'd change his mind.

Diana read the disapproval on his face and knew for

whom it was meant. "Bill didn't know a thing—he told me so. It was his wife's doing. She wanted to embarrass us because she thinks we're having an affair."

"But aren't you?" he asked gently.

"No. He's been a very good friend to me because of Jim."

"That's only part of it. Affair or not, he's in love with you."

"How do you know?" Though making an effort, Diana failed to conceal her excitement.

"A chief of neurosurgery doesn't easily make room for others in his life. There've been a lot of signs. If you've missed them, either you don't love him or you're denying his feelings for you. And you *are* in love with him."

Her surprised silence stood as a question.

"The day Bill returned from Nevis, I asked you what he thought of his vacation. I got one sentence on Nevis— all the others on Bill." Diana occupied herself with her cantaloupe and didn't reply, but Steve went on. "Anyway, I think he must be a fine man."

"You're not jealous?" She wasn't sure whether she wanted him to be or not.

"If everything works out the way I think it might, I'll be more happy than jealous."

"And how would that be?" Diana asked, curiosity aroused.

"Better left unsaid at this point. We wouldn't want to anger the gods."

They lingered over coffee, but, conversation exhausted, Diana couldn't help noticing his preoccupied stare. "You're not thinking about the Puissance, Steve."

He straightened in his chair and faced her with a resigned smile. "I wasn't going to mention anything till after tonight, but yesterday afternoon a letter arrived from the American Board of Pediatrics."

"What did it say?" Her tone held anticipatory delight, hope, *and* disappointment. After all, why wasn't Steve ecstatic?

"I haven't opened it yet."

"Why not!"

"I thought I should wait until after Puissance. I didn't want anything to interfere with your night."

"Steve, it's not 'my' night—it's our night, yours, mine, and Navarro's. We're in this together. Your letter means as much to me as any competition—no, more. It's your whole life. Now, please, I can't bear not knowing. Where is it?"

"My pocket."

Diana became aware of his reticence and softened her stance. "You said they'd say yes—Marshall Simpkins told you so. I hope you're not protecting me. If I fail to place first, it'll give me something else to celebrate."

"What if they turned me down?" He didn't attempt to hide his fear.

"Then I'll make a point of coming in first." She recognized the contradictory element in his thinking but understood why he felt that way. "Please, Steve, let's know now. No more delays, no need to feel guilty about . . . about anything."

Visibly pale, he pulled the long white envelope from his pocket, opened it, and unfolded the letter. His eyes jumped past the greeting to the phrase missing last time, when the door slammed in his face.

November 12

Dear Dr. Rodríguez:

It is a pleasure to inform you that after a thorough review of credentials, the American Board of Pediatrics has granted you certification. We deeply apologize for the inconvenience and delay to which you have been subjected, and have expunged the derogatory letter of reference from your record. Your certificate will be mailed under separate cover in four to six weeks.

Yours sincerely,
Grant Fisher, M.D.
Chairman

cc: Marshall Simpkins, M.D.

Seeing the pleasure on Steve's face, she jumped up. "Dr. Rodríguez, congratulations!" She put her arms around him and tears of happiness streaked down her cheeks. "How wonderful!"

He took her hands in his. "I don't think I would've had the courage to reapply if we hadn't run into Marshall Simpkins in Seville. I needed someone to tell me it wasn't my fault. And I would never have gone to Spain if it hadn't been for you."

"Don't credit Simpkins—or me—too much. After all, you gave me Navarro, and from the first you realized that his registration had to be settled. You knew—at least on some level—that you needed to go to Andalusia, and an inner compass directed you there at the right time." She took her seat and signaled the waiter for more coffee.

"You're sounding almost religious, Diana." He smiled.

"You're the religious one, not me."

"I lost my faith the day of the earthquake." His expression hardened as he spoke.

"And you've been trying to regain it ever since." He remained quiet as she continued. "You said 'lost,' not 'destroyed.' And what about the cross you bought for Jim?"

"He asked me to get it for him."

"Because he knew you were the person to ask."

"You're still sounding religious. I'm intrigued."

"Steve, I believe God works in strange ways." She paused, letting him think that might be the extent of it, then went on: "When he's working."

He laughed more loudly than Diana had ever heard him laugh before. "Very good, and in keeping with a certain historical—and healthy—tradition of Yankee skepticism." His face then turned serious. "I want you to have something that expresses what your friendship means to me. I was going to give it to you after tonight, but you've made me realize that there's no time more appropriate than now." He took a small white box from his coat pocket and placed it on the table in front of her. "Please open it."

Diana undid the wrapping, lifted the cover, and folded back the tissue—a pendant, three interlocking horseshoes set with diamonds on a gold herringbone chain. "Steve, this is so beautiful! It must have cost you a fortune."

"Just tell me you'll wear it."

"Of course I will." She got up from her seat and kissed him. "The three horseshoes are you, me, and Navarro, right?"

"Something like that." He blushed, but then a broad smile appeared. "Actually, I was afraid you might think it should have a fourth shoe and that the necklace somehow had thrown one."

"No, not at all, silly." She waved a dismissive hand, but her expression conveyed to him the depth of love she felt. "Tonight I'll wear this under my coat for good luck. It won't feel so lonely when I approach that first jump."

"If you do take down the wall—or a fence in the opening round—the necklace and what it stands for will still be with you."

The apartment was empty when Bill returned to gather more belongings and to collect Gritti, the only sign of Emily a necklace of seed pearls left on the bathroom counter. He called for the cat but she didn't come, so he decided to look for her after filling his suitcase. As he packed, he felt oddly secretive, akin to a thief in his own house, and then realized why: he had never really considered it *his*. Wedding present or not, it had remained in Emily's name. He'd turned down the apartment that came with his promotion, though far more convenient to the hospital, because Emily felt the neighborhood lacked sufficient prestige. Well, he wouldn't need to put up with that anymore. His lawyer had failed to persuade him to sue for half the property acquired jointly—Bill cared only about his neurosurgical library and getting away from Emily and the trappings of his marriage as soon as possible.

After he packed and took some records from his file cabinet, he looked again for Gritti, still mysteriously absent. Occasionally she'd decline to respond, and luxuriate in a particulary comfortable spot, but this was the first time she hadn't turned up eventually. A sudden uneasiness came over him when he walked to the hall closet and saw the pet carrier missing. Bill ran to the phone and dialed Briggs and DePrete.

"Good morning, flower shop." He recognized the falsetto sweetness of Margie Henderson.

"Margie, Bill Stanford. Is Emily there, please?"

She paused before responding, her voice hard-edged and unconvincing. "At the moment she's setting up a very special arrangement in the boardroom."

"Would you have her paged? I'll hold." He'd have called the boardroom himself if he thought Margie were telling the truth.

"I can't do that right now, Bill. I'm the only one here and a shipment of orchids just arrived. You know they need immediate refrigeration."

"Right." Quickly assessing his options, he decided to go directly back to the hospital to track down his wife. "Tell her I'll get in touch this evening. She knows I have to appear in court this afternoon." Bill had no intention of giving Emily an opportunity to hide. Thirty minutes later he walked into the Briggs and DePrete flower shop. "Where's my cat?"

Startled, Emily looked up from her arrangement of orchids and pine needles, but then her surprise shifted to controlled disinterest. "I thought you were giving a deposition." At this point Margie Henderson, all her antennae out, reluctantly put down the ribbon she was curling with scissors and exited the shop, leaving Bill and Emily alone.

"Where's Gritti?"

"I've had enough of that destructive creature—shredding my fronds, chewing my petals." She picked up a sprig of white baby's breath and twirled it between her fingers.

"Where is she!" Bill thundered. His deep voice rattled the glass refrigerator doors.

"At the vet's—that clinic where she got her shots." Emily hesitated, then went on. "To be declawed."

"What in God's name!"

"She gashed my Chinese juniper—it'll never be the same." Emily began to muster up some tears, but Bill remained unaffected. "You call that vet right now and stop him." He pulled the phone between them and handed her the receiver.

"She clawed my bonsai." Her voice begged understanding.

"I don't give a shit about your bonsai. This is just a postscript to last night, isn't it? You knew my cat was leaving today, and you saw me feed her late at night, but I'm sure you told the vet she hadn't eaten or had any water just so she might die under the knife."

"I never pay attention to her. How would I know if she'd eaten?"

Bill could barely control his rage. "Dial."

"I need to look it up in the directory," she replied, deriving momentary pleasure from the delay.

"Fuck it." He grabbed the receiver from her hand, dialed the operator, scribbled down the number, and quickly headed for his office.

Before Rose Pitzer could open her mouth to unleash a list of messages for the boss she hadn't expected to see that afternoon, Bill moved to preempt. "I'm not really here, Rose—just a figment of your imagination. I'm at Foley Square, remember?" He closed the door to his office before the miffed secretary could reply.

When the phone receptionist at Park Animal Hospital informed Bill that Gritti had not yet been declawed, he sighed with relief. She went on to say that they would now give her food and water and hoped he could pick her up as soon as possible—at least by five-thirty. Though this posed a problem—he had to be at the courthouse by one-thirty, and at Tiffany's before six to pick up a gift he'd ordered for Diana—Bill told her that either he or a friend would be in. Fearing that Emily might call the vet and countermand his directions, he called Madison Square Garden—seven times before he got through to the stabling-area extension.

* * *

"Why didn't you send for me when Bill called? I would have been glad to fetch her." Diana sat on the tack trunk and rested her back against Navarro's stall, poking her index finger through an air hole in the pet carrier to stroke Gritti.

"It was more important for you to relax than run uptown, and you told me you always wanted to see the hunter championship. I asked Mr. O'Dell's groom to watch Navarro again. Bill arrives around seven"—Steve looked at his watch—"in about twenty minutes to pick her up. He sounded apologetic—said he and his wife had crossed their signals about the cat going to the vet and that neither of them could pick her up by closing time. I didn't want you to worry about anything except yourself."

"But I can't just worry about myself. What sort of friend would that make me?" Diana turned and stroked Navarro's pink muzzle through the wooden slats. "You know, I see this animal every day, and every day his magnificence makes me catch my breath." She gave the stallion a lump of sugar and stroked his neck. "I'm very fortunate."

Steve put his arm around her and drew her near. "So am I. Tell me, have you had anything to eat since our breakfast?"

"No, but what a big breakfast!"

He frowned at her reasoning. "You wait here for Bill—I'll run down to Penn Station and pick up something light."

Diana stifled an impulse to check her tack—Steve said everything was ready, so she could trust it would be spotless and the leather tested for any weakness. She looked in the pet carrier—Gritti curled up sound asleep—and wondered what really had caused the disconnect between Bill and Emily.

"I'm looking for Miss Winston." A security guard matched the stall number against his list of exhibitors.

"That's me."

"A Dr. Stanford wants to see you, but he doesn't have a pass."

Diana realized that she'd have to leave Navarro to talk to Bill. "Can you let him through?"

"Strict rules. Sorry."

"He's my veterinarian and drove all the way from Massachusetts. Please. I could get him a pass but just don't have time. Look, I compete in an hour and he's got to check my horse."

The guard glanced at Navarro. "Looks pretty healthy to me, but then, I don't know these animals. I go to the dog track, myself. I'll bring him down." Diana waited nervously, hoping Bill wouldn't inadvertently blow his new medical identity. She so desperately wanted to see him, to be near him, especially after last night.

"How are you?" His voice was sincere and concerned as he took her hands in his and kissed her cheek. He looked impressive in a black topcoat, his face—still tan from Nevis—so vital even under the drain of fluorescent lights.

"I'm fine—just glad you managed to find me." She peered over his shoulder to make sure the guard had gone.

"Yes, and you can't imagine how glad I am." He smiled broadly. "I understand I'm now a large-animal doctor."

"You didn't say you weren't?" she asked anxiously.

"No. I thought you might be the one who rewrote my job description."

"You're not insulted?"

"Not at all. Besides, I've operated on some large animals from time to time—they just happened to have two legs." Bill spotted the pet carrier. "I didn't intend for Steve to race uptown. I'm very sorry about all this."

"He didn't mind. And I would've been glad to go too." She read the level of distress on his face. "Tell me what's happening—please." Her voice was soft and encouraging as she placed her hand on his coat sleeve.

"Emily and I are getting a divorce. I left her last night shortly after the dinner."

"Bill, I'm so sorry." She took his arm and held it.

He started to speak, but his voice faltered. Diana's sympathy had cut through the wall he'd built to shield himself from pain and loneliness, and he felt his eyes grow moist. Drawing a deep breath, he steadied himself and spoke again. "Don't be. It should have happened a long time ago. Anyway, as a parting shot, she sent Gritti to be declawed."

"Why!"

"Because she knew that cat was the only thing in the house I cared about, but the 'official' reason is that Gritti sharpened her claws on one of Emily's bonsai—her favorite one, in fact—after I walked out." He recalled that bitter cold and lonely night—before Nevis—when he'd picked up the stray at Les Sans Culottes.

"Gritti did that?" Diana couldn't conceal her smile.

"Anyway, until I get settled, she's boarding out. I need to drop her off now, in fact, but I'll be back in plenty of time for your event."

"Why don't you let me take care of her again? She's no trouble, and much happier roaming the farmhouse." Diana jumped at the chance to ensure seeing Bill after she returned to Massachusetts. "We're checking out early tomorrow. Leave her here, and Steve can sneak her back into the Algonquin tonight."

"I can't ask you to do that—everything's so up in the air. At the moment the Harvard Club's my home, but I don't know for how long. You see"—he paused—"I'm leaving Briggs and DePrete."

"But where are you going?" she asked, unable to hide her distress. New York was far enough.

"There's a fair chance Mass General will name me chief neurosurgeon. I won't know for two or three months, but patient commitments keep me here through May, so the timetable might work."

"Bill, how wonderful!" Now she made no attempt to contain her joy. "The place where the ten-year-old outfielder got his throwing arm back."

"You remember," he said with faint disbelief, more to himself than her.

"Of course."

They held each other's gazes and Bill ached to embrace her and cover her face with kisses, but life was too complicated and it paralyzed him—he'd just walked out on sixteen years of marriage, submitted his resignation, and had yet to receive one firm job offer. And he couldn't bear the possibility of finding out that Diana's hope and love for him were less than his for her. So he said what he'd come to say. "I have something for you." From his overcoat pocket he took a small turquoise box tied with white ribbon and placed it in her hand. Silently she opened it and gasped with surprise—a gold ring fashioned in the shape of a horseshoe, set with diamonds. "It's exquisite. You shouldn't have—"

"I wanted to. But I had to guess your size."

She slipped it onto her right ring finger, where it fit perfectly. "I'll wear it tonight. Thank you so much, Bill." She brushed her lips against his.

"I wish I could stay, but you must get ready." He reached for the pet carrier.

"Leave her here—please."

"Fine, then. I'll be in touch soon. Good luck tonight."

Diana glanced down at the ring. "That's what horseshoes are for."

"They are, indeed." He smiled, blew her a kiss, and left.

After she made a halfhearted attempt to eat her croissant and brioche, Diana dressed in the locker room while Steve tacked up Navarro. Handing her the reins, he stepped back to examine his two prodigies. "Navarro looks stunning and confident. You look stunning and nervous."

"I *am* nervous."

He checked his watch—eight-fifteen. "Let's go to the schooling area right now—you'll feel better once you warm up."

Walking past row after row of the top equine athletes in the United States, Navarro began to act up—ears pricked forward, he passaged and called out to each horse he saw or heard. "When it's the real thing, he always knows. Look at his coat—lathered already."

"He'll settle once you start to school." But Steve surveyed the energetic stallion anxiously. Navarro needed to be up, but not to exhaust himself before the first round.

Jammed with saddlebreds drawing spoke-wheeled carts at a furious clip, and with several Puissance competitors practicing over a single set of standards, the practice area seemed more constricted than its hundred yards. "This is crazy, Steve! We can't even fit into the chaos, let alone get a turn to jump." Her voice grew panicky.

"Stop it right now. This is Madison Square Garden— everything's congested. Forget about who's schooling and how many there are. I'll set the jump at four-six—take it once or twice, let him get an idea what's coming up. The first-round fences run between four-three and four-six— only an inch higher than the Newport Derby—but with no combinations, no Bank, no rain, and no mud. Concentrate on going clean. Forget this whirlpool—you'll only intimidate yourself."

Now in the saddle, Diana edged into the counterclockwise current of horses. Though excited, Navarro responded to her direction, and she thought he'd settle if she kept him moving forward—but after letting him trot on, she immediately had to restrict his ground-covering stride to prevent him from running down other horses. Navarro objected by tossing his head, evading her outside leg, and crashing sideways into Kent Rappaport and Nimrod, winners of the Puissance event at the Washington International Horse Show one week before. Diana felt her leg being crushed between the colliding half-ton animals.

"You watch it!" Kent barked, hustling the huge Nimrod out of their path.

"Sorry," Diana apologized, her word swallowed by the commotion. She maneuvered between two other horses, but as she passed them, the bay on her left laid back his ears, bared his teeth, and lunged at Navarro, who rose on hind legs to meet the challenge. Diana yanked on her right rein as hard as she could, and when Navarro came down, his hooves just missed their target.

"Are you crazy—coming from behind like that?" shouted the woman on the bay, now under control. It was Sheila James, Rookie Rider of the Year, on Night Flight, her new Irish import.

In the melee Diana's eyes searched for Steve, next to the schooling jump, waiting for a turn to set it up. She moved over to him and halted. "Did you see? We're out of control. I can't let him hurt himself or anybody else. How about putting him in draw reins to force his head down and round his back so he pays attention?"

"Canter, Diana—loose reins, strong inside leg." He ignored her request and went on. "When he goes forward, establish light contact with your outside rein. Don't restrict him."

"Christ, Steve! Look at the bits on other horses—gags, twisted wires, long-shanked pelhams—and here's Navarro in one that couldn't stop a toy poodle. This is no time for classical lessons from Xenophon and Boucher—my life's on the line."

"I know." His voice—soft, serious, firm—made her realize all his commands derived from understanding that her life was, indeed, on the line. "Remember Hampstead and what von Engerson said about style. Now, relax your shoulders and elbows, and move directly from walk to canter."

Riled, Navarro shook his head impatiently at the walk she requested. Short-strided and choppy, he was just waiting for the right moment to blow. Von Engerson, Diana thought—he seemed light-years ago. But she recalled the elderly German instructor—how he treated her with respect and elicited her best—without a cent to her name, but filled with the dreams of adolescence. "Style counts in riding just as it does in life. It is from the beauty of one's style that performance and ultimate greatness come. Jumps are goals, not obstacles. Diana, you could perhaps be the best. We shall see." Style could be the most superficial of things—and the most profound. Had she learned that?

"Go ahead, Diana."

She smiled at Steve's exasperated face, took up the reins, and applied the leg aids. Instead of tossing his head and charging, the stallion—now confident in Diana's manner—arched his neck, rounded his frame, and began his patented, easy canter. Yet, in the swirling ring, the simple airy jump appeared higher and more threatening than four-foot-six. When Diana cut their normal arc and headed toward it, she felt a jolt of electricity shoot through the flanks under her. Navarro remained obedient, but with every nerve alert, charged. One stride away—perfectly placed—he raised his forelegs and propelled himself up and over.

"Good. We'll stop at that. You've got fifteen minutes."

Though a Puissance event, unlike Grand Prix, is designed to facilitate jumping, all three initial riders incurred faults—the first and third took down the cedar rails, and the second nearly demolished a three-pole spread. Then Diana waited at the in-gate and watched Mark Willoughby on Cairo jump the course flawlessly. The solid wall, blocks of wood painted gray to simulate stone, hadn't posed a problem yet.

At the ring steward's hand signal, Diana and Navarro entered the arena on the tail end of Mark's applause. A whisper rose and rippled through the audience while she saluted the judges, circled clockwise, and headed for the first jump—a simple white vertical. They were the unknowns who'd won the Derby—a rider who hadn't been on the circuit long enough even to qualify as a rookie, and a horse who wasn't in the computer, let alone ranked. Diana could feel Navarro's concentration shift from the floor to the vast space and tiers of people above. Indoors he heard everything—sneezes and coughs, empty soda cans rolling, rustling programs, all amplified a hundred times—sounds he barely noticed outside. Sensing threats from above, he swerved from the arena wall. Diana drove him back with a strong inside leg and reassuring voice. Suddenly, with the fence now just three strides away, Navarro's ears flicked forward, his eyes focused, and she felt his concentration return to the vertical. With a burst of energy he lowered his back, raised his head, and lunged over with a foot to spare.

Confidence restored and looking for the next jump, Navarro allowed Diana to reassert control. Effortlessly, they took the three-rail spread and the flowerboxes filled with orange and yellow marigolds, then turned toward the cedar rails. On the approach Diana understood instantly why two horses had been fooled. From the ground—from a human vantage point—the obstacle contrasted with a white background. But from the level of a horse's vision the lines of orange and brown bunting blended with the rails, making it hard to gauge their height. Navarro would need a good long look. She half-halted with her seat and legs, and the stallion responded by collecting his gait. Another half-halt and he was cantering as he had in the warm-up ring—rounded and light—attention now focused on the brown rails. Clear again. In response to Diana's inner leg, he changed leads and headed to the white gate, giving the photojournalists a textbook shot. Like many horses, he preferred solid obstacles, so the last jump, the wall, proved easiest. At four-six it was still low enough to see over.

After the first round Steve came up to Diana, walking Navarro on a long rein to keep him relaxed. "Out of nine, six went clear."

"See our first jump? He doesn't think much of the seating arrangement."

"But you went clean. They're setting up for the first jump-off—three fences."

"Are the rustic rails gone?" she asked hopefully.

"Gone."

"But the wall's at six feet." Anxiety strained her voice.

"You knew it would be," he replied matter-of-factly. Yet when Diana and Navarro walked back toward the in-gate to face a height neither of them had ever cleared, Steve struggled to overcome his nausea.

The Michael Carney Orchestra played lively show tunes

and Diana watched the jump crew raise the wall a full eighteen inches. Just some hollow pine boxes six feet up instead of six feet under—she shuddered at her black humor, but recalled what Jack O'Dell had said about Puissance horses: even the marginal ones could clear six-six. And she'd heard him tell Bill that Navarro was a powerhouse with an excellent chance. She looked up at the darkened audience and thought about Bill, up there somewhere watching her, expecting her to win. Her eyes returned to the wall, solid and gray, with blue, white, and yellow flowers at its base. She had to win—she wouldn't be able to bear his pity or disappointment—but felt increasingly light-headed and distant, as if swaddled in a dream.

"All set?" Steve masked his nervousness with a light but businesslike tone.

"I don't feel quite here."

"You are here, Diana," he replied sharply. "About to go in a jumping ring with three straightforward fences—a simple vertical, a three-pole spread, and one wall." He stooped down for an instant. "Here, open your hand."

"I need to concentrate, Steve. I'm about to go." Her voice was hurried and distracted.

"Open your hand."

She complied, and he poured into it what he'd scooped up from the arena floor. "Dirt and shavings, Diana—earth and wood—excellent footing. Navarro's never tried six feet, but he's got what it takes—physical ability and courage. You and he formed a partnership, and you must trust him. He trusts you. Otherwise he wouldn't be standing here quietly waiting his turn."

From her gloved hand Diana let the dirt fall back to the floor. Steve was right. She recalled the violent force that a horse could use to register objections or fear—rearing, refusing to go forward, running away. In the end it didn't matter how severe the bit or how strong the rider.

The three of them stood silently at the in-gate until the orchestra fell silent. Then, as the announcer spoke, with just a touch from his owner's legs, Navarro walked into the ring.

This time he didn't overjump the vertical but cleared it efficiently, with just enough power to avoid brushing or bringing it down. They took the three-pole spread—now at five-foot-four—expertly too, with a perfect takeoff and light landing. Switching his lead and turning toward the wall, Diana felt Navarro evaluate the obstacle ahead. She closed her legs softly on his sides, conveying not only that she wanted him to jump it but also that he could. When they approached, his pace was even and relaxed, but five strides away and no longer able to see the other side, Navarro stretched his body and rushed forward. With all his weight now on the forehand, he couldn't use his hindquarters effectively. Diana half-halted in desperation, causing Navarro to overreact and come screeching to a near-standstill. Now she had to drive him forward with her legs. Two strides away and barely organized, the stallion gathered himself—every nerve ready—and at the sound of her voice, lifted himself over the wall, legs tucked, body rounded. As his forelegs touched the ground, applause filled her ears. Disbelieving, she looked back to see the wall standing as before, only from the other side. They'd go on to the second jump-off.

"Congratulations." Steve smiled and gave Navarro a hearty pat on the withers.

"He rushed it."

"But you regained control. This was your hardest jump, and you did it." He took Navarro's reins and tapped Diana on the leg. "Hop down. I want to talk to you." His tone had suddenly grown stern and irritated.

"Why? We cleared it. And I'm not going to overreact with a strong half-halt again."

"Diana, get off. Looking up at you hurts my neck. We're going to talk face-to-face."

She put her weight in the left stirrup and dismounted. "You're angry at me," she said softly, concern over their friendship crowding out anxiety about the wall.

"Only because you completely disregarded me when I said that was your hardest fence, and then went on to tell me why it wasn't."

"But Jack said any real Puissance horse can clear six feet."

Steve shook his head. "You're doing it again. Let me speak. Any rider who jumps five-foot-four can jump seven feet or more. Decades of training have shown that. But you must train each horse, and Navarro didn't know he could clear that wall until you showed him he could."

"But my half-halt—"

"The half-halt was a mistake—too rough and demanding —but he trusted you through it. Two strides away from the wall, he didn't panic—he listened to you instead. And that got him over."

"Now it's my turn not to see over it." While she spoke, Diana saw the jump crew straining to add the blocks that would put the wall at six feet, ten inches.

"As soon as Navarro lifts off, you'll see the other side."

"I just need to place him correctly."

"And confidently."

Four of the six remaining riders qualified for the second-jump off, with Diana last to go. But rather than wait and watch at the in-gate, she returned to the practice area and walked Navarro until Steve told her it was time, and that two of the three other competitors—Kent Rappaport and the Frenchman André Junot—had gone clean.

The audience fell into an eerie silence when she and Navarro headed for the now optional vertical. Over the fence, they cut a diagonal across the arena and headed straight for the enormous obstacle. Still thirty yards away, it loomed in front of them like a fortified wall around an ancient city. Charged up but responsive, Navarro's rhythmic stride told her he was ready—his body and his mind. Four strides away, Diana sensed their perfect approach. She just had to keep the pace regular until the final stride, when he would shorten, gathering strength. An explosion like a rifle shot shattered the silence. Wild with fright, Navarro careened away from the noise. Startled, Diana quickly tried to take control—her voice, leg, and hands, reassuring and firm, encouraging him back to the line of approach. But he surged forward to meet the wall. Two strides away, she half-halted—Navarro slowed but threw his striding into shorter, irregular lengths. Now one more would bring them too close to the base. They'd never get over. Quickly she angled his body and asked him to take the wall obliquely. Though it made the top of the obstacle wider, it gave them six precious inches at the takeoff. As Navarro arced over the six-foot-ten mass, the loud hollow sound of his hind hoof striking wood resonated through the arena. A collective gasp, just as audible, rose in response from the crowd. Trying to bring Navarro under control, she looked back. The gray block, struck hard and dislodged, but knocked at an angle against the others, had not fallen.

"What was that?" Diana asked, as she left the arena.

"Someone popped a paper bag." Steve took the reins and led them away from the gathering reporters. "If you'd knocked it over, I'm sure the appeal committee would have allowed you to jump again."

She imagined having to test herself and Navarro one more time because of some drunken lout. Her horse would still carry the handicap of his previous fright to the jump. "I hope security nailed him."

They heard the announcer tell the crowd that the wall now stood at seven-foot-two and that two of the three riders who had gone clean would compete in the third jump-off. André Junot had decided his horse had reached his physical limits and exercised the option accorded in FEI regulations not to continue. He would settle for third place or, in the event of a tie for first, he'd receive the second-place red ribbon.

"Seven-foot-two, Steve." Diana raised her eyebrows nervously, but then turned to Navarro and stroked his neck. "He can do it."

"And he wants to."

"So do I." Diana took off her gloves and handed them to Steve. "I should've brought an extra pair—these are soaked."

As Diana dried her hands on the saddle pad, Steve caught sight of the gold ring. "Where did you get that?" he asked politely, nodding toward it.

"Bill gave it to me this afternoon." She pointed to the collar of her white shirt, which hid the necklace Steve had given her that morning. "Exactly the same."

He looked at the diamonds on gold. "The fourth horseshoe," he stated quietly, respectfully.

Without another word, they walked to the in-gate just as Nimrod dropped his hind legs and crashed through the wall. If she and Navarro cleared it, Kent Rappaport would place second, and if not, they'd tie for first. She watched the crew restore a dozen blocks, and turned to Steve. But for the first time since he'd given her Navarro, he wasn't there. Diana spun Navarro in a circle, her eyes searching for the friend who'd always been at her side when she needed him. He was nowhere in sight. She walked her horse through the in-gate and glanced down the aisle that fanned out to encompass the ring. Strange faces that had come down from distant seats stared back expectantly. They returned to the in-gate, where a beautifully coiffeured elderly woman in an emerald-green evening gown wished her luck.

But as Diana watched the crew rake over the hoofprints of previous riders, panic welled up from the core of her being. Her breath came in short, shallow bursts and she felt disoriented, trapped in a tunnel. Her fingers grew cold and numb—an anxiety attack, just like she had had the night before. Diana quickly pulled out her stock, held it up to her face, and breathed into the soft silk. Feeling better after a minute, she recalled Bill's sweet assistance and the ring he'd given her three hours earlier. She looked down at "the fourth horseshoe" on her right hand, then with her fingers traced the outline of the three horseshoes beneath her shirt.

"Miss Winston, anytime." The steward had walked up after realizing Diana hadn't been watching him.

She nodded, took up her reins, and signaled Navarro to go forward, waiting for the applause to subside before they cantered. Moving past the optional vertical down the long side of the arena, she felt the necklace gently tapping against her chest in rhythm with Navarro's gait. She glanced down at her ring—the small diamonds flashed out despite the artificial light, and the gold glowed warmly. As they cut across the floor, she felt the stallion's body charge with power and saw his dilated nostrils pull in air, her hands and legs barely containing the energy and muscle beneath her. Now four strides away, she felt the force of a tidal wave carry her toward the massive wall before them. Navarro's ears lay pinned against his head as if flattened by wind. Two strides away, Diana looked up for a point of focus, but in the blackened space there was none. Ahead she saw only gray stone. Then, as Navarro rose up almost vertically, she imagined a star and held it up in the darkness for her eyes to see until she heard hooves strike the earth again, saw light on the other side of the wall, and knew she had won.

# Home
*Five Months Later*

"**A** Different Drummer—apt name for a restaurant on Thoreau Street," observed Steve as he and Diana took seats at a table looking out on the small wooden station at Concord.

"When's your train?"

"Eight-fifty-five. We've got almost two hours. I'll sleep at the airport Hilton and catch the seven-thirty to La Guardia in the morning. The flight for Mexico City leaves from Kennedy at eleven, so that should give me plenty of time."

"I can't believe you're going." Diana reached across the table and took his hand. She knew that their odyssey together—with Steve confronting and redeeming his past—was now over, but found it difficult to admit the end had come, and that it was time to let go. "So, when will you return to Stanford?"

"Not for several months. I need to dispose of the house and put my files in order."

"Do you really want to sell? You described it so beautifully—the arches and marble floors, the pool and garden."

"The beauty will remind me of what I've lost. Glad memories will trigger the sad ones." He paused in silence. "How's your drink?"

"Fine, Steve." The tone of her reply also answered his implicit request to change subjects. They went on to recall their year and a half together—the long, lonely fall

and winter of Navarro's recovery, that exciting spring
when he started to jump, then Newport, Andalusia, Jim's
struggle and death, and finally the Puissance. "Was the
show committee upset I didn't try for a new indoor
record?" she asked.

"Of course. They want satisfied spectators."

"You know, just before the last round—when I couldn't
find you—I panicked. It was as if you'd gone forever. I
completely forgot that you said you were leaving to tell
the committee I wouldn't try to break the record if I won
the final jump-off. But what did they offer?" She wanted
to know how much cash might entice a rider to attempt
an invalid record.

"Never got to that point. I just said you'd exercise the
option not to go on, and broke off any further negotiations. You won the class and that was just fine." Steve
called for another round.

"Did you know that effective tomorrow I'm managing
Hampstead?" She asked the incredible question almost
mischievously.

His dark eyes widened in amazement. "I heard after
the Snyders' divorce it went up for sale, but—"

"Not anymore. Lee Caudrey bought it outright from
Barbara Snyder yesterday—two and a half million. He
called me the day after we returned from the Garden to
ask if I was interested. I didn't say anything until it was a
sure thing. I'd been hoping for so long. Seems he's branch-
ing out into hunters and jumpers."

"You could have told me." His voice carried disappointment.

She reached across the table and took his hand. "You've
helped me so much—given me so much strength. I didn't
want to burden you with more of my hopes."

"Wishing the best for you is no burden. Your strength
gave me strength during a very confusing time in my life.
Anyway, I'm excited for you."

"Lee offered me a partnership—an even split of all
profits, no liability for losses—and the option eventually
to buy him out. Hard to believe—doesn't make much
business sense for him."

"Lee Caudrey's a near-billionaire who doesn't think strictly in cash flow. He admires hard work, honesty, and spirit, and he's been watching you ever since you stomped off to file a protest with the ring steward at the Newport Jumping Derby. Once, decades ago, he was an underdog too. It's great news, Diana. He's a terrific man."

"You knew him before Newport, didn't you?" she asked quietly, directly.

Steve recalled the orange dust of the monarch butterfly, the Day of the Dead, and the shattered glass of his discarded diplomas. He nodded. "The day I left Mexico I was delivering a horse to a Texan—Lee Caudrey—and I never went back. Lee took me on for a while, but soon I worked my way east. Texas was just too close to home." After a light dinner of salad and sole, Diana excused herself, returning a minute later to hand Steve a large flat package wrapped in silver foil and tied with blue ribbon. "What's this?" he asked, pulling out his chair and making room to open it.

"For a long time I've wanted to give you a present— some token to express how thankful I am that I've known you, traveled with you—but I couldn't think of anything until after the Garden."

The wrappings fell to the floor, revealing a large black-and-white close-up of Navarro clearing the wall—spectacular head, broad chest, forelegs drawn up against his belly like folded landing gear. Engraved in script on a silver plaque placed in the mat was simply "Puissance." "Don't you like it?" she asked anxiously, unable to interpret his silence. Without a word Steve took from his wallet a small photograph and placed it on the table for her to identify. "Navarro. But when was this one taken? I don't recognize the background." She examined the creased and yellowed likeness more closely. "And he's jumping. I thought he didn't do that until we got him."

"It isn't Navarro. It's his brother—Helénico." He answered her next question before she could form the words. "He belonged to us, to me and my wife. She trained him in dressage and I trained him to jump. I didn't even know Navarro existed. When they hired me at Hampstead, his appearance struck me, but I chalked it up to breed characteristics. Then, one night—you'd become involved with him by then—I reviewed his record in Sloan's office. And there it was—by Poseido out of Triana, same sire, same dam."

"Where is he now?" Diana asked, her voice hushed.

"After the earthquake I gave him to Laura de Bonilla, my wife's best friend. She was widowed in the tragedy and lost two of her three children. Helénico meant a great deal to her, she even showed him for Carmen on occasion." He returned the photo to his wallet. "You see, in the end, I never did get away from Mexico, or away from the earthquake and what I lost."

They sat in silence, each sensing the other's thoughts so completely that they felt no need to talk. Outside, snow had started to fall—heavy white flakes covered the steel tracks, telephone wires, and barren branches. Warmed by a second cup of cappuccino, they spoke again and their memories turned to the Restaurant Chapultepec and the cold but sunny carriage ride through Central Park. Suddenly the floor and table began to vibrate. Diana instinctively looked at her watch. "Must be an earlier train—we've still got fifteen minutes." She saw Steve's face—now suddenly pale—relax with relief.

He laughed sheepishly. "It felt exactly like the first seconds of an earthquake."

"Just the westbound for Gardner." She squeezed his hand. "Not yours."

"It seems strange that to return home I must first go east."

"But this time not as far as Andalusia."

He smiled and picked up the check. "No, only Boston."

Wet flakes had now turned to a fine cold sand sparkling in the streetlights as they walked down the sidewalk, padded with white. "Last snow of the year. Hard to believe it's April," she said, watching flakes melt on the sleeve of her coat. "We're to get eight inches."

"I don't like your driving in it."

"Don't worry about this New Englander. I grew up with storms." Shortly after they stepped out on the platform, an electric horn sounded. Diana looked westward but saw nothing—only snow and blackness. Again the horn, but this time they could make out a distant yellow light growing stronger and closer.

"That's it." Steve's voice was excited but sorrowful.

"Don't go." She impulsively threw her arms around him and pressed her head against his chest. Tears streamed down her cheeks.

"I must." He stroked the back of her head. "It's time." The train approached quickly, its metal tonnage unimpeded by the snowfall. He held her face between his hands. "Please, don't cry—the tears will turn cold and numb your skin."

"You're crying too." She half-laughed through her sadness.

He wiped the wet from his own face and smiled. "Do you believe it's melted snow?" Her pain cut through his attempted lightheartedness and he pulled her close. "Yes, I'm crying too." They heard the squeal of metal brake shoes on metal wheels, then the screech of metal wheels on steel tracks as the silver cars with their gold and purple stripes came to a stop. He drew a deep breath, backed away from Diana, and picked up his two suitcases.

"North Station, North Station—this train goes to North Station." The blue-suited conductor helped an elderly woman, the only other person on the platform, ascend the metal steps.

Steve gently kissed Diana's lips. "You know, as different as we are, we're very much alike." He mounted the steps, then turned to look down at her. The snow—sharper and colder still—framed a sad silhouette. He mouthed the words "I love you," then walked through the pneumatic door into a darkened car. The conductor waved all-clear, and slowly, laboriously, the train drew out of the station and the sound of its metal wheels filled the night again. Diana looked at windows that flicked by with increasing speed, but saw nothing. Then it was still except for the whisper of falling snow.

*        *        *

The next morning, after she released Navarro in the pasture and shoveled her walks, Diana drove to Hampstead. As she turned down the long driveway, a peculiar blend of uneasiness and excitement overtook her. It looked so familiar—four-board fencing, main stable and attached indoor arena, hunter course, and jumping ring—but it felt completely different. She wished Lee Caudrey hadn't canceled his trip to deal with some business emergency. The prospect of asserting herself without her partner and benefactor made her feel uncomfortable. He had told her that he'd informed the previous owner about Diana's position as barn manager and new partner, and Diana assumed that Mrs. Snyder had passed on the information. But when she walked down row after row of stripped stalls, her uneasiness continued to rise. She'd never been in a barn without horses, and it somehow reminded her of the time the steeple was taken off the local Congregational church for repairs.

She knocked on the door of the office and heard an all-too-familiar grunt. Walking in, she suddenly felt transported back to the time when she had little choice but to listen to the repugnant man in front of her and do what he wanted—almost everything he wanted—so she could ride. Anger shook her body.

"I thought you got enough lessons out of us," Bob Sloan commented brusquely. He didn't take his eyes off the mountain of folders cluttering his desk.

"Not quite," Diana replied, her voice controlled and her dark eyes fixed and unblinking.

"Whatever it is, take it to somebody else. I've got work to do."

"Yes, you do. This place is a mess—always was. Small wonder it turned into a money hole."

"I'm not giving out jobs anymore. Some loaded Texan owns Hampstead now. Probably go to the Arabs next, then the Japs." He laughed at his uninspired humor. "Anyway, there's a new manager coming in—peddle yourself to him."

Diana took a seat in Sloan's Scandinavian Design chair, which no employee ever used, and smiled coolly. "You mean to *her*." She watched the realization ring up on his primitive beefy face.

"You?" His voice was abrupt, incredulous.

"Me. And I want you out of here now. You've drawn your last paycheck on this property. This office belongs to me, and you're unsuitable decor. I'll give you an hour to clean up this mess—no more, no less." She nodded at the scattered files, loose documents, bills, and receipts.

"You can't do that. I need room to work, and the rest of the place—"

"Is unheated—that is, except for the Trophy Room. How well I remember. You just pile your things into cardboard boxes and finish up in there. I've got work to do too, and I'm certainly not going to stand around because you haven't done yours. Understood?"

During the next months, as Bill began to slacken or cut the strings that held him there, Briggs and DePrete became a difficult and lonely place for him. Patients he diagnosed requiring surgery he now had to refer to his colleagues—and that was hard, particularly when the patients' problems were grave and when he knew, of all members in his department, that he was best qualified to relieve them. There were petty insults. The chief of surgery now would ask him to operate on days he normally never had. Admitting started to assign his patients the shoddiest rooms—those facing north into a dark shaft between buildings, or overlooking the dumpsters. (He put an end to that with one angry visit and the threat of a memo.) Lou, the custodian in charge of the surgeons' locker room, had often met Bill coming out of a particularly difficult and drawn-out operation and offered to get him a sandwich, but lately Lou seemed out of sight. A worker in the mailroom who always would hand-carry *The New York Times* now busied himself with the chief of surgery's *Christian Science Monitor*. Bill's paper arrived with the regular mail at ten o'clock, when he was operating or busy with patients. And while colleagues ignored his domestic and professional cataclysm, some staff members—nurses, therapists, and secretaries—made ill-disguised passes which ran the gamut from opportunistic concern to an outright body grab by one physical therapist who "coincidentally" appeared half-dressed when Bill—after a heavy session on the PT Nautilus equipment—stepped buck naked out of the shower.

During this time Diana saw Bill only once—brunch at the Copley Plaza. Staying the previous night at the Parker House, he had attended a dinner with MGH's chief of neurology (an ad hoc committee member) and the acting chief of neurosurgery, a marvelous dinner hosted by a trustee in his home at 165 Commonwealth Avenue. Bill and Diana did speak occasionally by phone, and though it was clear that they cared deeply about each other—their career problems, private opinions—neither could express love or hope directly. Their worlds felt too fragile for more emotional risks.

In mid-June Diana flew to the exclusive Palm Beach Polo and Country Club to show a Grand Prix horse recently acquired by Lee Caudrey. Located on more than two thousand acres, the sports facilities of the twelve-year-old club were already legend—a dozen polo fields, each ten acres and large enough to swallow nine football games, Scottish links, twenty clay tennis courts, as well as two grass and two hard-surface, and racquetball and squash courts. The Grand Prix was the last event of the club's four-week Equestrian Festival, during which fifteen hundred hunters, jumpers, and dressage horses, valued at over 150 million dollars, would compete for national titles. After a hard day's competition, riders fortunate enough to know PBPCC members could look forward to relaxing at the health and fitness facilities or to watching a game of polo from the north end of the field in the air-conditioned dining rooms behind glass at the Players' Club. As the residential resort's name suggested, polo was the predominant sport. In little over a decade, Palm

Beach had joined the elite ranks of Greenwich, Deauville, and Sotogrande as an international center. Corporate sponsors such as Cadillac, Boehm Porcelain, Leica, Rolex, Cellular One, Coca-Cola, and Cartier would sponsor as many as twenty-two tournaments each year. Prince Charles competed regularly, including a 1986 match in which he rode on the Palm Beach team defeating the All-Stars, to capture the Princess of Wales Trophy. But that evening, as Diana dined at the Players' Club with some competitors and horse owners, glamour and corporate power only underscored her loneliness. She glanced at her watch—six o'clock—and wondered what Bill was doing. On a weekday he might be finishing rounds, but today was Saturday. He could be in his office completing the boring paperwork he'd mentioned, or maybe at home listening to the Turina record she'd gotten him in Andalusia and, perhaps, thinking of her.

Bill wasn't at Briggs and DePrete or at his apartment, but waiting in line at La Guardia to catch the six-thirty Boston shuttle. The evening before, Mass General had offered him the job, so Bill decided to fly up to meet with Bob Kniering, an MGH resident who'd promised him a six-month sublet on his North End apartment while he went to Minnesota on sabbatical. The next day, Sunday afternoon, he planned to fly from Boston to Washington, where he'd scheduled a meeting Monday morning at NIH to discuss a grant proposal. When Bill got to the gate, he took a seat and pulled out an article on recombinant DNA that a colleague had sent to his office. Normally Bill would have found the details of cell inheritance and insulin production absorbing, but he could barely concentrate, wondering why the news of his acceptance hadn't made him ecstatic. After all, he'd gotten exactly what he wanted—no need now to entertain a long move or the possibility of life in Texas or California. He had a job at a wonderful institution, in a city he loved, near the woman he loved. He glanced at the departure screen—TWA flight 453 for West Palm Beach would leave in ten minutes. Then he understood his edginess and depression. He was heading for Boston, but Diana was in Palm Beach. He returned to his article. Again he couldn't concentrate, but found himself taking his pen to the title—adding an I and an A—changing DNA to "Diana." A service representative announced that the six-thirty Pan Am shuttle to Boston was delayed due to "minor mechanical difficulties." Bill got up and looked at the screen again—he'd have to take the seven P.M. Trump Shuttle. The boarding block of the West Palm Beach flight, now flashing, caught his eye. Without another thought he picked up his bag, ran through the arcade to the main ticket counter, then followed the signs to gate eleven—the flight south to Diana.

He arrived in Palm Beach shortly after ten P.M., rented a car, and drove to the Breakers. He wouldn't try to find her until the next morning. After all, she didn't expect him. To show up on her doorstep this late would be inconsiderate, and he couldn't bear the thought of finding her with someone else. A male friend would be more easily explained between breakfast and dinner.

Diana was up early the next morning in order to get the horse she'd ridden groomed and ready for the van that would take him home to Massachusetts. Though Sacramento had come in only fourth, she was pleased with his performance. He'd had some very bad schooling with previous owners, and trust was a major issue, but he'd already made tremendous progress in the one week she had to get him ready for the show. After she and the groom gave him a bath, she led him down a gravel path onto grass near a polo field, then let him graze while his coat dried in the indirect but warm southern sun. The blue sky, still tinged pink, was soft but clear, and palm leaves rustled in the light breeze. How perfect everything seemed. At twenty-one, winner of the Newport Jumping Derby and Puissance, a successful competitor with a substantial independent income, she managed and was a partner in what would soon be a state-of-the-art facility, with some of the best horses in Europe now under her management, and the opportunity to make a continuing contribution to the world she loved. Most of all, she'd been open to friends and experiences: Jim, Steve, Navarro, Andalusia, even that cold but brilliant ride in Central Park—all had imbued her with sensitivity and understanding. She could approach life with the energy of a twenty-one-year-old, yet with the maturity and wisdom of someone considerably older. But why, then—just when she was succeeding in every way—why did she feel such emptiness? She thought about Steve, wondering if he was the cause. He'd called her on his arrival in Mexico and told her that he'd decided not to accept the job at Stanford. Though it would take time to reestablish himself, he knew Mexico City was where he belonged. It was home. Several letters followed, asking Diana to come for a visit when her own life grew more settled. So Steve's leaving was not the terrible loss she'd feared. Their friendship would continue, and they would see each other again.

Sacramento raised his head and pricked his ears forward. Diana tightened her grip on the lead shank and followed the bay's stare. Nothing but a grove of royal palms. Maybe someone coming out onto the field, but she saw no horses and no riders. The gelding returned to grazing at the sound of her voice and reassuring touch. Leaning her weight against the horse's shoulder, Diana closed her eyes and imagined she caught the ocean smell in an easterly breeze. Suddenly Sacramento moved away from her and looked again in the direction of the grove. A man in a dark sport coat and khaki slacks walked briskly toward them. She felt her heart quicken simultaneously with hope and disbelief.

Now running, Bill closed the distance between them, took Diana in his arms, and drew her close. "I hope you don't mind my coming to see you." His voice was anxious and happy.

"I haven't been able to bear this paradise without you." She buried her head in his chest.

"I felt the same way in Nevis." He raised her chin with his fingers and looked into her eyes. "I got the job. I'm moving to Boston."

"It's the best news I've had in my life." Tears of happiness and relief filled her eyes.

"I thought we could fly back together. I remember you told me you were leaving tonight."

"Bill, that would be wonderful."

"I love you, Diana." He placed his hand behind her head and brought her lips to his. With the gentle pressure of his mouth, his rough warm face against hers, voice deep and caring, all loneliness vanished.

"And I love you, Bill."

As they walked back toward the grandstand, his arm around her waist, four helmeted men in black shirts and four in white, mallets in hand, galloped past them and out onto the playing field.

When Diana and Bill landed at Logan that evening, they took a cab to the Parker House, where Bill had made reservations. They dined on lobster and champagne, then made love—not once, but several times through the night, and again in the early light of dawn, when they woke to find themselves in each other's arms.

Following breakfast of croissants and coffee they drove out to Hampstead. After a tour of the stables they walked to one of the back pastures. The June sky was deep blue and the sun strong.

"Is that Navarro?" Bill gestured to the white horse grazing in the distance next to a smaller black one.

"And Calliope," Diana said proudly. "She's in foal— due next April."

"I thought—like a lot of female athletes—she was having difficulty getting pregnant."

"It didn't look good. Even artificial insemination failed. But all she needed was time and a natural setting. Sunshine got her estrogen level up, and I think running free with Navarro took the pressure off."

Bill put his arm around her shoulder. "I'm so happy for you."

"Jim would be happy too," she said softly, more to herself than to Bill.

"Very."

She looked at Bill's rugged face, his gentle expression, and brightened. "You see that house under construction?" Now she was pointing toward the erect wooden shell of beams and planks. "That's where I'll live. This fall I'm going to plant bulbs—crocuses, daffodils, tulips. When next year's snow recedes, I want to see spring's earliest flowers. Then, in summer there will be roses, daisies, cosmos, marigolds."

"Sounds beautiful." Bill paused, then continued, "Are you keeping your Beacon Hill home?"

"I'd never sell it."

"But will you live there?"

"Someday. For now I'll keep renting it. And will you take that Louisburg Square house MGH offered you?" Though their voices were matter-of-fact, each knew they were talking about their future together.

"I don't think so. It does have a great view of the river, and on clear days they say you can see Mount Wachusett off in the west. But you were right about the tour bus and the megaphone—every hour on the half-hour."

A part of Diana wanted to tell him that her house on Mount Vernon Street offered the same view and was off the tourist track, but she held back. Tension was evident in their silence. "Let's go see the yearlings." She took his hand and led him through the stable to the front pasture. In a small herd, young horses were charging around, striking out at each other with their forelegs, ears laid back, teeth bared.

"They're fighting," he said anxiously.

"They're playing—getting fit, preparing for their futures."

Once again they fell silent and watched the energetic band break up and begin to graze. The shiny wet sweat of one black colt reflected an image of the sun. Feeling edgy, Bill broke the silence. "The grass is so green."

"Spring grass—richest in nutrients." She scolded herself inwardly for sounding like a vet manual.

"Beautiful day—gorgeous sun and too early for flies. Perfect for your horses. You know, today's June 20, the longest day of the year." He put an arm around her shoulder and drew her close.

"The summer solstice. I'd forgotten." She lowered her voice and cast down her eyes. "But there's something sad in it, the last day of spring."

"I don't see why. Spring is a promise, and the fulfillment of that promise—summer—begins tomorrow. I heard on the weather this morning that today we'll have more than fifteen hours of sunlight. That's something to celebrate. Also, I thought it might be the perfect day to ask if you'd—" He halted mid-sentence, closed his eyes for a moment, than looked at Diana directly, all the hope in the world appearing in his face.

"If I'd what?" she asked quietly.

"If you'd marry me."

Like a child unexpectedly lifted up high, Diana caught her breath. He took her hands in his. "Diana, will you marry me?"

She looked into his eyes—earnest and loving—her voice filled with joy and trembling with excitement. "Yes. Yes, I will."

He gently took her in his arms, and while they kissed, the yearlings engaged again in the rough play that would ready them for the challenges of life ahead.